emerge 22

ABOUT *emerge*

In its twenty-second year, *emerge* is an annual publication produced by students, alumni, faculty, and industry guests of the Writer's Studio. Students are assigned to teams and, over a four-month period, work with the publisher, editors, designers, our printer, and local booksellers to produce, market, and sell this anthology.

ABOUT THE WRITER'S STUDIO

The Writer's Studio is an award-winning creative writing program at Simon Fraser University that provides writers with mentorship, instruction, and hands-on book publishing experience. Over the course of a year, students work alongside a community of writers with a mentor, developing their writing through regular manuscript workshops and readings. Many of our alumni have become successful authors, and have gone on to careers in the publishing industry.

The Writer's Studio 2022 mentors:
Claudia Casper—*Speculative Fiction and Writing for Young Adults*
Leanne Dunic—*Fiction and Hybrid Forms*
Anosh Irani—*Fiction*
JJ Lee—*Narrative Non-fiction*
Kevin Spenst—*Poetry and Lyric Prose*
Emily Stringer—*Program Facilitator*

The Writer's Studio 2021–22 mentors:
Eileen Cook—*Speculative Fiction and Writing for Young Adults*
Saleema Nawaz—*Fiction*
Kayla Czaga—*Poetry and Lyric Prose*
Claudia Cornwall—*Narrative Non-fiction*
Stella Harvey—*Fiction and Personal Narrative*
Brian Payton—*Fiction and Narrative Non-fiction*
Tamara Jong—*Program Facilitator*

sfu.ca/write

emerge 22
THE WRITER'S STUDIO ANTHOLOGY

Jónína Kirton
Foreword

CREATIVE WRITING
AT SFU CONTINUING STUDIES

SFU PUBLICATIONS

Simon Fraser University, Vancouver, B.C.

Cover Design: Solo Corps Creative
Cover Illustration: Carrie Walker
Typesetting and Interior Design: Solo Corps Creative
Printing: Marquis Book Printing

Printed in Canada

LIBRARY AND ARCHIVES CANADA CATALOGUING IN PUBLICATION
emerge 22: The Writer's Studio anthology /
Foreword by Jónína Kirton

ISSN 1925-8267
ISBN 978-1-77287-094-7 (paperback)
ISBN 978-1-77287-095-4 (ebook)

A cataloging record for this publication is available
from Library and Archives Canada.

Creative Writing | SFU Continuing Studies
Simon Fraser University
515 West Hastings Street
Vancouver, B.C., Canada, v6b 5k3
sfu.ca/write

SFU Publications
1300 West Mall Centre
8888 University Drive
Burnaby, B.C., Canada, v5a 1s6

In memory of Isobel McDonald, a 2019 Writer's Studio graduate,
who taught us that writing is a joy, even in our darkest moments.
Her commitment to the craft inspires us to write
with persistence and passion.
1958–2022

"You have the itch for writing born in you.
It's quite incurable. What are you going to do with it?"
—L. M. Montgomery, *Emily of New Moon*

Contents

SPECULATIVE AND YA FICTION

Foreword

I have just returned home from the Denman Island Readers and Writers Festival. While there, I spent time reading this anthology and contemplating the power of stories. In *Women Who Run with the Wolves*, Clarissa Pinkola Estés, PhD, a Jungian analyst and storyteller, says, "Stories are medicine." She speaks to their power and the fact that "they do not require that we do, be, act anything—we need only listen."

Within this collection you will find what she calls "story bones," each one bringing us more of the "whole story"; a better understanding of ourselves and the world we live in. Estés says, "the more [that] subtle twists and turns of the psyche are presented to us ... the better the opportunity we have to apprehend and evoke our soulwork." I have found both writing, and reading or listening to the stories of others to be soulwork. Some speak of writing as bleeding on the page, but I prefer to think of ... the page as bone and the ink as blood; something that shows up in the title of my first book, *page as bone ink as blood*. As writers, we are nourishing the bone page with our life blood. Stories pour out of us, some fully formed, but many require the dedication to revision that is evident in this collection.

As a graduate of the Writer's Studio (in 2007) I know the work that led to this anthology and the stories contained within it. I also know that for many it may be their first publication—a publication that can not only lead to more, but also one that teaches us about book publishing and all the hands it takes to make a collection like this a reality. I recall the excitement of the launch of *emerge 2007* and the growing feeling that now I was a real writer.

The Writer's Studio is a community, one that continues as many alumni remain in contact and are there—arms wide open—to greet each year's graduates. Our first introduction to them is often this anthology.

Within this stunning collection we travel the world of fiction, speculative fiction, non-fiction, and poetry. There are life changing interactions with strangers, and adventures with a microwave that include cleaning tips from the talk show host Montel Williams. We meet Arthur the crow, the ghost of a dead father seeking restitution. Over and over again we find that remnants of the past can linger, and the effects are often disquieting but can become revelatory. Through the real and, at times, imagined lives of others, we are gifted with many story bones; the desire to be chosen by a cult leader, betrayal, feeling abandoned by people or God, questioning, if there is a God, what kind of God are they? We get glimpses into aging, budding sexuality, the loss of a loved one, and all manner of pivotal life events that we may have already experienced and need to make peace with. One poem speaks to the way that "histories [are] recorded all over our bodies as conjecture and conundrum." As storytellers, we are often confronted with what the body holds but the mind cannot accept. Adding to this is the conundrum of what lovers, friends, and families prefer remains hidden, and yet we feel called to share—often in hopes of lightening the load for others who carry similar trauma and loss in their bodies and souls.

This anthology is filled with good medicine; parenting while grieving; magic teacups; the special ingredient for Scottish shortbread. There are many "subtle twists and turns" that have the potential to not only bring us some joy, but also chances to attend to our sorrows. I cried more than once reading this collection. There is something for everyone here; it is filled with, as one writer posits, "raw and mutable wonder," the kind that evokes the soulwork that many of us are in need of.

—*Jónína Kirton*, New Westminster, the unceded
territory of many Coast Salish Nations, 2022

Fiction

Sharon Inkpen

Rewind

AN EXCERPT FROM A NOVEL-IN-THE-MAKING

I slide another VHS into the machine and press rewind. I can't help but wonder, would I, if I could, rewind my life too? To a time before pirouettes, pliés, and applause. Before ripening blisters, black toenails, and stress fractures. Back to swingsets, bruised knees, and training wheels. Back to twirling in the living room, bare feet on a shag carpet, and a high-flying skirt. Back to Dad's old record player, golden afternoons, and the gentle melody of "Here Comes the Sun."

Many talented dancers auditioned, the letter said. We are unable to offer you a place in our first-year class.

"Oh Beth," Mom had said that morning, her arms around me as I wept into her shoulder.

Clunk! The rewinder stops and ejects the cassette. Mike, the youngest store manager of all the Fresh Flicks' locations, is hunched over the shift schedule next to me. He chews the back of a ballpoint pen, twisting it between his front teeth. I slouch against the counter—our fortress of computerized tills, rolling drawers, and a swinging half-door.

Amber stands on the other side, between the drama and horror sections, reading the back of the videos she's supposed to be shelving. Confident and curvaceous, she makes our alarmingly red shirts look sexy without trying. The same shirt makes my body practically disappear. Maybe I can make it drape from my shoulders, like a Greek goddess, and show off my long neck. I stretch my collar, and three stitches pop.

"What are you doing?" Mike asks, staring down at me.

3

"The returns." I shrug, and my cheeks burn. I remove the VHS from the rewinder and scan its barcode. Its title, *Reality Bites*, appears in green block letters across the black screen. Amber loves this one. She says it's about our generation. But I didn't get it, and the only part I liked was the gas station scene when this boppy, watered-down punk song plays, and the characters shimmy, whirl, and hop to the overpowering call to move.

"Why are you bouncing?" Mike frowns at me.

I look down to see that I am, in fact, bobbing on the balls of my feet. The store's sound system plays a bubbly dance song with a high-pitched woman's voice singing the words "Barbie girl" over and over.

"I love this song," I say. I hate this song.

"Well, stop it." Mike turns down the volume. "It's distracting."

I lower my heels on the thin carpet and imagine the soles of my feet sinking deeper, beyond the floor, like my instructors taught me. I drop *Reality Bites* into a clear plastic case, file it in the drawer labelled "R–T," and put its jacket on the pile to be reshelved. I grab another video from the returns bin.

Outside, streetlights cast the empty parking lot in a dull orange. With our floor-to-ceiling windows and fluorescent lights, we're lit up and on display like a sealed terrarium. It bothers Amber when onlookers can see us but we can't see them. For me it's no different than standing centre stage, unable to see beyond the spotlight, but far less fun.

Clunk! The rewinder spits out another video. I scan, file, stack, and load another one. I sigh at the clock. 6:24 p.m. Tuesday night. Most customers are at home with their families. Their children are probably brushing their teeth in their "Ninja Turtle" pyjamas. Their teenagers are twisting telephone cords around their fingers and whispering to their first, and surely forever, true loves. Mothers are loading dishwashers, daydreaming about their dog-eared Harlequin romances. Fathers are arriving home tired after an hour stuck in gridlock, only to sigh when they realize they forgot their weekend rentals. They'll get back into their cars, drive here, and drop their videos off with their engines still running, each cassette landing with a hollow bang.

I rest my gaze on the plastic window of the machine and soften my vision. The spinning reels almost look like car tires. They remind me of a Dodge Caravan, the high school parking lot, and Amber phoning me in the middle of the night.

"Sorry," she had said, "but I just finished watching this trilogy ..." She babbled about trucks ripping through the desert and Tina Turner in a sexy chainmail dress. Then she said, "I'm going to try it, with or without you."

I should go, I'd thought. I should try to have more fun. I rolled out of bed, the phone cord nearly knocking the clock off my nightstand, and picked up a pair of jeans from the floor. "Give me ten minutes."

She arrived in her parents' van. A Smashing Pumpkins song, the one with a lulling guitar and haunting bells, played on the radio. She drove us to our old high school. Cement barricades bordered the parking lot, and the wet, black pavement shimmered white under the headlights. One graffitied payphone stood aglow in the corner, like a phantom reminding me that 911 calls are free.

"All I have to do"—Amber put the van in park—"is turn the steering wheel all the way and step on the gas."

This is a bad idea, I thought. I clenched my seatbelt, its edge cutting into my palm. Someone's going to get hurt.

"You ready?" Amber smiled at me.

"Sure," I said. This was a stupid idea.

She flipped on the turn signal. "Safety first," she smirked, and I laughed, not in the normal way, but in that erupting, busting-free-from-a-chest-made-stiff-from-shallow-breathing way.

Amber cranked the steering wheel. "Here we go." She stepped on the gas.

Clunk! The machine pops out the video. I scan, file, stack, and reload.

"You're bouncing again," Mike sneers. "Can't you just be still?"

"I'll try harder," I say. But I only feel still when I move.

I press rewind and the reels' mechanical whir is nothing like the screech of those tires when we spun. I remember sighting the glowing orange tails of the street lights in the billowing grey exhaust, like riding a carousel in hell. The inertia pinned my chest and pulled my heart into my stomach. And that cement barricade was getting closer and closer. And it was terrifying, horrible … but also strange and wonderful, and how can I feel that way again?

Amber braked in time. We couldn't stop giggling the entire drive home. She laughed so hard she cried. Then she wiped her tears, letting go of the steering wheel, and side-swiped a parked police car.

She's had to take public transit ever since.

Clunk! The rewinder ejects the movie. I scan, file—

"Wrong drawer," Mike said.

"What?"

Mike puts his pen in his mouth, pulls open the top drawer and takes out the video. "*Field of Dreams* belongs in the second drawer," he says, and his pen seesaws at every word. He puts the video in the "D–F" drawer, runs his finger along the titles, and takes another one out. "And *Reality Bites* belongs in the drawer on the right." He hands me the cassette.

I thought I had put it in the right drawer. Now he's waiting, and I stare at his short, side-combed hair, so encased in hair gel that it looks plastic. I'd like to knock on his head to see if he's hollow inside, but I slot the video next to *Rebel Without a Cause* instead.

"Are you for real?" Mike huffs. "It goes next to—"

Crack! Ink pools and pours down Mike's lips. His broken pen drops, splattering drooly blue specks across the carpet.

"Oh God." He cups his mouth, and I cup my mouth too, choking back my shock of giggles. He swings open the half-door and runs to the staff washroom.

Bang! I jump at the drop of a cassette landing in the returns bin. Outside, a balding man hurries back to his car, the engine still running.

When I grab another VHS for the rewinder, I hear the fast tapping of cymbals playing on the stereo. I turn the volume up and bounce on my toes. There's a sharp, synthesized clap, the heavy notes of an organ, and an airy voice singing. I swing my arms, and then Amber's eyes meet mine. She grins and vaults over the counter. Then the singer's voice explodes like a bomb, and we grab hands and whirl. My feet burn in my sneakers. I let go and twirl so fast that I think of vinyl records and sunlight bursting through living room curtains, and for a breath, I don't care about dance schools and rejection letters. And—

Thwack! Stacks of video jackets clatter to the floor.

Louise Dumayne

Thrown to the Wolves

AN EXCERPT

*Marie has come from England to work at a remote trapping homestead and
sled dog kennel in Alaska. A recovered heroin addict,
Marie hopes to reinvent herself as a wilderness guide.*

I arrived home just after dark, which was not late, about 3:00 p.m., and
unhitched my dogs. It was intensely cold, probably the coldest day I had
experienced so far. The chemical hand warmers I had stuffed into my
mitts were frozen, making my hands even colder. And my feet! Despite
the thick boots, it was as if the skin had been flayed from them and I
stood on bare bones. It must have been forty below, at least. A curtain of
icicles hung from the front of my hat into my eyes. I brushed them away
and pinched tiny crystals out of my lashes to stop my eyelids freezing
together.

Their cabin squatted into the snow, as if sulking. Usually, Martha
helped me put up the dogs or Hank came out to see how the run went—
who was listening to me, who slacked—but no one appeared.

I kept my eyes averted from the house and focused on the dogs, on
removing their harnesses, and smacking open the snap clips on their
collars with a pair of pliers I kept in my sled bag, as they were congealed
with frozen saliva. I led each tired dog to a kennel, thanking them as I
did so, and feeling a familiar weight of panic and sadness pile onto my
chest. An old feeling, a memory from childhood—outside the house, in
the backyard, standing with Dawn, my older sister who knew things I

didn't. I'd done something wrong. Everyone was angry.

Dawn's voice a searing whisper, "Stop crying! Mum'll get upset."

There would be another argument, and it was all my fault.

⁓

Two days after my return from the mountains, it was sixty degrees below Fahrenheit and still dropping. The air was so still, so brittle, the world seemed set in glass.

Hank didn't speak to me. He greeted me when I came into their cabin, but that was all. I gave a polite, "Hello," in return.

I had to go in to get soup for the dogs' morning feed—buckets of kibble soaked in warm water—but in the evenings we fed them from the fish cooker anyway, so I stayed outside, away from him.

Martha boiled up a broth of dried salmon, rice, and water in an old oil barrel cut in half with the top inverted and air holes shot in the sides of the lower piece. She made a fire in the bottom and tended it until the stew had cooked, then left it to cool. As we fed the dogs, smoke from the fish cooker was pressed down by the sinking, frigid air and drifted around our knees like dry ice, as if we were all characters in some spectacular stage show.

It was too cold to run dogs with the sled.

"It ain't good for their lungs," Martha told me. And they would all need to be bootied with nylon socks to stop the snow crystals cutting their feet like razors.

After giving them their breakfast, I plodded through the woods on the tennis racquet-like snowshoes Martha lent me, with a bunch of my dogs for company, letting the extraordinary beauty settle my heart.

The deep cold was like nothing I had ever experienced. It was tangible, a physical presence on the land. The air was thickened. I pushed my way through, following a trail to a ridge behind the homestead. Each breath sunk into my chest like gravel, sharp at the edges. Moving slowly, I inhaled only through my face mask or risked burning my lungs. Cold air carries less oxygen and I found myself almost suffocating, trying to draw breath, swaddled in my layers and layers of clothing, thinking, this must be what it feels like to be ninety.

I could not take my hands out of the enormous beaver fur mitts Martha had given me for more than a few seconds at a time. My fingers became painfully cold if I did, and I was not able to warm them again until I got home. Once, fiddling with my parka zip for less than twenty seconds, I got my hands so chilled I could not feel or clasp my fingers and rushed back, terrified I had frostbite.

If I touched metal bare-handed, a button or zip, it burned my skin—a white-cold pain similar to heat but more shocking for its unfamiliarity. The snap clips on the dogs' collars froze to their tongues as they ran, then tore off again, leaving blood beads that glistened like the cranberries I'd picked in the autumn. Everything broke. Twigs snapped when I touched them, plastic crumbled in my hands. The logs I usually struggled to split from my firewood pile with a heavy maul axe fell apart like matchsticks beneath my blows.

The stillness was so intense I seemed to smash through it. With each step, the snow squeaked and screamed, my clothing crunched and rasped. Something about the hard, frozen surfaces and the brittleness of the very molecules around me made my every movement so noisy it built to a steady roar in my ears. I felt like an old London bus lumbering down the trail. Sometimes I turned around, thinking Hank was behind me on their rattling old Ski-Doo. But as soon as I stopped, there was a silence so profound I could feel the pressure in my ears.

As we walked, a mist of vapour hung in front of my face and over each of the dogs. We moved like ghosts in our own freezing clouds of ice. I had the Ginger Minges, as I called them. Red, Palmer, Betty, Cougar, all with the same ginger colouring. For some reason, the red dogs liked to cluster at my knees. Maybe it was a genetic trait with this line of huskies. Other dogs would push on past me down the trail or rove off in the woods, leaping through the thick snow, but the Ginger Minges followed obediently behind. Red, my new best friend, had to be closest, of course, and barged any interlopers out of the way.

At the ridge, briefly, brilliantly, for a few minutes at midday, sunlight. The snow was a shimmer of flashing lights, each crystal gleaming silver, gold, and vermillion. With no sun in the sky, Martha told me, there is no red colour phase. The world is a palette of blues, which is why, I realized, every photo I took looked submarine, washed with a deep-sea cobalt. With the sun came the full rainbow blazing back into the world. I thought of outdoor raves from another life. The moment at dawn where darkness shifts into light and, high on pills, the world is radiant with colour. But this was real, not a mirage spun by some dodgy chemicals.

Looking to the horizon, I pushed my hood back from my forehead with my mitt to widen the view. On the rare occasions I'd glimpsed it since autumn, the sun was ringed by a solar halo, a glowing, white circle smeared into the air as the light was refracted through ice crystals. But that day, the coldest I had experienced so far, there were two suns.

The dogs saw nothing amiss. They nosed through the trees or sat politely behind me. They did not perceive anything unusual. Was I imagining it? Had the stress of the last few days, the weight of the cold, the tension of just staying alive outdoors in these inhuman temperatures, twisted my mind? No. There were two suns.

Sundogs. I had read about the phenomena. The reflection of light in airborne ice produces a mirror image of the star itself, sometimes two, just as bright. One sun was real and the other a phantom, but I was not sure which. I stared, eyes pierced, burning.

I was the sole audience for this unearthly show. I gazed until the cold began to bite. It was not a cold you could shiver at, nor could you jump around, swing your arms and warm up a bit. Once I felt chilled, I got colder and colder. The awful progression would not stop until I got back inside and stood by the fire. A twinge of panic: what if I trip and sprain an ankle? I could die of hypothermia right here on this ridge before anyone thinks to look for me.

I trod my snowshoes in deliberate, clockwork steps back to warmth and safety, marvelling that I had travelled so far from the world I knew that even the laws of nature were bent out of shape.

When I got back to the homestead, Hank was in the yard. The air was fixed as welded steel.

Hank hadn't spoken to me since our trip to the mountains, but he looked me full in the face now. "Fuck man, did you see the thermometer?"

I shook my head, sending a sprinkle of ice flakes adrift from my wolf fur ruff.

"It's 73 below!" Hank's eyes gleamed above his face mask.

Laura Mervyn

The Robbery

THE PROLOGUE TO THE NOVEL,
"LIONS AND TIGERS AND BEARS"

A drop of water fell from a wet curl and tickled down her nose. Cold in her wet shoes, she waited for the young clerk to notice her. He stood behind the crowded counter of the convenience store, absorbed in his phone.

"Ahem." Kate shifted her weight.

The clerk looked up, disinterested.

"I'd like a lottery ticket, please, 6/49 with extra." In her head, she'd already won. Miraculously work free, she'd drive through red rock canyons and desert, hot wind blowing through the open car window.

The machine clicked as it printed out the prize-winning ticket. The clerk laid it on the counter, eyes straying back to his cell. Somehow, he managed to scoop up the money and give her change, all without making eye contact. She sighed, used to the invisibility of being a middle-aged woman. She fumbled with waterlogged fingers to get the ticket into her wallet.

The jingle of the bell on the door accompanied a blast of cold air and the sounds of city traffic in the rain. *Snick*. Kate and the clerk turned toward the sound. Kate had a vague impression of an older man locking the door and turning the sign to "Closed." Then she registered the object in his hand. It was a gun, aimed at them, and shaking. Kate's brain stopped. In the life she lived now, this couldn't be happening. Her brain rebooted; her breath sped up. It was for real. The clerk, suddenly a scared kid, phone forgotten, stared at the gun.

"Hands up." The man's voice wobbled. He cleared his throat and moved between the overstocked shelves, out of sight from the street. "And put the phone down."

Kate swallowed hard, lifting her hands up in front of her shoulders. The clerk dropped the phone and threw his long, gangly arms high above his head. Time slowed.

The gun waved wildly as the gunman wiped his nose on his sleeve. Kate and the boy flinched. The man steadied the gun. He had an acrid stink of sweat on him. She knew that smell. It was fear and desperation. He looked ill under the toque pulled to his eyebrows. Huge, black-framed glasses obscured his eyes. Salt and pepper stubble too long to be fashionable sprouted from the rest of his face.

"Get behind the counter with him."

Kate edged closer to the clerk. The boy's eyes finally met hers, wide and terrified. She tried to reassure him with a smile but her face felt stiff.

Wrestling a roll of duct tape out of the pocket of his red plaid lumber jacket, the robber tossed it to Kate. "Both of you sit against that wall. You, ma'am—wrap the tape around his hands."

Kate's heart thumped in her chest but she had caught the tape and joined the clerk behind the counter. They slid down the back wall. It was a small space made smaller by a jumble of unopened boxes.

She twisted around to reach his wrists. It was hard to find an angle that worked, even harder to scrabble the end of the tape loose from the roll. Her hands shook. The tape whined as she unrolled it. She wrapped it as loosely as possible. Close to his face, she saw his skin was the colour of old parchment. His breathing was shallow. She gave him a small reassuring squeeze on his forearm.

"Now his ankles. Wrap it around his ankles. Please." In contrast to his rough voice, the robber spoke politely, as if he'd asked her to pass the peas.

He'd joined them in the already full space, close to the till. The gun loomed too close, the barrel huge. The boy's legs were long and his ankles hard to get at but she managed. Giant white runners looked ridiculously huge beneath the layers of tape over his bony ankles. He wasn't wearing socks and the tape clung to his skin and fine black hairs.

"Now yours."

Kate pulled the tape loose from the roll and wound it around the ankles of her damp pants. The robber watched closely. When she was done, he gestured for her to start wrapping it around her wrists. Laying down the gun, he reached over for the tape and finished wrapping.

She saw his eyes widen as he looked at her. He stopped, hands still, staring. His face was stricken. Visibly shaking himself, he finished by tearing the duct tape from the roll and turning away. He seemed to know her. Maybe he'd been one of her social work clients? There was something familiar about him.

And then it clicked. She remembered walking on hot pavement beside a young man with wild curly black hair and startling blue eyes. She felt the hope they'd shared. More than two decades had passed, but she knew him. This battered old man was the Jake she'd known so well. They'd spent weeks together, helped each other get through detox. When one struggled, the other encouraged. He was part of the reason she'd made it through.

But the smell of him, the grey skin and sniffling nose, the lines of pain at the sides of his mouth—she knew he was in withdrawal. He hadn't made it. Worse, he'd come to a place where holding a gun on Kate and the kid was possible. It was like a blow to her gut. How could this be Jake?

He turned the key to the cash register, fumbled the neat stacks of bills into deep pockets. His face sagged from weariness as he turned back to them. "I'm sorry."

Their eyes met in recognition. She saw his regret, felt it. Saw the question in his eyes along with sadness. A rush of grief for him filled her, followed by the familiar survivor's guilt. Fear left her. Kate answered the unspoken question with the briefest of nods, knowing she could never turn him in, right or wrong. It was a moral dilemma she'd wrestle with later.

They watched him push open the heavy alleyway door and fade into the weakening light.

She shifted her weight, trying to get comfortable. Her attention turned to the boy now struggling against his duct tape bonds to no effect. His face was regaining its colour.

"Are you okay?"

"Sure. No problem. Omigod, that guy stank!" His teenage cockiness was back, and the rush of relief and adrenaline had opened the floodgates. Suddenly he had a lot to say.

Kate gave him the half of her attention that wasn't in the past. When release came, when the interview with the police was done, Kate stepped out into the clean, damp air of early spring. Mixed with her relief was a heaviness. It could have been her. A longing grew in her to change it, to help Jake somehow.

Anna Cavouras

Wisp

A SHORT STORY

There weren't enough words for the look on Maryanne's face when she discovered a tiny three-year-old asleep in the family camper. A sleeping child is not that strange in and of itself, but this was not Maryanne's child. In fact, she'd never seen this child before. Adding to her shock was the dawning realization that she had driven over 300 kilometers since their last stop. It was nearly 11:00 p.m. and she had parked for the night in a Walmart parking lot.

The discovery occurred as Maryanne went to straighten the duvet on her daughter's bed. Ellie was asleep in her car seat, warm and dreamy. Maryanne's hands felt the worn luxury of a threadbare cover on the blanket, the pictures of bears and foxes faded into the fabric like ghosts in a fog. Her mind was elsewhere, thinking what remained of the loaf of bread and how she would turn that into a breakfast for her six-year-old daughter.

Her wrinkled hands, cracked from scrubbing out stains and spots not of her own making, looked like they belonged to a woman much older than Maryanne's 39 years. The battered camper was about the same age. On damp days, dormant mould bloomed behind the faded beige wallpaper, and the smell, that earthy, damp smell, made Maryanne briefly set aside her daily worries about tiny, toxic spores filling their bodies as they slept. On warm days, she could smell the dust living in the '70s brown and yellow dinette cushions. She knew she should give them a vacuum—maybe at the next truck stop.

The sleeping child who was not Maryanne's, clutched her daughter's stuffed owl in her left hand. The child was deeply asleep. Maryanne noticed a crumpled Twix wrapper on the bed, likely the one that she had bought her daughter at the small gas station they had stopped at that afternoon. A parental instinct to never wake a sleeping child irrationally took hold of Maryanne. With lack of clarity on what exactly to do next, she sat down at the dinette and looked out the window.

For once Maryanne could see the stars. Having spent a few nights in parking lots, she knew she was lucky tonight when she found a spot under a burnt-out light.

The death of her son had given Maryanne the push she needed to leave James. His obsession with "moving on" echoed in her mind when she tried to sleep. In the days following their empty-handed return from the hospital, she lay in bed, eyes wide open, wondering what had gone wrong. No consolation was to be found in the murmurs of her friends and family. No casserole made any difference to her state of mind. The only thing that resonated was James saying, "We have to move on," over and over, in various combinations of syllables and sentences. What Maryanne heard was, "Move on," and she held tight to that as an idea, which took root in the cracked landscape of her heart.

Tonight, she could see a sky that was so full of stars they seemed close, almost as though you could run your fingers through them. Sitting there, listening to the slow heavy breathing of a strange child, she allowed herself one big sigh but no tears.

It had taken Maryanne a few weeks to adequately come to terms with the state of her finances. She reviewed her account balance countless times, checking the line items for the past month. Her hope dimmed each day, eroding the belief that she might find an uncashed cheque or unused government benefit. Despite her efforts and her internal monologue of faith, the balance line remained stubbornly fixed.

When leaving James became more pressing than the practicalities, Maryanne bought an RV. A Kijiji ad read simply: *1982 Dodge Tioga Arrow for sale by original owners. Runs well. $5,200.* Maryanne loaded up Ellie in their old Volvo, packed some sandwiches, and drove out to meet the Johnsons, an elderly couple who lived in a rural farmhouse complete with a few chickens.

The Johnsons had welcomed Maryanne and Ellie with wide smiles and glasses of iced tea. The chickens flapped at Ellie's feet and she giggled while chasing them around the wide green lawn. Next to the barn sat a cream-coloured RV with small rivers of rust running down the sides. One of the tires sat low and a red tail light was cracked, revealing a small, old-fashioned bulb.

"There she is!" Bob's enthusiasm was sincere as he handed Maryanne the keys.

Maryanne dutifully climbed into the driver's seat and pretended to look around. She wanted to seem knowledgeable about RVs, hopeful she could knock a few hundred off the price. As the vehicle roared to life, Maryanne tried the wipers and the radio. She adjusted the heating and a faint burning smell came out of the vents.

"I'm not sure about that, Bob. Seems a bit questionable ..." she trailed off, not really sure what else to say about it.

"Yes, oh my. Happy to take it down to $4,900." Bob's eagerness to sell put Maryanne at ease and she smiled.

Getting up from the driver's seat, Maryanne looked around. A small dinette was right behind the driver. A bed with an old foam mattress sat directly above the cab. Further back was a small stove and a tiny fridge, a bathroom the size of a closet, another bed at the very back.

She was not bothered by the musty smell or the old cushions. Maryanne didn't flinch at the grease buildup on the stove or the foggy windows that needed scouring. To her these things looked and smelled like her new life. One without James. A life where she could keep her lost son close to her heart. A life filled with new air, inhaled from the open road and found in the creases of a map.

Bob and Caroline offered to drive the RV down to Maryanne's house the following weekend. She gratefully accepted, but asked them to meet her at a gas station a few miles from her house. Her plan didn't involve a lot of goodbyes and certainly no explanations.

The day of the funeral came and Maryanne packed a small bag for her and Ellie. Bob and Caroline were meeting them at the Quick Gas at 12:30 p.m.

Ellie adapted easily to life on the road. She loved the map and the chocolate bar treats. She didn't mind sleeping in parking lots and loved drawing pictures of the trees they passed. Clear skies meant easy driving and it was on the afternoon of the third day before they stopped for a picnic nearly a thousand kilometres outside of Toronto, on the shores of Lake Superior.

There were a few other people there—a large family having some sort of reunion, an older couple walking slowly along the beach, a group of young people taking selfies. After a short picnic and a rest on the beach, they left for Thunder Bay. They stopped once, at a roadside station for gas and a Twix for Ellie, before reaching the quiet parking lot of a Walmart Supercentre where they nestled near the perimeter under a spindly tree.

⤳

The sleeping child didn't stir as Maryanne sat down on the edge of the bed, exhaustion seeping into her veins. Maryanne felt her limbs sink into the worn fabric and she almost willed them to stop working, when Ellie's little voice called out urgently.

"Mama! Where are you?"

"I'm here baby girl, give me a second." Maryanne made her way to Ellie and sat down. "Ellie, who is sleeping in the back?"

"Mama, where is Ollie? I dropped Ollie!"

"Sweetheart, he's right here. I need you to tell me who is in the back bed. Was it someone you were playing with at the beach?"

"No Mama. I don't know."

Maryanne felt her breath catch. She got into the driver's seat and started the RV. "Okay, baby, someone must have crawled in for a nap. Let's go take them home."

Maryanne found her way to the police station. She unbuckled Ellie and went to the back to get the child. As she picked her up, stirring softly, the wisp of a child wrapped her arms around her neck. Maryanne thought she heard her whisper *Mama* but realized it must just have been hair brushing her ear. In that moment, she thought about turning around and tucking them both back into bed and driving off into the night.

Lisa Jones

Social Graces

AN EXCERPT

Sophie shouldn't nap anymore; it ruins her sleep. But the quiet moments are when I love her most. The clammy sweetness, the fact that I can't do anything wrong, that she doesn't demand things I can't give her. I watch the slow rise and fall of her chest, the little sighs and smiles of her dreams. We drift off beside one another and the parts of us that touch get sweaty, heated by the afternoon sun.

⌒

Our neighbour is singing opera when I wake up. She once told me she sings when she's lonely, and we hear her every day. I'm hazy like a black and white movie. Drool has saturated my pillow and the house is still. With the breeze gone I stick to the sheets as I roll over to reach for Sophie. But she's not there. Not even her imprint in the bedding.

My pulse thuds in my throat. When I yell her name, my voice cracks through the quiet. There's no answer. No patter of feet, no thrashing of toys, no giggles. There's nothing but dusk.

I stand frozen at the half-open bedroom door and will myself through it into the hallway. On our white walls there's a new purple stripe, like the too-low markings of a chair rail. I follow it down the hall to the living room, and a single line sprouts two and three colours, a mess of verve and Crayola. The cabinet beneath the sink is open and I lose my breath. I didn't lock it. I move past the couch toward the TV and see her on the floor. Laying on her side with her face to the wall. Unmoving.

My knees weaken and I brace myself as I edge closer. I'm so afraid to touch her. To see what I let happen as I dreamed of why she hates spaghetti and how I still give it to her because I'm tired and it's easy.

This is when she looks up at me with more concern than I deserve. She releases a purple marker from her grip and rubs her eyes. She toddles over and I fall to the ground to take her in my arms. Sophie touches my cheeks with her sticky hands and smears my tears around, then she pats my head the way I do hers when I'm reminding her things aren't really so bad. Like when I tell her the seam on her pants won't hurt her, and the doggy can't talk. I can see that my daughter is not dead from my negligence; it isn't the end of the world.

"Sad mum mum," she says, staring into my eyes like it's a challenge.

I clear my throat, clean off my face. "I was …" I lose my words, and the tears come again. "I was really worried about you." I wipe my nose, and she helps me. "I'm sorry, hon. Wake mama up next time, 'kay?"

Her frizz is backlit by the last ray of daylight. This wild, fiery thing that I decide might be okay despite me.

She smiles at my apology and says, "Picture," then turns to look at her art on the walls. The lines of purple dance with green and pink. In places, she's woven colours together in finger patterns. It's beautiful and I don't want to wash it away. I want to keep it there as a reminder of what I've done, what could have been, and what she is capable of without me.

She nuzzles herself onto my lap and says, "Hungry."

I stroke her hair, careful not to flatten the ringlets. "What do you want?"

"No pasghetti." I cry again and hold her so closely she yells, "Tight!"

As I take stock of Sophie's time alone, I hear the screen door creak and then the jingle of Tristan's keys. I want to scramble to my feet, but he sees me before I have time to move. Sophie breaks loose from my arms and runs to him.

He scoops her up without taking his eyes off me. "Want to watch Elmo?" he asks her, and pulls out his phone.

When she's in our bed again, where she was supposed to be as I slept, he comes out and sits next to me on the floor. He has trouble bending down because his suit pants are tight. He smells like the restaurant. Like grease and garlic and booze. I'm repulsed by it, but feel glued to the ground beside him.

"Can you tell me what's going on?" He motions to the walls.

I feel my eyes well, and I choke it back. "We had a nap, and she woke up before me."

He looks around the room. "For how long?"

"I don't know." I can't stand his stare. I want to grab Sophie and leave so he never looks at me again.

"You slept through all of this?" He stands and walks to the wall, swipes a strip of marker with his finger, then traces her handprint. I want to tell him not to touch it. That this is how our walls are now.

The sound of *Sesame Street* echoes out of the bedroom, and he shakes his head. "Has she eaten dinner yet?"

I look at the floor in embarrassment, and heat rises through my neck. "You can't ever bring us something home?"

He rolls his eyes and turns away, and when he pivots back, he's softened. I wonder about his chain of thought. If he perhaps remembered that I have no mother to show me how to do this. He stoops down and hauls me to my feet in an embrace.

Alone in the kitchen, I pick up the pot of congealed spaghetti we had for lunch. The sound it makes as I scrape it into the garbage distracts me from what happened. Then I hear Elmo say, "Elmo make mistakes sometimes, Elmo sorry," and I cry again.

⸙

Our dinner conversation is sad like the eggs and floppy toast we drown in ketchup. Tristan and I ask Sophie questions about her day and her favourite colour, hoping to fill the gaps in our love for one another with our love for her. He sits at the table like he's above us, slumming between work hours. His back is stiff and shoulders straight. He stabs at his eggs like they might run off the plate. I notice how I'm hunched over my food, and when he's not looking, I straighten myself.

He convinces Sophie to let him do her bedtime. It's easier for him because she has no fond memories of his tit in her mouth. With me it's always another snuggle, another song, don't leave mum mum, stay with me.

She's down in ten minutes. He comes to the couch with a glass of scotch and a tired face, and I suppress an eye roll. We listen to the sounds of cars whizzing by, of our neighbour humming by her window, and he speaks first.

"Are you okay?" He eyes me as he sips, and I feel guilty for how resentful I always am. The creases around his eyes have deepened and make him look more severe than when we first met. Like a serious man.

I nod. Wine has dulled my memory of the day. I put my feet on his lap, expecting a massage; and he edges a hand to the top of my foot but doesn't rub, just rests it there. His warmth makes me shiver, and I nuzzle my heel into his crotch. He shifts away and stretches his arms across the back of the couch, then shoots me a sympathetic look.

Fuck your pity. I pull some hair down from my topknot because he focused too long on my forehead, and tell him I'm going to check the mail then go to bed. I can't be around him when he won't touch me, when he doesn't look at me like I'm the evidence he struck gold.

It takes 37 steps to get to the mailbox. Sophie and I count them when we're bored. Every time I slide my key in, I expect to find a piece of my mom in there. Not a literal piece, like a finger or toe. But something. Some kind of proof that she's alive and every so often thinks of me. The slot is empty. Not even a flyer to raise my hopes. I stare into its darkness, inhale night air that smells like a family's roast beef dinner, and tell myself that if she were here, I could be happy. That it's her fault I'm failing at everything.

I count the steps in my mind back up to the house. He has his headphones on when I come inside. I want to reach out and rub the back of his head, to straddle him and ask if he could spare a moment. Instead, I walk to the bedroom without saying goodnight, and wonder when the next letter will come.

Adele Bok

Ester and Dinah

AN EXCERPT

*The twins, Ester and Dinah, are in their last year of
high school when Dinah disappears.*

Ester looked at herself in Dinah's dressing table mirror, her eyes once
again searching involuntarily for the necklace. She would have to tell Ma
tomorrow morning. Or maybe she would not have to, if Dinah showed
up in the middle of the night, smelling like God-knows-what. The
reflected image of her standing in Dinah's room made Ester feel all the
lonelier and she quickly picked up the last stray clothing.

When she had finished putting everything in the laundry bin, she
went back to Dinah's room to make sure she had left the light on. If not
for Dinah's return, then for luck.

⤳

That night Ester lay in bed listening for the slightest noise that could
signal Dinah's return. With every creak on the stairs, every hum of a car
engine close to her window, she lay infinitely still, holding her breath, to
listen more closely. She willed these sounds to be proof of her sister's
imminent presence. She reminded herself of nights that had finished exactly like this one would, with Dinah crawling into her bed, excited to tell
her about her nightly adventures and then falling asleep mid-sentence.
But with each hour that ticked by, her hope dwindled, as if someone were
plucking the stars out of the sky.

The next morning, Ester gathered herself to face the day that lay ahead. She would keep busy and Dinah would come when she least expected her. She washed the dishes, looked at the clock, vacuumed and dusted the living room, changed the bedding in all their rooms, looked at the clock, washed and hung the sheets outside, scrubbed the toilets, soaked the pile of clothes with tough stains, looked at the clock, polished her and Dinah's school shoes, heard someone fiddle with the kitchen lock and ran to the door with a whispered prayer of gratitude. But it was only Ma making sure the lock worked. Ester washed the black polish from her shaking hands and felt the gloom gathering, even as beams of sunlight still stretched over the kitchen counter.

"Ma, there's something I have to tell you." Ester could see remnants of hope warring with fear and resignation in Ma's expression. "Dinah never came to school to write the exam yesterday. They'll probably phone you about it on Monday."

Ma got up and then her legs gave out and she fell back into the chair. For a moment Ester feared that the chair would not hold this new weight that she had placed on her mother's shoulders.

"What?" Ma put her hand over her brow as if to shield herself from Ester's words.

"I don't know where she went after breakfast. I've been going over and over yesterday morning and … I don't know. I can't tell—"

"What did she say to you?"

"Nothing. She was just … very tired."

At this Ma raised her eyes to Ester's. It was a clear sign that, despite Ma's quickly-emptying bottle of antidepressants, she knew about the drinking and the absences of the last few days.

"Tell me everything."

She told Ma about the things that had gone missing in Dinah's room. About how unwilling Dinah had been to talk these past few days, about how sure she was that Dinah would come back yesterday. Last night. This morning.

They had been taught the statistics of rape in South Africa. One in four women. One in four women.

"What if something … happened to her, Ma?" Her voice was a whisper as she fought tears. "What if she was in an accident? Or she was … attacked?"

Saying the words out loud suddenly gave terrible shape to Dinah's absence. She had not in fact disappeared, she was somewhere and something so terrible had happened to her that she could not find her way home. Ester thought about Ouma San reading *Little Red Riding Hood* to them when they were kids. Their fear of their grandmother's growling portrayal of the big bad wolf as he seduced the little girl into telling him where she was going. How satisfying it was then when the woodcutter arrived and chopped off the wolf's head, saving the grandmother and the girl from an otherwise bloody fate. At this point, Ouma San would close the book with a resounding smack. "It's the two-legged wolf that you have to be afraid of in life," Ouma San would say fiercely, without any further explanation, leaving the girls with a goodnight kiss and a shapeless, bottomless sense of foreboding.

Ma got up slowly from her chair. "Why didn't you tell me? Why did you let me believe that everything was alright?"

Ester raised her hands to her temples and held onto her head, afraid that she might lose her mind, which was whirring with regret, with fear, with anger at herself. And yet she had only been trying to protect Dinah against Ma's anger, to stop Ma from worrying, to keep things as they were so that Dinah could step right back into their world with her turquoise-painted toes as if nothing had happened.

"If something has happened to Dinah—" Ma picked up the house phone and did not finish the sentence.

If Ester had told Ma earlier. If she had alerted the school. If the police could have been searching for Dinah already. She had made a terrible, terrible mistake. The enormity of the consequences of her inaction struck her and she knew that no matter what happened, she had failed Dinah, she had failed Ma and their lives, because of it, had derailed.

Ma put down the phone. "I need to go to the police station for a missing person's report." Ma put her coat on despite the warm day outside and looked at Ester. She must have seen the dazed expression on her daughter's face because she said, somewhat ashamed, "I didn't mean … it's not … everything is going to be okay."

Ester nodded at Ma's back, convinced that neither of them would believe those words again.

Shiva Bhusal
Stains of War

AN EXCERPT

There are three incidents in his life Sanjay will never forget. One of them was when he was eight years old, studying in grade three. He had just learned to play cricket and soccer, and had dabbled in dancing and caricature, mimicking Rajesh Hamal's moves in the famous Nepali film, *Deuta*. The family member he liked most was Grandfather, 72, whose face was unwrinkled but who had a head full of grey hair.

Grandfather was short and stocky and loved shaving his cheeks clean, but he kept a giant moustache and twisted it from the sides whenever asked to opine on a serious topic. His voice indicated no signs of his age, for it was full of command and authority like that of a military leader. He had lost one of his front teeth, not in a fight, but when he was tying a rope on a dry branch of an old Peepal tree to build *Ping* for *Dashain*. The branch creaked and Grandfather fell. He noticed blood oozing out of his mouth and felt a hollowness between his upper incisors. He never bothered to put in an artificial tooth. Sanjay loved being around him, especially during late evenings.

It was one such evening in December 2001. After having a cup of milk, three chapatis, and fried lettuce, Sanjay felt sleepy and went to sit beside Grandfather. Grandfather caressed Sanjay's hair.

"Okay, Grandson," he said. "Today I will tell you a story of a king. His name was Rana Bahadur Shah. He ruled Nepal 200 years ago. He was a cruel king."

Sanjay always heard stories of mermaids, fairies, and monsters from Grandfather, and for him, the meaning of "cruelty" was always something related to harming children like him.

Out of curiosity, Sanjay said, "Hajurbaa, did he kidnap kids? Did he beat them with a cane?"

"Yes, he kidnapped young girls from their parents."

"What did he do with the young girls?"

"He married them. He killed the girls if they resisted."

"Oh, he was such a monster!"

"Thousands of people died from famine, but he was always busy singing, dancing, and drinking. Our present king is not like Rana Bahadur Shah, but some people accuse him of killing his brother's family. I don't think that is true. Only God knows who killed the family. The new king recently visited our district. I saw him from a distance, and he sounded like an honest person in his speech. But one can be judged not by their speech but by their actions. He might also have evil intentions. Who knows?"

"How was the previous king?"

"Most of the people liked him. Even the Maoists were okay with his rule if he provided a little more freedom to the people. He made high school free. He reduced the budget allocated for the royal family and used that for people's welfare. He started giving an elderly stipend of five hundred rupees to everyone older than 65. He had an aura about him when he walked and talked. You know a king is a mighty person. Even if he is bad, he is still the incarnation of Lord Vishnu. We should never say bad things about him."

Grandfather hadn't completed his story, but he found Sanjay's eyes were closed. He placed Sanjay's head over the pillow and wrapped him with a soft blanket.

⌒

Sanjay was born in a remote village called Sarangdi in the western hills of Nepal. From a town called Kushma, one had to walk five hours toward the south to reach his village. There lived around twenty families, scattered over 100 acres. The nearest village was two hours of walking toward the east, and about a half hour of walking through dense jungle. There was a primary school nearby. There were 26 students in the school, with five teachers rotating their shifts. They didn't have electricity, and the only means that illuminated the dark nights were the kerosene lamps, wood fires, and fireflies.

The nearest high school was about two hours' walk away. High school students would leave home early in the morning packing their lunch and would return only in the late evenings. Since attending high school was a struggle, most boys and girls quit their studies after completing primary school and helped their parents in agriculture and raising cattle.

When he was six, Sanjay's family left the village in the western hills and moved to another village in the plains. The new place had a good road connection, the high school was nearby, and even the colleges were about an hour drive away. In the new school, he was admitted to grade one on a provisional basis. Sanjay did pretty well in grade one, so the teachers let him jump to grade three. There he had difficulty in math and english.

The math teacher liked Sanjay as he was the quietest student in the class. One day, the teacher gave a division assignment. Everyone did the assignment, and he began grading. When it was Sanjay's turn, the teacher saw that his approach was wrong. He also noted that it was similar to one of the graded copies. He pulled the graded assignment from the pile—it was Arjun's—and found they were identical. He called on Arjun and asked him to stand beside Sanjay.

"Did you copy your homework from Arjun?"

Sanjay's face turned pale. He bowed his head. "Yes."

The teacher demanded Sanjay and Arjun do ten sit-ups, right there. Then he turned and addressed the room.

"From now on, nobody will help this kid with his homework. He is new to the class."

After Sanjay's family moved to the plains, his mother, Sabina, got involved with a social engagement community called *Aama Samuha*. The group's primary purpose was to ensure women like her were empowered through access to fundamentals such as birth control rights, economic freedom, and social equality. Sabina bought two doelings, and after a year, they gave birth to two young bucks. Rabilal, the cattle specialist, came to their house from the neighboring village and castrated the bucks to make them wether. The castration process was extremely painful to the young bucks. Rabilal tied their legs with a rope and used pliers to disconnect the nerves between their genitals and testicles, during which the buck screamed so everyone in the village could hear.

Sanjay loved playing with the wethers. He would catch them with his arms and sing, "Mune mune patho yo!" No sooner would he finish the first line of the song than the wether would escape his arms and sprint across the field.

Before Sanjay completed primary school, politics entered his life. first came the discontentment and rage, then the promises, and finally the rebellion and fire. The discontentment and anger arrived in pamphlets and writings, through audio recordings and live speeches. The promise was of a bright future—a country where everyone was treated equally and a society that believed in rational thoughts instead of superstition. The promise was also of a strong economy where everyone supported themselves with jobs that matched their abilities. To fulfill these dreams, the path taken was full of bullets and guns.

Hundreds of people dressed in civilian clothes started marching in the streets. The walls of houses were painted with slogans overnight, but nobody was able to figure out who had painted them. Young men and women were spotted collecting donations from wealthy landlords, school teachers, and government officials. They threatened the people who resisted, and killed some of them without any hint or clue of who they were.

That year it rained a lot during the winter, and the rain brought tears to the farmers' faces. They had planted the paddies two months late, since June and July were dry. The late plantation delayed the harvest by a couple of months. The entire paddy plantation was destroyed while it rained cats and dogs—a bad omen. It was not the best time of their lives, and to make it worse, the civil war had officially begun.

Alicia Neptune

The Year of the Thunderstorm

When the storm came, no one knew what it was except for you.

We'd been living in the haze of wildfire smoke for weeks. Apocalypse sky, I called it, staring out the window at the eerie orange light. That's how it felt, watching the flames on the news every day. Our corner TV, usually all sports all the time, became our own personal wildfire monitoring station.

Then the thunder started. Like the gods dropped a bag of marbles. This glorious rumble that rolled across the valley. The storm was the exact opposite of that hot, dead haze. Wind blew in cool from the west. Purple lightning crackled in the air. Rain set every leaf jumping. I could breathe again. I switched off the news, sat on the front steps, and waited for you to get home.

It was not very sympathetic of me to be so excited. Would it make any difference to know I was holding myself back? You ran from the car to the sheltered steps with your jacket pulled over your head, and all I wanted to do was take your hand and run back out into the rain. Except you were shaking—actually trembling—and you crashed into me like we were long-distance lovers at the airport. We stood there with our arms around each other for ages before you let me free my arm to open the door.

I didn't get it. I get it now.

You being afraid of lightning is not like me being afraid of phone calls or spiders. It's not even like my fear of a meteor crashing into the Earth. If a meteor hit the Earth, we would all go together. Wrapped up in my fear is that one comfort.

36

I wish you had told me earlier, but I guess you tried to. It was right there on your profile under, "Something you should know about me." *I'm afraid of thunderstorms.* That sentence was doing a lot of heavy lifting. I thought it was sort of sweet. If a storm rolled in, we didn't go out. And for two years, that was just fine with me.

The thing about thunderstorms, the thing that always made them exciting and not scary, is that they end. They aren't like the rain or the haze. They don't linger. I expected to wake and find the wildfire smoke had finally cleared, leaving behind a picnic-ready blue sky. What I got was thunder, and you at the window, watching the lightning. And again the next day. And then it was Monday.

The storm's persistence had already worn down your nerves. You hardly slept all weekend. It was one thing for you to call in sick. It was another to ask me to.

"I know you don't like me going out in a storm," I said. "But I'll be fine. I'll go straight to the museum."

"Please," you said. "Just today."

I didn't have to decide, in the end. They issued a severe thunderstorm warning. We all stayed home.

How long can one storm last? The meteorologists debated while we learned to just live with it. That meant something different for everyone. For us, it meant a lot of time at home. More time than we'd ever spent together.

Before the routine went stale and things started to fall apart, you and I laid on the living room carpet and stared up at the ceiling. The curtains were open. Rain beat against the windows. And every so often, a flash.

"I got caught in a lightning strike once," you said.

"Jesus. You were struck by lightning?" I remember fumbling for the right words. "I'm sorry."

"Everything went white. Bright, like when the sky is covered with clouds and it hurts to look directly at it. And it wasn't raining anymore."

"What happened? Did you have to go to the hospital?"

"I thought I died. I couldn't feel anything. It was like my body didn't exist. I was just ... there. For a long time."

"You must have passed out."

"I didn't. I don't know what happened, but it took me someplace. Then it dropped me back here, and I'd been missing for two days."

"I don't understand."

"I just don't want that to happen to you."

I didn't ask you anything else. I didn't ask how old you were or what happened when you got back. I guess I thought if you wanted to tell me, you would just tell me. So I let the silence wedge itself between us, and we never really recovered.

⁀

The great flood. I called it that more than once, standing at the window in awe, watching sidewalk rivers flow past clogged storm drains. Goddamn. The imagery. Biblical curses have always been my favourite curses.

Trees came down on the power lines up north. It took ages to restore service because it was too dangerous to be doing electrical work. The soil on the ridge along Highway 98 started to erode and it brought boulders down onto a delivery truck. The province was taking a beating.

I set up my home work station in the dining room, where I could hear the rain on the skylight. You turned our closet into a mini recording studio, sound-proofing and all, and hid yourself away in there. We managed.

If the storm calmed down at night, and I was certain you were asleep, I would sneak outside to stand in the rain. The last time wasn't the first time. Did you know? You must have known. I'd been going out for ages.

We were trapped in this box together. I just wanted some space. I'm torn between remembering my need for solitude and regretting how much I took you for granted.

No one noticed folks were going missing at first. In the early weeks, there were hikers unaccounted for, sure. People in accidents, or stuck behind some landslide up in the mountain passes where there's no service. But then there were those folks, like, four months in who just vanished. Enough of them that people started to notice. People started thinking it was the rapture. I started thinking you were one of those people.

I found the throwaway account you made. The forum where you shared your experience and people didn't just believe you, they looked to you for answers. I'm so mad, looking back at it. Not at you—I'm mad at myself. I'm mad I didn't figure out how to talk to you about this. And okay, maybe a little mad at you for talking to strangers on the internet when you weren't talking to me.

But I didn't go out that night to spite you. Like I said, I'd been going out for ages.

You were snoring, so I figured I was safe. I crept out of bed and avoided the one squeaky part of the floor. I put my favourite raincoat on over my pajamas and pulled the hood up, and wore my winter boots, since I never did bother to get real rain boots.

It was warm out. We'd lived through the storm for three-quarters of a year and made it back to spring. I didn't go far, just up the street, around the cul-de-sac, and back again. The tree in our neighbours' front yard was looking the worse for wear. I scraped some leaves out of the storm drain.

There was a flash, and then a marvelous crash of thunder. Like it was right on top of me. I stood, rooted to that spot. It was a perfect crescendo. I felt it in my spine.

And then there was you, shouting through the rain. "Hold on! Don't move!"

You were holding my hand. And then—

flash!

—you weren't.

I *know* you got to me in time. When I think about it, I can feel your hand in mine, just like I can feel my teeth ache when I think about biting into an apple.

So why didn't it take me too? Did I let go? Did you?

It's over now. A year to the day it first started, the storm finally packed its things and left.

You said you went missing for two days back then. It's been a lot longer than that. I've had time to think about what I should've done differently.

I think what I should have said, that very first day, was, "Let's be scared together."

I hope you found all those other people. I hope they found you. I hope you're not alone, wherever you are.

I hope the lightning gives you back.

Caitlin McCarthy
A Fine-Toothed Comb
AN EXCERPT

*This novel follows three generations of related women who
come of age at different stages: young adult, mid-life, and end-of-life*

How many times had Bronwen sat in the back seat of the Crown Victoria and watched her grandmother fix her hair? Irene's knobby fingers
were covered in gold and amber jewellery. They looked like thick tree
branches seeping winter sap. With her skin-bark hands, Irene would
reach into her purse and feel around. There it was. The fine-toothed
comb. She'd pull it through her short, salon-curled hair; she went every
week. Smoothly at first, then the comb would catch on the tangled ends.

Her grandmother still had brown hair. Youthfulness: they had that
in common. Perhaps because Bronwen was short, or because she had a
round face, people always thought she was younger than she was. She
wondered what her hair would be like when she was as old as—how old
was her grandma, exactly? As old as time, it felt like. Because of her age,
Irene had a not-so-secret pride in her barely salt-and-pepper hair. She
must have been well into her eighties and regularly reminded Bronwen
that all the ladies at bridge told her every week they had long been using blue shampoo. Not so for Irene. But from her slump in the back of
the sedan, Bronwen could see Irene's hair thinning at the crown. *Did she
know?*

Crunch. Crunch.

Comb through.

Pat. Pat.

Put the hair in place.

She knew.

Bronwen fiddled with her French braid. She had finally taught herself, choosing to braid her hair rather than finish her Calculus 12 homework. Despite spending more time on her hair and the phone than on homework, she received a B on her final exam. And now it was summer break. She had to go on this road trip.

"It means a lot to your grandmother that we do this together," Linda had said, but Bronwen suspected the trip was important to her mother. In another couple months, Bronwen would be moving to Toronto and starting school, so this was a family send-off of sorts.

She looked out the car window and noticed her mom returning from the gas station bathroom. "Bronwen, when you walk, it's important to look ahead. Look where you're going and your feet will follow," her mom had always advised. Often, Bronwen looked down. She was prone to tripping. Linda's gaze darted from car to car, to the ground, and to the sky, where a summer storm was brewing. Easier said than done, it seemed.

Back at the car, Linda muttered to herself, "Okay, let me just get my sunglasses. And some lipstick. Where did I put my—oh, there. Everyone ready?" She didn't wait for a response before starting the car.

Bronwen turned her attention back to the magazine on her lap. She was hoping she could get in one more page before feeling carsick. It felt important to know the must-have items of summer 2003.

"Linda. Did you get those … what are those … they're …" Irene struggled to find the word, instead tracing a circle with her finger.

"Oh shoot. Sorry, Mom. Can it wait 'til the next stop?"

"What are they … for heaven's sake."

The car hit the highway with some speed, but immediately slowed to a halt. Traffic jam. Bronwen glanced up as her mom tried to peek around the cars in front to see what was making them so slow.

"My God, look at this. Bronwen, pass me the map in that—no, the plastic container—yes, there. Actually, can you open it?" Linda asked.

"A dough nut. Doughnut? Is that what they are?" Irene asked the car.

"Yes, Mom, we'll get you a doughnut," Linda confirmed.

Bronwen opened the map to the section of the highway they were on and passed it to her mom, who quickly tried to figure out if they could take a detour on country roads.

The three women had stopped in Kingston after finishing cream-of-something soup at Bronwen's great-aunt's apartment in Belleville. They made this pilgrimage every couple of years, stopping along Eastern Ontario on the way to Aunt Agnes' cottage near Algonquin Park. Spending time together felt like an occasion to watch each other from afar, not to enjoy quality time together. Bronwen's family liked tasks: doing dishes, reading the newspaper, running errands. Without their hands and minds occupied, they didn't quite know how to be in the world, let alone talk to each other.

"Can I take your plate?" Bronwen remembered Linda asking the last time they were at the cottage.

"Mom. I haven't eaten any potatoes yet," Bronwen had pointed out. Her aunt was an incredible cook, and she always saved the garlicky potatoes for last.

"Oh, sorry, dear. Do you want more? There's more. We should finish it."

Bronwen rolled her eyes as potatoes were piled on her plate. She wanted *time*, not more *food*. As Linda rinsed dishes in the kitchen, Bronwen and Irene sat at the table together in silence. Her grandmother finished everything and was eyeing the dessert on the counter. Her aunt and uncle had already left for their after-dinner walk, which was especially important that evening because her uncle Mark had a headache. Walking was their remedy for everything. Her dad had also come along for that trip, and after dinner resumed his station fixing the latch on the screen door. Bronwen remembered taking a bite of potato and realizing she might be able to finish the whole plate of them, after all.

The sun started to peek through the clouds and crept up Bronwen's arm through the car window. She smiled to herself as Irene pulled out an enormous pair of tortoiseshell sunglasses. Her grandmother's glamour always seemed accidental. Irene certainly had style, but her taste fell just shy of the elegance she was going for.

Bronwen didn't know this would be her last road trip with her grandmother. If she had, maybe she would have tried to ask Irene more questions. She also didn't know the specifics of the heavy air that always seemed to surround them all, the withheld information it had carried for her mother's entire lifetime. Maybe longer. A year from now, Bronwen's mom would call her to double check what time they were to meet the following day. Her mom's voice would sound more measured than usual. "We'll talk tomorrow," Linda would say, "not on the phone." And Bronwen would wonder what it all meant. But she wouldn't know what questions to ask until a long time after that.

Bronwen looked back at the service station's convenience store as it slowly disappeared behind them, trying to assess if they were far enough in their journey for Linda not to make a comment if Bronwen were to buy Cheezies at the next stop. The supply of almonds and raisins was quickly disappearing, and the sandwiches made at home six hours ago were definitely soggy. But Bronwen and the plush seat had become one, and she hadn't felt like moving at the last stop.

"Hmm?" Linda asked no one in particular.

"Didn't say anything," Bronwen replied after a moment.

They took the next exit off the 401 and hurtled down a regional road, the distance between them immense despite their proximity.

Cate Sandilands
Eleanor

AN EXCERPT FROM "DEAR JANE RULE"

A collection of short stories that imagine the many lives
Jane Rule (1931-2007) touched as a writer, mentor,
activist, correspondent, and friend

The first floor of the university library was bright with the mid-morning sun when Christine stepped off the escalator. The design of the new library had puzzled her when Ted brought her to the opening. Why enter from the bottom and that ghastly, dark corridor when there was such a grand welcome on the floor above it? Still, she liked the brutalist, first-floor space and how it provided an airy transition between the business of the hallway below and the quiet weight of the books above. Maybe that was the point?

Today, Christine didn't have time to ponder the architect's intentions. Ted was expecting her for lunch in half an hour. She strode over to the card catalogue, wrote down the call number she needed, rode up three escalators to the fourth floor, and walked down the aisle to the PS 3505 section: American Literature, 1900-1960. Why on earth did her book circle decide on an obscure novel by a long-dead woman when there were such interesting new titles in the bookstores? Still, she was grateful; even a story about farmers in Nebraska would be a change from fashion, or recipes for tricking children into eating vegetables.

She moved slowly down the aisle in search of the right shelf. Carson, Carter, Casey, Castle. There it was—Cather. Christine put her index finger on the spine of the first book and drew it along the printed gold titles. Toward the end of the row, her hand arrived at Chadwell, then Chandler. She stopped. Where was it? She tried again. She looked at the surrounding shelves to see if someone had put it in the wrong place. She checked the cart at the end of the row.

"Damn it," she said to the books.

She looked at her watch. Fifteen minutes before she had to meet Ted. She ran down the three escalators to the first floor and rushed to the circulation desk. There was no line, thank goodness, so she went right up to the librarian.

"Good afternoon," said Christine. She managed a pleasant voice despite her annoyance. "I would like to borrow a book that seems to be out on loan. Can you please help me? It's a bit … urgent."

She handed the librarian the piece of paper on which she had written the call number. The woman on the other side of the desk smiled at her. She had short red hair and wore no makeup. She looked very professional: smart jacket, green silk scarf folded neatly under a white shirt collar.

"I'm sure I can help you get your book," she said. "We can put it on hold. Could you please also tell me the author and title?"

Christine was suddenly aware of her appearance. She had dressed to please Ted, in the trim brown coat and dress he liked. Fashionable, not academic. She tried not to give away that she felt like an imposter.

"The book," she said, in a voice she hoped indicated seriousness, "is by Willa Cather, and it's called *O Pioneers*."

The librarian's smile widened. "Oh, that's an excellent book! I understand why you want to read it. But may I ask why it's so … urgent?"

Christine started to talk, hesitantly at first, then gathering into a gush. Despite her self-consciousness, she found herself telling the woman across the desk about her book circle, how much she craved the intelligent company of other women, that she would rather read the book by that new Morrison author, but Cather was the assignment.

"I think one of the circle must have borrowed it," she concluded, "because I'm not sure who else would want to read it."

The librarian grinned. She'd just said it was an excellent book. Christine flushed with embarrassment. How ignorant she must seem to such an educated woman, used to dealing with graduate students, not silly faculty wives.

To Christine's surprise, the librarian responded with encouragement. "As it happens, I know I just checked in *O Pioneers.*" She got up from her seat, revealing well-cut trousers. "If you can wait a minute, I'll get it for you from the back."

Christine was flustered and could only nod. She watched the woman disappear into the room behind the circulation desk. She looked at her watch. She was now perilously close to being late to meet Ted. Christine calmed herself with the thought that he'd encouraged her to join the book circle. Perhaps he wouldn't mind a slight delay in the interest of her reading? She adjusted her dress.

The woman returned with a red-bound book in her hand. She sat back down at the desk, wrote some details in a large ledger, and stamped a blue due date into the paper on the fly-leaf: November 18, 1971. She looked up at Christine. Her smile seemed warmer somehow. Christine felt a flutter in her stomach.

"Here you are." She pushed the book across the desk. "I hope you end up enjoying it. May I please have your library card?"

Christine hurried into her purse, found her billfold, and extracted the card: *External Borrower, Mrs. Edward Rideout.* She didn't want to dwell on the name, so she passed it to the librarian's waiting hand without looking at it. The woman wrote down the information in her ledger and handed it back.

Christine could have said a polite "thank you" at that moment. She could have turned and left. She could have been on time for lunch with Ted. In the months that followed, she wondered why she hadn't.

Instead, on impulse, she blurted out, "I hope you don't mind me asking, but as you said you like this book, would you be interested in coming to our little circle to discuss it? I'm sure someone like you would bring great insight. Of course, you must be very busy."

The librarian replied before Christine finished her sentence. "I'd be delighted. I love Willa Cather and I'd enjoy the conversation. Despite my job"—she gestured to the large space around her—"I don't get a lot of time to talk about books. I spend most of my time helping students find articles in social science periodicals. It gets a bit dull."

Christine felt the flutter grow. She would see this woman again. The thought of her company made Christine unreasonably happy. She allowed herself a wide smile back.

She dug a scrap of paper out of her purse and wrote down her phone number: *Christine, 539-8701. Book Circle.* The librarian responded with a pink university memo: *Eleanor, 486-7244.*

Eleanor asked about the circle and what other books they had read. Christine told a story about the last one, *The Bell Jar*, which had given her nightmares for weeks. Eleanor sympathized, and then laughed with her about how one of the other women in the circle insisted the book was a metaphor for class struggle. She was the wife of a sociologist. They laughed about that too.

Christine arrived at Ted's table in the faculty club twenty minutes late. To her relief, he was absorbed in a journal. He looked up to ask her where she'd been.

She answered, "The library." It was true, but it felt oddly deceptive. She held up *O Pioneers* to substitute for any further detail.

He didn't seem interested. He launched into an account of the article he was reading even before Christine had finished sitting down. She put the book, along with her purse and coat, on the chair beside her.

Ted had already ordered her meal. It was what she would have chosen anyway. As she waited for their entrees to arrive, she didn't really listen to Ted despite his obvious excitement about someone's views on British foreign policy. The sound of Eleanor's laugh played in her ears, over and over.

Resisting the temptation to reach out and touch the book again, she focused on the shapes Ted's mouth made as he spoke. He pursed his lips when he pronounced his *o*'s.

She tried not to think about Eleanor's phone number, carefully folded inside her wallet.

Chris Powell

Portside

AN EXCERPT OF A NOVEL SET IN
LATE 1980S BALTIMORE

Marion gives up an Olympic fencing bid to be a stay-at-home mother,
then a steel mill worker after her husband's workplace accident
forces them to reverse roles.

Marion's father, Carl, started driving her into D.C. to see pro basketball games in 1973, shortly after the Bullets had left Baltimore for Washington. She was only a child then but could not remember her father taking any of her four older brothers. Maybe she'd forgotten, or perhaps by then they had already left the house or were old enough to have moved on to their own interests. Her mother had never gone to any games either—there was no expectation to, and both husband and wife were relieved of that.

Carl required time alone, so had solo game nights for many years to afford himself time for introspection. One day, when his wife couldn't supervise young Marion, he begrudgingly took her to a game. Carl would have chosen to skip a game rather than take a fussy child, except he could not pass up a match between the Bullets and the Bulls.

It was that day Carl discovered his daughter travelled well. Marion didn't insist on idle talk, so they grew to enjoy each other's quiet company.

Sometimes Marion felt compelled to ask a question, as young children are. Sometimes her father acknowledged she had spoken. When he responded, she knew she had asked a good question. She knew she had asked a very good question when he answered with more than one sentence, so she tried hard to think of very good questions. Although Marion's lively young mind effervesced with wonder and was overflowing with unanswered questions, she had long recognized and accepted her father's reticence, so she chose her queries carefully. She had yearned to ask more but sat quietly, thrilled to witness the world revealing itself to her during their long days together, never wanting to risk losing those adventures.

As an adult, Marion always knew what constituted a good question and had never asked a foolish one.

When Carl found he was not obliged to entertain, he was content to have his daughter's company for the games. For the duration of each match, he would wedge himself into his seat like a boulder setting in concrete. While he sat motionlessly, the crevices carved into his stern, weathered face created shadows that emphasized broad, stone-like features. An observer would have suspected he wanted to be anywhere else, except for the odd expressionless nod to approve a good play or a grumble when his team had run afoul.

On about half a dozen occasions over the years, Carl had taken long routes to or from the stadium. Once or twice he stopped in the city for ice cream even though Marion never asked him to. He did not like sweets and was just as stone-faced buying ice cream in Georgetown as he was walking around the National Mall or visiting Arlington Cemetery, although she remembers him removing his hat for a moment while they were there.

Carl's second wife was much younger than his first, so when Marion, their only child, was born, she was ten years younger than her youngest half-brother. Carl was old enough to be her grandfather, yet rarely anyone suspected he was. He was charismatic, commanding a presence that projected a strong constitution, like that of a heavyweight fighter in his prime. His unwavering gaze conveyed confidence and fortitude.

Whenever Carl left home, he wore a tailored business suit, his tie centred and symmetric, and a distinctive wool fedora that asserted authority. He had deep, penetrating eyes that kept vigil under eyebrows that looked like crazy caterpillars, attached equally to his forehead and the brim of his hat. Those who didn't know him imagined him Mafioso and instinctively gave him a wide berth. He was not in the mob, but as a union leader, he dealt with all sorts and rarely spoke of his work.

At one game, Marion sat with her father in the lower stands, just above one of the locker room corridors where a team spilled onto the court. Had she reached out, she could have touched the men as they jostled through the passageway. She was astonished by the size of the players. From the upper stands, they looked lean on the court, but up close, right next to her, she realized they were giants. Their tremendous height had belied their actual girth. Their arms were dense and muscular, and each hand was broad enough to hold her aloft by her belly.

She never cared which teams played and never knew the rules, but Marion loved the games. Her senses ran wild amid frenzied crowds, frantic court action, swelling and ebbing cheers, the stadium's grandeur, throngs of people moving every which way, and the heady aromatic medley of hot dogs, burgers, and beer.

When Marion tired from shuffling in her seat, she would recline into her father to rest her head against his prickly camel hair overcoat and stretch her arms as far around him as she could—just about halfway. Once she had settled, her father would tuck her like a newspaper under his brawny arm. Occasionally, when she peered upward at just the right moment, she thought she caught a glistening in his eyes. But little girls have good imaginations. She was nine or ten at her first game, and his heart stopped beating just days before she turned twelve.

Marion still remembered the colourful birthday streamers, balloons, and the fabulous triple-layer cake, cleverly made with a doll standing in the centre. The figurine's lacy waistcoat spread out an inch or two atop the white frosting to form part of the fairytale wedding dress that appeared to have magically melted into sugary sweetness. The creamy dress looked to be draped over a farthingale, concealing airy white cake inside. When the cake had been devoured, the doll revealed its elaborate linen dress, safely rolled in paper, away from the stickiness of the vanquished cake and frosting.

Along with as many children as she could muster, Marion's mother had invited her own friends, some without children, and their husbands came, and the affair was grand for a child's party, and there were more presents than Marion had ever seen before. And late that night, as on recent nights before and many nights afterward, she lay in her bed alone and cried.

Nora Wood

Spring

AN EXCERPT FROM "KIT: BOOK ONE" OF
THE TRAGEDY OF THE COMMONS TRILOGY

CHAPTER I

It is generally believed that everyone must experience at least one period of solitude in life to find out what they are made of and what they might make of their delivered gifts. It has also been said that this solitude can be large and difficult to bear which is exactly why Kit found herself staring down at the lease agreement she held in her hands. Filled with the youthful determination of becoming the master of life on her own terms, miles away from anyone or anything she knew, Kit told herself that geography was the one thing large and tangible enough to separate her from the memories and pain of her past once and for all.

Her new home would be on the second floor of a three-storey walk-up in an old character building. When her favorite professor, Dr. Halldorson, heard she had applied to the environmental law program in Boston, he had reached out to a former colleague who had a place close to campus that would be conveniently vacant for the year. The professor hadn't bothered to look for someone to sublet his home while he was on sabbatical, so when David had contacted him, he thought, "Sure, what the hell. It'll pay a few bills while I'm away."

His indifference afforded Kit cheap rent in a prime location within walking distance of the campus she would attend in the fall. Or, *hoped* she would attend in the fall. Kit still hadn't received the acceptance letter. It was getting late, and she was getting nervous, but she had a plan, loose as it was, and wasn't going to waste the momentum. When she was offered a summer position at the law library, Kit felt the decision had serendipitously been made for her.

She didn't need to take much with her, which was fortunate since she didn't have much to take. Sentimentality for material goods had been a luxury Kit couldn't afford and one that had never served her well, anyway. The wheels were in motion and travelling light would be an advantage.

Staring down at the handwritten lease agreement that loosely formalized the terms and duration of the arrangement, she picked up her pen and signed her legal name: *Katharine O'Connor*. She slid it into the addressed envelope, placed a stamp in the upper right corner, and slipped it into her bag.

CHAPTER 2

Hunter shifted to his side, tossing Victoria's arm off him a little more forcefully than intended. He was hot. It was one of the many disadvantages of the old building he lived in. Doors that didn't close properly, floors that creaked inconveniently, walls that were too thin, windows that were drafty, thermostats that didn't work. He cracked an eye open. The light was starting to filter in through the blinds. He picked up his phone to check the time: 5:15 a.m.

Fuck, he thought.

He had slept later than he wanted. The drinks the night before definitely hadn't helped. Mornings like these were becoming an occupational hazard the more time he spent with Victoria. As he sat up, his head started to pound with a dull but growing thump. Hunter pressed his closed eyes into the heels of his hands, pausing before reaching over and shaking the bare leg sprawled next to him.

"Hey," he croaked.

There was no response.

"Hey," Hunter repeated, louder this time. "Wake up, I've gotta go."

"Ugghhhh." A disgruntled moan escaped the face buried in the pillow. Sandy blonde hair was heaped in a mess atop the accompanying head.

"I've gotta get to the site by six so if you want a ride home, you need to be dressed in five," he muttered, as he stood and made his way to the bathroom.

They had been seeing each other casually for the past three months—*casually* being the key word—but Hunter had the impression she didn't see it the same as he did. Victoria was a bit of a wild child, prone to violent temper tantrums when she didn't get her way—jealous with a short fuse was putting it mildly. He had found some early entertainment in being the one able to assuage the onslaught of her moods, but the appeal had worn thin. Hunter kept his distance emotionally, careful not to lead her on, which lately seemed to be having the opposite effect he'd hoped for. But if he was being honest, there were moments when they were in bed when Victoria literally made him forget his name, which more often than not gave the devil sitting on his shoulder the upper hand. He was aware he was walking a thin and dangerous line.

Hunter turned on the tap and splashed the cold water on his face, sending a jolt through his fuzzy head. In the mirror, he watched as water and disappointment streamed down his cheeks and dripped off his stubbly chin. He cupped water in his hand, threw back a couple Tylenol, and returned to the bedroom.

Victoria sat scowling on the edge of the bed, pulling her black knee-high boots up over her shins. Hunter grabbed his jeans off the floor, pulled them on, and dug a clean T-shirt out of the drawer. He slid his keys off the top of the dresser and strolled out of the bedroom.

"You ready to go?" Hunter called, not bothering to turn his head back towards her as he did.

⁂

"Well, well, well … Good of you to show up," Geoff chided, strapping on his work belt. Geoff had been his best friend since childhood, but Hunter's late arrival had become an annoying and increasingly frequent occurrence. "You do know there's a long line at the unemployment office full of bums waiting for a job like yours."

Hunter's uncle owned the construction company and had given him the job out of a sense of loyalty to his late brother, Hunter's father. It was hard manual labour but it paid decently while he tried to figure out what he was going to do with the rest of his life.

"Yeah, right," Hunter snickered under his breath.

"Listen, it's not like I blame you or anything. With that nice little piece of ass you keep on the side, it's no wonder you have a hard time dragging your sorry self here in the morning. I'm just sayin'… some of us gotta pick up the slack while you're at home getting off."

Hunter shoved him playfully. "Fuck off, man. You know it isn't like that."

"Yeah, yeah, I know it's not 'like that.' What's it like then? Huh?" Geoff shoved him back, chuckling, and walked away.

Hunter threw a sledgehammer easily over his shoulder and walked down to meet the rest of the crew. His gaze drifted over, yet again, to the words "Faculty of Engineering" emblazoned on the large, imposing building across the street from the work site.

His skin prickled with sweat. The spring had been unseasonably warm, punctuated by heavy downpours, and today was forecasted to be another scorcher. A tightness squeezed his chest like a strong fist; he felt his goals slipping further and further from reach. Hunter had just turned 27 and time was becoming an indecipherable blur.

Heaving a sledgehammer meant he didn't need to hit the gym anymore, which was good since there was little time or energy left for it after a twelve-hour day on the site. The constant, grueling physical work was also a welcome distraction from the rest of his life and the decisions he worked even harder to avoid making.

Hunter was dirty, sore, and exhausted by the time 6:00 p.m. rolled around. All he could think about was getting home, grabbing something to eat, hitting the shower, and falling into bed. But Victoria usually had other plans for Hunter. No matter how hard he tried to avoid this part of his life, he wasn't as successful at actually doing so.

He glanced at his phone as he walked to his truck. *Nope. Not tonight. Or any other night*, he thought. His jaw stiffened and he tossed the phone onto the passenger seat, ignoring the unread messages. The device continued its vigilant taser-like buzzing on the seat next to him, weakening his willpower with every demanding vibration on his drive home.

Niyanta Baniya
Goodbye

Nick raced home from Michaels with tubes of aquamarine blue, emerald green, and a bottle of varnish. Hopping out of his car, he unlocked his front door, took off his shoes, and ran upstairs to his studio. He had called in sick at work for the past three days to spend time on his first painting. Luckily, Lucy was no longer in his life to make any remarks about this impulsive decision.

Jumping over a pile of dress shirts, wrinkled papers, and emptied cans of beer, he placed the materials on the desk near the window. Nick set his easel on top of the desk and adjusted the canvas' position, mimicking a painter he had seen online. He sat down on a rolling chair facing the window and looked out to his muse.

Two redwood trees stood upright across the street in his neighbour's front yard, like gates to heaven. Every time Nick looked at the trees, he felt transported to a place where time stood still and the universe whispered blessings. It also reminded him of the summer he had spent climbing trees with his grandpa. A bear hug from him cured any falls or scratches.

Today, in the afternoon light, the trunks looked ethereal; lichen added a golden hue. The leaves gleamed as if a fairy had sprinkled stardust on them.

A loud honking brought Nick back to earth; a Dodge pick-up truck had pulled up to his neighbor Anderson's driveway.

But Nick wasn't going to allow this to distract him. He squeezed aquamarine blue from the tube onto the palette. With his brush he picked up the blue, then a little white, and mixed them vigorously in a circular motion. Nick smiled, feeling like a real painter. The colours lathered well on the brush. He spread it across the top of the canvas. His plan was to complete the sky, then add highlights and shading to the leaves.

Photographing the trees would have been easier but Nick had taken enough of them, of things that hadn't lasted in his life. This time, he wanted to try a different approach. One that would allow him to honour the subject and spend time with them.

The trees had been witness to his move-in day with Lucy and her move-out day a month ago. Alongside him, they had watched as she climbed into her new boyfriend's Jeep and sped away, leaving their eleven-year relationship behind. Nick had waved her goodbye and the trees had joined him, the wind swaying their branches.

He cleaned the brush in the water, splashing some on the desk and splattering a bit on the wall in the process. There was no one to complain about his mess. He looked at the trees again to examine the spots where the sun was hitting the leaves. Just then, three men got out of the truck and started unloading items on the sidewalk.

Within minutes, both the trees were fenced on one side by orange mesh, and construction cones and signs were placed on either side of the street. Nick paused in awe at the speed of the workers wearing hard hats and ear muffs. Anderson must be doing some work on his house, he thought.

One of the workers took out a chainsaw and approached the tree on the left. The roaring of the machine echoed through the neighbourhood.

Nick jumped up from his seat and screamed, "No! No! No!" His brush landed on the carpet.

He opened the window, yelling at them to stop, but no one heard him. A huge wedge had been cut into the trunk of the tree. He sprinted downstairs to his porch. Outside, Nick went straight for the man with the chainsaw.

"Move!" one of the guys shouted at him. Another shoved himself in front of Nick and pulled him aside to Anderson's driveway. Chainsaw-guy finally stopped after noticing him.

"Please don't do th—"

A loud crack interrupted Nick's protest, followed by a rumbling thud. In the blink of an eye, cut from her trunk, the fallen spirit lay flat on the road.

A shrieking cry prompted Anderson to come out of his house. He saw Nick sobbing near the head of the tree, clutching a leafy branch to his chest, paint on his face and hands. He could feel the eyes of the workers on him, hoping for some explanation.

Anderson motioned for them to gather around. "He is going through a lot in his personal life," he whispered. "Let's give him space."

The workers reminded him that they were only there for two hours. Anderson, who had gone through his own divorce, couldn't brush off Nick's state. He told them to take a lunch break. They shrugged and went back to their truck.

Anderson walked over to Nick and took him by the arm. He dragged him away from the road and back to his own porch. Anderson tried to console Nick by reminding him that there was more to life than one woman. A failed marriage didn't define a person.

"When I found my wife cheating, I ended the relationship." Anderson sighed. "I poured everything into my work after the divorce. Got promoted within months to site supervisor at the construction company. You know ... I turned my pain into something useful."

Nick slumped on the ground, half-listening. His divorce was different. There was no cheating involved. In fact, Nick was relieved that Lucy had found happiness with a decent guy. He himself had slept soundly once they finalized the divorce, after months of insomnia.

Even though they were together for so long, they had only been married for four years. Within a year of tying the knot, the couple had realized their mistake of settling with the familiar. They had invested so much of their time into the relationship that they were afraid of letting it go and disappointing their friends and family—they were the married couple that everyone admired, a chartered accountant and a lawyer, both successful at 36, and very much in love.

The reality was the opposite. Sure, they fought over silly things. But it wasn't until he found out that Lucy was taking contraceptive pills in secret that Nick understood they wanted different things in life. They had to separate for their own sakes.

He didn't know how to tell Anderson that it wasn't Lucy he was mourning. How absurd did that sound? A man wailed over his lover, his child, or an animal, but never over a tree. No one could comprehend that these two trees had kept him company just by their presence. Standing upright in the same spot every day, they had provided him a security that no other human being could.

"Anderson, are you cutting down the other tree, too?"

"Y—yeah. I—I got a permit," he stuttered.

Rage filled Nick. The redwood trees were irreplaceable. He wanted to punch Anderson. Instead, he walked towards the standing tree. He placed his hand on the trunk and closed his eyes.

"Goodbye," Nick whispered. He walked back to his house and closed the door.

When his grandpa passed a decade earlier, Nick had been on a remote tour in Peru and missed his chance to see him one last time. Now, he placed his hands on his heart as the second tree fell to Mother Earth.

Nick picked up his brush again and continued to paint. He reminded himself that only the fortunate had the luxury to say goodbye.

⁀

A couple of days later, Anderson was leaving early for work. He noticed something placed on top of one of the tree stumps and moved in closer to inspect. Somebody had left a beautiful painting of the two redwood trees.

Anderson looked around, but there was no one in sight. The red-woods reminded him of Nick; he wondered how he was doing after that breakdown. Anderson turned toward Nick's house, intending to check in on his neighbour.

But Nick's car wasn't there. Instead, a "For Sale" sign stood in the yard.

Amy Van Veen

Reunion

AN EXCERPT FROM A NOVEL THAT EXPLORES THE RIPPLE EFFECT UNSPOKEN TRAUMA HAS ON THREE GENERATIONS OF WOMEN

Ella

"This dress is itchy!"

Ella tugged at the black wool dress her mom had laid out for her. It was nearly spring, but there she sat, in thick black tights that went up past her belly button, black patent leather shoes with a strap over the top of her growing feet that would definitely leave a mark when she took them off later, and the black wool dress her mom had found on sale two Christmases ago and still made her wear, even though the hem was far shorter than when they first bought it.

"Why do we have to wear black, anyway?" she asked, as they drove down the highway.

"People wear black to funerals." Luke, her brother, played tic-tac-toe in the fog on the window.

"But why?"

"It's a sign of respect," her sister, Jane, said.

"Why?" she asked again, ignoring Luke's eye roll.

"Black is the colour of mourning," Jane explained. "We're in mourning."

"But it's after lunch."

"Not that kind of morning, you idiot," Luke piped up.

"Don't be rude, Luke." Their mom tightened her grip on the steering wheel and kept her eyes on the road. "Ella, sweetie, there are two kinds of morning. M-O-R-N-I-N-G is the time of day. M-O-U-R-N-I-N-G is how we feel when someone we love dies. Mourning is like grief, and sadness, and just—" she paused, "missing them."

"But I'm not sad."

"There are different reasons to be sad when someone dies." Their mom's tone made the children lean in to listen. "Sometimes we're sad because we loved someone so much and we'll miss them so much—like when Whiskers died."

Ella nodded solemnly, remembering when their cat was hit by a car the year before.

"And sometimes we're sad because we didn't get to love someone like we wanted to. And when they die it's too late." Her mom paused before quietly adding, "And that's sad."

Five-year-old Ella stared out the foggy window, trying to make sense of everything her mom just said. Before she knew it, they had pulled into the church parking lot. Ella's eyes went wide.

The building was grey and brown with sharp edges and front doors that, despite being made of glass, were dark. She wasn't sure why, but she felt like the church was frowning at her. Suddenly her dress felt even more itchy. She clung on to her hem to keep her hands still.

Maria

As soon as she walked through the glass doors of the church foyer, Maria could feel all eyes land on her in a condescending mix of judgment and pity.

She lifted her head and saw her mother at the oak double doors that led into the sanctuary—the sanctuary where she had spent too many Sundays as a child trying not to fidget. Maria had always had a hard time sitting still, but her father never had any tolerance for it. She used to sit on her hands until they lost feeling, and cross her ankles so tight the buckles would nearly break through her skin, afraid that if she moved a muscle, she'd catch his wrathful eye.

It was the only attention she seemed to get from him.

Her mother was a different story.

"Hi Mom," Maria said when she approached, one hand on Luke's shoulder and one wrapped around Ella's own small hand.

"Maria," her mother said, pulling her in for a hug. Maria closed her eyes, briefly letting go of her children to feel the parental comfort she'd been missing the last few years. "I'm glad you came."

Maria wanted to say how she was sorry, offer her condolences, anything, but she just bit her lip and nodded.

"Where will you sit?" her mother asked.

"I was going to sit at the back," Maria told her, holding Ella's hand for courage. "Just in case I need to take the kids outside."

"You should sit with the family. Up front."

"Ella isn't used to this kind of church," Maria said, giving her daughter's hand a squeeze and feeling awful for using her as an excuse. "She might get fussy."

Her mother gave her another sad smile but nodded in understanding.

As she sat down in the back pew, she was grateful there were no eyes behind her. She looked around the room to see couples of varying ages. Men and women sitting side by side, 'til death do them part. The only ones who were sitting alone were those like her mother—where death did them part. Divorce was rare and even more rarely accepted in that community.

From an oversized picture frame beside the pulpit, her father's cold eyes stared her down. The urge to fidget, even as a grown woman, grew under his gaze.

The pastor said a few words Maria barely registered. He then picked up the hymn book, nodded in the organist's direction, and music thundered from the floor-to-ceiling pipe organ, demanding Maria's attention. Without a word of instruction, the entire church stood in unison, their own hymn books at the ready. She had forgotten the effect such unanimity had on her. Immediately Maria felt uneasy, as if the social pressure was creating an emotional claustrophobia she couldn't escape.

The music ended and everyone took their seats. Maria listened as her three older siblings talked about her father's kindness, his courage, his tenacity. She shifted in the pew, feeling untethered from reality.

The man they spoke of was not the man she grew up with.

None of them mentioned his dark days. None of them talked about that shadow that lived inside the home when she was a teenager. They had all moved out when his episodes began. Her eulogy would have been far different; perhaps that's why she was never asked to share.

One of many reasons, she thought to herself.

COBIE

As she watched Maria and her three grandchildren walk through the crowd and out the glass doors, Cobie's heart broke. She hardly knew those grandkids; she hardly knew her own daughter anymore. And yet, her eyes remained dry. Through all the arrangements, Cobie had not shed a tear. She knew they would come when they were ready.

The day her baby brother died, she remembered the stark difference between her parents. Her father held nothing back as he wept for his son; her mother's grief was practical and dry-eyed, but—as she later learned—deeply felt.

After her youngest child's departure, Cobie made her way through the foyer filled with the people she saw at church every Sunday morning—her community, her friends, her family. She accepted the sympathetic head nods, the well-meaning handshakes, the chorus of "Gerritt was a good man." "Our condolences." "We're sorry for your loss."

After a while, the crowd began to disperse. No one ever knew how long to stay at a funeral.

Standing at the solid wood doors of the sanctuary, Cobie took a deep breath, as if the church itself was wrapping her in an embrace. She glanced down the aisle at the photo of her husband of 44 years. He stood in front of his prized roses, thick hair combed to the side, tamed by the trusty Brylcreem he'd used since he was a teenager. His hair stayed dark until very late in life before going grey. Cobie, on the other hand, had been dyeing her white hair since her mid-twenties and didn't reveal her natural colour until each of her children had their own children. Then she felt she could become a proper Oma with pure white hair.

She remembered the day she met him, tall but trying not to be, a wallflower who couldn't help but stand out. His loud friend had been trying to get her attention, but Cobie was immediately smitten with the quiet Gerritt. His gentle kindness had quickly endeared him to her, and they were engaged within six months. Weeks later, he left the Netherlands to be a nurse on the frontlines in Indonesia right after the war ended. The man who came home to her was different.

The move to Canada had been one of desperation. She knew he was running away but she hoped that it would help bring back the man she had fallen in love with. And it did, for a little while. By the time her three oldest had moved out and started their own lives, Gerritt's had slowed down enough for the ghosts to return.

She and Maria were the ones with the front-row seats to those dark years.

Cobie chose that photo of him in his garden because his eyes were the closest they had been to the eyes she fell in love with all those years earlier. It was in that garden where he pieced himself back together. The garden where, day by day, he dug his way out of his own darkness. The garden where she had found him, finally at peace.

Cristina Fernandes

The Ones You Love the Most

AN EXCERPT

Is there a boys-only class in school that teaches sex as the answer to every question? While us girls squirmed beneath colourful diagrams of ovulation cycles and fallopian tubes, they took the lads for lessons on the healing powers of their penises. Bad hair day? Here baby, let me soothe you with a quickie. Kids pissing you off? A blow job'll relax you.

My husband must have aced that class. I wish now that he'd been out sick that day. Maybe then he never would have dragged his sleazy little secrets through our lives, leaving none of us untouched.

⁓

Blinking one eye open, I found myself still in pretend paradise. Lounge chair nestled in gritty sand, roaring slate ocean stretching for miles. Despite the summer sun high in the sky, I shivered inside my fleece and fur-lined booties. An Oregon Coast wind turned August to autumn in one gust. A stray curl lashed my face like a whip. It was unsettling to be this cold on a beach in summer.

I flicked the pages of my half-read novel before tossing it aside, casting my gaze to Marcus. Star pupil on the dick's magical properties of dicks and the reason we'd driven three hours down the 1-5. The brochure he'd waved at me claimed this Marriage Healing Weekend was going to fix us.

Marcus grinned from his chair—oblivious to my silent condemnation—and pointed at my discarded novel. "Does that mean you're finally ready for some fun?"

I rolled my eyes and he sighed. Probably crafting his own case against me. *Ungrateful bitch. Can't she just be happy? And fuck me senseless.* It wouldn't be hard for him to find a sympathetic audience. Twelve jurors who would turn my sharp comments and disinterest into a conviction.

The first year or two we'd vacationed on the Oregon Coast, I'd loved it. I'd pretended the ocean mist clung to the green cliffs of Ireland, the wind whipped the waves into a froth off some far-off village with an unpronounceable name. The wild magic of this place tapped a romantic bone I'd misplaced in the years since. The wonder disappeared as it did with anything you start taking for granted.

This trip cost more per night than our mortgage payment. Enough to pay for a real holiday. I yearned to cross items off a bucket list I hadn't bothered to write. Marcus' pamphlet replaced my secret printouts of shabby apartments just within the circle of Paris *Arrondissements*—dingy studios offering little more than a bed, which I could afford if I ate nothing but baguettes slathered in creamy brie. I'd clicked over to the retreat website and scanned the resort's on-site restaurant menus. How could I not? This was Marcus' first turn suggesting a marriage lifeline.

Everything was different—for him—with Ginny's bomb wedged in our lives. *I have cancer.* He had to re-examine things when his only sibling was dying. But my priorities weren't as shifty. I'd put in seventeen years. My responsibilities almost met, debt paid. I'd do anything for Ginny. Almost.

Marcus reached for my hand, drawing lazy circles around my thumb. My insides crawled into a ball in my chest, shrinking from the obligation in his touch. He flinched, but didn't pull away, and I had the decency to blush.

Forcing the smile he'd expect, swallowing around the lump in my throat, I tried to be reasonable. "Give me ten minutes? You know how much I love the ocean."

My allotted time passed in an instant. When it was over, Marcus didn't ask if I was ready. Just stood, holding out a hand, certain I'd follow. Which I did. A promise is a promise.

Trudging through deep, soft sand, I linked arms with Marcus. He goes from anything to sex without transition, but I need build up. Connection.

I nudged him with my shoulder. "So, what did you have in mind?"

The wicked smile that used to make me melt lit up his face. "Well … those big windows in our room?" He leaned in to whisper the rest against my ear. "I'm going to press you up against them naked and fuck you from behind."

His raspy arousal plucked at my primitive core. A thrill spiraled from between my legs to unravel my spine. I turned to find his lips and we kissed like we meant it. Hungry and urgent.

Stepping into the glow and warmth of the hotel, the thrill dampened. Fizzling under forced polite smiles at the valet who held the door open, a sidestep around the stroller parked just inside the lobby. I looked to the lounge, longing for a little extra blur.

"Let's have a drink." I tugged Marcus toward the bar, throwing my own wicked smile over one shoulder. "You know what booze does to me."

"There's beer in the mini-bar upstairs." He tugged me back, mouth turning down at the corners.

"I'm in the mood for something hot and foamy." I let go of his hand and marched on alone. He sighed, exasperated, but trudged behind.

Settling at a corner table with a view of the entire room, I made amends with a sly hand slid along his thigh. Teasing, stopping just before inappropriate, as the spent-looking server wound her way to our table, tapping a pencil against her order pad. I chose the most ridiculous thing on the menu—hot chocolate, peppermint schnapps, all drowned in whipped cream—ignoring Marcus' eye roll, while still shivering from the beach wind. Hopeful the sweetness would rush through me and wash away my sour skepticism. It was hard to believe a sex marathon and a psych-prof-turned-counselor from UDub could right something that had always been wrong.

A few minutes later, I sipped the hot, sugary drink dumped on our table, savoured the burn trailing down my throat, and scanned the room for someone else's life to dissect. One of our few shared pastimes, indulging in petty storytelling about random strangers.

My focus landed on a young couple in an argument, their tense body language giving them away. He pulled her hand toward his lips, she yanked it away, tossing a curtain of dark hair to one side and avoiding his gaze. He tried again, whispering soothing words, but she slid back in her chair and scrolled through her phone. He persisted, clearly the one in the wrong. Tickling her arm, he enveloped her balled fist between his large hands and played up begging for forgiveness. She cracked a smile and the argument was all over. They went through the motions of hurt feelings and apologies, paid the bill and raced each other out of the bar to make up for real.

I jerked my chin after their retreating, entwined bodies. "What do you think? Did he forget to book the couple's massage, or tell her she should slow down on the Long Island iced teas?"

"Fool if he did. No, she wants a honeymoon baby and just found the super-sized box of condoms in his luggage." Marcus chuckled, crinkling the skin around his eyes. Making him seem harmless.

"Maybe. I wonder who'll win upstairs."

"Poor bastard doesn't stand a chance."

"More of a chance than we did." I tipped the last of my drink into my mouth. The joke hit too close to the decision taken out of my hands at seventeen.

"Well, sure, but that didn't work out too bad. Right?" He waited for my nod, then pushed his empty pint away, stood, and tugged me into his arms. We stayed that way for a moment, before he tilted my chin with one finger and brushed his smile across my lips. "I'd say you made out pretty damn well actually."

We stumbled through the slate and timber foyer to the elevators, where the chance of being caught meant we couldn't keep our hands off each other. Flirting with exhibitionism—our other shared interest. Even amid our frantic kisses and clawing hands, my mind wandered to the younger couple in the bar. Longing for days when problems melted away as easily, instead of lurking in the background, building and mutating, gaining the strength to destroy me.

Tamar Haytayan

The Alarm

The sound of the house alarm blares through the night. Sylvie jolts from bed and looks over at the clock on the wall. It reads 1:45 a.m. She dreads this the most, to be alone in this big house, with her children sleeping in the second bedroom, and the alarm going off late in the night.

Sylvie runs over to the alarm keypad. She lets out a sigh of relief on seeing that the zone where the alarm was triggered is by the back door of the garage and the office window. She feels safer knowing that the problem has come from outside and not from a motion sensor in the house.

The phone rings. It's the alarm company, calling to verify all is okay, and Sylvie lets them know that it is.

The security of this knowledge envelops her for a second, until she hears noise coming from within the house. With the phone still in her hands, Sylvie frantically dials 911. She interrupts the operator.

"Intruder in the house, please come quick!"

Sylvie then calls her father, Arthur. Her arms are shaking; she cannot hold the phone straight to her ear. All sorts of scenarios run through her head. She suddenly remembers the kids and runs to the second bedroom. Anthony and Jilly are sound asleep. It never ceases to surprise Sylvie what deep sleepers they are, just like their father.

"Thank you, God." Sylvie has never been good in stressful situations.

"Hello?" Arthur's voice is on the other end of the line. He sounds gruff, definitely woken from a deep sleep.

"Dad, come quick. I'm scared." It's all Sylvie can say. She knows her dad will not ask questions. He will just get up and come over. He owes her too much.

As she waits, terrified, Sylvie has one last idea to keep her sane. She presses the talk button on the phone and dials a number in Lebanon.

The receptionist's response is immediate. "Good morning. Elonex Corporation. How can I help you?"

She sounds like a robot, Sylvie thinks, knowing too well she is the gorgeous blond her husband, Tim, and his partners recruited recently; all legs and boobs. The last receptionist was nice, but she was clearly not blond. Sylvie's thoughts return to her current situation.

She does not know how Tim will be able to alleviate her fear from thousands of miles away, but she asks to speak with him anyway.

Tim answers in his business voice. Sylvie is too engrossed in her thoughts to respond to him immediately.

"Hello? Hello, can I help you?"

"Oh, Tim!" Sylvie says. "I am scared. The alarm went off. I heard noises in the house … yes, yes, the police are coming. I called Dad, too." Sylvie's heart is pounding fast and loud. Hearing Tim's voice makes the fear protrude from her body, harder and faster, with every beat. "I am so scared, honey."

"Sylvie, darling, calm down, calm down."

Sylvie can hear the worry in her husband's voice.

"Are the kids alright? Are they awake?"

Their conversation is cut off by the arrival of the police, followed by Sylvie's father.

"Honey … okay, I'll call you as soon as things are settled … bye, honey."

The two policemen ask Sylvie some questions and search the house. Arthur searches too. They find nothing.

After the police leave, Arthur decides to stay with his daughter. More than anything, he wants to alleviate her fear. He is very uneasy. This is the house where his daughter grew up. This is the house where he shared sweet moments with his first wife, Sylvie's mother.

Deep in his thoughts, he does not see Sylvie stealing a glance his way. Her glance lingers too long. Sylvie knows her father is not comfortable in the house. It is filled with too many memories for him. If she could get through the night on her own, she would not ask him to stay.

"Dad, I really need you. I need you to sleep next to me. I cannot sleep in that bed alone tonight."

Arthur looks at Sylvie. His eyes say it all. He cannot get the words out. He knows he cannot fail his daughter again. He just cannot.

Two hours later, Arthur lays next to his daughter, on the same bed he shared with his first wife for 25 years.

Life takes funny turns sometimes.

He cannot sleep. He lies on his back, facing the ceiling, his eyes wide open. Too many thoughts flow through his mind, making sleep more unreachable by the minute.

Sylvie lays next to her father, thinking of her mother.

Mum, I wonder if you are watching. Dad is here, where you always wanted him. But you are not next to him. He is here, that is what matters. Dad, are you in turmoil? Do you feel the memories creeping through the hidden cracks of the walls?

Sylvie turns towards her father. A teardrop trickles from the side of his right eye.

"Are you not able to sleep, Dad?" Sylvie asks.

She instinctively places her right hand on her father's chest, something she did as a child. Arthur cannot hide his emotions and starts sobbing uncontrollably.

Sylvie moves toward her father and embraces him. Father and daughter remain this way for a while, knowing too well that too many things will remain unspoken, even as they feel hopeful for all that they have to share.

Eliane and Perla

AN EXCERPT

I could hear her step out of the painted metal garnet tub. The water splashed.

From the small patio of the apartment she rented, I watched the sunset, the sky becoming a marmalade orange, transitioning to a periwinkle purple, fading to indigo. I was jotting down this moment in the teal journal, the one she had purchased for me after I convinced myself not to buy it. A single teardrop fell onto a blank page. I was leaving her against my will in a few hours and she would have to stay behind. A melancholic wave of dread came over me as I sat, staring down at my feet. My toes were freshly painted a vibrant coral to match my tanned skin.

The buzzer rang, signaling that my taxi had arrived early, but I dared not turn my head and acknowledge this present moment.

Instead I rose and headed over to the bathroom, climbed into the tub, and sat down across from her. She leaned forward to hold me and there we stayed a little longer in delusion.

⸏

One morning when I was seventeen, I arose to the sound of creaking hinges—the ancient door frame of my 100 sq. ft. room, which was bare and musky. Father entered with a suitcase, flicking on the single bulb hanging from the ceiling.

Soon I was waving goodbye to the daffodils that stretched over the vast Pyrenees of Bordeaux, France, a city I was just beginning to call home.

My father and I moved to a northern region of Spain called the Basque Country. Father has been an international pilot for as long as I could remember. Until I was old enough to be on my own, it was my aunt who raised me while Father was away, which was a lot.

On one rare occasion Father had to stay in a small coastal town in the Basque Country due to his flight being delayed. He instantly fell in love with the architecture, the warm Spanish sun on his face almost every hour. He realized how much he had grown tired of France and knew right then and there that we would move. No questions asked. The coastal town didn't get many tourists and felt more comfortable that way. Where I grew up in France was constantly overloaded with American tourists. Father always had a spontaneous soul, so it wasn't a surprise when he wanted to uproot our life again. We stayed in a hostel for a few days until we moved into a 17th century apartment a few blocks away from the bustle.

I spent my days in Basque Country reciting Spanish and hiding under wide holm oak trees to avoid a potential future of becoming pinker than a young piglet.

⁀

Born in Ireland, I was carried over to France before breaking into my second year of life. Looking at pictures of myself from those early years in Ireland, every photo featured a grin stretched across my face from ear to ear. My hair looked as it always had: long, curled, and cinnamon brown.

Picking up a pair of silver kitchen scissors one midday afternoon, five inches of weight fell upon the pearl-tiled bathroom floor. A new Eliane stared back at me. I was as shocked as I was thrilled.

I explored the town. There were lots of small markets, a few restaurants—that was mostly it. And a beach. I stopped along the boardwalk, saw couples, families, and groups of friends laying on it. A stand at the far left where umbrellas could be rented. Large cherry-red umbrellas that many people were using.

Climbing down from the boardwalk, I relaxed my hands against the smooth sandstone surface, and at the velvety shoreline, I excused myself from the bundles of noise. Swishing toes across, clawing back sand. Waiting, waiting, waiting …

Occasionally a couple strolled by, arms interlocked, with uncomfortably wide smiles, as I sat, curling into my knees. I knew I had to do something, although wracking my brain for what usually led to slumber. I rose and walked down the beach, looking to the Cantabrian Sea. It was windy this afternoon; the waves came up to my knees as I entered the ocean. I wandered slowly back to the empty apartment waiting for me. On nights like these, I couldn't hold anything in and although no one could hear me I still quietly whimpered in my bed.

I had purchased a journal to jot down my thoughts, though they never changed.

I feel lonely.

I don't know who I am.

When will this circle end?

Father would have a few days to help around the apartment to make it feel more like "home" before he had another flight. From my observation of him, I think he liked to believe that I would follow his orders, and that I enjoyed my "solitude," as he called it. Father mentioned to me a social event happening in one of the town plazas and we were invited to go. We did.

Being the exotic bachelor pilot that he thought he was, Father spent the evening chatting with every woman who looked his way.

I sat on the outskirts sipping sparkling grapefruit juice, when a boy dressed in a blue polo shirt and white bow tie approached me. I was already preparing the dialogue in my head of what I would say to let him know I wasn't interested. Or I'd speak in French to throw him off.

"The cake here is fantastic, if you haven't tried it yet." The boy spoke in an excitable manner. "It's the only reason I visit these events; it may make your time more enjoyable."

"You don't think I'm having a good time?" I replied.

"I mean, all I'm saying is every time I've looked over at you, you have slumped yourself more and more into this chair. You'll be on the floor pretty soon." The boy smiled. "Oscar is my name."

"Eliane. Do you visit these events often?"

"Almost weekly at this point. It's a place for families and kids to connect. We have a bonding circle and every circle is different. It's a way to bring all ages together."

"I'm glad to have missed it," I said.

"Not the chatty type, are we?"

"More of the bang-me-over-like-a-jar-of-pickles type," I responded. Oscar looked over at me, puzzled. I clarified. "You really have to crack me open to get anything."

"Interesting, you almost say that with pride."

"It makes me mysterious. I've been told people love that."

"Who are you here with?" Oscar asked.

"My father. He's over there in the corner, where he's been all night."

Oscar kept asking questions, almost as if he was in a rush to know everything about me. I told him of my pilot father who was never around and how I didn't know who my mother was. Upfront honesty wasn't what I was used to but I felt compelled to talk to him. Strangely at ease with him. Or, possibly, I was desperate for a taste of human interaction.

"He leaves tomorrow but he'll be back in 48 hours," I continued, "and then he'll be on break for three days."

"Do you miss him when he's gone?"

"At times, but I've mostly gotten used to it. I was five when he first left. I saw him for a total of two months in five years. My aunt Alieen became my full-time caregiver. She had to figure out quickly how to have a career and raise me."

"That must've been difficult for both of you," Oscar said.

He continued to speak, but I tuned out. I watched a tall woman across the plaza, slipping in and out of conversation, covered in coral linen. She swayed so delicately, pearls flashing about the room.

I sat back, sipping slowly, observing the woman's every move like a curious lion hidden in lush grass. With narrowed eyes, I studied every angle of her.

In a separate reality, I'd walk up to this woman and ask her to get lost with me tonight. Into the shadows of an alleyway, I'd press her up against a wall, feathery touches, sparks crackling as we melt into granite blocks laid by broken hands centuries before.

Oscar invited me to have dinner over at his place the following evening. I said no, that I had plans. He knew that wasn't true but didn't press me. Eventually he vanished from the shell of my existence.

April dela Noche Milne

All the Ones That Remain

A SHORT STORY

I walk past a girl at the airport as she says to the friend sitting beside her, "You only get proposed to once. You need to make it special—" and a tension prickles in my chest.

Sitting down in front of my gate, it is clear that collectively, as separate travellers, we have all tried to leave as much room around ourselves as we can.

I adjust my new Doc Martens that made my feet bleed for a week, white platforms that still require me to wear Band-Aids on the back of my heels. I call them my break-up boots. For the next half hour, I Face-Time with my cousin until my phone's battery gets too low to ignore, then I pull out my book: *Beautiful World, Where Are You* by Sally Rooney.

Across from me, a dad looks at his phone as his coffee spills, the cup next to his leg pouring onto his chair.

"Ahh, get up, get up, get up!" His wife quickly reaches for the cup, righting it.

The dad stands and there's a large wet spot on his pants, near his back pocket. He rotates one way, then the other. He wears glasses and a toque and has a pleasant face. I see a hearing aid in his right ear.

"Heh, nice," says their daughter. She's a teenager, wearing black platform shoes and tight yet comfortable-looking black pants. Her frizzy hair is a number of different colours: purple, green, yellow, blue.

"I'll throw this away," says the mom, holding the cup.

"Well, that's gonna be fun," the dad says.

"It's not that bad."

"I'm gonna go dry this off in the washroom." And the dad disappears.

The mom, standing, waits for the zone to be called, looking at the attendants by the gate. She's holding a passport and a boarding pass. Long thick parka, smooth grey hair tied back.

After a little bit, the daughter says, "I kind of have to pee again but I just went. Should I go? Or should I …"

The mom says something I can't hear.

"Where's the bathroom again?"

"It's that way," says the mom, pointing.

The daughter goes off in the opposite direction of the dad.

The mom remains standing, still waiting. She calls out eventually, "Where's your dad?" to the girl, now returning but still far-off.

"I don't know. I thought he would have been back by now."

"Can you–can you text him? We're boarding."

"Yeah."

The girl sits down and texts. "It's only so people next to the window can board, but it doesn't really matter," she tells her mom. There is a boarding announcement.

"He's coming," the daughter says.

I realize there are very few people left waiting to board. I stand and get on the plane. I have a window seat.

⌒

The family arrives after a little while, and they are seated in front of me. The mom handles putting the luggage on the top shelf on her own. "You guys go in," she says. The daughter shrugs off her coat, sits by the window, and the dad sits in the middle.

"What a white Christmas! We spent most of it in the airport." The daughter laughs, looking out the window. She turns to her father. "Are these different pants?" She slaps his knee affectionately.

"No, I just took them off, put them under the dryer."

The flight steward makes an announcement, talks about masks, and would like to wish us, by the way, a merry Christmas.

It is snowing, big white flakes, and I take a video of the airline … taxi? coordinator? I don't know what they're called—as they guide a Flair Airlines plane onto the tarmac. We are headed to LA, and though I've been there many times, it's been so long since I've gone anywhere that it feels like I am a tourist and have never flown in a plane before.

The daughter is explaining to her dad that if she moves her arm, "It's not 'cause I don't wanna be close to you, I just—" then I can't hear the rest.

The father and daughter mimic various French words from the French version of the airline announcement.

"So, Patricia wants us to wake her up when we get there, but I told her it'll be late, we'll just see her in the morning," says the dad to the mom.

"I'm kind of traumatized from trying to wake her up, it's not—" says the daughter, but I miss the end of her sentence. The dad agrees with her.

Outside, the sky and ground are fully grey-white. Lights glow like little havens in the full emptiness of it.

Why is it that no matter what time you washed your hair that day, your hair always feels limp and greasy as soon as you get on a plane?

Finally, we are taking off down the tarmac, red lights from the plane flashing onto the wing. Faster and faster.

"It just looks like it's melting already," says the girl about the snow.

"Well, the heat from the plane—" says the dad, expounding.

We've come to a stop now.

They are spraying the wings with chemicals to melt and stave off the snow. Looking through the tiny window at the huge clouds of water steaming up off the metal makes me feel like I'm in a spaceship and aliens are working to successfully get us off the planet.

The daughter and dad discuss what's happening outside, while the daughter uses her phone to photograph what's going on. They continue to have a loving, lively back and forth.

"He's in a tiny room. It's like a video game for him." And she is recording a time lapse. "He's looking right at me!"

I take my own photo of the workers for posterity. They spray green on the wings.

The mom has been silent this whole time. At one point later during the flight, I will get up to go to the bathroom and though a movie will be playing on the mom's screen, she won't actually be watching. Her hand will be covering her face.

In both seating arrangements, while waiting and on the aircraft, the dad sits in the middle.

As we make our way down the tarmac again, I stare out the window at the snowstorm, praying for safety and feeling like I am flying directly toward the Omicron strain. I do not realize that I have stopped blinking until my left contact suddenly goes dry and I have to blink rapidly. I need to pee again.

I remember how excited my roommates were for me to get into my writing program versus Ryan's reaction. I rotate all the rings on my fingers—all the ones that remain.

We are speeding down the runway. Can I pinpoint the exact moment the wheels lift off the ground? Yes. We are in the air, angling up. At this altitude, the roads look like tangled cords. I have not had this viewpoint in a long time: two years and two months.

Gradually, bumping through the sky, we make our way out of the snowstorm and into the clear black of the night. The plane's wing shines out of the darkness, illuminated by its own lights. The lights don't feel cold, or soft, or warm; they feel matter of fact. They feel practical. They are the only thing that I can see.

Chase Boisjolie

Things are Alright

AN EXCERPT

Allie followed her father into the living room and said a final goodbye. She waited at the window until he had packed into the car and pulled out of the driveway before going to the kitchen. She opened the fridge and took out the milk jug. It maybe had enough in it for one bowl of cereal. She unscrewed the cap and pressed the opening to her nose. The faint sour smell made her wince, but she set the bottle on the table anyway, along with a bowl and spoon. From behind the door, she got a step stool and unfolded it in front of the pantry. As she reached for the cornflakes, she caught sight of her reflection in the glass of the microwave door. She took in the sight of the bright red hat for the first time since putting it on. She tilted the bill until it was just above her eyelids. There were words stitched out on the front in bold, white words. Allie squinted, running her finger over the raised lettering as she tried to read them in the backwards image, but only made out the word *America* before Henry's voice from the doorway startled her.

"Is he gone yet?" His voice cracked on the last word.

Allie nearly dropped the box of cornflakes. "You just missed him," she said. She hopped off the stool. At the table, she sat down and fixed her bowl, filling it to the brim before dumping in the milk. She shook the bottle to free every last drop.

"Great," Henry said. He was all dressed up in his work clothes: a black pair of jeans and a plain white T-shirt. There was a hole in his left sock that revealed his little toe. He walked into the kitchen and looked in the fridge. "Did you seriously just take all of the milk?"

Allie dug up a big bite and put it in her mouth. She struggled to keep her face from scrunching up. "You snooze, you lose," she said, chewing.

Henry grabbed a spoon and came up behind her. He reached over into the bowl and took some of her cereal, jamming the spoon into his own mouth before she could protest. He immediately recoiled and turned around to spit it out into the sink. "That's awful," he said. He took the bottle from the table and studied it. "No wonder. It expired five days ago."

"Tastes fine to me," Allie said. She took another bite. With all of her might, she kept her eyes open, but there was a twitch in her eyebrow that betrayed her.

"Sure," Henry scoffed. He took a box of waffles from the freezer and placed two of them in the slots of the toaster.

Allie got up and went over to him. She picked up the box and looked inside. "No more?" she said.

"You snooze, you lose." Henry stuck out his tongue and depressed the lever.

"Whatever," she said. "As if I wanted one anyway. It's so hot, I don't know why anyone would want something from the toaster. That's just crazy."

Henry ignored her; he opened the cutlery drawer only to shut it right away. "Cool hat, by the way," he said, waving a lazy finger in the air in front of her. "Where'd you get it from?"

Allie perked up. "Daddy gave it to me."

"Well, it looks stupid on you." Henry had turned his back to her and was rinsing out some old dishes that had been sitting in the sink. "Does no one around here know how to clean up after themselves? There's never any goddamn clean forks around here."

"You shouldn't talk like that," Allie said. "And it does not!" She felt her heart beating in her ears. "Red is the best colour on me. Everyone thinks so."

"Keep telling yourself that." Henry hoisted himself up and sat on the counter. "I bet you don't even know what those words on it mean."

"Do too." Allie took the hat off and placed it on the table in front of her. "America is great. And you're just jealous."

"I wouldn't wear that thing if you paid me to."

The toaster popped. Henry took his waffles and a bottle of syrup and sat down at the table across from Allie. He turned the bottle up and poured the syrup until the waffles were not only drenched, but swimming in a puddle of thick, sticky liquid. Allie hadn't touched her cereal again, and her mouth began to water as Henry stabbed the first one with his fork and took a bite. She could hear the moist sponginess of it squishing around in his mouth as he chewed. As their eyes met, Henry sighed. He stuffed the last of the waffle into his mouth and leaned back in his chair, pushing the plate forward toward Allie.

"Here," he said. "You have it."

Allie looked down at the plate. The waffle looked soft and soggy, just as she liked them. Her stomach grumbled. "No, it's yours," she said. "I snoozed."

"Just take it for Christ's sake. I know you want it—and I know you know that I know that," Henry said. "I'll just have a muffin or something when I get to the café. That beats the hell out of this, anyway."

Quickly, Allie took the plate and picked the waffle up and, folding it in half, began shoving it in her mouth. As she bit, it seemed to resist her teeth, but the sponginess gave in as she ripped and pulled.

"Did you hear how hot it's going to get?" she asked in between bites.

"Hot as hell," Henry said. "I don't care. I wish people would stop talking about the weather all the time. All day I have to hear about it, because the café is apparently the only place in town with any goddamn air conditioning."

She ignored him and went on: "It's going to be over 100 degrees." Allie wiped her sticky fingers on her pants. "Me and Miguel are going to cook ramen on the sidewalk."

"What?" Henry looked up from his phone and scrunched his eyebrows together.

"Water boils at 100 degrees. We're going to put the pot on the sidewalk and make lunch."

"No, it doesn't," Henry said.

"It does! We just learned it in school."

"I promise you," Henry said. "If those are your lunch plans, you're going to be hungry." He got up and went to wash his plate off.

"If it doesn't, then why would Ms. Clancy lie?"

"She didn't. You just don't know the difference between Fahrenheit and Celsius. It's really a shame you missed the end of the school year. If you don't even know something as simple as that, sixth grade is going to be tough for you."

"You'll see," Allie said. She got up and stomped out of the room, heading for the stairs. It was just like Henry to flip-flop. He could never just be nice. She may not have been the smartest in the house, but at least she wasn't rotten and mean.

Allie skipped every other step as she went up the staircase. Her to-do list kept growing, and she wondered how she could fit everything into one day. First she'd go to the store where she'd find Miguel opening up with his dad. Then the two of them would look for the cat a bit. That would take them to midday, when the sun would be high enough to guarantee the perfect conditions for cooking that ramen. Of course, then they'd have to go to the Oceanview Café and look around back. She had heard all about the crazy man who had drawn over just about every inch of the walls. Henry had spent almost a whole shift trying to scrub it off, but the chalk stained into the paint, and there was no way it could be gotten rid of entirely without having to be painted over. Some of the other kids tried to figure out what it was he had drawn, but no one was sure anyone had got it. Allie knew she would be able to figure it out at first glance without even trying.

It was going to be a perfect day.

H. E. Scott

The Highwayman

AN EXCERPT

On Wednesday morning, December 28th, 1774, keys rattled against the bars as a turnkey opened the cell block door. Four constables slapped their batons into their hands in a rhythmic, threatening display. Two others burst into the cell to chain the convicts together, two by two at their ankles, their hands chained in front of them. Their journey to the New World had begun. They shuffled across a large, dark courtyard and into the street beyond. The quiet in the street was disturbed by the rustling of chains and the swishing sound of the men's shoes on the slippery cobblestones.

The streets of London were awakening to a day of business and trade as the convicts plodded from Newgate to Blackfriars on the River Thames. Many people watched, contempt on their faces, as the prisoners passed by.

The day promised to be wet and cold. The stifling smoky air made breathing difficult. It mingled with the stench of garbage, feces, fish, and amongst those odors wafted the aroma of fresh-baked bread. The prisoners had been fed stale bread and a thin gruel for their breakfast. The only way to chew the bread was to soak it in the gruel, making an unappetizing breakfast indeed. The gruel created a lump weighing down Lawrence's stomach. The lump threatened to leap out of his throat with every step.

People spat at them and jeered as they passed. Young boys, with nothing better to do, threw rotten fruit and vegetables until a quick slap of the constables' batons warned them away. The sense of dejection their actions caused made Lawrence silently berate himself for being a fool.

Some of the bystanders called out as they shambled past, wishing them a safe journey—friends or family of one or more of the bedraggled herd of men. Others, with their hate, the cruelest of all, lobbed dirt and screamed, "Hang him, hang him."

Lawrence turned to see who they treated so mercilessly; it was Daniel Bishop, a young man a few steps behind him.

Daniel Bishop had beaten his sweetheart to death. Lawrence wondered how this man would also be transported for such a horrible crime. The more the crowd jeered at Daniel, the more he responded with laughter and jeers of his own. The crowd hurled rocks and dirt at him.

A rock hit Lawrence, grazing his temple. He stumbled and the man chained to him also fell. They collapsed in a heap on the ground. Lawrence's knees smarted from smashing against the slimy cobbles. The crowd's laughter and hoots at their misfortune pierced his heart.

A nearby constable, having not seen what happened, began beating Lawrence and his partner. "Get to yer feet you loiter-sacks, the tide don't wait for no cowsons such as you." He yanked on their wrist chains and pulled them to their feet. Both men leaned heavily on each other as they staggered to catch up to the rest of the group. Each step an agony as their shackles abraded their bruises, cuts, and sores.

The masts and rigging of the ships in the harbour towered over nearby buildings. Lawrence's stomach revolted and he gagged. He had never been on a ship before. The smell of tar assaulted his nostrils, a more pleasant tang than the filthy streets, but it stirred the lump of gruel in his stomach.

They made their way along the docks until they came to the ship, ironically named *Freedom*, and moored some distance away from the other ships due to its stench. A huge seagoing vessel with guns lining its sides, men in the rigging, and barrels, boxes, and animals being loaded into the hold.

Gulls flew overhead, their raucous calls competing with the shouts of the men working below. The constables allowed the convicts to wave their goodbyes to family and friends. Many broke down in tears. None of Lawrence's family came to the port. He did not expect them. He asked them not to come. As he gazed into the crowd, Lawrence glimpsed a man in a heavy woolen cloak—the hood pulled low over his face—who stared back at him. Lawrence wondered if the man was staring at someone else, but when he turned to look no one stood behind him.

The man resembled Jack's father. Self-consciously, Lawrence pulled at his beard, grown long and unkempt during his incarceration. He had worried Jack's father would pursue him but realized his appearance was much changed since Edward Griffiths last laid eyes on him. His hair hung lank and dirty around his face. He looked like every other man in the convict line. His dirty, ragged breeches were so loose he had to hold them so they would not fall lower than was respectable, but there was a glint of recognition in Edward Griffith's gaze. Lawrence tugged his canvas sack closer and turned away when he realized Jack's father recognized him.

At a signal to board, the convicts were unchained from each other. In single file, they shuffled crablike up the steep and narrow gangplank. It bobbed from the weight of too many men. Lawrence held the railing in a fierce grip as he slid his hand along. He slipped his feet forward without lifting them. A huge splash and a loud whoop of satisfaction from the crowd on the dock distracted him. Daniel Bishop had fallen from the gangplank into the river. He flailed, attempting to keep his head above water. His face was white and his mouth wide as he screeched in fear.

A constable threw Bishop a life buoy. Bishop looped his arm through it. When he reached the dock, he grasped the constable's arm and they both fell into the water. For reasons only Bishop would know, he wrapped his wrist chains around the constable's neck and pulled him under. A small skiff rowed to where they struggled and fought, but by the time the skiff reached them and the constable was pulled from the water, coughing and gagging, it was too late for Bishop. He floated face down and lifeless with his arm still looped through the life buoy.

The constables rushed the rest of the convicts up the gangplank. Expressions bleak and eyes hollow from what just occurred, the convicts gazed around to see as much of England as they could, before descending into the hold. Cool and dark, the hold was less than five feet in height. Lawrence stooped as he hobbled into the darkness.

The sounds of bumps and shouts from the sailors loading the last of the supplies continued and then a whistle shrilled. Footfalls sounded to and fro across the deck, as if every man had an urgent purpose. Lawrence perceived no movement of the ship but then felt it jerk and bob with the fast rolling movement of the Thames.

Panic took hold of Lawrence. His heart pounded. He was below-decks, chained with no way out. What if the ship sank? They would all drown. He wanted to scream. The walls of the ship closed in on him. He shuffled towards one side of the ship, sat down with his back against the wall, and wedged himself between two men who already occupied the space.

"Hey, look out where you're steppin, mate. You crushed me fingers," said a scruffy man, his bulbous nose pointed up at Lawrence in accusation.

"Sorry. Sorry. I need to sit down; I can't breathe."

"Ah, that'll pass, don't you fret none. I hear the passage is a bit rough now and then, but you'll do."

"How do you know?" he asked. "Do you know of someone transported before?"

"Well, me father, some years ago now. He sent one letter to me mum. After that we heard nothin' from him but in that letter, he told us not to get ourselves in trouble so's we need not make the passage like he did."

"After that advice, what did you do to get yourself on this ship?" said Lawrence.

"Well, that's an interestin' story. I was just passin' by a house, mindin' my own business and two men came runnin' out, hell bent, they knocked me down on the sidewalk and while I lay there rubbin' me behind some-one came up and accused me of bein' one of the thieves. No one vouched for me honesty and so they arrested me. 'Acause I didn't have any of the goods on me and the lady of the house, bless her soul, couldn't identify me they decided that perhaps I was an innocent bystander, but the con-stables were acquainted with me. The judge decided I needed a lesson and gave me passage on this here ship."

He chuckled and Lawrence knew the man was lying. The story he just told probably was more interesting than what really happened to him. If he had been in prison for any length of time, he would have had some time to invent it.

Denise Unrau

Men Who Wear
Black Nail Polish

AN EXCERPT FROM THE NOVEL
"THE SAVING OF IDA MAE WIENS"

Ida drives to the warehouse-sized drugstore at the edge of the city on
Saturday morning, when she knows the traffic will be lighter. She is nervous about driving on the 75. Cars rush by her even though she stays to
the speed limit, and when she gets to the city, she feels the pressure of
the vehicles behind her at every intersection, sure every honk is directed
at her.

She parks in an empty bank of spaces a considerable distance from
the entrance, so she will not have to back out afterwards. After taking a
deep breath, she gets out and locks her car. She pulls the door handle
to make sure. Upon entering the store, she is momentarily disoriented;
normally, she heads straight to the pharmacy counter in the back. It's
never occurred to her that the store might offer her anything beyond the
pills that bring relief to her chaotic head.

Her sister-in-law had suggested lotion. "Lotion? Aisle five," says the
clerk stacking cans of Coca-Cola on a display stand at the entrance when
Ida plucks up the courage to interrupt her.

Aisle five is overwhelming, not what she expected. Ida brings her
hand to her mouth when she is confronted with the long array of lotions
that promise to renew, soothe, repair, restore, soften, and hydrate with
soothing aloe, nourishing honey, hydrating coconut, and anti-age glowing lavender. One assures relief for extremely dry, cracked hands; another

95

says it will smooth and protect; and yet another boasts of ultra-care and fragrance-free, pure and natural help for working hands. Although her body is fixed to a spot in the centre of the aisle, her hands are beginning to tremble, so she grasps one with the other in an attempt to steady them and her anxious mind.

A ponytailed blonde wearing sturdy brown boots and an ankle-length, camel-coloured cardigan hurries past Ida and reaches down for a bottle, almost without stopping. Ida is reaching for one like it, when a man with a black baseball cap over his eyes stops beside her and takes a bottle from the top shelf with equal certainty. Ida hesitates.

Usually, in times of crisis, she calls her friend Frieda. Frieda is a no-nonsense girl who knows how to shut down Ida's worries.

When Ida is undecided about what dessert to bring to the church potluck, Frieda says, "Personally, I like that carrot cake you make with the cream cheese icing," and that is that. Decision made. Anxiety allayed.

But Frieda is out of town, on the first solo vacation of her life. Freedom Fifties Tours advertised a trip to Florida to escape the last gasps of winter, and Frieda decided to expand her view of the world.

What would Frieda do? She asks herself now, then feels badly because she's substituted Frieda for Jesus, who should be her number one go-to. The thing is, she's not at all sure Jesus is interested in helping her choose suitable gifts for nurses.

At the end of the aisle, a young man is restocking toilet paper. After a moment of indecision, she clears her throat, adding a barely audible "Excuse me?" at the same time he rips the tape off a new box. The sound sends her back a step. Not sure how to proceed, she turns back to the shelves.

"Do you need help?"

Ida whirls around and has to catch herself, gripping the orange cardboard display for sunscreen, which wobbles a little, then holds steady. So the young man has heard her. His button-up shirt hangs over a pair of black jeans. He has an earring dangling from one ear, a pierced eyebrow, and black fingernails. Ida has never seen black nail polish on a man.

"I ... I need to buy some gifts," she says, and then clarifies, "for people I don't know." The young man raises his eyebrows, encouraging Ida to go on as he continues to unload toilet paper onto the shelf from a large box. "I'm thinking of buying lotion." She waves her arm across the assortment before them. "But I really have no idea ..."

He starts to flatten the cardboard box.

"Wait." Ida reaches out for the box, then pulls her hand back because it's shaking, a poplar leaf in still air. "Maybe we can use that to put the gifts into," she says, unable to help herself. Boxes are so hard to find.

"So, a lot of gifts."

"Yes, for all the nurses at the hospital," she blurts out, like a child sent to the corner store with a list. "There are twenty, including the aides, at Mordel Hospital."

It was Elsbeth's idea. "Ida, I've been thinking," she'd said. Ida had felt a lurch in her gut. "What do you think of buying gifts for all the nurses?" It was more a decisive statement than a question. Elsbeth had made a life of taking charge, teaching literacy and ESL on three continents. When it became clear that she was dying, she returned to Rosenfeld, disposed of all her worldly goods, and settled into the hospice room at the local hospital. Then she hired Ida, an old high school friend, to help her notify her friends and acquaintances—of which there were many—of her imminent departure.

The letter writing and phone calls had been one thing, but this was a whole other matter Ida did not sign up for. "What will I get?" Ida's panic welled up like bile from her gut.

"You'll know." Elsbeth had waved her arms around limply, too tired to be firm. Ida was sure she wouldn't know. She was hopeless at choosing. And she didn't spend money on indulgences. The disability cheque she received for her anxiety disorder (words she equates with not trusting in God) paid for the basics: groceries, rent, and gas, but not much more. Ida rationed everything, spent sparingly.

☞

"My sister works at that hospital," the young man comments, then shrugs and wanders down the aisle. She follows close behind, fuelled by this revelation.

"Is she a nurse? Does she use lotion? Do you know what kind?" Ida shoots the questions out like a contestant in a game show, hoping one will result in the prize she seeks.

He stops. "Maybe this one?" He points to a white bottle with the name written in dark green letters on the front. Sensible looking. Clean. $4.99. And just like that, the voices competing in her head leave. She feels lighter.

"That's perfect!" The lotion comes in many scents, but the hospital is a scent-free zone so this last decision is easy. Her hands are clasped at the top of her sternum, quiet and beatific.

"Wait here. I'll be right back," the young man says as if reading her mind. He returns moments later with a cart and a small cardboard box inside it. They load up, or rather the young man packs the box with four neat lines of bottles. "The sale on these ended yesterday, but I'll ask the cashier to give you the discount since you're buying so many," he says.

"That is so kind of you," Ida says, digging in her purse for her wallet. She doesn't like to keep customers waiting in the line behind her and likes to have her money at the ready. She looks up when he does not respond, but he is already off in some other aisle, restocking toothpaste perhaps. As she walks out to the car, pushing her cart, Ida wonders what kind of young man takes the time to paint his fingernails black.

Elizabeth Moira

Forever the Want

Is there a place I can hang my hat? This place, that place? England or Canada? Which is mine?

❧

The night before we left England, I was wakeful. Filled with anticipation and nostalgia, I lay in bed clutching my child tight—a need to hold on to something truly belonging to me. And he did that. Belonged. Darkness smudged outlines of cozy furniture, while half-packed luggage stood like intruders in the familiarity of my childhood room, the room where I spent my final night.

Night became dawn. I heard the distant moaning of early traffic. Our milkman replaced empty bottles with full ones. The empties jangled jauntily and grew faint as the cart receded down the long driveway. Our letterbox clattered, *The Times* thudded to the floor. The perky whistle of the paper boy faded. All as it should be.

Would it ever be all as it should be for me again?

❧

Belly heavy with late pregnancy, I clutched my two-year-old's hand. Music droned through the loudspeaker at Toronto airport. The chorus from Abba's "I Have a Dream" filled the terminal.

I did not believe in angels or anything good in what I saw. No. I saw nothing but pain. My pain. This move to Canada.

Oh how I did not want to come!

But he'd insisted. And with the baby growing inside me, and a fierce love for my son, I had no choice. No wish to pull our little family apart.

⌒

My baby born, I'd awake soaked in melancholy, wallowing in idyllic English scenes: Cumbrian fells caressing lakes, serene summer concerts at Kenwood House, the Hunt Ball, singing Jerusalem at The Last Night of the Proms...

Many times I'd awake. I'd awake and scrunch my eyes tight closed.

If I imagined hard enough, I'll awake in England.

I never did. The sheets were the same ones I'd put on the night before. The curtains, the dresser. No. Nothing had changed. When the dull ache swelled to searing pain, I'd whisper to my son:

"You are my British boy. Always my British boy."

⌒

I hurled a shoe at the wall. "I hate it here!"

My son dropped his plastic penguin and stared at me, confused.

Damn nostalgia!

I was ashamed. This was his new country, his future. What right did I have to behave like that? And everyone had been so welcoming. Kind. I was unfair.

Who'd think it would be that hard? To adjust to a country *so* like my own. Same language, legal, and political system. We shared a similar culture. But that's the surface. What lay beneath was harder to explain. Canada had a persona all its own. Related to England, yes. But did the two countries share the same inner core, what the English knew as *Englishness*? I didn't think so. Canadians had their own identity; they were proud of it. And I grew to understand the distinct separation.

A friend recently asked me about this.

"England's a far cry from Canada," I replied.

"You could go back if you wanted to."

Sure I could, but my kids won't come. Full grown, very much Canadian, they'd stay behind. I had been in Canada for a long time. So long it had become a habit. After all, I had been here more years than I was in

England. The depth of my pain had softened. A scar with little to show for itself. At first it was impossible to believe the festering wound could ever heal, but time buried the blow in a deep place. A place I thought of less frequently over the years.

༖

Is it the plight of immigrants everywhere to live in Limbo? Never to be a bona fide member of the new country? *Unauthentic.* Not like someone born there. Apart. Then there's the accent, sense of humour—even the way one moves, certainly the way one thinks. I've never pushed my Englishness, but that's how Canadians view me: English.

And the old country? I'm no longer part of that. Like a divorce.

While in Canada, England freezes to the day I emigrated. Stuck in that time like a dusty model village in a museum. And when walking the streets of England, I expect young people to think I'm one of them. A quasi Rip Van Winkle. Older folks *cannot* be my age. But they are. Life has moved on without me. Buildings have come and gone. Political ideas and values have evolved. I've read about them, talked about them, but I've never experienced such changes in the same way a resident of England would.

But that's not all. When in England, visiting relatives and friends leaves little time for anything else. And those visits are not reality. If I move back, we'd meet once or twice a year—perhaps all we had in common were memories, anecdotes, and the family stories we repeat each visit.

I'd be terribly lonely.

And I don't do lonely well.

༖

Am I to travel through life like those lost souls forever wanting? Craving for something I cannot have? Ford Maddox Brown's painting, *The Last of England,* brings tears to my eyes. A nineteenth-century clipper ship off to America. The emigrants bid farewell to England with a gaze of blank resilience and loss. What fortitude those brave souls had. Stoic, never to return. Thrive they may have, but some part of them is forever trapped in the want. The want for what was. There is something unbearable about that painting.

It's a hot, humid August day in England. My palm runs down a cool stone pillar inside an eleventh-century church. The pillar is a monument to a thousand years of strength. Hard, unsentimental, it has withstood change. I close my eyes and breathe in the smell. The smell of 'before.' The smell only old churches have. A residue of *oldness* impervious to the passage of time: musty hymnals, wafts of candle smoke, and hints of incense—scent of specters.

Nostalgia. Hold it in your palm a moment. Grasp it. Close your fingers. Never let go. Like I let that dragonfly go as a child. My feet firm on the ground, the dragonfly was mine for that moment. Mine. I owned it. But it escaped and flew away—a smaller and smaller speck. And then? Nothing. Nothing until I captured another. Not the same one. Not *that* one, the precious one. The rest were replicas.

And my memories are like that. Phantoms from another time, moments I experienced. Once. When it was real. Memories, stuck in my head where 'now' is not. My body, trapped in real time, has no tolerance for such rootlessness. It has moved on.

I might wrap such moments in layers of silk and lay them away in a hope chest to cherish in the future. But like my body, recollections wither. And are the recollections truthful, or have they rusted? Nostalgia craves the past, but it cannot take me there. Nostalgia burnishes memories, and oh, how they shine. And me? I drift with the poignant sounds and lingering scents nostalgia scatters like fairy dust. To loiter is to be a pitiful child watching others play, knowing she's not welcome.

Entao Liu

Woman With a Lightning Scar on Her Left Breast

AN EXCERPT

AGE 25, SURGERY WAITING ROOM

The surgery waiting room was immaculate. All patients were seated. Two nurses at the front desk, one young, one older. The most important thing in the room was the wireless printer.

Whoosh, whoosh, whoosh, it spat paper out, freshly printed pages with the result of a breast tissue check.

A woman reached for the hot paper from the printer with trembling fingers. Just a few minutes ago, she tried to start a conversation with me. She told me if she could survive, she would get a boob job, D cup this time. She smiled with dry, cracked lips .

"Not yours!" the older nurse yelled at her. "I will let you know when your results come." Just moments ago, the same nurse had quieted weeping women by saying, "Crying does not help your illness."

The woman sat back down—the gauze wrapped around her chest had dried blood on it.

Soon after, they took her to the operation room. On the printer paper, the result of her breast tissue indicated malignancy. The older nurse was much nicer this time, and she patted her back as she walked her to the surgery room.

When another piece of paper came out, no one stood up. The younger nurse was typing and seemed to not notice. All women in the seats held their breath, hoping and not hoping their names would appear on the paper, seemingly burning hot.

The woman next to me studied my face and said, "You will be fine since you are so young." I looked around the room. I guess I was the youngest person there. The younger nurse stood up, took the paper from the printer, studied it, and said something in a gentle voice. It took me a few seconds after the nurse repeated herself to realize that she was calling my name.

Oops. When nurses, doctors, and cops suddenly talked to you in soft voices, it usually wasn't good. That was a lesson I learned a long time ago.

I followed the nurse and entered an operating room that was too clean, too white, and too bright to keep my eyes open. Everyone talked to me in kind voices, which meant things were worse than I expected. I don't remember much after that. When I woke up, I found myself alive and without a left boob. I knew it, the one that always hurt more, the naughty one. My mom came to visit me with my step-brother. She sat crying for a while before I sent her away.

Salesmen sometimes came to visit the sickroom. One day, a man with an athletic build took out something round and soft from his suitcase. He passed the silicon pieces around the room. The cost of a boob job never gave me any thought of doing it. The man stood next to my bed, nearly begging me to take a look. He handed it to me through the bed curtain, and then our eyes met. Years ago, the same pair of eyes looked into mine; he was saying,"I love you, I love you so much."

This was the way things ended and started. Me, in debt because of the surgery, with aching stitches crawling over my chest. Him, wearing a wrinkled suit with a mismatched tie, his bag bulging with silicone implants.

I remember my mom's acid words. "Those who have been to the park won't have a future." Even though I knew she was talking about the loss of my virginity, somehow I felt it was a proper description of the moment ...

AGE 15, MIMOSA PARK

Once upon a time (only in this story, once upon a time means years ago, when I was a teenager), an accident happened in a park named Mimosa on a cloudy Sunday. For days, people were talking about how children had fallen from the Ferris wheel like splashing raindrops from a giant, rainbow-coloured umbrella. A lot of people had witnessed it, but I did not. In my memory, I only heard talk of bodies being broken into pieces, how gruesome that looked. People bent over and scanned the ground, carrying black woven bags in gloved hands. Everyone knew what they were searching for. Thereafter, the Ferris wheel paused in the position of its last rotation, and Mimosa Park became abandoned.

The main road in the park soon elicited a haunting imagery: a twisting path in the thick wall of a well-forested park, a natural disguise for inappropriate things. When the sun went down, some teenagers stepped onto the road and disappeared in pairs, diving into the lushness.

In the school washrooms, students gossiped about the night events in the park. The girls in the centre of the washroom conversation were the ones who wore glittery blue eyelashes to school and low-neck tight shirts beneath the boring school uniforms. These girls always had tattooed boys waiting for them outside the school gate. The boys dyed their hair platinum silver. They were involved in fistfights because of love affairs. They rode motorcycles, and no one asked where they got the shiny vehicles. In one version of the story, some of the girls they dated secretly swallowed abortion pills and cried in their own blood.

The boys talked openly about the park in a "wow" way. *He took so many girls to Mimosa. What a hero! Congrats, buddy! Wink, Wink!*

Under the shade of the trees, in the depths of the bushes.

Human bodies twisted together like an octopus's tentacles. Curved arms, scissored legs.

One of the pairs was us.

The smell of sweat, cheap cologne, and rubber. Bless those who remember to steal some condoms from the drawer of their parents' nightstand.

The click of buckles, the rustle of clothes. A sack of human flesh crashes into another, creating moans and screams.

The glossy leaves, the branches, and the soft petals—some dropped, some withered on the dry stalks.

We were one of them, the inappropriate, the degenerate ones.

In my second year of middle school, I thought I'd foreseen the hardships of my life. The dimming future of women of OUR kind. My mother worked for a pharmaceutical factory. I've seen her wear a lab coat from her manufacturing unit home. She wore it on rainy and dusty days, making local painkillers with bare hands just like all the other workers in her unit. If a pill fell onto the ground, they would pick it up, blow the dust off, and put it back on the table. At least that's what I heard. People of my grandma's age loved the local painkillers. They believed pills from the local factories were a better fit for the locals. A stronger kick. They swallowed a handful of pills per day.

I told my mom that I wished I was one of the children who fell from the Ferris wheel. She slapped my face and my cheek burned for a long time. Our relationship became worse when she discovered that I went to Mimosa with a boy in my grade. I chose him because I was obsessed with the way he was obsessed with me .

My mother pointed at my nose. C-U-N-T. She said it in such a slow way, as if it was more of an observation than an angry slip of the tongue.

Lauren Galbraith-Gould

A Song by the Seashore

AN EXCERPT FROM "THE IN-BETWEEN"

It was well past midnight when Cora locked the apothecary door and set out for home. She had scrubbed, sorted, and straightened until the shop was spotless, but her mind was still preoccupied with Ailsa's news of Angus' proposal. In truth, she had been expecting this, or something like it. She had noticed the way Angus treated her sister of late, and suspected that his generosity and goodwill were not innocent. Cora doubted there was a man in the village whose eyes weren't drawn to Ailsa when she walked by. But why must her eyes be drawn to Angus?

Bright moonlight washed over the buildings lining the street, which was empty except for Cora. She was glad for the solitude. She didn't have a mind to chat with neighbours at the best of times, and she was certain that word of the forthcoming marriage had reached many ears already. Gossip and rumours spread like rampant weeds in this town, and Cora could imagine what people might be saying about her, the speculations they would be making about what she thought of the man she was once meant to marry now choosing her sister instead.

Patches of cloud lay overhead like a threadbare blanket, the sparkling of the stars visible only here and there through gaps in the cover. Although it was the peak of summer, a cool breeze flowed from the sea. Cora drew her shawl closer. The sharp tap of her footsteps filled the night air as she made her way down the street, past the cobbler, the smithy, the tailor. Her family's apothecary was miniscule compared to these buildings, many of which had not existed when her grandparents were children.

Several decades ago, the bay had become a small port on an important trade route, bringing in goods from all over Europe and beyond. The village economy had soared overnight and fallen just as quickly only a handful of years later. It was during this boom that many of these buildings had been constructed, but the Murdochs' apothecary had been a fixture of the village for over a century prior. Merchants still visited their shores, but luxurious foreign goods were harder to come by these days. The last monument of these prosperous times was the cobbled church that capped one end of the main street, built when the Kirk decided that the town was bustling enough to require absolution of sin.

A thick clump of clouds passed over the moon as Cora turned down a darkened lane. The wind danced around her, stronger here as it was funneled into the narrow space. As the gusts whistled past her ears, they carried with them a faint, familiar tune that slowed her steps and quickened her heartbeat. Cora turned around, face to the wind. She tilted her head in the direction of the noise, which grew stronger with each passing second until she could pick out the melody. It was her mother's song, the verse she had sung as she walked into the waves that overtook her. The words were just as foreign and the sentiment just as sad as they had been that night.

After a moment's hesitation, Cora surrendered to the lure of the voice. She sprinted back toward the street and turned in the direction of the ocean. The clatter of her footsteps echoed behind her. As she reached the end of the street, the moon burst forth against retreating clouds, bathing the edge of the village in silver. The tide was out, and the rocks on the beach shone like beacons. She ran along the sandy path toward them. The song grew louder, playing in time to the crashing of the waves.

Approaching the shore, Cora slowed her pace, turning her head this way and that. She scanned the beach for any sign of another person, of her mother. But she was alone, just as she had been every other time she had chased this song to the sea. Her heart thumped in her chest, blood rushed in her ears. Steps from the shoreline, her run became a walk, and she sat on the nearest boulder to rest.

The melody quietened as her body grew calmer. With every steady breath of salt-laced air she took, the notes became harder to discern, until there was nothing to be heard except the cadence of the waves. Cora was no longer devastated by this sudden silence; she had learned that it was inevitable. The song was leading her toward the water, and it died when she would go no closer than this. She hadn't felt so much as the spray of the sea since it had taken her mother from them, and she was not going to follow that song, of all songs, into its depths.

The first few times she had ended up here, she had waited on the beach until the sun rose, convinced that something remarkable was about to happen. When nothing did, she had trudged home in despair, exhausted and unable to explain to anyone why she had spent the night alone by the ocean. She knew how it would sound and was not yet sure that she wasn't imagining the song. The first time she had heard it calling to her, she'd thought she was going mad. Years later, Cora still didn't know if it was real, but she had stopped being disappointed. She could not resist the pull of the song, would never be able to remove the hook it had buried in her heart, but she didn't stay anymore. She had enough to think about tonight and didn't need the distraction of whatever this was. She rose and made her way home without looking back. The song did not follow her.

The house was asleep when Cora tiptoed in. Da's snores filled the air, interspersed with the snapping embers of the dwindling fire. Gran was curled up close to the hearth, her wizened face smoothed by the soft light. Cora paused to slide the quilt farther up her grandmother's hunched shoulders before heading into the small alcove she shared with Ailsa. She could just make out the shape of her sister's body under the thick blankets. Undressing quickly, Cora slid into bed next to her. Her side of the bed was warm, as if Ailsa had rolled over only moments before. Ailsa's back was to her, and Cora considered wrapping an arm around her sister, a gesture of apology for her poor reaction to the engagement, but the thought was fleeting, and she turned away instead. As she laid her head on the pillow, Cora noticed that it was damp beneath her cheek.

Bing Jie Jenny Liu

The Engagement

CONDENSED

Wang Mei was 52 when Mu Bing re-entered her life. She lived with her 24-year-old daughter, Ling Ling. Their days began with Wang Mei massaging and stretching Ling Ling's limbs. For breakfast, they drank a bowl of soy milk and ate boiled eggs and buns. To strengthen Ling Ling's muscles, they took slow walks around the complex. For work, Wang Mei cleaned homes in their neighbourhood and walked children home from school, the only job she could find that allowed her the flexibility to be with Ling Ling most of the day.

Ling Ling loved helping with things around the house, like pouring scoops of rice into the rice cooker—counting every scoop out loud—and cracking freshly boiled eggs against the edge of the table. While her mother worked, Ling Ling napped and watched cartoons. She loved when the characters slipped on banana peels or smacked themselves with a frying pan. She liked drawing, although she had difficulty gripping a pencil. When she felt restless, she leaned against the front door, waiting for the sound of her mother's footsteps.

Wang Mei became a mother via an agonizing delivery, fraught with complications. Soon after coming home from the hospital, Wang Mei and her husband received a letter from the government granting them an exception to the one-child policy, citing their "extraordinary circumstances" —the same exception given to parents who lost children in the Sichuan earthquake. Wang Mei took it as an apology for the hospital mishandling her delivery, not as a sign that the government didn't register their daughter as a full person.

The older Ling Ling grew, the smaller Wang Mei's world became. Ling Ling was clumsy, slow in speech, and prone to pulling her own hair when she felt overwhelmed. Wang Mei's friends felt uncomfortable around her daughter and grew distant. Her husband couldn't handle the shame of having a daughter who was different and relocated to a different city. He continued to support Ling Ling's medical expenses through his company's medical benefits, but the coverage will end when she turns 25, leaving Wang Mei responsible for the costs.

Teachers didn't want Ling Ling in their classrooms for fear of slowing down other students. And kids who played with Ling Ling received perplexing and contradicting lectures from their parents about generosity but also instructions to associate only with those who are accomplished and academically gifted, lest they be dragged down. To be anything less than excellent was to be sifted out.

The isolation was painful. Wang Mei was never alone, but always lonely.

Mu Bing grew up in the same neighbourhood as Wang Mei. They attended classes together throughout elementary, middle, and high school. Everyone expected the two friends to get married, but Mu Bing's parents thought he could do better, so they sent him away to college and introduced him to other girls. He married a woman his parents chose for him. The marriage lasted barely a year. His wife met a foreigner through work and had an affair, trading up for a chance to be a white man's wife. When news travelled about Ling Ling's problems, Mu Bing's parents murmured that, at least, divorce was better than getting tangled up in Wang Mei's bad luck.

More than thirty years after they graduated high school and had lived out their separate lives, Mu Bing decided that he had to see Wang Mei. His parents had passed away; there was no longer any reason to stay away. He regretted all the years he had wasted out of obedience, ashamed that he'd let his parents hold so much power over him as a grown man. He had never known how to reach out to Wang Mei beyond exchanging formal New Year's well wishes and customary inquiries after each other's families. It had been easy back in their school days—he teased her about how slowly she ate, they discussed what their teachers did at home and ate for dinner, and she always zipped up his backpack when he slung it over his shoulder with the contents hanging out.

He took a taxi to her neighbourhood that day, carrying a pack of sunflower seeds—her favourite—then grew worried that he didn't plan a big enough gesture. Unsure about what he was going to say when he saw her again, he asked around to find out which building she was in. As if by some cosmic choreography, Wang Mei and Ling Ling were out taking their slow walk.

The two old friends felt an immediate sense of comfort and ease that time apart hadn't erased, like the scent that lingers on an old shirt. They never talked about what compelled him to visit her on that day; they simply fell into a routine as if they had never been apart.

Ling Ling quickly grew attached to Mu Bing, whom she affectionately called Uncle. He brought over a huge roll of paper that he spread out on the floor as her canvas and gave her thick crayons and markers she could grip with her whole hand. They watched cartoons together and he laughed at the same parts she did. She hated when he had to leave. One rainy day, she threw his shoes off the balcony and excitedly said that Uncle had to stay. She burst into tears when she saw the look on her mother's face. Mu Bing wore rubber slippers home that day.

⁓

Wang Mei was once approached by a man who said he was a matchmaker and asked her if Ling Ling was of good health and could possibly have a baby; if so, he might have some interested parties. How dare he, she'd said, spitting out the words. She cried all the way home.

Wang Mei never allowed herself to dream of her daughter getting married or having a family. She hadn't been invited to a wedding in two decades. A part of that came from good intentions: people not wanting to burden her with the obligation of giving a gift when she had no opportunities to receive any. No one could think of a milestone, like graduating high school, that Ling Ling would ever celebrate.

But it was easy to make Ling Ling smile; she needed so little. She didn't crave designer items, attention from boys, or meals out like other girls her age, yearning only for company and routine. Ling Ling loved Saturdays. She waited by the door, hair combed and shoes already laced, for Mu Bing to visit and take her to the park. Sometimes Wang Mei joined them, the three of them appearing almost like a normal family. Other times, Wang Mei stayed behind to cook lunch for them and steal some rare time alone.

For Ling Ling's 25th birthday, Mu Bing took her to the zoo while Wang Mei decorated their apartment with balloons. The three of them ate cake, popsicles, and blew bubbles off the balcony. It was the first time Wang Mei and Ling Ling had celebrated with a third person in a long time. It was a joyous occasion, but heavy in Wang Mei's mind was the issue of paying for Ling Ling's future medical bills. While Ling Ling napped after the day's festivities, Mu Bing and Wang Mei cleaned dishes. Mu Bing, her friend of almost fifty years, reached out and touched her arm.

"I think we should get married," he said softly.

Wang Mei patted his hand on her arm. "Come on, I'm so old," she said, not meeting his eyes.

"Let me take care of you and Ling Ling."

"You already do so much for us."

"Can we sit down and talk? Let's tidy up later." Mu Bing nudged her toward the dining table.

He held her right hand with both hands as they sat quietly next to each other.

"If I marry, my spouse gets my healthcare benefits and also my pension," Mu Bing explained.

Wang Mei listened. They sat in silence, listening to the sounds of their neighbourhood while Mu Bing massaged Wang Mei's hand. Suddenly, he stopped and looked up.

"Wang Mei, what if I married Ling Ling?"

Wang Mei's eyes opened wide. "Does that mean ..."

"Ling Ling would get my medical benefits."

"Mu Bing, I can't ask you to do that."

"I want to."

"Ling Ling will be so excited. She's seen weddings on TV before. I can make her a dress." Wang Mei started crying, struggling to find the right words. She started to thank Mu Bing.

"Family members don't need to thank one another," Mu Bing said. "We can hire a professional bubble blower for the wedding." He chuckled.

"Can you imagine Ling Ling's reaction?" Wang Mei laughed, brushing her cheek with the back of her hands.

Stephen Douglas
Homage
AN EXCERPT

Settling into the tufted green armchair, I felt grateful that Stewart had opened his office window. Just three weeks earlier, a cold front had descended from the northwest, blasting the city with a horizontal sleet that stung my eyes and made my daily walk treacherous. Winter's last punch. But on this day, the sun was radiating warmth.

A slight wear on the Persian rug from the door marked the steady daily path of clients. With my back to the window, I relaxed to the chirps of wrens and robins and the sweet potpourri of the viburnum's white blooms outside, anointing our counselling appointment. It was my tenth session with Stewart, according to my diary.

One title on his bookshelf drew my attention each time: *In the Realm of Hungry Ghosts*. I had no idea what the book was about, but that phrase seemed to describe how I felt. Therapy was like that. I didn't always get why it helped to talk about old hurts and failings, but I *was* beginning to feel better about myself, even while sadness lingered. I didn't have to stuff that feeling down anymore. And this made it a bit easier to stay sober.

Beside the writing pad upon Stewart's desk sat an emerald mug, a thin vapour still rising from his tea. I could picture him sitting there after I left, making notes about our session. What impression did I leave? It seemed silly to me, childlike in a way, but I wanted to matter to him.

The rug, the book, the mug, each were touchstones connecting one session to the next. Little things, perhaps, but their presence reassured me.

Stewart took his seat opposite me, attentive and welcoming as ever.

He had a kind face. Though angular, there was gentleness to it. Soft eyes, that's how I would describe them. Patient. Genuine. And with this sense of being cared for, one hour each week, I allowed myself to simply feel again, to slowly loosen the knot that had bound me all these decades, memories thorned with guilt.

"It's good to see you, Seb. How are you feeling today?"

He always gave me space to unpack.

"I don't know," I sighed, tuning in. "Unsettled might be a good word." I lied. At that moment, I was actually feeling calm. But I remembered how unsettled I felt the day before. I still thought it was important to tell him the difficult stuff, not the good stuff. I didn't believe that I had earned that privilege yet.

"Okay. I invite you to go into that a bit, Seb, if you are willing. What is 'unsettled' like for you? Where do you notice it in your body?"

By now, I understood, start with the feeling, see where it takes me. I could tune back into yesterday's mood, but I struggled to place that feeling somewhere inside myself. Because my body felt empty.

Oh, right.

"There's just space, a big emptiness, I'm feeling alone."

This was old and familiar. I could go there anytime.

"Like in your dreams?"

"Yes. Mmm …" I scrunched my eyes. Something tugged within.

For as long as I could remember, I journeyed solo in my dreams through strange landscapes: paddling upstream in a canoe, wandering abandoned castles, streets with no traffic, in and out of vacant houses … emptiness was safe.

I felt my brows furrow as I attempted to reach further inward. Unnecessary effort was counterproductive, Stewart had suggested in an earlier session. Relaxing my body, I remembered a dream from just a few nights before. The following morning, I scribbled a couple of sentences, quickly forgotten among all the journal notes I kept. Until Stewart's remark prompted me. Was this what my unease was about? Perhaps.

Carefully anchoring myself to the start of it, I returned to the rug, to the cup, and to Stewart.

"I had a dream this week. It was a little bit different," I offered.

"Okay. If you'd like to, tell me about it."

I had learned that almost everything I shared in session was capable of releasing a demon or two. I had gained faith in our weekly scavenger hunt. And this dream still had some life to it. It felt worth exploring.

"I was standing on the edge of a cliff overlooking the ocean …"

"Can you try saying, I *am* standing? …" Stewart invited me to step fully into the dream.

"Right, thanks. I am standing on the edge of a cliff. Faintly, I can see a small boat below. There is fog, lots of fog, but I can still see it. Just sitting there, a bit offshore. It's starting to ebb away, like it's being carried out by the tide. Almost out of sight. But I recognize him, Dad's in that boat! I know it's him." The dream returned vividly to life for me.

"I'm calling out, 'Dad, I'm here!' But … my voice is stuffed, or muted, or … like the fog is too thick, he can't hear me."

"He can't hear you and he's ebbing away."

"Yes, um …" I paused. "There isn't any more to it. That's when I woke up."

Stewart let me sit with this for a few moments, allowing the yearning to sink in. Four decades had passed since the explosion. All those years, I never stopped wanting him to teach me, to encourage me, and when things got too scary, to feel his hand squeezing my own. Just a simple pulse that said, I'm right here. Tears, relics of this vision, trickled down my cheeks.

"What do you need?"

I went with it, pushing beyond the familiar despair of my dream. "I have to reach him! Dad! I'm here!"

Only Stewart could hear me.

"I'm feeling … um, I'm feeling panic! This is my last chance, he'll be gone. I … I …"

In my mind, I tumbled down the bluff and sped across the rocks, so fast and light, my feet barely touched them. Then the thick wet sand slowed me to an agonising crawl while my father drifted further away.

"I'm at the water." I brought Stewart back into my vision. "I jump in. I start churning away with my arms and legs, speeding through the water." *Like Aquaman!* I thought, as if six years old again.

I stopped, in the vision, my head bobbing as I looked desperately about.

"I can't see him. I can't see his boat. I … ah …"

I was too late. Though my eyes remained closed, I knew Stewart was with me. In my mind, I scanned the stillness of the water. Finally, I admitted defeat. "Dad's gone."

I pulled a clump of tissue from the box and blew into it forty years of snot and tears, my throat tight, cheeks red with the sting of salt.

Then, whether the words came from Stewart or some older part of myself, I couldn't tell, I heard a gentle invitation, "Keep going."

Treading water, I was caught by a current. The harder I tried to swim back, the farther I was pulled away from shore. I saw my mother, sister, and brother all standing atop the cliff. I struggled to keep my head afloat with the chop splashing over me, and I lost sight of them, along with memories of the life we once had together, our laughter and teasing, birthday cakes and hugs. The life we once had with Dad.

"Something is pulling me down," I cried out. "A rip tide. I'm being pulled underwater!"

While in one corner of my mind I knew I was safely anchored in Stewart's office, I was also gripped with the fear that I might die.

I became a turbine churning water. My arms paddled furiously. I couldn't keep it up, though. "The current, it's stronger than me. I don't know which way is up!"

My lungs felt ready to explode, when suddenly, my hands struck sand, and I discovered that I was in a mere three feet of water. Gasping, I simultaneously stood up from that armchair and rose out of the water. The sky was clearing.

When I opened my eyes, I was standing in Stewart's office, my shirt soaked in perspiration. He didn't ask for any more detail. He didn't need to. My father was gone. That certainty had finally reached the core of my being.

Stewart offered me a hug, which I gratefully accepted. He held me as I sobbed and shuddered. I had emptied myself. And I made it back to shore.

Dianne Kenny

Bathing

AN EXCERPT

Every muscle, each fibre of connective tissue, ached. Claire couldn't pin-point one precise area that hurt more than any other. Today was just the weariness; tomorrow would bring real pain. How strange that fatigue and damage, at this extreme, were so similar. She pulled her stiff legs out of the car, and step by step, coaxed each up the stairs.

She balanced on the edge of the bathtub, wincing in pain as she reached to turn on the faucets. The rushing water reverberated around her small bathroom, almost angry, unlike the gentle tumble of the mountain stream that had been today's soundtrack. As the steam rose, she pondered what she had been through that day. Her first technical climb on an actual mountain—farther up that route than a novice should even try. Gareth, with his unnerving sunny-side-of-the-street look at everything, called it her "accomplishment." She blamed him for the risk and resulting trouble, yet had to thank him for stopping her fall. Her fingers trailed across the top of the water. Dido, her cat, leaned on her shins for attention.

She peeled off her clothes. Stretching to pull off her sweater and t-shirt felt good. Each sock was crusty with sweat, dirt, and blood.

Ouch. She hadn't noticed the stubbed toe and blisters. The thought of hot water on open wounds and tender skin made her pause. Pain was all she could feel; was more necessary?

She hobbled into the kitchen and poured Merlot into an old pewter beer stein. Back in the bathroom, the air was thick with steam and the scent of bath oils. The water was a touch hotter than usual, but soon the heat would seep deep into her, revive her calves and feet, wrinkle her toes. Lowering herself inch by inch, she smiled at the perfection of it all.

Bathing was her go-to for relaxing both her mind and body. Her arms, legs, and buttocks settled into their usual tub pose. She closed her eyes, her right hand a neck cushion, her left cupping the old pewter mug. She stilled herself to see if the water could be made entirely calm. This would be the ultimate moment of peace.

Her mind drifted as her limbs gained buoyancy, and she sank a bit further into the water. Something slid against her skin, tickling her spine. A little air pocket, defying gravity, was floating to the surface, sliding around everything in its way in a life-defining act to burst through the surface and become one with the air. A smile grew across Claire's wind-burnt face and she cheered the little bubble as it sped toward the top, proud of its accomplishment.

She adjusted her position again, lifted her chest slightly to pull her shoulder blades away from the porcelain, releasing another bubble. Without hesitation, it followed a similar path as the first, seeking elevation, until it burst. She repeated the movement, releasing bubble after bubble to cascade upward from the base of her spine, along the ridge of her curved back until each reached the air. Some tickled more than others, some travelled further. The most urgent, insistent bubbles reached highest up her spine, along her neck, caressing skin at the base of her hair. Like little climbers with tiny hands, rising to their destiny, and like the hands that last held her back, saving her from falling. Her mind attached bodies and then faces to the hands. Into focus came a particular face. Her eyes flew open. It was the wrong face.

She rose hastily from the tub and stepped over the edge. Dido hissed at the splashing water. Claire wrapped the towel around herself, rubbing it vigorously across her back. She bent to grab her robe from the floor and felt suddenly hot-sick.

Shit. She'd stood up too quickly, causing her blood to rush around, so now she was dizzy too. She knew better.

Michelle Greysen

Shunned

AN EXCERPT

PROLOGUE

She sat so purposeful in the lap of her maternal granddad. He in his cable-knit sweater and after-church pants, she in her Sunday best with her favourite pink hair ribbons dangling in the sway of the gliding rocker.

"What makes us a family, Grampa?" she questioned out of nowhere, in that all knowing, all wondering way of a curious five-year-old.

He took a moment to savour her candid innocence, while he contemplated his own existence through the child's eyes.

"Well, I'm your family, honey, and so are your mommy and daddy and your new baby brother, Conrad."

"But Gramma's not my family anymore, right?"

He steeled his emotions, swallowing the lump in his throat.

"Of course Gramma is your family, but she lives in Heaven now. Remember?"

"But she is not baby Conrad's family, right? 'Cause she moved away to Heaven before he was born, and she never saw him and she can't come for dinner or to my ballet recital, and that is what families do, right Grampa?"

He sat motionless, stuck in the memory of his recent loss. He wished he could go back to the times he had rocked his own little pigtailed daughter on his lap. Now, her the mother, and forty years passed, this new twenty-twenty decade made it all a lifetime away.

"My friend Lisa's dad doesn't live at her house anymore, and she said her family is just her and her mom now. If my dad moved to his own house, like Lisa's dad, then he won't be my family anymore either, right?"

The child's unsettling questions were overwhelming for the old man with too few answers. Her wisdom was wonderfully simple. Perhaps, he thought, over the years we have all confused family history with being-a-family. Maybe they are not the same thing? After all, how can what one generation said and did a century back make any difference to what another generation may or may not become in the future?

With her out of questions and him out of answers, the pair quietly rocked. Rays of warm winter sunshine blanketed them, peaking across the room from the worn outer edges of the shades. Watching his precious granddaughter drift off in the glide, he longed for a catnap and a break from her haunting questions now sinking into the pit of his gut. That dark spot where he tucked away the sorrow of his late wife not meeting their new baby grandson.

He couldn't help but wonder where one's sense of family came from. In his half-awake state, he pictured family history just hanging in the air, ghost-like, waiting, hovering patiently, readying to affix to the next generation.

Recalling the day his daughter, his family, had been given the gift of this adopted little angel, he softly cradled the child sleeping so peacefully safe in his arms. He pictured her true family history drifting around, lost and unable to find her, missing the opportunity to settle into her soul and carry her through life.

The glider slowly eased itself into stillness as he and his granddaughter, family-but-not, napped together in the sunshine and sweet silence.

In the year 1920 …
ONE

When the weekly list became too long to put off any longer, Abraham rose early, well before his father was up, and started the laborious process of readying the Ford for a full day to town. In the shivering early hours, under moonlight streaming past the edges of woollen blankets covering the windows, he headed down the narrow creaky staircase. Abraham's thick wool socks padded across the board-floor.

Stopping in the kitchen, he slid the poker under the copper boiler pan of cold water into the old black cast range to shake down the ashes, then loaded more coal, in hopes of firing up a searing stove.

While waiting for the rolling boil of the kettle it was time to shovel. The snowdrifts, piled high against the doors, took some getting past, but once cleared, Abraham went to the pump for fresh pails of water. Returning to the kitchen, stopping long enough to warm up somewhat and light the lanterns, one for mother coming down to start the morning meal, and one to take along himself, he ventured out again to the frigid barn to tackle the task of starting the car.

Wedging a block against the front wheel, Abraham went around the backside jacking up one wheel behind to allow the gas to flow forward. Relying only on an old paint stir he stuck in the crankcase, his experience determined enough oil. Around the side door, he reached past the frozen old seat cushion, already mended twice now, much to his mother's ire. Unscrewing the gas cap, he poked in the other end of his makeshift dipstick, gauging that the level of gas was also sufficient for the long day trip ahead.

Shivering in the cold, Abraham headed back to the kitchen for the now-hot water needed to fill the radiator and pour over the iced mechanics in hopes of an easy start. His father, David, was now sitting at the table in silent prayer as Abraham dipped water from the stove top boiler into the bucket and headed back out.

Abraham cranked with all the strength of his one arm and the choke wire in the other as he made his first attempt. He thrilled in the success of getting the used Ford to start on the first try. Turning the key on the old coil box under the windshield, the car took on a rumbling hum and all the hard work was not in vain. Never skip one step, take your time, and things should go well was what Father had taught him; it turned out he was always mostly right. Not that Abraham, or Abe, as he preferred to call himself, mentioned it much to his father.

He tossed the choke and his makeshift dipstick into the toolbox, grabbed the jack and hopped into the car. Backing out, he chugged the car to the front of the house where he left it to warm up, as he ran inside to do the same. Abraham joined his father for a morning reading and prayer before a quick meal. Mother had by now readied for the men before their journey to town.

His father, always sounding so stern, delivered the morning devotional on a modest life.

"Romans 12:2: And be not conformed to this world: but be ye transformed by the renewing of your mind, that ye may prove what is that good, and acceptable, and perfect, will of God."

It was not by accident, thought Abraham, that his father had picked this exact lesson before heading to town. He had often lectured all his children on the sins of the outside world. The sins that lead to a broken life. In their trips to the city, David had noticed Abraham and his younger sisters glancing at the young people wearing their sinful ornamentation and fashionable dress. He wanted none of that for his children, especially his son he now needed beside him to farm and care for the family.

As fast as the men could echo "Amen," Mother arrived with full plates of hot breakfast and steaming coffees. Coffee was a new taste Abraham had yet to fully appreciate, after his young years of enjoying the sweet, chocolaty malt flavour of Ovaltine or Postum on cold winter mornings.

Armed with a carefully plotted list of supplies and deliveries, Father readied himself in the right passenger side while Abraham tucked a full cream can on the floor between his father's legs, and then on his lap, gingerly piled a dozen wooden crates of eggs. Gently closing the doors, Mother then passed through the window a lovingly warmed quilt from beside the stove. Wrapping it over their legs and draping it around the egg boxes piled to the windshield, the men were at last off.

"The driveway, sloped downward from the road, was better backed out of first thing in the morning," David reminded Abraham. "So as to let the fuel run down to the engine and lessen the chance of a stall-out so early in the day."

"Yes, Father, you have mentioned that a hundred times before," replied Abraham.

David ignored the backtalk and lectured on, "You wouldn't want to have to restart the car all over again now would you ... all that hard work."

Clearing the driveway, they bumped over the winter ruts onto the ice-packed dirt roadway, breaking their first egg of the day. Venturing onward in the cold crisp hint of first morning light—God's light as Father had said many a time—Abraham and his father David were at last on their way to town.

Kim Dhillon
The Mirror

The girl went to the bathroom as soon as she got home from school. She locked the door and looked at herself in the mirror. Holding out her forearms, she was relieved to see that, at least, they weren't overly hairy. Fine hairs, almost blond from the sun, sat against her arm. Her skin was still darker than its usual brown with the end-of-summer tan that hadn't yet sloughed off. She leaned close to her reflection and examined her nose and upper lip. Small, black hairs poked out from her nostrils. Turning her head to the side, she could see the fuzzy moustache of pale brown hair on her upper lip. She hates that Rebecca had been right.

What kind of sixth-grade girl had a moustache? Even the boys in her class didn't have moustaches yet, except for Cory, who not only had a crop of downy hair on his upper lip, but whose face had also begun erupting in swollen red spots. She would stare at the red lumps, fascinated, during math class. She wanted to reach out and squeeze them until they burst. The other girls in class had skin that was fair, hairless. They could flip their head back and laugh and their inner nostril was a pristine extension of their peachy complexion, almost translucent. It was as if their insides glowed from within, pure and unspoilt. She looked at her face in the mirror: her nose straight and long, skin brown, and those hairs. How had she never noticed them before?

Her mum would be home soon. She didn't have long.

Opening the left-hand bathroom drawer, she found hair elastics and brushes. In the under-sink cupboard, there were only cleaning fluids and a sponge. She had seen commercials on TV for a cream that seemed to magically dissolve hair for girls who wanted to wear "short shorts," but there was none of that in the drawer, and she couldn't ask her mum to get any in the grocery shopping. She was pretty sure it was for legs anyway. Her mother wouldn't understand: her skin was pale and freckled with only fine hairs like the other girls. Her mother didn't share the dark pigment or unwanted hair that the girl had inherited from her Punjabi side.

In the right drawer was the first aid kit. Opening it, she found Band-Aids, iodine, scissors, and a pair of tweezers. She placed the scissors in her hand, her thumb and forefinger between the plastic circular handles. Opening and closing them, the shears pressing together made a satisfying cutting sound. She looked again in the mirror and held the scissors near her hair before placing them back down.

Picking up the tweezers, she leaned into the mirror again. With her left forefinger, she pulled the tip of her nose—long, not button-like like Rebecca's—to the left. The hairs poked from her right nostril like thorns on a rosebush. Pinching the tweezers around the base of a hair, she squeezed and pulled. As she plucked out a single hair, her eyes filled with tears. Her nostril burned. She looked at the tweezer. The solitary hair was now removed from its rooted bunch. Leaning in again, she went for another. Again, a burn of pain, followed by tears, now trailing down her cheeks. Her nose filled with snot, and she turned to grab a wad of toilet paper and blow. The clear mucus filled the paper, which she placed in the bin. This would not work. It was far too slow, the pain too much.

Looking to the bathtub with its standing shower, she spied the orange and white Bic razor that her mother used on her legs. She picked it up and examined it in her palm. The handle was cheap plastic, still wet from the splashes of her mother's bath. The blade was a thin silver strip of metal held in the flat head. Soap scum sat in it. She turned it over in her hand.

Facing the mirror again, she examined the hairs once more. Small, but black and wiry, they descended on the inside of her nostril. She knew from the commercials on TV that you needed water or soap to shave, you couldn't do it on dry skin. Running the tap and patting her fingers in the soap bar that lay slimy in its dish, she smeared a small amount of lather on her upper lip. It smelled of lavender. She could hear the TV down the hall, where her brother, oblivious to her task, sat in front of it. Placing the razor blade gingerly on her upper lip, she pulled it down over her skin on the left side of her upper lip gently. Too far from the skin, her pull was too light. Nothing came off. Her neck began to cramp from this close examination. Taking a deep breath, she lathered again and repeated the action, pressing a bit more firmly. As she moved the razor away and looked at its crop, a row of small hairs, fine and curved as they separated from their follicle, lay on the blade. She rinsed it in the tap and examined her upper lip. The skin now looked rosier, more bare.

Good, she thought. She was only going to do this once. It wouldn't be a regular thing.

She lathered and moved the razor over her upper lip on the right. Examining the results in the mirror, she was pleased. Hairless, it looked better. Smoother and paler. There would be nothing for her friend to make fun of now. Except for the hairs in her nose that remained from her abandoned tweezing. She used her left hand to push her nose to the side, exposing the inside of the nostril more clearly. She dabbed with the razor, gently, to cut the few hairs that stuck out. *There, better.* She approached the other nostril in the same way.

As she finished, she relaxed and drew her hand away. Then there was a sharp sting. The blade had grazed the tip of her nose. A deep red drop emerged. She dropped the razor, which clattered on the counter. She sucked in her breath from the sudden burning in the skin from where she had cut. She had a bloody slice—the size of a pea—where the razor had left a rupture of pink flesh. She grabbed a piece of toilet paper and ripped a small piece off, placing it on the blood. It darkened like blotting paper with a deep red dot.

Downstairs, she heard the door open and close. Her mother was home from work.

"Hello?" her mother called. "Are you home?"

"I'm in the bathroom!" she called back. "Out in a minute."

She peeled the bloody tissue piece off her small wound. The dot of skin beneath was raw and quickly refilled with blood. She heard her mother's heavy footsteps in the kitchen now, opening cupboards and banging pots as she started dinner. In the bathroom, she ran the tap and dabbed her finger on the cut again, trying to clean it off. *Stop, stop,* she willed it. She opened the drawer and swept her tools back in to hide the evidence.

"Can you come help me with the rubbish?" her mother called from the kitchen.

She dabbed at the blood again. It stopped and in its place remained a round pink slice. *Maybe Mum won't notice. Maybe she won't realize what I've done, won't ask me why I've done it.* She went to the kitchen.

Her mother was bent under the sink, emptying the bin which was overflowing. "How was school?" she asked without turning.

"Fine," the girl said. She held her right hand in a fist near her nose, as if about to sneeze.

On the counter sat a colander of peeled potatoes, their skins piled and waiting to be put in the bin. Next to them was a thin knife, its wooden handle worn from use. Her mother pressed the contents of the garbage down with her bare hand, and then tied the black bag. She turned, looked up, and gazed at her longer than usual.

The girl's hand hesitated and dropped slightly from where she held it by her nose.

Her mother opened her mouth as if to say something, and then stopped. Instead, she turned to the sink and shook her hands into it. A thin scrap of pink ham from a half-eaten sandwich in the bin fell off her finger. She rinsed her hands under the tap.

"If one of you would empty the bin before it's overflowing, that would be a big help," her mother said, wiping her hands with a tea towel.

She cleared her throat. "Mum, can you …" She paused.

Her mother looked up from the sink.

"Actually, nothing," the girl said. "The garbage …" She shielded her face again. "Right. Sorry."

Her mother turned back to the sink.

The girl picked up the bag to take it to the carport and then, backing out of the kitchen, she said, "I have homework."

Her mother glanced at her. "Hey," she said.

The girl looked up.

Her mother hesitated.

"Dinner will be ready in half an hour."

Jennifer Scarth
The Bridge

1: POSTCARD

The postcard propped against the salt shaker has made me sit down with my third cup of coffee. I'd take a shot of whiskey if it wasn't ten o'clock in the morning. The photo side is the sunset-lit Ponte Vecchio, with "Ciao, from Florence" in brush script along the bottom. The flip side, a brief jot addressed to me, has caused my heart to race up the rungs of my spine, squeeze through the hole at the base of my skull, and take up a hammer behind my eyes:

"Hi, Dad! You'd love it here. Doing great! Love—MoMo"

It is the unmistakable hand of my daughter, my only child; I taught her to write. Mona died from a fentanyl overdose two years ago, on the 18th of April. Over the years before that, she was slowly abducted from us. We paid out a heartsore ransom of driving around looking for her, doing food drops whenever and wherever we found her, and buying her cellphones that she lost and sold. So while the words on the postcard are powerful enough to knock the scab off my grief, they are also meaningless. It's been a very long time since Mona was "Doing great!"

Below that line, near the address, there is a scribble that I don't recognize:

"Found this in a bag Mo left here—T."

I don't know who the hell T. is, or where "here" is. Gail knows, I'm sure. She probably texts with T. on Mona's birthday. And death day. When I ask her, Gail will tell me that T. was Mona's rehab partner, or halfway house supervisor, or lover.

I'm alone here in the house I used to share with Gail and Mona. Alone but for Beau, our ancient spaniel, who tracks me around the house with his sense of vibration—the only sense he has left. Gail moved out last year. She needs a break from her talking about Mona, and me not. Last week, she texted that we need a "check-in" for the first time in months. We're having coffee this afternoon, but now I'm thinking drinks might be a better idea.

Gail and I were older, cresting forty, when we had Mona. I was the stay-at-home during the pre-school years. Gail told me to relax, to enjoy Mona, let go of my "inner engineer." She didn't understand how much I loved it. I developed systems for the bottles, the laundry, the groceries, and teaching Mona to read and print, all the while marvelling at each passing milestone. At some point, I started to blur around the edges; I lost sight of where I ended and Mona began. I took credit for her self-assured opinions, her precocious wit, her inspiring commitment to her emotions—whether it was sudden joy or a cloudburst of tears. Later, when Mona went out to play in the real world, I took the blame for what she found there.

A few weeks after Mona died, the police delivered a bundle of her belongings; everything she left behind fit into a bag the size of a pillow-case and smelled of ash and mice. Gail cleaned them up and packed them into a dresser in Mona's old bedroom; we've never touched them since. I should put the postcard with the rest in the drawer. But for now, I slide it into the pocket of my jeans.

II: TRAP

Raccoons are my latest project. They rattle the garbage can lids of my brain, whether I sleep or not. They knock the trash over and tear the bags open with their simian hands. They pick out the bits of egg, the crisp fish skin, the porkchop gristle and fat, and all the things I've squandered from the fridge. They show their disdain for me by tossing the rest of it all over my yard.

I plan to make a trap. Google says raccoons like puzzles and tunnels, so I'll give them a puzzle, with a can of tuna as first prize. I have a pile of lumber, stacked and tarped in the backyard. It's an ex-treehouse that Mona outgrew long ago.

I stare at the boards and window frames and it comes to me fully wrought—the best idea, the best feeling I've had in years. I take the postcard out of my back pocket and salute Taddeo Gaddi, who built the masterpiece Ponte Vecchio almost 700 years ago. It has sturdy, closed spandrel supports and shops and apartments built right into both ends of the bridge. It will do nicely to attract the attention of the trash bandits.

In the postcard photo, the bridge is ochre yellow and reflected in the slow, flat river. I imagine a clutch of tourists at the balustrade in the central, open part. The out-of-towners jockey for position; some raise their cameras above the crowd on a skinny arm. I hear them curse the tall ones at the front. I know that Mona never once left Montreal during her whole, short life but there she stands, looking through the camera lens at the people on the bridge, sunset warming her back and lighting up the blond spirals of her hair.

The trap will run from the fence post, diagonally across the yard. There will be rooms, four on each end, with windows and shutters. The centre section will be glassed in to give them a view, but no chance of escape.

I get as far as a raccoon-scale sketch and begin to select and measure the materials—my favourite part. Dorothy from next door comes out to her back stoop for her three o'clock cigarette.

"New project?" Dorothy squints, as if she could make out the details from where she stands. I nod.

She blows a straight stream of smoke in my direction and talks through the last of it.

"Good for you. Keep you busy," she says.

III: T R I P

I pull up to the Moustache Café late, at quarter to four. A quick look in the rear-view mirror confirms that a shave would've been a good idea. Gail sits at a table near the window. I can tell by the way she puts on her lip balm—four quick rounds of her lips—that she's worried, or peeved. She takes out her phone, and a moment later, I get a ping: *"are you coming?"*

I wave to her from the door and go to the counter to order her decaf non-fat latte. For my first meal of the day, I order soup, scone, and pasta salad.

"Hungry," Gail observes, as I unload the tray.

"Busy day," I say. "Sorry about the scruff."

"That's good." She takes a pull of her coffee. "The busy day, I mean. And the scruff suits you." She smiles.

I concentrate hard on finding the corner of the foil on the butter package. Mona's postcard is warm in my breast pocket. I should share it with Gail. She would love it. But I hesitate because she's wearing a dress and earrings that I don't recognize. I open my mouth to remark on her new haircut.

"Michael, I'm seeing someone," she says in one long word. She covers her mouth, as if she's released a belch.

"Oh. Okay. Wow," I say. I spit out a wad of scone into my napkin and drop the whole thing in my soup.

"I thought coffee was better than drinks?" she says.

"That's okay. That's okay." I stop myself from saying it again, but it pinballs around in my head: that's okay, that's okay, that's okay.

The silence sits between us like a bog.

"I'm going away," I say. This is a surprise to me.

"You are?" Gail sits back in her chair. "Well. That's great. Really great, Michael. Where?"

"Italy. Florence, actually."

"Are you—have you got someone to go with?"

"No, but I'm—I'll be meeting up with an old friend," I say.

Gail has every right to raise her eyebrows; we both know she's the oldest friend I have. But what if? If I take the postcard with me, tucked in my passport? I'll go to Taddeo's bridge and admire the view. If I can find the spot where the photo was taken, I can stand where Mona stands. With the sunset warm on my back, I'll have Mona's hand, small and soft as paper, enclosed in mine.

Ethan P. Yan

Beef?

What sound do you think it makes?

"Guys, look."

The wonder in Denzel's voice reached Falco and Sibus despite its softness, calling their attention. The three boys gathered by the second-story window of the orphanage, pressing their faces against the glass, eager to spot what Denzel pointed out.

And there it was, passing the white picket fence to the grassy field and below the early morning sun: a large, spotted cow. It was being herded into the orphanage's grounds by a couple of large farmers who, from the size of their shoulders and arms, were likely men. It was the first time the boys had seen a cow, as well as grown men.

"What sound do you think it makes?" Sibus asked the question as if it was the prompt for a political debate. The oldest of the group, he towered over the boys at six feet, scratched at his smooth gold hair.

Falco looked up at Sibus, baffled. "They moo, no? We've all seen cows on TV, why are you asking—?"

"Because we don't know *for sure*, right?" Denzel answered swiftly, blue eyes still fixed on the animal. He periodically had to brush aside his lengthy dark brown bangs with slender fingers just to see. "We've never seen a real one. What if real cows sound just like chickens?"

"Then tell me, genius," Falco retorted, stroking his chin lightly as if his pubescent facial hair was thicker. "How do we know what chickens sound like?"

"Because we have a real chicken coop, dingus."

"Oh, right."

Sibus gave the boys an encouraging smile. He ruffled Falco's smooth chestnut hair as he backed away from the window. "Good try, Falco, but Denzel gets my point." He sat on his bed, its springs squeaking beneath his large physique. "I've been spending a lot of time in the library, but I still can't believe a lot of what I've been reading about the outside world. Machines that fly people around? Buildings twenty times taller than this three-story orphanage? I'll believe it when I see it. Until I see the world in those books myself, I'll keep my assumptions to myself, and that's my advice to both of you for when I'm gone."

Falco and Denzel stared at him in awe. It was as if their head orphan had just conducted a brief graduation speech before crossing the stage to adulthood.

Because that was exactly what it was.

"This sucks."

Falco was the first to say it, although the words had been lingering in Denzel's mind for months now. However, if he said it out loud, he would cry before he could say another word. Falco pressed a hand against the window, eyeing the world beyond the picket fence which revealed only hills, trees, and dirt roads. "Let me come."

"Falco, you have to wait for your own papers—"

"But they won't come for most of us!" Falco slapped the glass. Denzel jumped at the impact, though it was not nearly strong enough to crack the glass. "Why are we trying to pretend like this is a good thing, throwing a party and eating beef just to celebrate you going? Deratrix picked you because you're the golden boy, but it still took you being sixteen to get out! Denzel scores the highest on knowledge exams. Miriam crushes everyone in speed assessments. And I rank second highest in endurance tests, right below you. But what about the rest? How long will it be before kids here realize no one is adopting them, and we'll have been here for nothing!"

Sibus shook his head. "Look, Falco, I get your frustration, but you have to trust me that things will work out. Let's talk about this again later, before I leave—"

"Easy for you to say when you're the only one going!" Falco dug his nails into his palm and threw his fist at the window. The thin glass exploded at his strike. Denzel gasped. Sibus sighed.

A cowbell rang.

Distracted from the smashed window, they gathered around to inspect the animal through the new opening. The cow made several noises, having now neared the entrance of the warehouse next door. A cowbell, strapped to its jugular, chimed in the air again. Several of the other orphans could be heard spilling out onto the yard to admire the animal, with some exclaiming that it looked tasty already. Denzel sighed to himself in disappointment, "That's lame. They really do moo."

"Let's hope beef really is good, then." Sibus ran a hand through his perfectly golden, golden boy hair. "After sixteen years of chicken, I'm excited—"

Deratrix's raspy cadence thundered through the PA system, stunning them: "Sibus, it's time. Pack your things and say your farewells. Your parents are here early."

The trio stayed silent for a moment. Sibus, with the foresight and intellect to act swiftly, immediately told the boys to sit down and be silent—especially Falco, who looked ready to move on to smashing walls. They all knew what was going on and were each processing it in their own ways. These were Sibus's final moments in their dorm, and he wouldn't even get to try the fabled "beef" they were looking forward to.

Despite Sibus's request, Falco still spoke up, "No way I'm touching that cow meat."

Anticipating this, Denzel added, "It's not right. The party was meant for you, Sibus. You should be here—"

"That's enough. Falco, your hand." Sibus pulled a bundle of tissues from his nightstand. "Wipe the blood. I know you probably don't care about infection, but at least don't get my mattress dirty right before I'm gone."

Falco gave a heavy sigh before taking the tissues, dabbing away at the cuts on his knuckles. As he did, Sibus went on, "Just promise me two things. Both of you."

When the boys nodded slowly, Sibus spoke, "The first promise is that you both will stick through it all—whatever you go through here, or anywhere. It can't be for nothing, and I want you both to promise that you'll remember that. Yeah?"

Another slow nod and Sibus went on, "The second thing that I want you to promise me—and this is more important than the first—is that if I'm wrong, if this orphanage really is a setup for failure, then you do whatever you can to get out. No matter what it takes. Fair?"

"Fair," Denzel replied instantly.

Falco puckered his mouth at first. He tossed his bloody tissues in the trash before biting down the bitter words on his tongue. He gave a reluctant answer, "Fine. Fair."

The boys let the conversation taper off there, giving their farewells with wordless hugs and vows to see one another again. Sibus took his luggage, his contributions, and his regrets with him out the door.

And they thought it was the last time they would see the golden boy's golden hair. Rather than participate in the "festivities" that night, Denzel and Falco decided to instead retrieve a bitter trophy in Sibus's memory: the cowbell.

They wormed their way into the warehouse beside the main building during dinner. Despite the warehouse requiring a passcode, Denzel pointed out easy entrances via the open skylights. They kept watch on their tail, ensuring nothing was touched or tracked as they cut down to the underground slaughterhouse. Shelves and boxes gave way to knives and cleavers as they zipped past a strangely unlocked iron door leading into the slaughterhouse. Entering a kitchen-like room illuminated by bright white lights, the pair found themselves surrounded by steel tables, white tile walls, and splatters of dried blood. Though nervous about this unsettling environment, they were ready to get what they came for—

which presented itself as a cowbell rang in the air.

The two boys froze in their tracks, staring at each other as if one of them had made the noise.

Despite being the more timid of the pair, Denzel was the first to overcome his shock. He crept around the corner of the hallway leading out of the room, walking slow and steady toward the source of the sound. He placed a hand on his chest to quell the pounding in his heart and soul.

When Denzel cleared the hallway, he involuntarily drew in a sharp gasp—so sharp that he had to inhale a couple more times just to ease the shock of it.

"Falco, look."

Falco snuck up beside his friend. He hated the expression on Denzel's face because he'd never seen it before. In all their years together, Denzel was the boy who could figure anything out and come away from all problems with an accomplished smile. This was why, when Falco discovered what Denzel was looking at, he could only wonder what his genius friend was thinking behind his disgust. The question that came out of his mouth was, "Is that the cow?" and then, "Why is it still alive—?"

An ugly suspicion nestled itself in Falco's own mind. Horror settled into his face. Beside him, Denzel was trying his best not to vomit.

Sure enough, the cow was alive and well. It glanced at the two boys from inside a fenced corner, cowbell still jingling from its collar. Across from it lay a long wooden table, with a cleaver buried in it like an executioner's axe—and beside it, the source of their horror.

The carved scalp lay in a pool of dried blood, still curled from the shape of a head. The flesh was barely visible, covered by a nest of what the boys recognized as golden, golden boy's hair.

Heather Morgan
Private Conversations
A CONDENSED VERSION

They rehearsed their lines at their usual corner table, rotating in and out for cigarettes. She regretfully pondered why on earth she had invited her parents to see this show, starring her and her secret lover. Dan was an older businessman who wore custom-made tailored shirts. He had a daily cocaine habit she had originally seen as fun, but had now seeped into her life too.

She smoked a second cigarette to prolong the walk over to the venue. She stared at Dan, his shirt tucked in highlighting his small belly, which she liked so much. He had told her that he didn't like to wear his work clothes to class and every week wore the exact same polo shirt. When he didn't have time to change, his work clothes seemed to provide him with an air of arrogance, which she accepted as a challenge to soothe after class. Emily felt both infuriated and eased by his presence, a swirl of emotions she had grown quite attached to. She kissed him once more. His gruff stubble rubbed against her upper lip; she inhaled the smell of his cologne. He carried it around in a miniature bottle, she assumed so not to smell of alcohol, though she quite enjoyed the taste of it on his breath.

At the venue, he ordered his third pint. She thought he would be fine so long as he didn't start on the cocaine. They reserved that for after class, except for that time he laid it out on the cistern, hidden under a single piece of toilet paper. She had thought about flushing it, but only briefly.

Emily walked up the backstairs to the small, dimly lit room, spotting her parents. Her mother was dressed for the theatre, not for some tiny room above a pub. She hugged them and asked about the train ride and their hotel. She said hello to her friend, Terry. He was her office gossip buddy and wanted to know which was the older man that was keeping her out on weeknights and ever increasingly late for work. She enjoyed being a source of entertainment for him and nodded towards Dan, who was pacing alone.

"Mm, thought so," Terry said smugly.

The class gathered at the back of the room, ready to make their dramatic entrance, a whole ten feet to the stage.

The host, dressed as a ticket inspector, announced the show. The class walked through the applauding crowd, onto the stage where they swayed, holding imaginary handles as if they were on a bus. Her scene started—a phone call about a date with a man whose mother walked in on them having sex, only to offer them a cup of tea as his head raised from between her legs. She questioned what she was doing on stage, until she heard the audience laugh. Emily shifted back into her space, pretending to be on the bus again. Her scene with Dan was up next. He had devised the plot too close to reality for her liking. She was a young intern studying law. He was a successful business developer who recognised her from a meeting and asked her out for a drink. He bungled his line, they panicked, and skipped to the punchline. It flopped and they endured the silence spattered with echoing pity laughs.

The post-show buzz filled her body. Her mother left, it not really being her scene. Emily eagerly asked her dad what he thought of the show, while Dan neatly slid a pint of Guinness beside her, and again in twenty minutes. She shooed him away with her stares.

"Who's that?" her dad asked, as Dan's skirting around the edges became more obvious.

"Just the guy from my scene," she said, feeling weird about lying to her dad but quite certain she would not be making introductions. She had warned Dan not to talk to her parents. She couldn't tell if her dad knew or chose to ignore it. It was surprising Dan had kept it a secret this long. They finished their pints, hugged her dad goodbye, and joined her class to celebrate. At some point, Dan interrupted the festivities to share a story.

"And I pay her salary," he shouted about one of his employees being late for work. Retelling it over and over, waiting for an acceptable reaction. Everyone ignored him. Emily was embarrassed for him, and herself. She couldn't resist, so she pulled him outside to calm him down. She consoled him for messing up his lines. His seductive veil was falling, fast.

"I think I'm going to head home," she said.

He grabbed her and pulled her close, teasingly. She rubbed his chest and lightly pushed him away. She wanted to tell him how annoyed she was, but she would do anything to avoid a confrontation.

"Are you *actually* leaving? We haven't had any fun yet," he said as he pulled a little white bag from his wallet.

"I guess I could stay for one more."

The delight returned to his face, his eyes regaining their mischievous glint.

"You should go easy on that girl, you know."

"Who?"

"Your PA. You're definitely not an easy man to work for." She smirked.

"I pay her fucking salary. She works for me," he said through gritted teeth, and close to her face. She didn't want to soothe him anymore. She wanted to run the fuck away.

"I'm only joking." She pulled him in for a kiss.

She could do it for one more night.

Kathleen Newson

The Visit

Molly sits alone in the waiting room. The morning sunshine squeezes through the small window, making a neat square on the floor. Her legs are crossed at the knees and entwined at the ankles to keep the jittering at bay—a consequence of sobriety.

She's familiar with rooms like this; she has waited in many over the years. As a kid, her life was punctuated by meetings with social workers—her de facto parents. But this waiting room is different. She now waits for decisions about her daughter. It has been ten months since she's seen Ruby—ten months since the social work boss said she was not a safe parent and Ruby was given to her dead boyfriend's mom. Since then, there has been an endless pause in state intervention. For the first time in Molly's life she wanted The Fucking Social to knock on her door and see her clean. Alone and waiting.

Tomorrow at 10:00 a.m. they will allow her to see Ruby. She has been counting down to the visit, life moving in agonizing slow motion. If she continues to be good, they will allow her a small window of strictly supervised time with Ruby each week. Eventually, a judge will decide if she is fit to be a mother and have her daughter back.

"Hello Molly." At the doorway stands a tall, tired-looking woman.

"I'm Debbie." She beckons with her head down the hall, a stack of files in her arms. Molly rises and follows her to an office.

Debbie directs her to sit down and pulls a file from her stack. Although this is their first meeting, Debbie will know everything about her; Molly's nineteen years are well documented, a thick scrapbook of forms and notes.

"I will be managing the visits up to the court date," Debbie says this more to the file than to Molly who stays silent. She's met enough social workers to know that Debbie is part of the machinery; her compassion was extinguished a long time ago.

"I see you have made some decent progress," Debbie says looking up from the file.

"Yeah, I'm sober and I got a job and a place to live."

Debbie smiles a practiced smile at her. "Good. You stay sober and you get to see Ruby."

Molly says nothing, digs her fingernails into her palms.

Debbie goes on to explain how the visits will work. Set times, on set days, at the office, under Debbie's supervision. Debbie says Molly should bring things for Ruby: a *healthy* snack, an *age-appropriate* activity.

Molly looks down at her hands. She uncurls her fingers; crescent shaped fingernail marks line her palms. "Ruby will be two next month, her birthday isn't on a scheduled visit day ... *I'm her Mom* ... can I please see her on her birthday?"

Debbie, irritated by the deviation from the script, looks hard at Molly. "We'll see how the first few visits go. If you stay clean, I'll talk to Helen and see if we can work something out."

Fucking Helen. Helen who never liked Molly, who now hates her, blames her for her son's death, lays claim to Ruby because she's Greg's mom. Helen who has money and a lawyer, and a home with furniture and *healthy* snacks. Molly manages a nod and fights back her tears.

After her appointment she walks to the second nearest bus stop. The nearest one takes her down the road past the drop-in center where her old crew can often be found. In rehab they drilled into her the need to avoid old influences. Sometimes she catches a glimpse of friends; sometimes she's spotted and she'll duck into a store. It feels like a betrayal. She hates herself for it.

At home in her small apartment, she puts Debbie's sheet of goals on her fridge. At some point in her rehab journey, she acquired a magnet that says, *You are worthy of love and belonging*. Why she has kept it she doesn't know; the message stings. Greg is dead and Ruby is gone. But there it is, this empty message, holding up things she should do to prove she is worthy of getting her daughter back.

She lies down on her single bed that is both a bed and a couch. She tried so hard when Ruby was born. She sobered up; Greg did too. Mostly. Sometimes Greg disappeared for a night or two, but he always came back. She belonged to two people and two people belonged to her. A family at last.

But they had fucked up. That one night. Friends came by. Ruby was asleep and she convinced herself she was in control now and could have a little. She lost them both—a toxic supply and Greg was gone. The paramedics called child protection and Ruby was taken away.

Thick with grief and nowhere to go, Molly went back to the street until she was convinced by an outreach worker to go to rehab.

She often lies in this bed remembering Ruby's soft pink cheeks and her beautiful baby smell. Little arms reaching out whenever she picks her up and Ruby's soft breath on her neck as she cuddles in. She wants to be more to Ruby than a crumpled-up picture at the bottom of a bag, dragged from foster home to foster home—what Molly's mom had been to her.

Before her shift at the grocery store, she wanders down the aisles of the toy store in the mall. Does an almost two-year-old colour? Scribble with crayons? She fingers a colouring book with a small pack of crayons attached. Ruby can sit on her lap and they can colour together. At the end of the visit, she will tear out one coloured-in page and take it home to put on her wall.

She wanders through the remaining aisles. She finds a night light that projects blue and purple stars onto the ceiling to create a magical starlit room. Ruby always needed to be in Molly's arms to fall asleep at night. She was a real mom in those moments. Molly stares at the picture on the box: a baby in a cot, smiling and reaching for the stars. She will light up the office tomorrow and make it magical. Ruby can have it in her bedroom, fall asleep under the stars each night and think about Molly.

She tucks her purchases away in her locker at work. Her shift is long: stocking shelves, replenishing produce, mopping a spill in aisle five. On her break she goes to the staff room. There are two girls there, probably high school kids; she doesn't know, no one talks to her. Molly sits at the other end of the room and picks at a sandwich. She hears the girls laugh on their way out.

After work, she walks out into the cool night air. A light rain falls. Her body has been quietly vibrating all day. Living with so little hope requires so much strength. She wills her body to move. The feel of the hard pavement under her feet is real and familiar. The rain comes down harder and she stops under a shop awning. Across the road, a block down, she sees a group of people huddled in a bus shelter, talking and drinking from cans. She recognises a laugh, sees someone's dog. They are from her life before Ruby. From when their lives wove together and they watched out for each other on the street, shared their daily dramas and the little they had.

Molly wakes to her phone ringing. Her head is thick. She gropes towards the sound and peels her eyes open. The phone stops ringing. She props herself up on an elbow, wipes her eyes, and checks the screen again. Two missed calls from Debbie.

The time is 11:32 a.m.

She looks around the room. There are people passed out on a sofa, a bean bag, the floor. In the centre of the room is a coffee table laden with cans, pipes, needles, a bong. In the midst of the filthy rubble is Ruby's magical nightlight. Molly collapses back onto the floor. In the late morning light faint blue and purple stars circumnavigate the ceiling.

Nicole Dumas

Light Sleep

"I don't wear clothes. So I won't." Diana stands just inside the door of our shared room at the International Student Hostel. There is a single bed and a double bunk. Over thirty candles burn on a small wooden table near the window.

"You've got the bunk," she says. "I don't like having anything over my head when I sleep." She smiles as she speaks, but it is not an invitation to compromise. Her hair is sleek and rests just under her chin. Round glasses frame her eyes, like searchlights, as she sizes me up.

"Where's the shower?" I ask.

Diana notices I don't have a towel and hands me one of hers out of a plastic bag hanging on the door. I wash off the twenty-hour bus ride and dress in the stall before returning to the room.

At night, the candles illuminate the space with an anxious light. Their heat is unbearable and I open the window while Diana sleeps undisturbed. The next day, I rent an extra flat sheet from the front desk, and hang it over the top bunk as a curtain.

"We usually just get locals living here," the manager Dahndi says. "They can't beat $95 a week. By the way, Diana's had that room to herself for a while."

Diana comes and goes from work, discarding her office wear the moment she crosses the threshold of our room. Men living in the hostel seem to know when she is home and often come to the door to see if she wants to talk. Each one pretends that there is nothing unusual about her lack of clothing as they sit on the end of her bed discussing things like community gardening or the Grateful Dead.

One morning, I awake to a new voice. "Oh, God. Oh, God. I don't want to have a baby. I've never done it without a condom before."

Diana laughs.

"You're such a boy," she says. "I'm 31. I know my cycle."

I shove the makeshift curtain aside and pull on my jeans. He is still on top of her and rolls off to hide under the blanket. Diana sits up and leans against the wall. She stares at me without saying anything as I put on my sandals and leave the room.

At the front desk, Dhandi grins when I tell him about the wake-up call.

"Go confront her," he says. "Someone needs to." I exit the front door instead.

Chess players are out on Mission Street. I'd like to play, but I keep walking, pondering why I have come to San Francisco in the first place. A familiar existence exchanged for experiencing the unknown? What does it mean to be alive? There was the history of humanity right in front of me: generations of people fucking and wanting or not wanting babies. Have I expected something more profound? The mess of the city is all around me, contained in families, bodies, apartments, and histories. What kind of container can hold me when all I do is escape? Escape, a distraction, like the flash of hot sand on bare feet, permeating all thought with its intensity.

A large banner picturing Rauschenberg's *Bed* hangs across a nearby museum's exterior. A site of sleep and intimacy confronting the public. His real bed hangs on a wall inside the museum, but I am stuck outside the front door. I want to make work that nestles up with his but can't even afford the price of admission. It is his hunger for investigation I want to live with (as well as his success). I want to matter.

Heat radiates off the sidewalk and surrounding buildings. I lean against a tree in Yerba Buena Park, sliding off my sandals to feel the shaded grass.

"Hot enough?" says a man sitting a few trees away.

"This sun is too much," I reply.

"Do you know sunlight makes hair lighter but skin darker?" He tells me that hair is dead and skin is alive. He talks about nerve endings and the power of life when held by death. He moves a couple of trees closer as he speaks.

I lie down on the grass and wish for silence; not to be alone, but to not have the space filled with facts. I can already feel the fact of the heat edging into my shade. It is enough to contemplate. He seems to understand.

"You have nice feet," he says. "I'm actually really good at foot massages. It's like a gift."

I search for the boundary that should be there, but it is missing. My need for touch is embarrassing. He looks surprised when I offer him a foot. He moves closer to grasp it in both hands, so gently, like he is delivering a small animal back to her mother.

"Are you sure this is okay?" he asks a few times before falling into what seems like a foot-worshiping trance.

After a while, I tell him I have to go home.

When I get back, the room is empty and the candles are burning. I lie on the bed and sleep.

I dream about being held up naked to a fire by hands of different sizes. I don't feel afraid. I want to see what lies beyond the flames.

Diana is on her bed, reading a book.

"What's with the candles?" I say.

"Those?" she says. "One for each month I've been here. I'm going to be getting out soon."

Gerald Willams

Under the Hat

It is the nice train.

The two other train lines run through the lower-class areas. My train, the Hankyu train, is the true middle class train and offers Osaka passengers whatever greenery is available. Lawyers, doctors, business executives use this line and are proud to live in a society where everyone is equal. Those who work as teachers or middle managers don't live near the Hankyu, but do live close to the JR line. They say "everyone is equal" but actually know the truth. So, they overspend at the *right* universities in the hopes that their children will be lawyers and doctors, and thus, slightly more equal. The third group. The others. They live closest to the factories and large warehouses and they use the Hanshin line. These are the ones who spend 50,000 yen on a wallet by Louis Vuitton or Paul Smith because they know debt is a sure sign of being middle class.

I'm on my way to a Sunday afternoon party at the house of a consulate official from the government of Yugoslavia. A country embodying equality. Diversity held together by an acceptance for all. "All" excludes homosexuals, of course. Equality that includes everyone wouldn't be considered fair by the middle classes.

It is the spring of 1991. In a few months, the differences that hold that country together will be shredded by the people who destroy in order to get less than what they have. The country will disappear, leaving the consul with no job and an impotent passport.

It is a secret party because the consular official is gay. All the guests are gay. I am gay. The pedophile, I had thought was gay, but I'm not sure whether a pedophile is gay or straight. Which side claims the pedophile as their own? Who will argue that the pedophile is *one of us*?

I'm travelling to the party with someone I've met at parties before. He has telephoned, "Shall we catch the train together." He tends to declare questions rather than ask them. It is off-putting, but I haven't mastered how to refuse.

I arrived at the platform late and he'd been waiting. Before cellular phones, we existed on patience and trust.

On the train, we are sitting on a bench-seat with a large panoramic window behind us and a matching bench-seat and window combination across the aisle. The seats are a kind of soft velour in a version of purple I've only seen on a train. The colour feels like a failed monarchy. A once royal purple diluted for use on the nice train.

He is tall and broad. He looks like he has played football, but has the stillness of someone who spends time thinking. We have never been interested in each other, "that way." I realise this is the first time we are together without others from our social circle.

I am in my late twenties and he is exactly 42. It is, coincidentally, his birthday.

"Oh, well, happy birthday."

"Thank you."

"Do you have any special plans?"

"Just this party."

"Well. Happy birthday."

Previously, we've had casual conversations at social events, and he once lent me a book I didn't want to read, then asked me about it every time we met. I eventually read the last chapter so I would have something to defend myself with.

It was an intellectual book. I am not an intellectual.

"Look at the guy in the hat," is how he begins.

We speak English, which is the only language I speak, though he is fluent in Japanese and French, I will learn from his obituary. We aren't embarrassed talking about which guys are good-looking on a public train. English is not common amongst the Japanese, even among those taking the nice train. The ones who do speak English almost always make a point of staring like a hungry cat, so are very easy to spot.

I look at the bench-seat across from us. I look at the guy in the hat.

He is well into his sixties, wearing a charcoal suit and dark tie. And a hat. The hat would have looked good on any gentleman attending the 1963 Kennedy assassination, or on a hipster in Kansas City in 2021. The Japanese man is distinguished the way photos from the 19th century show corpses looking distinguished.

I don't know my companion well. He isn't the topic of much gossip beyond the facts that he doesn't date much, he imported a Harley-Davidson motorcycle from his hometown in the States, which means he has money, and he spends most weekends driving around the countryside alone. Foreigners with driver's licences are not common, foreigners with motorcycles are unheard of. He is odd in an acceptable way.

"Oh. You're into older guys."

I am proud of how I keep judgement out of my voice. "Why would anyone want to date an older guy?" is what I'm not saying. All gays may have been created equal, but we are not required to live that way.

He laughs to show he understands my unspoken disdain for age.

"No. Not *that* guy."

His judgement of older guys is clear. We share a smirk of contempt for the thought of dating anyone older.

To clarify for those who may not understand homosexual parlance of the early nineties, *dating* means sex. Sometimes followed by conversation.

"The guy in the blue cap. With the shorts."

I look again. The blue cap, the shorts, the awkwardly large leather school bag. The image is universal in Japan.

It isn't uncommon to see primary school children take trains by themselves. There is a collective understanding that everyone is responsible for the safety of children.

I look at my seatmate, inviting him to deliver the inevitable punchline. He's looking back at me and I wait. I keep waiting.

He looks forward again. Across the aisle. The look on his face states that there is no punchline. This is not banter, this is conversation. A confession.

"I wanted to tell someone."

If there is a correct way to respond to this, it is not in my repertoire, and I become aware that we are in a very public space, and I don't want to be near him.

"Oh."

"I haven't told anyone else."

His confession teases me into halted conversation.

"That's probably ..."

"I've never done anything. Never."

There's an edge to his voice. I've never experienced desperation spoken, but it makes the words cling to me. I become afraid he will break apart, and I don't want to handle the pieces.

"Oh good. Yeah. That's good."

"I just need someone to know."

"Ok."

"I've never done anything."

"Yeah."

"And I won't. I know I won't."

"Well, that's good. Right. I mean, that's good."

Together, but apart, we walk to the party.

⌒

It wasn't the worst party I've ever been to. The worst ones became funny over time. About half the invited guests were already there. Being fashionably late was in vogue, though if you arrived too late no one cared.

I went home early. The consulate guy was trying too hard. Being gay was hard when you can only do it on Sundays. The pedophile offered to refresh my drink a couple of times, trying to pull me aside for further insights into his life.

"Thanks, but I'm good."

He left Japan within the year. He went to one of the middle eastern countries where they used to give academics unreasonably high salaries, while providing no oversight.

He needed oversight.

It was less than three months before he deserted the desert and returned to his alma mater on the east coast of the United States to take up a sessional teaching position. His university was a prestigious one so I won't name it. If you need to know the name, think about which ivied university might have a pedophile on staff. You're probably right.

The obituary his sister wrote didn't mention the silver handgun or the small basement apartment where he concluded his difficult life. It listed his respectable academic qualifications, his teaching positions, and his notable publications. Also his love of motorcycles and the freedom he felt speeding down highways with no destination. Freedom to run from his demon living under the small blue cap.

I know he never felt comfortable on the Hanshin, the JR, or the Hankyu train lines. And besides, which train lines' passengers would have accepted this pedophile who never acted? Who chose self-exile on a motorcycle rather than a commute with a community?

I've wondered what he wanted from me. I think he wanted acceptance, for me to recognize him as my friend. I don't know if there is room in the definition of equality for pedophiles who never act but only dream. Maybe our equality only works if everyone stays on their own trains, and those who don't fit in get basement apartments and make decisions for us.

Speculative & YA Fiction

Sierra Guay

The Change

"These are delicious!" John said after biting into a strawberry. Juice dripped down his chin as he ate a second, and then a third. It wasn't until he'd emptied the carton that he realized what he'd done. "Oops," he said, as his wife entered the kitchen.

"You ate *all* of them?" she asked.

"They were so good," he explained.

He went to the bathroom and washed the stickiness from his face and hands. He looked in the mirror as he toweled himself dry. His eyes were bright red. "What in the world?" he said. "Honey, come here!"

His wife walked into the bathroom and gasped. "We're going to the hospital," she said.

At the hospital, John and his wife waited in a crowded room. By the time a nurse called John's name, the skin on his face had turned red, too.

"This is certainly odd," the doctor said, after she ran many tests. "I can't find one thing wrong with you."

John laughed. "See, honey, that's what I've been saying for years!"

On their way home, John insisted they stop to get more strawberries. "You've got to try them," he said. "They are unbelievable."

In the store, people stared at him. "Gross!" a child said.

John's wife furrowed her brow.

"The doctor said it should go away soon," he reminded her. "Not to worry."

They paid for five pints of strawberries and left the store. It was dark when they arrived home. John's wife parked the car and turned on the overhead light. She screamed.

"John, what have you done?"

He counted five empty cartons. "No ..." he started. "How ..." he stopped.

"Your arms, John!"

He looked at his arms. "What's happening to me?" He was red all over. "Help!" he yelled as he watched his gut stretch outward. His belt snapped in two and his abdomen grew as big as the space would allow. His wife put the car in reverse and drove back to the hospital.

This time, they didn't have to wait. John could hardly walk due to his size, so a team of people loaded him onto a double-wide stretcher. His heart raced as doctors and nurses swarmed around him. There were pokes and prods, and plenty of words he didn't understand. There was incessant beeping and a "Ma'am, you need to wait outside." After what felt like forever, the crowd dispersed and things began to calm.

One doctor remained by his side. "We took a sample of your skin, John," she said. "I'm not sure what to make of this, really, but you've become ..." she hesitated. John's wife entered the room. "Good," the doctor said, "you'll want to hear this."

"I've become what?" John asked.

"It seems you've become part strawberry."

"Excuse me?" John's wife asked.

"We've never seen anything like it, but we have no reason to believe that it's harmful. Your other tests came back normal."

"I'm a strawberry?"

"Yes," the doctor said.

"For how long?" John asked.

"There's no way to tell. Maybe forever." The doctor's pager buzzed. "Anyway, you're free to go. Have a nice day," she said as she left the room.

John and his wife were quiet. She helped him sit up. He caught sight of his reflection and felt faint. He was red all over and speckled with seeds. His body, save for his arms and legs, was shaped like a strawberry. His hair had turned green. He held his wife's arm to steady himself as they left the hospital. He struggled to fit in the car.

When he woke the next morning, he was still a strawberry. He rolled from side to side to get momentum enough to sit up. When he did, he saw that the blankets were covered in red. *Strawberry juice.* The thought turned his stomach.

He wobbled to the kitchen and found his wife cutting fruit for a salad. She grinned as she approached him with a knife and cut a slice from his side.

"What are you doing?" John asked.

"Making breakfast, Dear." She cut the slice into smaller bits and added it to the salad. She took a bite of his flesh. "Delicious!" she said.

"Stop eating that right now!" he yelled.

Her eyes were turning red. John tried to grab the salad from her, but his reach was hindered by his round body. He watched her, horrified. She continued to eat and her face turned red.

She finished the salad and spent the morning sneaking bites from John's body. By midafternoon, he had lost several inches from his waistline and her transition into a strawberry was nearly complete. When she got her seeds, John was unable to resist tasting her. "Just once," he told himself.

He took a bite and became euphoric. He began to salivate. He needed another bite. And another.

The pair spent the rest of the day taking bites from one another until there was nothing left but one mouth—one set of lips and teeth. *Poof!* The mouth transformed into a single strawberry.

No one heard from the couple for several days. Finally, a neighbour called the police. Two officers knocked and then broke down the front door. They were met with an overwhelming sweetness. Everything was covered in red. The floor was tacky, and the officers' boots stuck to it as they tiptoed through the house. On the couch, they found a single strawberry.

"What is all of this?" the first officer asked.

"A sticky situation," the second officer said. "We'd better call for backup."

On the way back to the front door, the first officer plucked the strawberry from the couch and popped it into his mouth. "Delicious!" he said.

Si Mian Melody Sun

The Library

AN EXCERPT

The bell announcing the end of the last period rings. I grab my tote bag and rush out of the suffocating classroom before anyone else. Several white boys run and jump in the hallway, their backpacks dropping to their butts. After the boys leave, I spot Vivian Zhou surrounded by some girls who are taking selfies next to their lockers. Vivian holds a black compact mirror in front of her face, carefully examining her matte, dark-red lipstick and thick mascara. Her black, wavy hair tumbles over her shoulder. She wears a plaid mini-skirt and a pair of over-the-knee boots.

I've heard a lot about Vivian since the orientation. Some say she once vandalized Coach Miles's car, some say they've seen dozens of condoms in her locker, and others say she's from a super rich family in Shanghai, so she doesn't have to worry about school or anything. She's never spoken to me. To be frank, I don't think she knows me. It's okay. I don't think we'd be friends either way. I hate wearing make-up and taking selfies. A big wave of students comes out of the classroom beside me. I put on my grey hoodie and head to the exit, knowing exactly where I want to go.

When I arrive at the public library, I stop at the entrance to look at the posters on the bulletin board. Many exciting events are happening, and I'm glad they're all outside of the school. Among them, I find one particularly interesting—a book club for Mandarin speakers. I pull my binder out and write down the information, although I'm not sure if I will attend. I step forward, and the automatic door to the library slides open.

The espresso machine in the tiny coffee shop on my right is making a crackling noise, a contrast to the overall silence. I inhale and exhale slowly. The smell of old carpet and coffee is familiar and familiarity means safe. My mind finally calms down. I feel relieved that no one in the library notices me when I enter.

I have spent most of my after-school hours here, ever since I came to Vancouver in September. My school counsellor, Mr. Jones, once told me that I needed to do some extracurricular activities. "I don't understand what that means. Isn't reading an extracurricular activity?" Mr. Jones didn't seem happy with my answer. He wanted me to join a sports team, sing in a choir, or volunteer for a fundraising event, but I don't like any of those activities.

The shelf labelled New Releases and Fast Reads stands right in front of me. I pick up the book *Mockingjay*. I read the first two volumes of The Hunger Games back in China after they were translated. Not a big fan of the series, but I remember the writing isn't too difficult, so I'm sure I will understand the original text. I flip to the first page to read, but after a few pages, I give up. It's not that I don't understand the words individually, but when they are put together in sentences, they become riddles to me. English is so weird. And hard. Frustrated with myself, I slam the book back down on the shelf.

That leaves me only one option—the underground level. It's where the library keeps Chinese books. I walk past the information desk, the magazine section, and the book sale table to find the stairway that goes to the basement. I hop down, my heart lifting when I hear the soothing sound of a running stream. One of the walls in the basement is decorated with an artificial waterfall.

I stand in front of the Chinese section, my fingertip swiping against the book spines as I tilt my head to read the titles. I see some of my favourite Chinese authors: Eileen Chang, Lu Xun, Pai Hsien-yung … There are also quite a few new Chinese releases. I'm always amazed by how fast the library can get them.

I sit on the ground to browse the bottom level. Half are Wuxia novels while the other half are all romance. *A Billionaire CEO's Little Sweet Wife. Rebirth of a Vicious Consort. Capturing My Runaway Bride.* I gag at the sight of the titles. I sincerely hope the librarians don't understand Chinese. These romance novels are just too embarrassing.

I take several books I'm interested in to the corner beside the window. They are Agatha Christie's *Death on the Nile*, Haruki Murakami's *Norwegian Wood*, and Eileen Chang's *Love in a Fallen City*. When I open each book, I put them close to my nose and inhale the old book scent from the pages that have already turned yellow. This is a ceremony for me.

The basement of the library is only partially underground. When I get tired from reading, I look out the window and count how many cars pass, though I can only see their running wheels. A few people come down occasionally, but I've never seen anyone from school before. I'm surrounded by books and strangers. I couldn't be happier.

As I'm about to continue reading, my nose catches a sudden whiff of cigarette smoke. I turn my head to look around. Vivian walks past my seat. Why is she here? I've never seen her at this library before. What's she doing?

She swiftly moves towards the Chinese section. Just like me, she touches the spines and tilts her head to read the titles. Like what I did, she opens a book and smells the pages. But how is it possible?

A sudden anger takes over me. She's supposed to be the pretty and cool girl everyone talks about. She should only be good at wearing makeup and taking selfies. Reading is *my* thing! Being nerdy is *my* thing! This hidden corner at the library is *my* place!

I bet she just wants to take a picture and post it somewhere. Or maybe she only reads trashy romance. Oh, please, let her just read trashy romance.

I pretend to put the books I was reading back on the shelf. On my way, I crane my neck to sneak a peek at what Vivian is reading. I am shocked at the sight of the cover.

Anna Karenina.

I haven't even dared to try the challenge of Leo Tolstoy yet!

I put my books back and stomp out of the basement. Before I leave, I grab another copy of *Anna Karenina* and check it out at the kiosk.

Leena Khawaja
Cardboard Toast

That bastard turned on me. He was the size of a golf ball when I found him in the fragments of twigs and leaves, and carried him in my palms from the pavement onto the grass. Falling with the nest had saved him from a crushing death. Well, the nest and me.

Now, I am no bird specialist so I can't say for certain he's a male crow, but based on how he has been torturing me for the last year I know he can't be a female. Females love me. From my dog, Billie, to my mom, to my sister, to all my ex-girlfriends.

I also know he is the ghost of my dead father who hated me from the second my mother told him she was pregnant. Nana told me the whole story during my last visit to her at the nursing home. She didn't want to go to the nursing home but Mama could not take care of her anymore. I felt guilty that we lived in her house and in the end booted her out, but Mama said it was for the best. I think Nana told me the story to get back at Mama.

Papa was mostly away for work. He sold the Weight Watchers Step Climb Program to bored housewives across the Midwest. Our house was filled with pamphlets and frozen meals he got from work for half the price. It worked well for us because Mama did not like to cook, so Janine and I would come home from school, throw the frozen packets in the microwave and eat in front of the TV.

"I don't get it. Why do women buy this shit from you? It tastes like cardboard," I said one day at breakfast. I really didn't care about how the food tasted. With the amount of ketchup Janine and I added we could barely taste anything else. I just wanted him to talk to me. Acknowledge me. Say anything. He put down the newspaper, took a sip of his coffee

169

and walked out of the backdoor. It was not uncommon for Papa to ignore me. He returned a few seconds later with a piece of cardboard which I knew was from the recycling bin because I had taken it out last night. He pulled a plate from the cabinet, set the piece of cardboard on it, slathered it with ketchup from the fridge and placed it in front of me.

"Eat," he said as he settled into the seat next to me.

"James don't be silly," Mom said from behind me.

"Eat, Kyle," he repeated in a calm voice.

I stared at him. There was a lump in my throat.

"James. Stop torturing him. He's just a kid." Mama walked over to grab the plate. Papa held her wrist. The grip was tight because I could see her skin redden around his fingers. My ears burned. Mama yanked her hand away, threw her apron on the floor and stormed off. I remember wishing she had stayed.

That night I went to bed knowing two things for certain. One, ketchup could not make everything taste better, and two, my Papa was a monster.

⌒

I named the crow Arthur because there was something king like about him. Arthur was black as night and his eyes were the same colour as his coat, just glossier. His claws were long and sharp. He attacked me many times with those claws and I had scars to prove it. The first time I felt a tap on my head, I thought for sure it was bird shit. I touched the round of my cap. Nothing. The next day it happened again and I looked up just in time. I recognized Arthur by the white dot he had on his forehead. That was the only part of him that wasn't pitch black. He sat atop the silver pole by the entrance caw-cawing at me. I was happy to see him. I thought he was trying to say hello.

In the coming days and weeks, the taps on my head got more aggressive. Arthur was getting bigger and stronger each day. Once I was late for work, I ran out of my car holding a bagel in one hand and coffee mug in the other jogging towards the entrance. I didn't see where he came from but everything happened very quickly. With my cheek kissing the cool pavement and the coffee mug rattling on the main road, I looked up to find Arthur two feet away from my face, picking apart my bagel.

"Why did you do that Arthur?" I said looking at my scratched-up hands as I lay there feeling a pulse in my knees.

"Because you deserved it." With that he looked up and swallowed the last piece of my bagel and flew away.

～

No one at work believed me when I said this crow was attacking me daily. Except for James. Wanda, the front-desk bitch, laughed when I occasionally showed up at work with disheveled hair and coffee stains on my shirt.

"Loser," I heard her say every time under her breath.

Mama said I ought to stop eating on my walk from the car to the gym entrance. I did, but that did not stop Arthur from attacking me. Neither did wearing a hat, walking urgently, running from my car to the entrance, or wearing a wig to fool him into thinking I was a woman. He pulled that blonde wig right off my head and managed to get some of my real hair too with those dirty claws.

My buddy Eric, who worked as a personal trainer, said he would ride with me in the morning one day to meet this *alleged* attacker. Of course, that day Arthur left me alone. I looked around for him while walking with Eric, barely listening to whatever he was going on about. Nina, our supervisor, said I had something called PTSD. I had no idea what that was so I looked it up on the computer. It made no sense.

James was the only person I could trust to not make fun of me or call me paranoid. So, I asked him to walk me to my car every now and then when our schedules aligned. I told him about how I met Arthur when he was small and sticky and how I saved his sorry ass.

"Crows imprint. They are very intelligent. They remember people.

Did you know they made tools?"

Of course, I did not know they made tools. I did not know shit about crows other than the fact that they were black and made a horrible sound.

I searched for hours on the internet looking for ways to get rid of Arthur. I was not very successful because I always got distracted by porn. But this one time, after watching thirty seconds of a Busty Betty video, I wiped myself off and returned to a Reddit thread open in another tab. Everything I read was unhelpful. I couldn't carry a spray gun because I never saw him coming and even if I did, he wouldn't consider water a threatening weapon. He had attacked me in pouring rain for Pete's sake. I could not shoot him with a gun because I did not have money to buy a gun and Mama wouldn't give me any cash. I could not hold his leg and yank him on the ground HULK style because he was too fast. I decided Arthur and I needed to chat, man to man.

I went to work well before the gym opened on Sunday to reason with Arthur. As a peace offering I brought an Eggo waffle and sat cross-legged in front of my car with my hips on the pavement and legs on the road. I lay pieces of waffle next to me. He landed within a minute.

"Arthur, this needs to stop. You've been torturing me for the last year. What did I ever do to you man? You need to leave me alone. I hate coming to work every morning because of you. I need this job. Mama said she will throw me out this time if I don't work."

"No," he said as he held the waffle down with both claws and ripped a piece of waffle with his beak.

"Why not? What did I ever do to you? Why do you hate me?"

"You know." He tossed a piece of waffle into the air and caught it in his mouth.

I could not take it anymore. "It's not my fault she cheated on you Papa! It's not my fault you were gone lots for work and she was lonely. It's not my fault you couldn't love me. I loved you."

"We were so happy before you came. The second she was pregnant with you, every day was torture for me. Every day. So now I will make every day torture for you." Papa laughed and shook his whole body like a dog out of water.

"You want me to quit. I'll quit this job."

"I will find you everywhere you go." Papa started walking away.

"This is not fair Papa. You cannot hold me responsible," I shouted behind him.

"I hold you responsible? Or do you feel responsible?" Papa turned and flew away.

The next day I quit. I didn't need this shit in my life. To be tortured by a fucking crow. Eric said it was a pity because it was the first job I held for a whole year and that I needed to grow up and stop finding excuses to escape responsibility. Whatever the fuck that meant. I told him to fuck right off. He was dating my sister Janine and I didn't need her knowing or she'd be on my case too. So, I told him if he told Janine I quit, I would tell Janine he cheated on her with Wanda in the women's washroom at our gym.

I decided not to tell Mama. How would she even know? She left for the hospital early and came home late after visiting her boyfriend on the other side of town. I'd pay her rent from my savings and by the time that ran out, I would find another job. She'd never know. And Arthur would have to find someone new to torture.

Julie Lynn Lorewood

Senior Year and Other Catastrophes

AN EXCERPT

What I should have done is beg Seerit to tell everyone I was too sick to make it.

What I really, really shouldn't have done is agree to consider this a date with Mason. And yet here I am, and for some inexplicable reason, so is my best friend and two of my least favourite people, Marissa and David.

Seerit steps up to the counter to order while Marissa and another classmate, Carrie, complain about how many calories are in peanut m&ms. Mason puts David in a headlock, grins and looks in my direction.

"Dude, get off," David says, but he's laughing.

I bet they worked this routine out before I arrived. What can I say to get out of this situation? *I'm not feeling well. Maybe I should go home?* It isn't even a lie.

"Peyton?"

The sound of his voice hits me in the stomach like a fist of butterflies driving up through the centre of me before fluttering outwards—reaching my fingertips, my toes, my lips. Blood rushes to my ears and mutes the sound in the lobby.

I turn and there he is.

Gabe.

The boy I spent days trying to find stands in front of me. He looks so much better than he did at the hospital. His pants are charcoal grey today, a burgundy button up sticking out from under the black hoodie he had on the last time we met.

"Gabe?" I say, finding my voice, though it comes out in a squeak. "You're here. I mean, how are you here? I mean, I guess you live in Newport, and it isn't like there are other theatres, but I've never seen you at this one before, and yet here you are."

I bite my bottom lip to stop the word vomit. Gabe chuckles and the butterflies do an encore. *This* is how it's supposed to feel.

"Would you think I'm a weirdo if I said I was looking for you?" He shoves his hands in his pockets and shuffles his feet on the multicoloured carpet.

"You were looking for me?"

Gabe smiles, his gaze flickering between me and the floor. His eyes are bright, the colour of melted chocolate, and he no longer looks like a boy who is going to fall apart at the lightest breeze or the gentlest touch. I lean forward, wanting to close the distance between us.

He's here.

"Yeah," Gabe says, one hand reaching up to rub the side of his neck. "I went to the rec centre first, but I didn't think you'd be doing the aqua aerobics class and the taekwondo was all kids."

I let out a breathy laugh, at a loss for words. He had been looking for me. *He* had been looking for *me*.

"I left a note for you, actually. In the storage room at the hospital," Gabe continues. "I figured the cleaners would find it if I left it in grandpa's old room. I guess you didn't get it though. Or ..."

"I didn't! I didn't even think to look there. I should have—" I jump as an arm drapes over my shoulders.

"Who's your friend, Peyton?" Mason asks.

His arm is heavy and with him standing this close, the smell of body spray makes my eyes water. I gape at him for a moment before my brain successfully restarts and I can answer.

"M-Mason, this is Gabe. He's a friend of mine." I want to shrug his arm off my shoulder, but his grip is firm, and he is *supposed* to be my date. I turn my gaze back to Gabe, trying to formulate an explanation.

He blinks a few times before his smile returns. "Nice to meet you, Mason," he says, extending his hand.

Mason looks down, arches a brow, and then offers a quick, loose shake. "Yeah. You too, man," Mason pulls me towards the counter. "Come on. Our movie's starting soon."

A surge of panic washes over me. *How will I find Gabe if I lose him again?*

"Wait!" I call out, placing a hand on Mason's.

Rather than stopping, he takes another step, dragging me along. "Our friends are waiting for us."

"My movie is about to start too," Gabe says, moving past us to join the queue for tickets.

I realize our friends stand at the end of the counter, watching our spectacle unfold. Seerit's eyes are the size of dinner plates, and the look of amusement on Marissa's face makes blood rush to my cheeks.

Please, just let the ground swallow me up.

"Let me buy you something to eat," Mason says, letting go of my shoulders in favor of holding my hand, unphased by the fact that it's balled in a fist.

"I'm not hungry."

My mind is reeling. *Gabe left me a note.* The day in the hospital *had* meant something to him. And now he's here. Mason's hand is tight around mine, as though sensing my urge to flee.

"Then I'll just get you a drink," he says, moving to the counter.

I've given Marissa enough of a show for one day, so I keep my mouth shut. Mason purchases three drinks and two orders of extra large popcorn, one for himself and one for David, who presumably doesn't have a part-time income.

Is David his date too?

Mason hands me a cup filled with something orange—*pop or juice?* He didn't bother asking what I wanted.

With food and beverage in tow, Mason can no longer keep a death grip on my hand. I follow him into the theatre and, at his urging, sit down beside him. I lost sight of Gabe at the concession, but I'm determined to find him after the movie. At least this time my search area is limited to one building.

I turn to whisper to Seerit, leaning over the armrest towards her. "You'll never believe—"

The words dry up in my throat. It isn't Seerit sitting beside me. I'm leaning over the armrest, peering up into Gabe's eyes, the lights above reflecting in the dark pools, dancing with his amusement.

"What won't I believe?" Gabe whispers back.

Rather than filling out the end of the row, Carrie, Marissa, and Seerit have moved to take the seats in front of us.

Seerit must be pissed that I didn't tell her about Gabe.

The lights go down in the theatre and the movie trailers start. It takes another ten seconds of staring before my brain catches up with my body. I watch the slow transformation on Gabe's face as his features soften into a shy smile, his gaze dropping to my lips. I quickly sit back in my seat, facing forwards, heart thundering in my chest. I steal a glance at Mason. It's only a matter of time before he realizes Gabe is beside me.

Crud.

I barely notice what the movie's about. David and Mason howl with laughter beside me, popcorn spilling onto the floor as they shake, so I assume it's a comedy. By contrast, Gabe's chuckles are lower, breathier. I lean towards him, wanting to familiarize myself with the sound. The last time we met, he'd been subdued. He was livelier at the restaurant than the hospital, but the sight of his stiff back as I dropped him off had left the stronger impression.

I jump at the press of Mason's leg into mine. His hands are switching between shoving fistfuls of popcorn into his face and drinking his pop, so he's found an alternate means for claiming me. I want to move, to pull away, but if I swing my legs to the left, they'll be pressing into Gabe's. An elbow bumping against my arm sends a thrill through me. For a second, I wonder how boys can take up so much space, and then Gabe's hand is moving down the length of my arm, and I stop breathing.

My heart hammers so hard the sound of laughter around me is muted by comparison.

What is he doing? Mason is right there. If he doesn't stop… God, I hope he doesn't stop.

His hand makes the rest of the trip down the length of my arm before wrapping around my own. I have a brief impression of long fingers, heat, and something pressing between our palms, before he squeezes my hand and pulls away. He's given me a small rectangular object. I lift it closer, using the light from the movie. It's a breath mint from Big Al's Waffle House. Either he thinks I have terrible breath, or he's trying to remind me of the day we spent together.

Or maybe he's thinking about kissing you.

I force my brain away from that train of thought, thankful the darkened cinema hides my burning face. A glance at Gabe shows me that he has a mint too. Our eyes lock and we exchange secret smiles. My whole body heats. I hold the stare for as long as I can, bathing in the warmth, before I lower my gaze and turn back to the screen.

Nikki Berreth

The Enigmatics

AN EXCERPT

Imagine you were once some bright, young *thing*. That's right. Your sexist mother—who pretended you had potential—always referred to you as a *thing*, an object. Did she do that to either of her sons? No. She did not. She always referred to them (and still does) as humans. Not just any humans, but *super*-humans. Those who serve and protect.

Garbage.

To prove yourself to both her and the world, you worked your ass off. Not in a girl-goes-to-the-gym-to-transform-her-body-and-therefore-her-life kind of way. That bullshit doesn't work, no matter what diet marketing tells you. No, your way is more—girl crushes it in school, gets into an Ivy league on scholarship, spends eight years earning her PhD only to crash and burn in her final year, and end up here. In a shitty car that stinks of meatball sub, on the side of a dinky secondary highway, in the middle of bumfuck nowhere, watching an empty cabin through the best pair of binoculars the RCMP can buy—which isn't saying much.

Despite this situation, you don't question yourself. After the year you had, you deserve a little *je ne sais quoi*.

Why?

Well, picture yourself dragging your sorry, depleted, mentally-broken ass home from the UK. You just spent six weeks in a psychiatric hospital for a nervous breakdown, followed by another eight weeks attempting to (very poorly) reintegrate back into university life and … it wasn't pretty.

Eventually, the university tells you that your scholarship funding will be placed on hold while you take at least one year of leave.

So, you return home, looking forward to the moment when you can fall into your mom's embrace and have her hug the pain away. Only you remember the moment you lay eyes on her through the living room window, where she is red-faced and obviously in the middle of some yelling match, that she is *your* mother. Not the mom your friends gush about at school who sends care packages. No, she's the type of mother who hears your accomplishments and successes only to tell you some tall tale about a mediocre thing one of your brothers did "because he is a well-respected officer of the law." Fuck.

It only takes five days of living in her house before you realize that this can't be your life. Action needs to be taken and it needs to be taken *now*. You really want to return to school and finish that degree when this year is up.

But …

Your mind is fickler than ever and despite your best efforts, it slips back to that damn fateful day, nearly five months ago, when your supervisor was injured in the lab. You found her on the floor with her back covered in deep lacerations, but as you bent to speak calming things in her ear, you watched her heal. Each deep scratch formed by tiny stone shrapnel that sheared through layers of cloth and skin, then sealed itself up in minutes. Kind of like a skin zipper.

Is this some superhuman? A *real* superhuman and not some third-rate cop working in a seedy town arresting teens for smoking weed. "It was not real," you cry. "The mind likes to make stories," you chant. You tell these things to yourself, following the coping mechanisms your psychiatrist gave you to *return to reality*.

Now, loosen your fists and think!

If you tell yourself these things and start to believe them, how do you trust the difference between story and truth? You don't. So, you stop telling yourself these things because these things are *toxic* and you're a badass scientist whose memory has never been in question.

Besides, you notice your psychiatrist looks a lot like Sigmund Freud, and when you tell him that, he gets weird, disappears, and some new psychiatrist takes over. Now, you're extra suspicious. So, you use your meagre phone privileges to call your best friend.

And she believes you.

You find out she's also seen some unexplainable stuff in her own science lab. Success! You're not crazy. Now to convince the rest of the world.

So why the RCMP?

Well, you can imagine that it doesn't take long living in your mother's house for you to desperately need work. And, whose incredible "superhuman" brothers are able to hook you up with a desk job at the local precinct "because they are so well-connected and respected"?

Your brothers, of course!

Lucky for you, it's merely a month before another similar (and better paying) position opens with the West Coast RCMP, thousands of kilometres from your mother's (and brothers') homes. Plus, during your time on the West Coast, you do some light sleuthing with your special access and find your old lab supervisor was seconded to Oxford from a little science organization, Scoden Scientific, located right here on Canada's West Coast.

Perfect. Cue shitty beater car.

Of course, the RCMP wouldn't allow some desk jockey out on surveillance, so you've got to do it on your own time and hope you don't get caught. You considered becoming a cop, but you didn't want to share more than DNA with your brothers. Fuck that. Likewise, when you told your mom, thinking she'd be delighted, she simply asked you what self-respecting man is going to want to date a "girly cop"? Thanks for that.

You forget your mother because you have bigger fish to fry. You have only a limited number of years before you need to return to your PhD or you lose all your fucking hard work. Yet, that slippery superhuman supervisor of yours is playing house here at Scoden Scientific—

Home of the Superhumans. It's terribly difficult to get in there because of their heightened security.

Hmmmmm, you wonder, now what?

Then, you find this strange little cabin, tucked away just beyond the edge of Scoden's property. It's owned by their alleged CEO, Ellen Doherty, and it just sits there. Alone. On the edge of a moderately busy road with no other cabins nearby.

Yet, each day the cabin's lights turn on and off at the exact same time and, I mean, it's down to the millisecond. Then, Ellen, who never seems to stir at night. Bladder of steel, you suppose? Or maybe she has superhuman night vision and lights are redundant? Well, she comes out of that damned cabin at exactly 7:35 a.m. each morning and she returns at 4:25 p.m. each afternoon. Like a very precise old-timey grandfather clock.

Who does that? It just seems … improbable.

You follow her to the nearby community on her days off and the woman is meticulous in her interactions, tracing the exact same pattern step-by-step-by-step before returning home again.

What if they don't have Gala apples one day, Ellen? How the fuck will you deal with that? Now, it's crossed your mind that she is just extremely Type A or maybe even a little OCD. 'Cause you know, scientists can be like that.

However …

You feel something odd in your gut that's squirming around trying to tell you something. It says those lights are automated and Ellen isn't staying in that house at night. It's telling you she doesn't ever leave the house at night, but she also isn't fucking in there. Then, where are you *Ellen*?

Okay.

You tell yourself to relax because you're here in your shitty beater car and you're doing the only thing you can at this point. Watching. Well, you're also consuming enormous, and potentially unsafe, quantities of caffeine chased with anything coated in cheese dust.

But, most importantly, you're watching.

And pretending that your disappointment-on-wheels is broken down on the road, which isn't a stretch because you bought it when you first moved back, and you had nothing but pennies to your name. And you don't want to replace it because it still technically runs, and climate change is real and—fuck.

All you need to tell yourself is that you will find the superhuman's secret. You know it. They will mess up someday and you'll be here to catch it. But you're going to need help and—

Oh shit.

You spot some smiling buffoon getting out of a Canada Post truck and ambling across the road to your car. Double shit. You need to stop counting your curses and act, starting with this guy and the deflated tire you stabbed with the switchblade you stole last year from your brother.

Ha! Take that, Ian.

Now take a deep breath. Put on a smile. Get out of the car.

You got this!

Kirk McDougall

Three Supers Walk Into a Bar

FOR MY LOVELY WIFE, ANGELLE

Beeble Boop, a serving drone at the Super Hero Public House on Hawkins, received an emergency alert from an anonymous Phantom Agent. "Imminent assassination. Supervillain: Event Horizon. Target: unknown. Location: SHPH."

The tiny drone's lubricants ran cold when he glanced at the stage and realized Virtuoso was likely her target. There was bad blood between the pair since their split back in '29.

Horizon could sneak into the bar through a wormhole, but she would require a singularity receiver on the other end. To plant the device, she would need an asset on the inside, and the only customers were Gravitate, Quantum, and a tarantula named Twiz. One of them had to be working with the supervillain.

Beeble set his sensors on high and connected the external cameras to his feed while he was on his way to serve the sole table of patrons. "Good afternoon, supers. Did you hear that Gargantua walked into a bar? It's rubble now."

Beeble's lonely laugh echoed.

Twiz transformed into a lithe translucent witch. She swayed back and forth. "If toil is no trouble, I'll have a newt double."

Gravitate smiled. "Something light. Toast with a whole avocado on top."

Quantum kept fazing in and out depending on whether or not her velocity was measurable. "I'll have Schrödinger's—"

Twiz gasped. Gravitate narrowed his eyes.

Quantum continued, "—Schrödinger's fish."

Everyone relaxed and Beeble said, "Okay, that's a Twin Rhubarb, Happy Hipster, and Flavour Special."

Gravitate had the ability to make a receiver weightless, so Beeble scanned the ceiling and dismissed the super when he found nothing suspicious. That left only two possibilities.

"Order up."

Beeble checked the external cameras for signs of Horizon's singularity receivers as he delivered the customers' selections.

Twiz downed her newt and disappeared completely, which was odd, even for her. Gravitate made the avocado heavy enough to crush itself and spread evenly over his toast. Quantum uncovered the fish and popped an entangler onto her plate. A shimmer of light travelled toward her mouth.

Beeble said, "A Phantom Agent walks into a bar and nobody notices."

Twiz's voice came from nowhere and everywhere. She said, "Phantoms are entities with real feelings. Making jokes like that is hurtful."

Beeble slipped into an empathy algo. "Sorry, ma'am. I was trying to lighten the mood."

Gravitate chuckled. "Hey, changing the gravitational constant is my thing."

Beeble let out a happy *boop* and turned his attention to Twiz. She could disappear, change form, and parts of her could disengage from her body. It would be easy for her to plant the receiver.

But there was something about Quantum's method of eating. A piece of fish moved from her plate into the shimmering tube and reappeared inside her mouth. It was spooky action at a distance. Except, it wasn't. That's not the way entanglement works. She must have a singularity receiver on her plate. Horizon wasn't planning to transport into the bar; she was already here!

Beeble yelled, "Quantum is Horizon."

Gravitate raised his hands, but Horizon created a portal that yanked the super outside before he could act. Twiz's arm solidified for an attack but disappeared with Gravitate. She remained a phantom to avoid the same fate as her appendage.

Unopposed, Horizon threw the receiver at Virtuoso to create a double-entry conduit. She tossed a bullet into the portal and stepped aside. The performer would be pulled into the other end and collide with the cartridge at such incredible speed it would be the same as being shot. A textbook reverse shooting.

Beeble sped forward and crashed into Virtuoso, pushing them out of the path of the wormhole. The heroic drone set his rotors to maximum as the gravity well pulled him in. He moved ahead one centimetre as his rotors screamed. He was about to escape when his left-rear rotor seized. The tiny drone gave Virtuoso a farewell *boop* and vanished into the passage. The bullet pinged against metal. The conduit vanished. Beeble clattered to the floor.

Horizon locked eyes with Virtuoso and then glanced at the receiver. Before the supervillain could retrieve the device, Virtuoso grabbed a piccolo, aimed, and launched it like a spear. It missed the mark, but a clarinet followed close behind.

Distracted by a flurry of woodwind instruments, Horizon didn't notice that Gravitate had snuck back into the bar. He inched along the back counter carrying Twiz's disembodied arm in his left hand. When the supervillain dodged an oboe and dove for the receiver, he increased her weight enough to lodge her in the indentation created when she landed.

Twiz rematerialized. Gravitate tossed the limb toward her. She detached her other arm and sent them both to secure the evildoer with power-dampening cuffs—the type that only an undercover Phantom Agent would use.

Virtuoso raced to Beeble's side, their extremities shaking. "Beeble! Speak to me."

Beeble groaned and held up a serving tray with a bullet-sized dent. His voice was soft when he said, "A supervillain walks into a bar, and I get shot."

Isaiah Papa

Weave Into One

AN EXCERPT

Moments like this were dangerous. Yulafina knew she had to focus on the certainties—or risk losing herself.

So, she looked at her hammer. She had swung it, brought it crashing down, and embedded it in the roof. This was hers—of that, she was certain. This weapon, she could put away now, for she had finished what Brightbloom had ordered her to do.

Mio was dead. Yulafina had killed her.

She gripped the hammer's long, stone handle and *pulled*, dislodging it and scattering ash and shattered clay tiles across the roof. Some of them, the ones that weren't completely disintegrated from the blow, turned colourless and brittle, their edges still sizzling from being near the prismarium that comprised her weapon.

A thinning, prismarium mass—like a small, stray fog—lay where she had struck her hammer. But this wasn't her prismarium. This was Mio's, glowing a faint shade of purple and emerald, touched by clouded moonlight.

This was Mio's fading corpse.

Yulafina exhaled sharply, felt her shoulders grow tense.

Mio was a Lumina like herself—another certainty she could hold on to, yes, and she did. Their bodies were made of prismarium from which they formed their weapons. And like their weapons, once Lumina had been used, they needed to be put away.

Mio was dead. Yulafina had killed her.

Their hands incandescently entwined. Her kiss tasted like fading sunset.

Yulafina's quartz pulsed with colours like a beating heart, shifting through her chroma and the memories that had formed them. It shook her staff as if trying to separate from it. She closed her eyes, took in the smell of coming rain. Certainties—she had to focus on the certainties. No doubts, no emotions, none of them.

So, she opened her eyes and looked at Mio's quartz; it lay broken, smashed into dull, crystalline pieces by Yulafina right before she turned her hammer on Mio. The chroma that were stored inside it—however many she had left—had long faded by now.

Dead and without any chroma, everyone would forget Mia. The process slow at first, but becoming more precipitous every passing hour, until all traces of her, all associations she had to anyone and anything, were wiped from existence.

Even Lumina would forget. Even Yulafina. Many of them believed Brightbloom was ruthless. Yulafina believed that it was simply merciful.

Her quartz stilled as it reverted to a clear, colourless crystal. Inside it, she sensed her chroma dim, one by one.

What little remained of Mio's prismarium corpse dissipated into wisps. They rose and danced in the air for a few moments, glittering in purple, rippling in emerald, and then they faded away. Slowly. Finally.

Mio was dead. Yulafina had killed her. Mio would be forgotten.

And all that Yulafina had to do now … was let go.

"Brightbloom thanks you for your service," a voice called out behind her.

Yulafina turned and looked up at Vikavos, her gaze sharp and steady. He perched on an agrionne panel that loomed over the roof and cast its vibrant colours onto the rotting wooden walls of the surrounding tenements and the puddle-ridden streets below. She sensed the prismarium coursing inside the panel like playful tides; it lit up the agrionne, producing various moving images within the crystalline matter.

New Lumina-branded fizzlejugs available at all apothecaries sponsored by Brightbloom. Images of a new merchant district under construction at the former Brittleback Housing and Refuge. Ludavido's infectious smile and wink promoting another Ceruleans recruitment call—the latest collaboration between Lumina and the city's enforcement institution.

And sitting on top of the panel, with a knee raised and an arm resting on it, Vikavos didn't let his snakelike grin falter against Yulafina's gaze. Why would he? Brightbloom had been busy growing its businesses, showcasing its products and services through the panels, expanding its influence—and she'd just handed it another boon.

Mio was dead. Yulafina had killed her. Mio would be forgotten.

Vikavos shifted his gaze to the crowd of people down at the streets. "You two put on quite a show. Look at them, still buzzing with fresh memories. It's a shame that there's no way for you to harvest them."

"I've done my part." Yulafina let go of her staff; it floated in the air, twirling ever so slowly around her. Her quartz glittered in the moonlight. She closed her brown cloak and put on the hood. "Now make your end of the bargain quick."

Vikavos sighed. He tilted his head and looked at his misshapen quartz, affixed to his staff like a mushroom sprouting from a tree. "Guess I just have to put on a little Session of my own, then."

"Is this really the time, Vikavos?"

"It's quite a crowd, Yulafina. Look at it. Might as well, right?"

Yulafina regarded the crowd, mostly to humour Vikavos. At the peak of dismissal hour, people were still carrying their mining tools: helmets made from copper, rusted blast-picks, and depleted agrionne lamps that swung loosely from their waists. A lot of them were children—glee in their eyes, soot on their scarred hands.

One miner, a burly, grey-haired man, offered a bucket of almost wilted wildflowers to a woman with small hammers in her apron. She laughed and took it, and—

Her kiss tasted like fading sunset.

A cool breeze touched Yulafina's cheeks. Her lips quivered, and she remembered—

"You don't like them?"

Yulafina glared at Mio, then closed her eyes and turned away. Her face felt hot. "I don't like flowers. Especially purple ones. Like these."

Mio smirked. Her hair, long and straight and purple, flitted about with the wind. "Well, I insist. People seem to really enjoy giving them to those they love."

"Then insist," Yulafina responded, more quickly than she liked. "But know that only a fool would ever give me these as a present."

"You are such a joy to be around with."

"Easy now, Yulafina," Vikavos' voice cut in, a knife from nowhere. "Your burden will be over, soon enough."

Yulafina blinked and caught her breath. How easy it was to get lost, even after all that had happened.

Up above, still on the panel, Vikavos tilted his head and smiled at her, the lights from the panel making his face bleed into shadows. Thin, green, prismarium wisps dissipated from his body and he channeled them into his quartz; the crystal came to life, contorting on the staff, a small mass of shimmering, colourless edges.

"I take it that this is a mining district," Vikavos noted. "Hm—what to pick, what to pick." He snapped his fingers, and Yulafina sensed prismarium surging in him as he started tapping into his selection of chroma.

His quartz turned grey; fierce yellow flames burst out of his body, his eyes and mouth turning into nothing more than thin black slits, an infernal regalia trailing behind him.

"No, too flashy," Vikavos said and then sighed. His mouth slit, scattering embers.

His quartz turned green—his flaming body was extinguished and replaced by a towering mass of feathers, from which long, crooked fingers protruded and swayed in a beckoning motion.

"Hm, not quite."

His quartz turned brown—the feathers and fingers gave way to a stark black cloak, standing upright as if it was being worn by some invisible force. A rusted pendulum swung inside it and churned the abyss contained within.

"Too existential. Not the right time and place."

His quartz turned yellow and red. Vikavos' human form returned wearing a court jester's torn and sagging attire. Numerous eyes writhed within its many holes, their pupils darting up and down, left and right.

"This should work. Not too lighthearted, but also not too mundane." Vikavos dropped down from the panel and landed on the rooftop's ledge. He turned and faced Yulafina, twirling his staff with one hand. "Why don't you come and watch my Session? We are the arms of Brightbloom's business, after all, and business is *booming*."

He smiled, the many eyes in his chroma outfit closing shut—and then leaned back and fell.

Shelby Sharpe
A Deception at Sea

AN EXCERPT

"You going to finish that?"

Mara's gaze darted up to land on Callen, who was pointedly staring at the sugar-dusted pastry sitting on the table beside her lounge chair. Sighing, she gestured for him to come take it, eager to return to her spot in the book. Callen jumped up, grabbing the plate to return to his spot on the couch to her left.

Crunch.

The hairs on the back of Mara's neck prickled with irritation at Callen's loud eating. Once again, her concentration had been broken by her twin, who seemed to have little regard for anyone but himself, at least where food was involved. Mara pointedly turned the page to remind him that he was not the only person in the room, but that also went unnoticed as he started to lick the sugar off his fingers and smack his lips with satisfaction.

"Did you lose all your manners during your travels?" Mara finally said, closing her book with a snap.

Callen smiled sheepishly and looked around for a napkin or handkerchief. "Sorry, it's been a while. They just don't taste the same everywhere else." He settled for wiping his hands on his pants. "Homemade is always the best."

"No arguments from me there," Mara said, laughing. "I'd never willingly leave Ms. Laurette's baking."

"It was a bit hard at first." Callen smiled. "But I got to try so many new things. I can't wait to get back out there."

"So you're leaving again then," Mara said flatly.

"Well … yeah, you knew this was a temporary visit. I have a life out there. Responsibilities," he stated, nodding and looking as if he was puffing out his chest.

"Oh please. You balked the first moment Andras mentioned responsibility here, and then next thing we knew, you were on a ship off to gods know where," Mara said.

"Just because what I want out of life isn't on this island doesn't make me the bad guy," Callen said. "What do you want to do anyways?"

"I just figured I'd probably teach. We were fortunate enough to have a good education. I think it would be nice to share that with children on the island."

"You have no teaching experience. Mar, you don't even have life experience," Callen said, with a perplexed look on his face.

"There are books for that, you know," Mara said, rolling her eyes. "Plus, Andras taught us many subjects, and he had no formal education." She purposefully refrained from mentioning the tutors that were hired for all the subjects Andras didn't teach.

"Mar, Andras has traveled all over the archipelago, even to the east, and between cooking and sword fighting, he knows how to do almost everything," Callen said, his admiration clear. "He is the definition of life experience."

"As I said, there are books for practically everything now," Mara said defensively. She stood up, clutching her book to her, unable to remain seated while her cheeks started to flush and her stomach turned within.

"Mar you don't leave the island, do you really think books are enough? You're limiting yourself."

"I hear enough stories from the sailors and merchants that come this way," Mara said, hating that she sounded as though she was second-guessing herself. "They talk plenty about their travels. I can use that."

"So, second-hand. Mara you're not even getting it from the source. How can you trust what you're hearing?"

"If you don't like the idea just say so. I don't need you to pick it apart and tear me down while you do it!"

"Gods, Mara, I'm not trying to, but it doesn't sound like you thought this through," Callen exclaimed as he ran his hand through his hair, turning away in frustration.

"I have so! I was good in my studies, I'm a decent listener and can write. What would you have me change?"

"*Leave!*" Callen shouted facing Mara head on. "Leave this island, and go out and learn, and explore yourself! Mara there is so much out there that you don't even know of. I know you're smart enough to make it out there. Why not try?" He looked at her as though he saw all that she was capable of, and she was doing the equivalent of simply breathing.

Fighting off tears that had started to well in her eyes, Mara said as calmly as she could, "I'm tired of talking about this to you, I'll see you in the morning if you haven't run away already."

"'Night Mara. Let me know when you decide to be brave again," Callen replied in a flat tone, walking down the hall towards the bedrooms, turning into his and closing the door without another sound.

Mara angrily stomped after him and turned to the left into her own room before slamming the door shut behind her. The tears she had been holding in with all her strength ran down her face as she leaned back against her door.

She was angry at Callen for not understanding that she was satisfied with her life. At the same time, she felt this deep anger and disappointment in herself for not wanting more. What had happened to the young girl who dreamed of excitement and adventure? The child who would try to climb palm trees, skinning her hands and knees as she fell, only to get up and try again. The girl who explored the rainforest behind the house with only paper and ink. The young teenager who discovered temple ruins with friends just outside of town.

She'd grown comfortable in the familiar life she kept, however mediocre it was. Knowing what each day would entail, with a few manageable surprises splashed in. The simplicity and privilege of not worrying where her next meal would come from, that she would be taken care of even if she decided to sit in a chair the rest of her life.

Not that I would want to, nor would Andras let me.

Having Callen home brought up all of these memories and feelings that she had suppressed, not wanting to risk the life she had for one of uncertainty. What did he know, anyway? He left home as soon as possible, looking for any excuse to avoid responsibility. So her ambitions changed; there was nothing wrong with letting past aspirations of discovery slip away.

Even if it was a life you once dreamed of? asked a soft voice in the back of her head. She was beginning to grow resentful of that voice. It had re-emerged in the past month, asking gentle questions about her happiness or adventure, and then disappearing for days, leaving Mara to wonder where the thoughts had come from.

As Mara laid in her bed, falling asleep with tears gently trickling down her face and onto her pillow, she dreamed she stood on the edge of a ship in the wide-open sea. Wind blew past her as she peered over the ledge, only to lose her balance and fall into an ocean that swallowed her whole.

Kieran O'Connor

Elise's Path, Chapter 5

AN EXCERPT

"Greetings, Master," Elise said formally as she walked through the doors of the sparring hall. She shook herself, trying to rid her long grey tunic and short brown hair of the droplets of rain that were beginning to soak through uncomfortably.

"Hello, Elise," Sarana, her new master, replied softly. She was a stockier looking defender, with dark leather armour and long black hair that was tied back. "Did you sleep well?"

"Very well, thank you." Elise crossed the long wood floor of the room to the spears on the far side, grabbing one to begin practicing her moves. She wanted to be fully warmed up before Fayla, the other trainee, arrived.

Sarana smiled at her, watching curiously with her lush, vigorous green gaze. There was a scar on her cheek that barely missed her left eye, but made it twitch occasionally. "I'm surprised at you," she commented. "From the way Protector Maela spoke, I had thought you might be a lost cause. She was worried she'd made a mistake appointing you as a defender. I'm glad you've proven her wrong these past weeks."

"Thank you," Elise said, her round face beaming from the praise.

"Master Flynn said you were never focused during your training sessions with him. That you never seemed to put any effort in." Sarana observed her questioningly. "Something's clearly changed."

Elise froze. "Well, uh ..." she began. "You're a good teacher."

"And Master Flynn isn't?"

Elise felt a lump in her throat. "Well ... he's not ... I mean you're just ..."

"I'm flattered, Elise," Sarana stopped her. "But whether you like it or not, you will have to return to Master Flynn very soon. I know his teaching style is very different from mine, but that is no excuse. If you put the same effort into his lessons that you've put in here, I'm sure you'll do just as well. He will be proud of you if you do."

"I don't think so," Elise replied doubtfully. She leaned her spear against the stone wall, sliding down and sitting on the ground beside it. "No matter how hard I try, I've never heard a single compliment from him. When I first began training, I was so excited. And I tried so hard to do my best. But he pushes me down even when I've done nothing wrong. And then, in our last session, he taunted me and said terrible things about my mother."

Sarana's eyes widened in surprise. "Terrible things? Like what?"

Elise swallowed, her gaze dropping to the floor. Protector Maela hadn't believed her story, trusting the word of Master Flynn over hers. *Would Master Sarana be any more understanding? Or would she think I'm lying and get mad at me?* She sighed. Now that she'd brought it up, she didn't seem to have a choice anymore.

She launched into the tale of her last day training with Master Flynn, reluctantly reliving the memory once more. She could hear his taunts ringing through her head as he ridiculed her. She ran her hands over her arms, feeling the bruises hidden beneath her tunic. She remembered every one of them, every blow he had ever dealt. Then she recalled the surge of anger as he spat upon her mother's memory, the dark claws sinking into her mind as she lashed out and smashed his head from behind with her quarterstaff.

When she was finished, she took a long, deep breath, forcing herself not to cry like a child in front of her new master. *I'm stronger than this*, she told herself.

Sarana's gaze clouded with worry. "I had no idea. What you describe sounds nothing like the Flynn I know." She paused. "I don't agree with his methods, but that doesn't excuse what you did either. You should have left and told Protector Maela what happened instead."

"I know," Elise said sullenly.

"Words can hurt more than any weapon. But you cannot let them control you. Any foe could taunt you like that on the battlefield. Giving in to those words, and letting them force you to recklessness, could be fatal. Keeping your cool and focusing instead of lashing out is what separates good warriors from great ones. Maybe that's what Flynn was trying to teach you."

Elise nodded hesitantly. "I suppose," she mumbled. *Would I be able to keep my cool if it happened again?* she wondered.

Sarana stepped closer and sat down beside her, crossing her legs. "I know it's hard," she said softly. "I miss your mother too. She and I were good friends, you know."

"Really?" Elise had never thought about it before. They did seem to be about the same age.

"Yes," Sarana continued. "We grew up together, playing in the gardens every evening as the sun went down." She smiled, staring off as she relived a distant memory. "She was the troublemaker. Always treading on someone's feet, getting in the way. One time she set up a trap outside her house, and the cook who was bringing in food that day tripped over a rope she'd set up and spilt vegetables everywhere."

"I never knew." Elise laughed, trying to picture it. It was hard to imagine her calm and tender mother as a mischievous prankster. She frowned. *Maybe I didn't know her as well as I thought.*

"Yes, she was a handful, that one," Sarana continued. "But she never really thought her pranks through to the end. She laughed so loud that she was immediately caught and given a stern talking to. I got roped into the punishment as well for being her *accomplice*. But I never blamed her for it. I don't regret a single day we spent together."

"That sounds ... wonderful." Elise let out a deep breath. "Having someone like that."

Sarana's smile faded. "It was. But then the day came. We both reached twelve years of age and went our separate ways. I became a defender. She became a healer. We didn't have time for our mischief anymore. I only ever saw her when I got roughed up from training. But even when I did see her, she wasn't the same person anymore. The scheming and troublesome girl I grew up with was gone. She'd devoted herself fully to her duties as a healer." Sarana paused for a moment, shifting her legs. "She always worried that she would never be good enough, that no one would ever take her seriously after how much trouble she had caused in her early years."

Elise swallowed uncomfortably. "I know the feeling."

Sarana sighed, her gaze dropping. "There was a time when it became too much for her. After her own mother died of illness, I found her staring off the edge of the plateau in tears. She blamed herself because she felt that she'd failed her duty as a healer. She told me that she wanted to leave the village, because she didn't feel as though she belonged. That she wasn't enough. That she was just a burden. But deep down, I think she just wanted to feel loved and respected."

The room went quiet for what seemed like an eternity. Elise tried to speak several times, but the words kept sticking in her throat. "I ... I've been there," she managed to choke out finally. "At ... at the edge of the cliff. So many times." She clenched her fists. *I failed her ...*

She felt Sarana's comforting hand on her shoulder. "You remind me so much of her, Elise. It took her a long time to come out of that darkness, but when she did, she was stronger for it. I remember seeing her for the first time after you were born. And that smile ..." Sarana closed her eyes, letting out a long breath. "It wasn't anything like the smile she had when she was getting into trouble. I could see more joy reflected in her eyes when she looked at you than I had ever witnessed. I couldn't have been happier for her. After that day, she never spoke of running away again."

For a moment, they sat in silence. Elise felt something building inside of her, something attempting to break free. Finally, she could hold it in no longer. Before she could stop herself, she reached out and embraced Sarana. "I miss her," she cried. "I miss her so much."

Sarana seemed taken aback. At first, Elise wasn't sure if she'd be pushed away or ridiculed by her new master. But then Sarana smiled, embracing Elise in return. "So do I," she said quietly, her voice as warm and soothing as a mother's. "So do I."

A. J. Hanson

Parallax Error

AN EXCERPT

DAY ONE: NINE DAYS REMAINING

I'd always imagined my landing would be graceful. Don't get me wrong, sometimes in my wakeful dreaming, I'd picture my ship burning up during atmospheric entry or exploding into fragments as my body was ripped apart, atom from atom, in the vacuum of space. But overall, I pictured a gorgeous landing—the feet of my ship sinking gratefully into a puff of dust as they settled onto a new planet.

This had been something else entirely.

The last thing I remembered was the lid of the sleep pod closing and the momentary panic before the meds kicked in.

Why hadn't I woken up before the landing?

Groaning, I clutched the back of my head and blinked open my eyes, expecting the dull ceiling of my spacecraft above me.

Instead, an unfamiliar sky glared down.

I skittered backwards, scrambling on my elbows and digging my heels into the softness of the moss that cradled me. Above, where the ceiling should have been, gnarled tree trunks led up to crowns where strands of gelatinous purple beads spilled over, reminiscent of the branches of weeping willows back on Earth. Through the canopy of purple tendrils, a red star eclipsed the majority of the sky, bathing everything in a rosy glow. I breathed deeply, trying to calm the stuttering of my heart.

I'm not wearing a spacesuit.

The realization slammed into my brain, derailing all other thoughts.

How am I not dead?

Clutching at anything that felt familiar, I curled my fingers into the thick, damp moss. It squished like rotten meat beneath my fingertips.

Letting out a yelp, I scrambled to my feet and nearly fell over. I caught myself, grabbing fistfuls of the thorny underbrush.

Where's Griffn? I cursed my friend again for following me onto the ship. *He would've been better off on Earth than wherever this is.*

"Griff! Where you at?" As soon as my voice left my throat, I tried to choke it back. Who knew what kind of dangers were here? No good would come of calling attention to myself.

In the patches of dappled starlight, pieces of the ship reflected the menacing glow. The main cockpit of the craft lay behind me where a breeze rasped branches along the top. I waited, letting my lightheadedness subside before I crept to my spacecraft. As I drew closer, the carnage came into view. Where the middle of the spacecraft should have been, jagged edges of metal truncated the hull.

If the front of the ship is here, where are the sleep pods? Griffn would have been in a sleep pod too when we crashed, right?

If I was going to find Griffin, I needed answers, and the Interstellar Log would have them.

Ducking beneath the sharp edges of a hanging strip of metal, I crawled into the cockpit, careful not to scrape my knees through the tears in my pants. The console flickered, barely bright enough to read, as I brushed off the spattering of leaves that had settled on the screen. With a trembling hand, I selected the most recent recording. Goosebumps prickled on my arms as I heard my own voice say, "This is Daisy Plymouth, resident of Earth."

Why do I not remember this? And when have I ever called myself a "resident of Earth"?

My voice continued, launching into a bizarre list: "Insect of genus and species *Drosophila melanogaster*, arachnid of genus and species *Latrodectus mactans*, two packs of freeze-dried mushrooms of genus and species *Agaricus bisporus*, 1.9 trillion bacteria of genus and species *Lactobacillus acidophilus,* ..." More words I'd never heard droned on for several minutes until their chilling conclusion: "... two humans of genus and species *Homo sapiens.* Lifeforce count: thirty-nine trillion, seven-hundred and eighteen."

What does that mean?

Metal clattered behind me and I whirled to face my attacker. But I found only Griffin's lanky frame blocking out the rosy light of this planet's star.

"Mother of spaceflight! Don't sneak up like that. You all right?"

"You're alive!" He ran and enfolded me in one of his big bear hugs. I stiffened. He was always faster to forgive than I'd ever been. "What happened? Where are we?" He paused, releasing his death grip. "Are you okay? You look pretty banged up."

I touched the spot on my forehead that he was staring at. My fingers came away sticky. *That explains the headache.* "Nah, I'm good."

"Were you talking to someone? I thought I heard your voice."

"What? No. Maybe you hit your head too." I gave Griffin my best everything-will-be-all-right smile.

He nodded, his dark hair falling over his eyes. "Maybe."

As soon as he turned to look at the torn edge of the ship, I pressed the button to delete the last log. *It would be easier to figure that out on my own without him getting freaked out about it.*

"How did we survive that?" Griffin continued. "The ship is ripped apart worse than cars at a scrapyard." He tapped on the edge of the metal.

"Don't know. More importantly, we need to figure out where we are."

If we could signal Earth, we could ask for our coordinates and let them know we found a planet with breathable air. For the first time since I'd awoken, a shiver of excitement ran down my spine. *Is this an undiscovered exoplanet?*

"The communicator will be here somewhere ..." Griffin scoured the walls, running his fingertips along the sleek metal until he found a compartment that popped open at the touch of a button. The communicator stared back at us. It was about the size of a small backpack and lay on its side as though it had come loose and tumbled around during the crash.

He pulled it out of the compartment and immediately attempted to broadcast, "Anybody read me?" Only silence replied.

"Is it broken?" My heart dropped as I felt the threat close around my dreams of returning as a hero.

Griffin turned the contraption over in his dirty, cracked hands. "Nothing I can't fix."

Of course, he'd say that.

He looped the strap of the communicator over his arm and we continued searching the ship. Unfortunately, the cockpit yielded nothing more of use.

It would take time to fix the communicator and even more time for a second expedition to arrive from Earth. We would need supplies. I ran through the checklist in my head: water, shelter, food. I stumbled out of the cockpit and back into the rosy starlight. Ducking under the vines of purple beads, I surveyed the surroundings, trying to view this as just another salvage mission. There would be time later for panic.

In response to a rustling noise above, I threw my hands over my head and crouched, muscles tense and at the ready. I looked up. A small grey bird perched on a branch, tilting its head, appraising me. Its eyes held an unsettling intelligence.

"Hello?" My voice came out thin and was swallowed up by the dense foliage. The bird tilted its head again and gave me another piercing look, then sprung off the branch and was gone in a flurry of feathers.

"You talking to yourself again?" Griffin joined me in the starlight, resting a hand on my shoulder.

"No, I just thought—" *that the bird had wanted to tell me something? How hard did I hit my head? Focus, Daisy. Focu*s. "Never mind. We need to find water and food. And some shelter. Looks like we'll be here a while."

Our safest bet would be to find the supplies that were hopefully stockpiled on the ship. We searched through the thicket, and I tried to ignore the way my feet sank into the moss and the dampness seeped through the tattered soles of my sneakers. Every time the red starlight winked off another piece of our ship, I ran to it and scoured the area for any traces of supplies. Near the left wingtip, Griffin stumbled on a freeze-dried food pack, but there was no trace of water. *Guess I should've checked the inventory* before *I stole the ship.*

Though it felt like hours had passed, the rosy star still glared down, unchanged from the moment I'd awoken. *Was it possible this planet was tidally locked?* If that was the case, it would always be light on this side.

With fatigue settling into my bones, I turned my attention to the last thing on our survival list: shelter. Unsure whether the dangers would lie in the trees, in the sky, or underground, I chose the only familiar option.

I began to dig.

J. R. Chapple
From the Ashes
YA NOVEL EXCERPT

Sadie sweeps into my chambers with far too much enthusiasm. She's going on about the new guest, saying she had opportunity to chat with him when he arrived and she found him sweet and charming. She says he was curious about me and eager for our meeting. I don't know where she gets the energy for this positivity. Each time, she finds something nice to say about these arbitrary visitors. Each time, her eyes shine with a hope that seems near insanity at this point.

I don't change my clothes, but I ask her to pin my hair up. I look a bit feral when I let it swing over my shoulders and work its way into tangles, but I like the feeling of it. I imagine I can hide behind it like a curtain, drop my chin to fade into the wallpaper and swing it over my shoulder when I need to reappear.

Tonight, I don't want to hide my face for this new guest. I'd like him to fully survey the damage. If he can't look at me, I'll do as Caleb suggested and send him away immediately. Putting weeks in with someone who won't get past my appearance is a trial I can no longer tolerate. No more veils and slow reveals. I've come to the point where I want to get the shameful part over with in the beginning.

When I arrive at dinner, Caleb and the guest are already seated. It looks as if Caleb hasn't made any effort to welcome the boy, despite his insistence that I work to put him at ease. They both rise as I enter the room and take my place at the head of the table in silence.

"Be seated," I say softly, and we are still as the food is served. Once the table is set, I raise my wine glass and wait as they join me. "A toast,"

I say. "To our guest. I am glad for your company tonight." I do my best to smile in his direction.

I can tell that Sadie has gotten him ready for dinner. She's dressed him in a simple coat of slate grey with silver piping running down the clasps at the front. It's a nice choice, complimenting his skin tone and bringing out the flecks of gold in his dark eyes. He is very handsome, or perhaps pretty is a better word, as his youthful features have a bit of a softness to them. I suddenly realize I don't even know his name. What did Sadie say? I don't recall a word of what she told me about him.

He sees me watching him and nods pleasantly. He does look nervous.

"Tell us about yourself," I say, cutting into my meat delicately.

He clears his throat. "What would you like to know?"

I lift a forkful of food to my mouth and chew slowly. I can't very well admit I don't know his name. I catch Caleb's eye and he mercifully saves me.

"Well," he says with a smile. "I didn't get the brief, so I don't know the first thing about you."

Our guest looks at him with a crooked smile. "Forgive me, Sir, I don't know who you are either."

Caleb laughs and takes a drink from his wine glass. "Right, well I'm a first cousin to Lillian on her mother's side, a grand duke and an interloper here at the palace. You can call me Caleb."

Our guest lowers his chin in a polite nod. "My lord."

"None of that," Caleb replies, stifling a giggle.

The boy didn't even use the correct term to address him. I suppose he has no etiquette training at all.

"Well, my name is Sev, Sevrin actually, but no one calls me that." He glances from Caleb to me. "My father is a merchant but I'm the second child and I regret to say, lacking in education because of it."

"Oh, I like a man who is forthright," Caleb chuckles.

I shake my head at him. How uncouth he can be sometimes.

Sev looks my way seriously. "I was told to be truthful." His eyes are searching and I can see that he is working out some question about me. There is no telling what kind of rumours he's heard. "If this is indeed a way for you to connect with the common man, there is no use in my trying to pretend I know my way around a royal court."

"Exactly right," I reply as Caleb smirks into his wine glass.

"Perhaps we like this one after all," he says to me, and I bite back my annoyance. He's already downing his drink as if it's a competition. I don't know if I can take his buffoonery tonight.

There is a lull while the click of cutlery fills the awkward silence, and I choke down my meal. The offerings are appropriately lavish—lamb and quail, fresh vegetables, and a selection of fruits and nuts. Sev looks properly enamoured by the opulent spread, but each bite seems to turn to ash in my mouth.

"So you won't be inheriting the family business," I say, trying to sound interested. "How do you pass your time?"

He blinks and looks at his food. "Truthfully?"

Caleb and I glance at each other. "Yes," I say slowly.

"I've spent the last two years with a traveling band of thieves. I came home because I ran up a gambling debt that I couldn't pay."

Caleb slaps the table and howls with laughter as I struggle to maintain my composure.

Sev looks back and forth between us, trying to gauge our reactions.

"Honesty is a virtue," I say, fighting back a smile. Sev catches my eye and his shoulders relax an inch or two. He picks up his wine glass for the first time and drains half the contents in two big gulps. It used to be only nobles called to my court, but over the years the situation has changed. It's been necessary to move toward people who won't be missed. I can see now that we have reached the dregs of society.

"What did you steal?" I ask conversationally, as if I've hosted criminals at my table many times before.

"We'd rip off shipments in transit. Whatever goods we could. If you can get the manifest, it's easy to get in and out at the ports without much hassle."

He wasn't joking about being truthful. I take a sip of wine to keep my face from misbehaving. I don't know how to proceed with this conversation at all.

"How old are you?" I ask and he chokes on his food. I suppose he is imagining asking me the same question.

"Eighteen."

I glance at Caleb, and he is grinning like a fool. Sev looks young. Still with a trace of that gangly looseness that accompanies a carefree adolescence or, I suppose, one spent traveling with a band of thieves. I know I look the same age, but I feel excruciatingly old and tired. I can't recall a time when I had that kind of looseness.

Staff sweep through the room, clearing plates and refilling wine glasses. Sev puts his hands on his lap and looks as if he is having a difficult time keeping from fidgeting through these quiet moments.

"May I ask you questions?" he says to me.

I tilt my head. "What would you like to ask?"

"I don't know yet. But I just thought …" He rests his elbows on the table, and then quickly removes them. "Well, if we are going to be spending many evenings together, I'd like to know if you are looking for a conversation or an interview."

I swirl my wine. I've already drunk more than I should tonight, but I'm feeling more apprehensive than usual. Though I've been telling myself it's just paranoia, my correspondences with neighbouring kingdoms have felt increasingly fraught. I'd much rather be at my desk deciphering political tensions than here trying to play hostess.

I look over my glass and see that Sev is staring at me. He doesn't fidget or look away. He seems resigned to my horrific appearance already. Perhaps a man who spent time with thieves is less delicate than the nobles I dealt with for so many years. Maybe I should have tried the dregs sooner.

"Ask me what you want," I say.

He smiles, much of that previous nervousness seeming to melt away. "I want to know if you'd like our future interactions to be conversations." He glances down at the table and then to me again. "I'd like to know if you will also be truthful."

Caleb leans back in his seat and tosses his serviette on the table. He raises his eyebrows at me, amused by our guest's impertinence. I'm not sure a commoner has ever addressed me in such an impish manner. Caleb might be expecting me to crawl over the table and stab this boy right now.

I take a slow sip from my drink and Sev holds my gaze. I don't think he even realizes this is no way to speak to a queen.

"If I'm being honest," I say, "I'm not sure."

Maria Myles

The Art of Time Travel

AN EXCERPT

They kept giving me poems

On the end of days
Up to the moment I left for the future
Some gave me more than one
Weaving words on the tip of their tongues
Prophecies of things to come
The doom of future passing

At the end of oblivion

I should preface by telling you this hasn't happened yet. Not really. Not out there. This is all still a dream. But it's going to happen. As far as I know, we can't stop it.

"T-MINUS-3-SECONDS." A metallic voice rang through the cabin. At that moment, I knew Seguaeno saw me. Gaping through the window linking the laboratory to his office, years of certainty on his face were washed away by a look of dread I shared, but for the inverse reason. His cold eyes that devoid the world of morals widened. His lips parted. His word was law—and I'd made a play outside his rulebook. I knew I'd made a mistake. I just hoped it was the right one.

"T-MINUS-2-SECONDS." I thought back to yesterday and the days leading up to this moment. I glanced at the wheel as it spun shut and locked into place inside the space capsule. Then I looked back through the bullseye window. He started to raise his hand. Was this my grave and casket? The thought drained the world of meaning and hope. A glimmer in his eyes, a hint of a smile. He reached for the intercontrol panel outside his office. I jolted toward the cabin door, but there was no way to override the countdown—the energy build-up surrounding the capsule was too great to dissipate into the present. Something inside the cabin screeched. I looked at the destination interface. I was still going to my pre-programmed time and place. The future. The smell of jet fuel permeated the air. My mind had raced through all the possibilities of what he had done.

"T-MINUS-1."

A memory flickered. Or rather, a boy from my childhood ran across the laboratory room. A ghost. A reality at the end of a dark tunnel. My past. A laboratory beaker tilted from the metal table and shattered; viscous black liquid simmered and seeped onto the epoxy resin floor. Seguaeno's eyes remained fixed on mine, like a predator zoned in on his prey. I clung to the cold metal grips behind the leather seat. The whir of the capsule dissolved into the recession and soft approach of a wave.

Rolling pebbles shush *through the salt water seiche as it slips back into the lake stretching to the horizon. I feel the cool summer breeze travel from the water and billow through the pine and green maples behind me. The cold metal I was gripping now feels like the surface of a large rock. Back here, evil is just a theory. My Sketchers dig deeper into the ground as I press my back into the bedrock, wishing to be invisible. Footsteps approach. The willful clatter of two boys determined to claim victory their own cut through my line of vision. The more I try to quiet my breath the louder it sounds.*

"We can see you!" A curly top of a head of blond bounds towards me. I close my eyes, as if my inability to see could make me invisible. Worry drains my legs from the will to run as I stay frozen, my body glued to the large rock. I can't

outrun them anyway, I think to myself. As quickly as the footsteps near, they recede past the rock, onwards along the shoreline. Moments later, they dissolve into the far rustle of trees. I dive back through the pines and into the forest. Cutting through the undergrowth I hear a branch snap. My breath wavers as I lower myself into a small trench. I lie still and dig my fingers into the soft, cool earth. Then, a fluttering of whispers approach. Jolting my head back, my worries dissolve as a girl and a boy from our team crawl towards me.

"Are they nearby?" she asks.

"They sent a group to our side."

"How do you know?"

"I saw them run past the lake."

The girl looks back to the boy and he shrugs. A scream sounds in the distance.

"One of us?"

"Probably."

I lift my head and scan the periphery.

"No sight of the flag?"

"I don't think they're guarding it. I can't see anyone."

Rustling branches sound right above us. I look up. One of the camp guides, a reserve marine, holds a finger to his lips as he looks down. In his other hand is the bright green flag. I almost let out a laugh at our luck. Incredulous, we wave at him and point toward the trail a few steps ahead that leads a direct route back to our side of the campground.

He shakes his head. "It has to be one of you."

I look over to the girl next to me.

"No way!" She whips her blond braid back.

I slowly stand, scared to make noise, and reach for the tattered neon cloth.

I start to creep toward the trail head. I look down, tiptoeing past branches threatening like land mines.

I hear whispers growing behind me, "Go! Go! Go!" as I reach the trail.

I break into a run. It is silent at first. The forest holding its breath. Only the scrape of my running shoes digging into the ground. Then. An eruption of noises.

"Go! Go! Go!" A frantic commotion builds behind me, and I hear shouts and

branches snapping from both sides of the trail.

A stampede of running feet grows behind me. The ground seems to shake. I grip the cloth fabric tighter as my arms swing. I run harder. The trail breaks into a clearing, a grass field with a makeshift line cut down the midline by school bags and orange sport cones. Shrieks of bewilderment sound from our side of the field. I feel desperation behind me. Running footsteps drawing nearer. I push my legs to run harder than I had ever ran before. As if this is the last thing that matters. My lungs burn like there's no more air to breathe.

I cross the line.

Elation sweeps over me with warmth. I did it. The cheering roars transform into engine sounds.

⁀

Tears stung my eyes as the past and the future became one. The faint outline of laboratory tables glimmered again past the round capsule window. Seguaeno had said that moments from our past could radiate through time when we travel to the future. *Memory strings.* The past crumbling, dissolving, leaving the lonely traveller to their own devices.

With momentary dread I thought I was back where I had escaped from. But the time was different. It was dark, the laboratory empty. The presence of the man that controlled years of my life haunted the room in memory.

I was still that child in the forest, still running from the world. But I was also here, with no forest to hide in, no victory flag to hold. The objective wasn't clear, and I was hoping against hope that this would work, despite dreading what was coming.

I looked out the bullseye window in horror. When you fall through time, everything around you shifts; it groans, it creaks, it ages. There is nothing that can protect you from the accelerated movement of time, the displacement of reality. You feel it crawling on your face and skin like a million tiny bugs. My lungs constricted. A sharp electric pulse ran through the wiring of my brain. I screamed but all I heard was the ringing in my head. Light blinded my eyes.

I grasped at any semblance of existence, of any feeling beyond excruciating pain. I grasped onto a single word. I held onto it like it was my last piece of sanity.

And then. Nothing.

Reality slowed, but my head was spinning. As the throbbing in my chest subsided, a tiredness set in that I felt couldn't be replaced by rest. I only remembered one word. A name. Your name.

As I lay in the rubble of a past life, I ran my tongue over the five-letter word, not because I was certain it would lead me where I needed to go, but because I couldn't remember anything else.

Darian Halabuza

Follow the Leader

AN EXCERPT

This isn't right. This isn't. Why is it so quiet already?

The warm, pleasant, orange tint of sun spreads along my closed eyelids, swallowing me whole. A humid wind crawls along my bare skin, rushing past me as it howls in my ears and travels through my head. The small birds along the tops of distant trees call out to each other, singing happily to a song only they know.

But this isn't a happy day. This isn't pleasant, no matter what the scene is telling you. Don't believe everything I say; I'm not to be trusted. Or, at least, that's what everyone kept telling me before. Before all this occurred, before this day, this moment that I'll never forget. And now, neither will you.

With every breath I take, warm air hits my lungs like I'm breathing in smoke—choking me, burning me. I'm the only one breathing in this air within the field, although one hundred people surround me. I can't see them, but I know they're here, their bare skin turning cold by the second as they lay next to me. Their eyes remain closed just like mine, but they aren't pretending. They really are dead.

"Don't do this, Sue. Don't do this. Join us, we all belong together in the other world. That's why I chose you, and you chose us. Because all your life you knew you were different, misunderstood. You didn't fit in anywhere, not until you came to us." Your voice rings in my head, an echo away. As if you just spoke this seconds ago, unlike hours. The hum of your deep, husky voice lingers in the air, amongst the breeze. But I have to ignore this now; I have to push you away. Because you aren't here anymore, I know I'll never

hear your voice again. A voice wrapped up in power, held above the rest of ours like you owned this land, owned this group, owned *us.* The way you held your head high as you stood in front of the crowd near the podium, spewing beliefs that soon became ours. But they weren't just your beliefs, were they? No, they were the truth, they had to be. Otherwise, what was all of this for?

"This day, my lovely people, we will make history." You said this hours ago. You said it, do you remember? Is this what you meant by "make history"?

"We will make a stand to the world that we will no longer follow their set rules that they've placed on us, on society. For all these years, they've made us look like fools, like we're nothing, like we're just a bunch of children with wild dreams and big imaginations of this other world. We've all seen it, haven't we? The news articles, the reports, they think we're idiots. And the reason they've done this and outed us to the world, is because they know we're right, and they're scared of us. Scared of what we're capable of, scared of our knowledge."

Your ramblings haunt my head, as if it's burnt inside. My heart beats quickly, slamming against my chest as the sun brightens, beaming higher in the sky as midday approaches. But I can't lay here any longer and let your voice drive me insane. This needs to end. I have to leave.

Finally, I welcome the blinding sun into my sight. Silent tears leak from my eyes as I stare at the brightest part of the sky for a moment, letting out an exhausting breath that feels like it's been held inside me for so long. A breath I've been holding for years, not just a few hours. Birds fly ahead, continuing to sing to each other. The wind chimes surrounding the hut dangle, clinking together. And the silence of the others around me pollutes the air, along with their decay.

It shouldn't be this quiet already. It shouldn't. How are they gone so quickly?

Taking a sharp, uneasy breath, I sit up carefully, wearily, waiting for someone to call my name, point their finger, and direct the unwanted attention towards me. I wait for their stares.

"Look! Look at Sue. She isn't dead! She faked it. She didn't drink the lemonade like the rest of us! She's a fraud. She was never *one of us!"*

But after seconds, I'm met with silence yet again; only the warm wind makes its way to me instead of harsh, judgmental stares. And as I peer around, the tears only rush down my face harder, my stomach twisting so harshly I swear it will rip in two.

They lay here. Do you see them too? Some on their stomachs, their hands covering their faces, as if sleeping peacefully within themselves. Others cuddle up to their children. Their partners. Their family members. Their friends. Some with their mouths wide open, as if they're still trying to gasp for air. A deep, red liquid drips from their mouths, escaping the death inside. Their skin draining colour. Their bodies lifeless. Their eyes fading, foggy, and grey. Their clothing and hair the only things moving in the field other than the tall grass and weeds among us. Other than myself, the only surviving member.

It didn't have to go this way. You know it didn't. Why did you have to do this?

Finally, I shift my feet under myself, standing with shaky legs and nerves that feel like they're eating me alive. The tall grass brushes against my bare legs, goosebumps rise, and my dress blows back in the wind. I ball my fists as my nails bite into my palms, trying to calm the nerves but that never helps. Swallowing hard at the knot in my throat, I try to blink the tears away, but they only blur my vision more, turning the sky, the grass, and the bright clothes the bodies are wearing, into colourful orbs. I watch my step, shifting through groups of bodies that look as if they've turned to stone, even in the heat of this summer day.

"I'm sorry. I'm sorry," I whisper to no one, weaving in and out of the pounds of decomposing flesh. The smell of the damp grass and weeds and wildflowers nearby mingle with the stench of corpses beginning to seep through the air.

What am I apologizing for? For stepping over them? Or for letting them down.

I don't think about this for longer than a second. I can't. I can't be here anymore. I can't look at them. I can't think about them. I can't let myself remember the sound of their dying words. Their coughs of blood.

Their painful screams that haunt this field as the poison-laced lemonade was poured down their throats.

Don't think. Don't think. Don't think about it.

But how can I forget when these things are replaying in my head like a burnt tape?

Taking in another staggering breath, I continue forward.

One step.

Over Terry's body.

Two steps.

Over Barbara and her husband.

Three steps.

Over Amanda and her ... her *three-year-old* daughter.

No. Don't think about it. Don't think. Don't think. Don't think.

But then the fourth step comes, and this time, I can't let myself forget. I can't *not* think of this one. I have to. Because here you are. Lying among the group, directly in the middle of this sick circle, the leader of them all.

Here, you lay. The man I thought I knew so well. The man I thought I trusted with my life. The man I thought loved me unconditionally. The one, I thought, I loved more than life. Here, you lie. The same red trickle leaking from your mouth. Your dark hair half covering your face, hiding one glossy eye as the other stares dully at the sky and the birds flying freely, hoping to join them.

Have you joined them yet?

"Oh Sue, I thought you loved me. I thought you loved this group, our family, just as much as I did. I loved them so much I died for them."

I can almost hear your voice speaking within the wind, calling me out, trying to get through to me. And the tears once again rush down my face.

"Why didn't you die for them too?"

Nikica Subek Simon

Touch the Floating Stars

AN EXCERPT

A rumble shook the ground. Kamíya and his friends stared at the mountain in astonishment and stumbled backwards. A crack appeared and grew wider by the second; a thunderous trembling compelled the group to retreat further as they watched the mountain fracture. The steep cliff ripped itself apart and revealed a vaulted doorway—a gaping entrance into the unknown.

⌒

Kamíya took a deep breath, squeezed the torch hard, and stepped into the pitch-black uncertainty first, as was his habit. Stomping the smooth, hard surface, he marvelled at its firmness. All other discovered hideouts had earthen foundations.

Standing still and straining his eyes to infiltrate the dark expanse, he willed his mind to focus on the task ahead and not dwell on his disquiet.

Derra approached, reached up, but couldn't touch the ceiling. "It's high. Not cramped for a change," he said.

The rest of the group huddled together at the entrance with their torches lit and ready.

Kamíya turned around to face his friends. "This is what we've been hoping for." He took a deep breath and raised his arm. His torch burned with a steady flame. Moments later, a grim veil of darkness enshrouded him. Comforted by the shuffling footsteps of his friends, Kamíya advanced with caution. Surprised at the absence of odours and the usual earthy smells, the peculiar emptiness raised questions.

No skeletons. Was that a bad sign? No skeletons, no treasure.

With a knot forming in his stomach, he pressed on. How far? Will it end like this? What was here to be scavenged but a vast nothingness?

Behind the slight bend, a vaulted rotunda opened up like a large community square fit for dancing. Dark pathways led in different directions and further into the unknown. Kamíya stopped, waited for his friends to catch up, and pivoted to count the options. "There are seven more passages besides the main one. Let's do what we always do and meet back here when we get thirsty. If anything unusual happens, use the danger signal."

The group split into pairs according to how they travelled in their steam vehicles.

Kamíya and SenLin marched into the passageway closest to them, past a smooth oblong sign affixed at eye level. It read Gallery B. How long would it take to explore the entirety of the underground pathways? Likely, more time than they had—too many mysteries and too few expeditioners.

After several unopenable doors, Kamíya found one with a handle. "I can open one," he called out to SenLin. He hesitated, but then reminded himself that apprehension was normal. After all, it was his calling to rescue valuable resources from Before.

The moment he pushed the door open and stepped in, the familiar smell of old books permeated the air and spellbound him. Wall-to-wall shelves were stacked with hardcovers, softcovers, and manuscripts. As Kamíya passed by the shelves filled with paper treasures, his heart skipped a beat. So many books in one place. The community had been scavenging items left behind by the world of Before since his father Naji could remember, yet the Finders' Place contained a trifle of the wealth amassed in this single room. Time stopped as Kamíya cleared cobwebs and pulled one book after another off the shelves, careful not to let the flames lick the precious finds.

In the corner, a dusty armchair beckoned. Kamíya pulled it to the middle of the room, placed a stack of books beside him on the floor, and sat down. His fingers brushed over a canvas cover as if touching a delicate flower. For the first time on this expedition, a found book didn't smell mouldy. Enchanted, he turned the pages one at a time, inhaled the scent of the ancient paper, and lost sense of the time.

From afar, the sound of an owl hooting penetrated the thick walls. Kamíya perked up. A pile of books towered on each side of the comfortable chair. He placed the book he had just perused on his right and picked up a new one from the left. Shouts could be heard, feet stomping and more owls—the danger signal.

"He's here," SenLin's voice echoed outside the room.

Azul stormed in out of breath. "Kamíya, you won't believe this." She rushed to their leader and pulled on his sleeve.

"What's wrong?" Kamíya rubbed his eyes. "Can it wait? Look." He pointed to the open book resting in his lap to show his friend a green valley with yellow flowers and white peaks in the background.

"I'm amazed," Azul said, but her voice took on a high pitch. "Forget the books."

Others crammed into the shelf-filled space, nodding in agreement as Azul attempted to drag the leader out.

Having found an important resource the community would cheer for, Kamíya couldn't fathom what could be more critical. But the group was adamant and determined he must see the surprise with his own two eyes.

"What is it, Azul?"

"You have to see it," she said and pulled the book from Kamíya's hands.

Kamíya sighed and followed his friends.

The expeditioners retraced their steps from the paper treasures chamber, through the long corridor, and toward the rotunda. Scurrying, almost running, they covered the distance in the fraction of time it had taken Kamíya and SenLin to explore it earlier. Azul led Kamíya through another tunnel bearing the sign, Gallery c. Shortly, the expeditioners reached a dead end and stopped in front of a large double door.

Azul stepped ahead and planted her finger on the thick glass. "See for yourself."

Kamíya looked back at his group. Flames threw shadows onto their stoic faces. He pressed down on the door handle and pushed the door open in slow motion, revealing a large hall.

It couldn't be, but there they were, right in front of him—a sea of glass beds arranged in rows, with a narrow space between them, enough for one person to pass through.

On the beds were people—children, women, and men. They looked at peace. They looked asleep.

"Are they dead?" a voice from behind squeaked.

The expeditioners filed in one by one. Bewildered, they stood among the sleeping people. Incredulity and questions swirled in Kamíya's mind like a cold season tempest.

"Oh, my bright stars. We found the Lost," said Breeze with a cry.

"The Lost are fighters," said Kamíya, shaking his head as he tiptoed among the beds and stopped at one.

Dome-shaped glass enveloped the entire person reposed on the narrow cot. Kamíya lifted the edge of his tunic and wiped clear a circle of dust above the person's face. His sneeze caused others to follow suit in a ricochet of violent bursts.

The woman in the glass bed remained still; the noises around her caused no movement of her limbs nor twitching of her eyes. Her long hair—an unusual and unfamiliar colour, like the morning sun—rested upon one shoulder. She wasn't breathing but didn't look dead; that was not a face of a deceased person. Kamíya knew death, and this wasn't it. He turned to Azul. "It looks like they're in a deep sleep. Look at the skin. It's so pale, but not grey. What do you think?"

Azul shook her head. "I don't see any steam valves, there is no fire anywhere, and nothing is moving, but something keeps them alive. How can someone sleep for long without waking up?"

Derra stepped forward. "Are these the people of Before?"

Kamíya looked at his best friend and shrugged. His friends were right; this was more important than books. He stood in one spot and observed the others wandering around. In the twilight of this peculiar room, flames flickered, blurring the real and imaginary. Listening to the breaths and murmurs of his friends as they wiped the glass covers to see who was underneath, Kamíya's gaze followed Azul. If anyone would understand, it was her.

She lingered in a far, dark corner. Kamíya strode toward her and the faint red light she was observing. The thin red lines glowed and scintillated close to the floor.

Azul crouched. "These lights are hovering in the air. I don't understand, but Anan would know." Her hand came close to the shimmering crimson streak.

"Our scientist is busy with his experiments at home," said Kamíya. "Don't touch!"

Azul looked up, but her hand had already broken through the light. A hissing sound spread like a wave, and a series of loud clicks pierced the eerie silence.

"You triggered something with your hand," said Kamíya and straightened his back, focusing on where the sounds were coming from.

Breeze rushed to their side and started crying. "You woke up the Lost."

Ruth Midgley

The Runner

AN EXCERPT FROM A LONGER WORK IN PROGRESS

Daphne lives off the grid in the foothills of the Rocky Mountains, withdrawn from society. But the arrivals of a mysterious girl from another world, and a powerful stone, force Daphne to confront her mistrust of the system, and propel her into fighting for a world she wants.

It only bothered her when they touched her face. The tickle of the spiderwebs was pleasant on her bare arms and shins, less so on her cheeks and nose. They caught on her goosebumps, her clothing more suited for the heat and sweat she knew was coming, not the current, cool, early-morning dampness.

Daphne was trying to beat the crowds and the sun, and because of the invisible spider silk she was cutting through, she knew she was succeeding. She was the first to travel this trail today, running back and forth on the switchbacks that lead to the top of the mountain. In the night, spiders had floated across on their strands, creating a crisscross of single-line webs only noticeable when they touched her skin as she passed. The spiders themselves were long gone, but the path they took remained. Evidence of no one. If she kept up this pace, she would have the ridge line all to herself.

As the trail steepened, her run slowed to a fast hike, legs pumping in short steps. Cinched at the waist and chest, her small daypack sat snugly against her back. As she walked, she sipped water from the plastic tube that snaked from her pack onto the shoulder strap. When she had left her campground that morning she could still see the stars, but now she clicked off her headlamp. The trees were shorter and more spread out as she approached the treeline, letting in more of the brightening sky. Wisps of hair that had escaped her ponytail clung to her sweaty neck and forehead. Her strong thighs and calves started to burn but she coaxed herself on, always promising her legs and lungs that they could rest at the top of the next crest in the trail. See that rock there? Just get to that rock. Then, inevitably, some strength would return as the trail leveled off, and she would find herself running on.

Daphne had seen almost all of this patch of the Rocky Mountains from the top of one peak or another, had run or hiked all of the signed trails and most of the hidden ones, and knew every campsite. She liked to think that if someone knocked her out, spun her around, and plopped her down in a random spot, she could find her way back, no problem, and be sitting with her feet up by her campfire come nightfall. No compass required.

When the trail turned from roots to rocks and her feet began slipping in the loose scree, she lost her rhythm and came to rest. She bent to untie her shoes and fish out the grit that had accumulated in the heels. A few steps off the path a cluster of green stuck out against the grey-brown of the slope. Some mountain sorrel had taken root in the protective shadow of a small boulder. She plucked a couple of leaves and chewed them, feeling the sour tang release onto her tongue. Her breath slowed, and in her stillness the subtle sounds of the mountain came into focus. From up here she could hear the shape of the landscape as the currents of air ran up the windward side of peaks, crested over the top, and rushed back down to swoop through the valleys beneath.

As the gust of wind died, there was another sound. The soft scuff and crunch of feet on the trail behind her.

Muttering under her breath, she quickly re-laced her runners and continued diagonally up the slope, hoping she could outrun whoever it was and have the peak to herself. Daphne stole glances down as she climbed, taking care not to lose her footing. She could see part of the trail below through the sparse trees but did not spot the other hiker.

Coming to the end of another switchback, she turned and saw the man, who was running at a trudging pace. He had already reached the sorrel boulder. Was he gaining on her? She fought for the top, pushing up and up, no longer any energy to spare to look back. Only her feet existed. One in front of the other, in front of the other, in front of the other until …

Blessed flatness. Doubled over, hands on knees, Daphne took in the view, breathtaking even for the hundredth time. A panorama of peaks, the sunrise turning the limestone to glowing amber.

"I've been trying to catch up to you." A panting voice behind her. "You're pretty quick."

She straightened and turned. The man was tall, and wore the usual runner's array of neon-coloured polyester and nylon. His tanned sinewy calves were caked with sweat and dust. He looked like he was a bit older than her, maybe forty. His teeth seemed to pop out of his face when he squinted, which he was doing now, looking at her.

Daphne shrugged. "Yeah." It was all she could muster. This was the first human she'd spoken to in days and the word felt weird in her mouth. Daphne's feet shifted in the scree as she considered whether or not to continue running before he caught his breath. She wasn't sure she wanted this man at her back for the rest of her run.

"You training for a big race or something?" the man said between sips of water.

"Nope."

"Just run up mountains at sunrise for fun, eh?" He laughed a little and smiled at her. The teeth thing was actually kind of endearing.

"Just don't like … tourists," Daphne said.

"Oh, I hear you. Worse every year."

For something to do, she bent down and retied her shoe.

"Really running those into the ground, eh?" he said nodding toward her abused trail runners. Her left big toe was beginning to poke through the mesh revealing her sock beneath.

Daphne forced a chuckle and an affirmative. What did he want from her? She took off her bag and stowed her headlamp inside while she waited to see if he would continue on or, hopefully, go back down. But he stood there looking out, taking it in. Which she couldn't blame him for, she supposed.

"Want to run the ridge together? I think you need someone to pace you if you're doing the whole loop. Speedy Gonzales, over here." He was laughing again. He had a nice laugh.

It was time for a more direct approach. "Actually, I'm enjoying running solo today."

"Say no more, I get it." He put his hands up and dipped his head in surrender. "I'm a talker, what can I say? Have a good run."

She watched him for a while. When he was about half way along the ridge she followed, picking her way through the rocks, running slower this time, so as not to catch up.

~

In her tent that night, when Daphne lay her tired body on her mat she thought about the man. She thought about what might have been if she'd said yes instead of no and ran the ridge with him. Maybe it would have been nice. He seemed like a good guy. Perhaps she'd judged him too harshly, her hackles always up. Maybe back at the parking lot they would have got to talking about food and how ravenous they were. She could have offered that her campsite was nearby, and lunch might have turned into afternoon fishing. Perhaps, afternoon would have turned into evening and talking to silent caresses. But this was only one scenario among a thousand others with less happy endings.

Daphne tried to put thoughts of the man aside and fell into a doze, but as the night darkened she grew cold. In her half sleep, she zipped her sleeping bag all the way up, but it was not enough. Her body ached unbearably. Not from the run or from the cold. It ached with awareness, awareness of where she ended and the world began. She yearned for touch, for there to be something between her and the night, for a body, any body, next to hers to keep the pressing expanse at bay. She wrapped her arms around herself, and still, it was not enough. Her heart reached out its tendrils and found nothing, nothing for miles on which to cling or ask its questions and find answers. Out and out it searched, past the trees, past the sky, and all the way into the void of space. But there was nothing, and her body ached all the more.

A thunderous crack woke her from this dream for a moment. In a stupor, she poked her head outside the tent and listened. No rain or wind disturbed the silent forest around her. As she lay back, she wondered briefly about the possibility of a flash flood and the creek that ran in the canyon below rising and rising until it carried her tent away like a boat. The thought was strangely soothing, and she fell into a deep sleep.

Sarah El Sioufi

Light Between the Lines

AN EXCERPT

The hospital cafeteria is empty except for a few nurses sitting at the far end. Uncle Khalid left a while ago to get a change of clothes for us, so it's just me and Aunt Sami. I feel sweaty and gross, and Sami doesn't look much better. Her eyes are heavy, and her hijab slips back on her head, letting some of her brown hair peek out.

We were full of anxious energy on the drive over but once we saw Mom sitting up in the hospital bed, talking and only slightly worse for wear—the relief flooded through us, any remaining strength depleted.

I've always done what's best for you, Nour.

I roll my eyes at the memory of her words from when I sat in her hospital room. Leave it to me and Mom to find a way to argue in any circumstance.

I refocus on the napkin doodle I made of Sami and add some shading to the bags under her eyes, then slide it across the table. She looks down at the drawing and chuckles—she's happy for a moment before her smile falls and she returns to staring into the distance. I reach for the drawing and stuff it into the back pocket of my jeans. We sit across from each other in silence while she drinks her coffee and I pick at a stale muffin.

⁀

As the elevator doors open, I hear "code blue" over the speakers and wonder what that means. My curiosity mounts, and a rush of worry courses through me. When we get to Mom's room, there's a swarm of people inside and my knees wobble as I realize the code blue is for her. It's a flurry of beeping and bodies swirling around the bed, moving wires and iv bags. *Oh God, what's happening?* My stomach threatens to expel the muffin.

"On three. One. Two. Three," a man's voice says.

They lift Mom onto a stretcher and wheel her out of the room, pushing past us. I stand there, frozen.

Sami follows until she's stopped by a nurse. "You can't go in there."

"What's going on?" Sami demands, grabbing the nurse's arm.

"She had another stroke."

Sami releases her grip and watches the nurse run down the hallway, the doors slowly swinging shut behind her.

⁀

It feels like days before the doctor emerges. His hair is disheveled, and his mask hangs off one ear as he approaches. Sami squeezes my hand and stands, bringing me up with her.

"She had a second embolic stroke. A larger artery was blocked off and too much of her brain was affected. There was nothing more we could have done. I'm afraid she died."

I hear nothing else he says after that. A scene from a medical drama plays in my mind. In it, the doctor explains to his interns that they need to be direct when communicating with a patient's family. They can't say someone has passed away or any other euphemism. They have to be clear.

"She died," I whisper back to him, the words escaping like air from a deflating balloon.

⁀

The next twenty-four hours are a blur. Sami and Khalid bustle around our condo, making phone calls and cleaning. They move around me while I sit in my chair and wonder how things would be different if my dad were alive—if I had ever known him. I'm not alone, but I feel lonelier than I've ever felt in my whole life. No parents. No siblings. Just me, Sami, and Khalid.

I stare at my phone on the table; the last text I sent Sloane was from the hospital before everything went to hell, and I can't think of how to tell her what happened. I get tired of trying to find the right words and finally decide to be direct, telling myself I'll explain more to her later: SHE DIED LAST NIGHT. I'LL BE OKAY.

Sloane calls almost immediately, but I silence the call, unable to take in her reaction when I haven't even processed my own.

⸙

"Why do we need to do this right now?" I ask Sami, looking at the door, almost expecting Mom to walk in.

Sami takes a deep breath and speaks, her voice barely above a whisper. "Your mother would have wanted a Muslim funeral."

"But why? I've been to a few funerals, and they're always a week or something after the person dies. This is crazy, this just happened and we're going to bury her within a day?"

Sami sighs and runs a hand over her long curls. "We don't use any embalming or preservatives on the body, so we need to bury her as soon as possible. It's what she would have wanted."

"If you say so," I mutter. I want to run past her and go to my room, but I know that if I'm alone right now, I'll start crying and probably never stop. I look down at my cereal and move the cheerios around with my spoon. *My first Muslim funeral will be for my own mother.*

⸙

The three of us walk through the parking lot toward the mosque. It's a white building with long glass windows and domes on the roof. Each dome has a thin piece of gold metal on top, leading up to a small crescent.

Uncle Khalid brought me once when I was little, but we weren't allowed to pray together. He told me that the men had to pray in the front and the women in the back. When I asked him about it, he said it was to protect a woman's modesty, that there was so much bending and kneeling, it would be *haram* if the women were in the front. Even at ten, the gender segregation inside such a holy place didn't sit right with me, and I never went back, until now.

A man with a long beard, wearing a white cap greets us. He shakes our hands, and I stand aside while he speaks with Sami and Khalid in Arabic. I zone out, staring at the intricate carpeting and eventually follow them into a room. There's a small stand with a box of tissues in front of a beige sofa.

My heart sinks to my stomach when I see her lying on the table at the other end of the room. Verses of the *Qur'an* play softly over the speakers as I walk up to her alone. She's wrapped in a white sheet, naked underneath, her long black hair tucked into a white head wrap. She looks strange without make-up; I rarely see her without her dark winged eyeliner. I want to take the head wrap off and shake out her hair so that it can cascade down her back and around her shoulders like it usually did. No jewellry, no clothes, nothing—just her body under some cloth.

I finally understand what people mean when they say the body is only a vessel. She looks hollow. Tears fall onto my hands, and I drop to my knees. I can't say goodbye. She's already gone.

⌒

At the burial site, it's a clear summer's day, and the sun beats down on us while we stand around the grave. It feels like I'm in a dream. A whooshing sound engulfs me, dulling the noises, like getting water stuck in my ears after swimming. Moisture builds up under my bra, and my pantyhose itch like crazy. It's taking all my self-control not to take them off in front of everyone.

Sloane is there with her parents, and I see a few friends from my old school huddled together—none of them able to meet my eyes. I imagine my dad standing across from me on the other side of the grave, his head down and his hands clasped together. I've only ever seen a few crappy pictures of him, but I always imagined him to be tall like me, with the same jellybean birthmark on the back of his neck.

The image vanishes and I watch two men wearing *galabeyas* approach the wooden casket. For a brief moment, I envy their outfits. The long, flowing white cotton robes seem more forgiving than my stuffy black dress and pantyhose. One of the men is carrying a shovel, and the other opens the top part of the casket, revealing Mom's face, as still and pale as ever. He gently lifts her head—I stifle a sob. The man carrying the shovel thrusts it into the fresh soil, then brings the shovel closer to Mom's head and tips it into the casket, letting the dirt fall in before resting her head down over the earth, like a pillow. Sami explained to me earlier that in Egypt they put the body in a shroud and place it directly into the ground, but in Ontario, for an Islamic funeral, we had to comply with provincial law. So even though she'll be buried in a casket, she'll still technically be touching the earth.

I hate myself for caring, but my friends would be freaked by all of this, and I avoid looking at them for confirmation. Sami moans loudly as they lower the casket into the ground. Her cries remind me she's the only family I have in Canada now, and I swallow a feeling of resentment toward Mom—that she kept me from my family in Egypt. She always said she'd explain it to me when I was old enough, but now it feels like her secrets are being buried with her. I want to hold Sami's hand or hug her, but all I can do is stare at the soil pouring into the grave until every spot of wood is covered.

Rachelle Jones

A Simple Spell

AN EXCERPT FROM THE NOVELLA
"CHASING STREET LIGHTS"

"I want him to be loved," I began to sob. "Just not by me. It can't be me anymore."

Maddie wrapped me in her arms and let me soak her T-shirt with tears and snot as I muttered, "It can't be me," over and over.

"Let's go," she said when the worst of the storm had passed.

She drove along dark back roads, high beams illuminating gentle curves and slow warning signs. We stopped in the parking lot of Kalcoola Beach. I opened the car door and threw up before stumbling out, wrapping my arms around me even though there was no chill in the air. The water whispered my name and I walked into the waves. I had no intention of stopping, but Maddie grabbed my hands and held me back when the water reached my thighs.

"That's far enough," she said.

She leaned backwards while holding my wrists tight, so that I could lean forward—feel the falling, feel the surrender. There we stayed, our two bodies leaning in opposite directions swaying with the waves. The water was so black and inky that I couldn't see anything below its surface.

All of a sudden, I was alone. Maddie was gone. My feet were sinking into the sand. Thick scarlet red veins emerged from the water, each moving independently like tentacles. They looked like heartstrings, strong and elastic, searching for a heart socket to plug themselves into. They climbed my legs making their way to my torso. I tried to rip one off, but a searing pain shot through my body like a bolt of electricity. With all my strength I pulled my feet free and scrambled onto the beach in a panic. On shore, the heartstrings dried up and I brushed them off as easily as dried seaweed.

"Let's take you home," said Maddie. She was by my side again, brushing the hair out of my eyes.

She drove through empty streets, ignoring stop signs and traffic lights until we reached my driveway. I felt so weak that Maddie had to help me into the house. We landed on the cold kitchen tiles, sand pooling around us. I closed my eyes and leaned my head against a cupboard.

"Where did you go?" I asked her, keeping my eyes closed.

"When?" she asked.

"On the beach. You left me." I opened my eyes to look at her, even though I felt lightheaded.

She looked confused. "I was with you the whole time. I never left your side once."

That night I dreamt I walked into a tumultuous turquoise sea with a horse strapped to my back and helped it give birth to an octopus. The octopus was too small to ride the waves alone, so I kept it close to my heart.

We had waited three days for the new moon.

"Where did you learn about this?" I asked Maddie as we carried our supplies from her house to the river.

"The internet." She shrugged. She had found a witch's spell to make Tyler fall out of love with me, and at this point, I was desperate enough to try anything.

At the river we placed a tin bucket on the ground, and Maddie placed a piece of tumbleweed inside.

"Did you bring a photo?" she asked.

I slipped my favourite photograph of Tyler between the thin tumbleweed branches, his smiling face looking back at me. Maddie pulled a cigarette lighter from her jean jacket and lit the kindling, softly blowing on it to encourage the flame. She reached over with a small pair of scissors, cut a piece of my hair, and threw it into the tin bucket. The sulfuric smell of burning hair filled the air. Then, she opened four small containers holding dried bay leaves, rosemary, cloves, and salt, and sprinkled them into the flames. Her movements were swift and confident. The dried bay leaves burst and crackled, causing the flames to reach higher as the photo melted.

"Do you remember the words I taught you?" She kicked off her flip flops, squishing her feet into the grass.

I nodded, also removing my shoes. Maddie lit two long taper candles, handed them to me, and then lit two of her own. The uncharacteristically calm night was absent of any wind to threaten the flames. She stood across from me, the tin bucket fire between us.

"Ready?" she asked, steadying herself. We circled the fire, always facing each other, holding a candle in each hand.

"Ah—Ala Goya, Hoy—Ala Goya, Oi Oi Ah Yah Ta," Maddie whispered.

My voice joined hers and we got progressively louder as we continued circling the flames, "Oi—Goy Eye Yah Ta, Goy Goy Ah Ya Ta."

Maddie continued to chant the sounds as I layered new words on top, "Oh, great magic sleeping in the sea, wake and rid me of his love, set his spirit free. Oh, great magic sleeping in the sea, wake and rid me of his love, set his spirit free!"

"Go!" we screamed to the heavens as we stopped and lifted our candles into the sky. Frozen in that position, we channeled all our energy into the night sky.

The next morning, I woke to banging on the front door. Tyler stood at my doorstep. He wanted to say goodbye before leaving for camp. He put his hand on my cheek and slowly kissed me, like an ivory silk slip slipping through mud. I was hit with a wave of relief when he turned to walk away. The tension in my body melted as his truck drove out of sight.

I sat at the kitchen table and picked up my pen. Words splashed from me like the blood of my first period—over confident and slightly indignant.

Shantell Powell

This is the Time Just Before Spider Woman Meets Kiviuq

My hut is sodden without and within. The sod roof is drenched with the mist which always shrouds this vale of scrubby trees and sphagnum. And the inside? Ah, that is the moisture from my cooking pot.

Men are stacked around me in neat piles. Today is the boiling day, when marrow bone femurs seep their flavours into richness. The meat isn't fatty enough, so I add seal oil until it swims on the surface. Round floating islands grab at one another in a large amber slick, then scatter like lemmings when I stir the pot and poke down any protruding bones.

I sing to myself while I cook. My eyebrows hang down over my eyes, blinding me to all but my work. Off to my side, I hear a moan. The men stacked like firewood speak to me. "Push us into the cauldron," they say, but they shall have to wait their turns. Spiders creep like lichen across my arms. They are my children, and tonight we shall sup well.

The roof is always making sounds. Bugs burrow in, making nests, making worms, until on the rainy days water and maggots patter down onto my earthen floor. I scoop them up and eat them by the handful, or feed them to my children.

This is the best time to be alive! I have no use for the frozen times, so I die, we die, and when the rains come to melt away the snow and drench the bogs with water and larvae, I resurrect myself and weave an orb as a cradle for my youngest.

The sounds of the creeping things bring me comfort. The sounds of my fire bring me joy.

The sound I hear now brings me confusion. What is that great noise? I don't know it. It is not the sound of my stew, of my crackling embers, my shaking fire, my sprinkling rain, my moaning stack of corpses. No, it is something new.

I look up, but my eyebrows dangle in my way.

No matter. I don't need them on my face, anyhow. I slice them off with my ulu, pop them into my mouth, and look up into the shocked face of a living man.

Forced Birth

EXCERPT FROM A NOVEL IN PROCESS

Dry was the womb that birthed me, all dust and sharp, ragged edges. Windblown, windswept haboob, raw as Mars. Dragged from my mother by callused thick hands, the hands of the celestial carpenters, plumbers, sheet metal workers, and general labourers of the antediluvian eon. Layered in brittleness, stacked atop fossils, my starving soil only grew the thorny things: the venomous, the blood-hungry lamia, the things which eat, and the things which are eaten.

Dragged forth from the nether reaches of Eden, detritus from the original building project, tectonic birth pangs, the unwanted parts of creation, stacked together hurriedly, like something made by the lowest bidder, born in pain, and destined to pain.

The humans were bounced, barred, never to return to the mother from which we're removed. Fresh new mortals, they cowered in newly learned fear, an essential emotion if they expect to survive on me.

I am the badlands, the malformed child of Eden. I am the firstborn earthborne, born in landslide, shale, and gravel. I am continental drift.

The humans looked for somewhere to shelter. They had to work hard. The ground shook beneath their feet as I spasmed in pain. Scorpions chased their shadows. Spiders bit their flesh. Lice found succour, and the humans learned how to kill.

Casual cruelty is the way of things here. Eat or be eaten. Kill or be killed. They fashioned weapons from my bones, throwing rocks at small animals. They made tools from my teeth, napping chert into edges sharper than scalpels. They learned to cut and slice, stab and club. They peeled animals like fruit to eat the insides. They brain-tanned skins and stitched them together. They ate any creature they could kill while avoiding the ones they could not.

Lions stalked the badlands for meat and tepid water. Though it rushes in rivers through the atmosphere, water is a treasure on my skin. Shelter is a treasure. A full belly is a treasure, and treasures are rare, hard to find, and harder still to keep. These humans would never be rich again, but perhaps their progeny will.

Will I ever be rich like my mother? She was blessed before she was locked away and forgotten, a memory hidden behind a flaming sword. I was born dying, doomed to countless deaths, bound to die myself, to be the site of wave after unending wave of death.

I was made as a punishment, a prison, a Hell, a Gehenna for the burning of refuse, but if I must burn, let me be a crucible. May I find ways to create beauty in fleeting life though I am made to devour souls. May I find the beauty in death. The blood shed by hunters, the blood poured onto me from birth, these feed me. And the piss of fear, the stinking shit of predator or prey, they feed me. I eat these unclean things, and I transform them into life. From death springs forth new life. Trees grow, fed by rot, manure, the mouldering leaves and leavings of their predecessors.

I am a necromancer, raising the dead again and again. Petroleum blood rushes through my veins. I break out in tar sands and erupt volcanically.

The wary humans watched me. They learned my fresh new secrets. They hunted, they killed, they learned to grow. They toiled and bled and grew thin even as one grew round. She squatted and dropped a mewling baby, and somehow, both survived. Each child she grew is a new beginning. A new pair of eyes and ears to watch and listen for danger and food. But each new child is a gamble with her life. Each new child is a new mouth to feed.

They begged to be allowed back into Eden, but I will not beg. I will not pray. The god who made me is not my god. I am a cursed land, bound to an eternity of colonization. I was created to be used as a stopping point, a resting spot on the journey to heaven or hell. I'm a filthy bus stop, neglected and filled with blunt hypodermic needles and shattered bottles, with dried blood and a pool of sticky urine. No one wants to stay here any longer than they must.

Non-fiction

Jackson Wai Chung Tse 謝瑋聰
The Virgo
WRITTEN WHILE EATING CHOCOLATE
PEANUT BUTTER HÄAGEN DAZS

My dad cuts up eggs and toast into bite-sized pieces and skewers them together before putting them into his mouth. He grows the nail on his left pinky finger long and uses it to part the hair of the clients he services, crouching down with his scissors and comb to meet their scalp with his height. He insists on making the bed every morning and sleeps like a mummy in the tomb. He loves collecting stamps and coins, and no matter which Chinese restaurant we go to, he always orders ham yu gai lup chow fan. Salted fish and chicken-fried rice.

He sorts VHS tapes for fun, peering at the labels through Coke-bottle lenses, a tuft of silver hair tickling his eyebrow. He wears tube socks he's worn for over a decade, and all of them have holes in them. His wallet, keys, and pocketbook live in a Tupperware container next to the TV, and he doesn't like it when I rest my elbows on the dinner table, knocking the wood surface twice with his chopsticks, *tack tack*. Every day, he dresses himself in a down sweater vest and cargo zip-off pants. Every night, he goes over the day's receipts and makes notes in his accounting book, long after I've gone to bed.

⁓

When I am thirteen, all I want is to eat ice cream. On a Saturday afternoon in January, Dad invites me to go. I suspect something is wrong for three reasons. First, when I was seven, I won a piano competition and I begged him for a Dairy Queen Buster Bar, but he refused to buy me one.

He got me a mechanical pencil instead. Second, when it's scorching hot in the middle of a Calgary summer, he stocks our fridge with knock-off Freezies from Costco. It's cheaper. Third, icicles are crystallizing on our nostril hairs and he is more chatty than usual. My dad never says more than he needs to, so I pull on my boots and pile into the backseat of our robin's-egg-blue 1999 Toyota Camry.

He keeps looking at me in the rearview mirror. We're not heading for the closest Dairy Queen, but I enjoy the ride. I don't get a lot of quality time with him. Maybe we're going to the fishing goods store first and he'll let me pick out some lures.

"哥哥."

"Yes, Dad?"

"I have something I need to tell you."

I meet his eyes in the mirror. Have his kidney stones flared up again? My stomach drops.

"What's wrong?"

He concentrates on the road. We cruise down Deerfoot Trail at 100 km/hour while 88.9 Shine FM blares "Lord I Lift Your Name on High" by Hillsong United. It looks like we're leaving the city to get ice cream in Red Deer, the next town. Am I being kidnapped?

"I've been wanting to tell you for a long time."

"Are you sick?"

"I am deciding to tell you against your mother's wishes. It's important you hear it from me."

My brow furrows. The seatbelt seizes around my chest, and I wiggle to give myself more breathing room against my parka.

"What is it?"

He is as silent as these miles of fence posts along snow-covered hills. Is he cheating? Leaving us? The knot in my chest gets tighter with every worship song we listen to. He clears his throat.

"You said that you've noticed a few times that there's a smell coming from the garage."

My bedroom window is right above the garage, and sometimes I smell something sharp late at night. It's not the Chinese medicine that my mom boils. It comes in a moment, and then is gone the next. When I told my parents about it, they looked at each other but didn't say anything.

"Uh huh."

"That smell is coming from me. I smoke."

His eyes are fixed on the road, his hands tight on the steering wheel. Mom always tells me to plug my nose whenever we pass a smoker. It's bad for your lungs, she says, waving her hand in front of her face. How has Dad hidden this from me for so long?

"You smoke cigarettes?"

"Since I was your age. I wasn't good at school, so I dropped out and washed dishes at a restaurant to make some money. Everybody smoked back then."

His voice starts to waver.

"I've tried to quit all my life, but I haven't been able to. Your mom was so mad. I hid it from her too, till we were married. She threatened to divorce me."

He is quiet for a moment, steadying his tremor. I notice tears running down his cheek.

"Before you were born, she made me promise never to smoke around the house, to never expose you to it."

We're taking the exit into Red Deer and heading to the Little Ice Cream & Soda Shoppe.

"I wish I never started. Sometimes I wonder if your bronchitis was because of me." His voice trembles again.

"I'm so sorry, 哥哥."

I feel my pulse between my ears, three beats for every light post we pass. Dad never cries or apologizes. I open and close my mouth, my tongue as clumsy as a rainbow trout.

"It's okay, Dad."

He pulls into the strip mall parking lot and turns off the engine. We sit in the car, our breath fogging up the windows, the radio silent.

"Have you tried nicotine gum? I've heard it works really well."

"It doesn't work for me."

We fall silent and stare at the storefront. Little Ice Cream & Soda Shoppe is empty today, except for one server behind the cash register. The wind is howling outside, but it's warm in the car.

"Thank you for telling me."

He blows his nose into a napkin and opens the car door. "Okay, let's get ice cream."

I follow him inside and choose my favourite, Rocky Road. He gets vanilla. We must have looked like a peculiar pair: two bespectacled Chinese men in Red Deer, licking their ice cream cones in the dead of winter, not looking at or talking to each other.

Aimee Taylor

I Love You So Much With My Hurt

AN EXCERPT

It is only 8:00 a.m., and my child has already had me in tears twice, and has no doubt woken the landlords upstairs. I have an ongoing fear of getting evicted from our basement suite due to the Chicken's outbursts, even though I put up with the landlords' preschooler stomping back and forth above my head all day. I had all but begged for the place when I'd come to view it, shortly after my wife left us, gaining the woman's empathy when I explained how hard it was for a single mum on disability to find a spot to live in this city. Nobody wants to rent to us. And now, I realize maybe it's for good reason.

In spite of having an advanced vocabulary, the only sound that has come out of the Chicken's mouth this morning is either a yell or a no, or a yelled no. I have an ongoing joke with some mum friends that it won't be the cancer that kills me, it'll be the parenting. Today, I don't doubt this statement.

Her toast was cut wrong, I pressed the coffee grinder button before letting her help, I told her she needed to wear pants when she insisted on shorts, she wouldn't let me brush the rat's nest out of the back of her hair, and now, she is screaming at me because I wiped the jam off the table so she wouldn't continue to finger paint with it. My mother has told me again and again that I need to be firmer with her, to scare her a little bit, so that she submits to me. What my mother doesn't know, despite me promising myself that I would parent differently than she did, is that

I spend my life screaming at this child, completely out of control to the point that I scare myself. Even so, it does not seem to matter whether I hold firm boundaries or let her run amok; this child is completely out of control. I have no idea how to parent her. And I am doing it on my own.

Nobody knows how hard it is, because I haven't told anyone, for fear of their judgment. Everyone knows it's the mother's fault when her kids don't have any respect for her authority. I have tried everything: reward-driven parenting, gentle parenting, punitive parenting, to name a few. But it doesn't matter what approach I use, I am horrible at it all. And she knows it.

There are some days when I think the Chicken is the biggest gift I have ever been given. Then, there are moments when I truly struggle to like her. I hate myself in these moments. Today is filled with them. Compared to this, my morning chemo will be a breeze.

The Chicken finally stops screaming. She sits at the top of the three steps that lead down from our front door into the ground of our dank basement apartment. Her small hands cup her jam-streaked face.

"You okay?" I ask, taking a break from the dishes. My heart softens when I see her face. "Are you feeling nervous about Mummy's chemo today?"

She lets out a sigh big enough that the top half of her body sinks into her lower half.

"I just love you so much with my hurt," she replies.

I swallow a large ball of shame. No matter what I am feeling, I am the adult and should have the capacity to manage it. This tiny human in front of me has no such ability. I sit next to her and pull her onto my lap. She turns her body so that her face is against my chest. A tear falls from my eye onto the top of her head. I smooth it in before she feels it.

"That's called empathy," I explain. Name the emotions, all the parenting books say, so that she learns to validate them and decrease emotional reactivity. "Empathy is when you love someone so much that you feel what they feel, and today you are feeling sad because Mummy has to get yucky medicine that is going to make her feel sick and she's sad. It makes you feel sad, too. Thank you for caring so much about me. I care about you so much, too."

This. This is the child I boast about and tell the world about. This child, who is so connected to my pain that she feels it in herself. The child I can forgive for creating such havoc in our every day. We take a moment to cuddle. I remind her that it is not her job to worry about me. It is her job to jump and skip and discover new things. I wonder out loud if the ducks have hatched at daycare yet. She reminds me that it will be another four days.

Sir arrives with her clippers, Xander with his camera, and Chelsey and Ashley, my two closest cancer friends, for moral support—they've both been through this process and will support me through my head shave. My hair hasn't fully fallen out yet, but the clumps of it on my pillow when I wake up, and in my hands when I rinse out the conditioner, push me to be proactive. I'm not upset about it. I have very few feelings of loss, which I know are common.

The Chicken, however, is visibly uneasy, though the other people in the room don't notice. She is clingy and quiet; her fingers wrap around mine and her jagged nails scrape against my wrist. I make a note to trim them after she falls asleep tonight. Xander sets up his lights and angles his camera on the tripod to capture the moment. His photos will go in the legacy box that I've started for the Chicken. Chelsey places a stool in the middle of the room, on which I sit, suddenly self-conscious. Chelsey and Ashley hug my shoulders, one on each side of me. Xander clicks his shutter, Sir sets herself up behind me, the Chicken at my front. I am flanked on every side by my chosen family. A warmth moves through my chest and my vulnerability scares me. I break the quiet.

"How many heads have you shaved before, Sir?" I ask.

"I was a dyke in the '80s, Aimee. I got this." Her gruff laugh echoes through the suite. I study her handsome features. My mother's greatest fear with this head shave is that I will appear too masculine. She has suggested wearing dangly earrings so that people can still read me as a woman. In the binary world of queerdom, where the dichotomy of "femme" and "masc" still prevail, I land more on the femme side of things, though I am intrigued at whether I'll be able to experience some gender fluidity with this newfound baldness.

Sir turns on the clippers and the Chicken scurries up on my lap in a panic. I see a fear in her that is so unfamiliar, it is shocking.

"Wait!" I hold out my palm to Sir. The buzzing and clicking and talking stop instantly. I look around the room at all the compassionate faces. "Can you give us a minute?" The room clears out as my friends respect our space. The Chicken is wrapped around me like a koala now, her lips at my ear.

"What's wrong, love? It's just hair," I say, stroking hers. "It won't hurt me."

She pulls away from me just enough to look me in the eyes.

"Will Mummy's face still be there?"

"What?" I ask, not understanding her question.

"Will Mummy's face still be there, after Sir shaves her head?"

"Oh, love." I wrap her in an embrace, finally realizing why she's been so alarmed. She has no context for a head shave. She has imagined that every feature on my entire head will be erased under the razor's edge, never to be seen again. A faceless parent. "Of course. I'll be the same old Mummy."

This, and the promise of a mango popsicle, is enough to persuade her to climb down and play with Ashley and Chelsey while Xander captures Sir shaving my head. Ashley and Chelsey are starting the process of fertility treatments to get pregnant with their own babies, after cancer stripped them of the ability to do it without interventions. Chelsey will go on to have three beautiful babies, twins via surrogacy and then one more, which she will get to carry herself. Ashley will die shortly after freezing embryos with her husband.

Sir holds up the mirror in front of me when she's finally done. Everyone is silent, waiting for my reaction. I look a bit ridiculous bald, but feel somehow liberated and fierce. I smile and thank them all so much for being here. The Chicken, now fully convinced that my face isn't going anywhere, loves the feel of the soft bristles that are left on top. It quickly becomes a new calming strategy at bedtime: rubbing my cue ball of a head to get to sleep. Whatever gets us through.

⁀

Chemo is relentless. I feel as though I am stuck on a ship in the most horrible ocean storm, and I can't get off for a week each time. I have never felt so exhausted in my life. The Chicken demands all of my attention, setting up elaborate make-believe scenes where she is the mum and I am the baby. When she shouts at me, berating me for any behavioural misstep, I know I must start doing better.

I realize that so many of my efforts over the last year have been veiled attempts to change her. To make her less anxious. To make her more respectful. To make her less angry, less impulsive, less needy of me. But what if I stop and instead accept her as she comes? What if I truly allow her to shine as she is, even if she's not the child I expected to have?

I hang on to hope that she will be too young to remember this time, but that, somehow, she will remember me. The good moments. Which seem fleeting.

B. A. Cyr
Girls Don't Ride Motorcycles

DAY 6 OF 14 / 1,824 OF 7,000 KILOMETRES

Through the window, I see the sun rising and the rays reflecting on the motorcycle tank are a blessing to my sore muscles. I put on my well-stretched jeans, my necessary sports bra and a white T-shirt. On the motel bed, I roll my few clothes back into my duffel bag. I slide into my ankle boots and zip them up. I pick up my leather chaps, buckle them, then painfully put one leg on the chair and zip it up, followed by the other leg and zip that one, too.

My body is feeling the reality of the trip; I am more aware of the different muscles every day. I stare at myself in the mirror, my eyes look tired and my cheeks are red and puffy. I tie my hair, creating one long thick braid. I gently put sunscreen on my face. I fold my black bandana meticulously to form a two-inch wide rectangle. With the ends in each hand, I bring the middle of the bandana to my forehead, stretch my arms out and tie a knot in the back. I make a second knot looking at my clear brown eyes, preparing my soul for the ride.

⁀

I start the bike to warm it up and strap my duffle bag on the tail. I look around; I am alone. The parking lot is full of family cars and motorcycles for two; people seem to be on holiday or a romantic ride. The sound of the motor is a warning that I am ready to saddle in. I put my black leather jacket on, breathe in to zip it up over my boobs, and tighten my helmet. I

256

swing my right leg over the purple bag and the bike, like it was nothing. I feel invincible. I put my feet on the gravel to back up, and slip. I barely touch the ground with my boots, and now fear is sneaking in. I slowly back up and put it in first gear. The vibration of the engine warms my heart. A smile appears on my face; I twist my right wrist. The roar of the motor confirms that I am no longer a guest at Mystic Isle Motel.

It's just me, the sun, and the road. I pass Wawa and White River. The road is hot; I can feel and smell the asphalt steaming under the sun. It follows Lake Superior. It's easy to relax; no choices to be made, just ride. The green of the trees reflect on the open water. I can hear the waves crashing on the shore over the engine's sound. I vibrate with the bike and the winds. I continue to marathon before taking a break.

I stop to fill up the gas tank; the gas station stands in the middle of nowhere. Two big trucks are parked farther along, and a few people are pumping gas. The total comes to $13.56. I walk toward the store to pay, and notice a young girl and her father coming out my way. We meet at the door, and I hold it open for them.

"Dad! Look at the bike!"

"That's her motorcycle."

"Girls don't ride motorcycles!"

The little girl's comment surprises me. "Girls don't do what?" It hit a nerve. It's like my spirit woke up and was ready to fight.

The dad continues, raising his chin at me.

"Yes, girls can have motorcycles. Look at her; she owns that bike."

She studies me. She stares at my boots, then my chaps, jacket, gloves, and helmet. She seems to be trying to find a flaw that would prove her dad wrong. She looks at my face and my head with the black bandana holding my light brown braid. She stares. She takes a second to look deep into my eyes.

I continue inside the store. The clerk is in a glass cage on a platform, five inches higher than where the customers are standing. I put my left arm on the high counter and look for money in my right pocket. I observe the little girl. She has stopped in front of the bike. Her head is barely higher than the seat. Her delicate nature stands out in contrast with the black motorcycle. The blue ribbon that ties her blond ponytail looks perfect from my angle. I put the cash on the counter, waiting for my turn with the clerk, keeping my eyes on her flowery ruby dress flowing in the wind. She has little sandals, not made to run. I wonder if this was a mom's touch. A perfect little outfit by design.

She looks at the bugs in the front light and the mud in the fender. She examines the shininess of the chrome pipes and the engine. It is still hot, and smells like gasoline and rubber. The bike is so much bigger than her, so much dirtier than her. She's dressed like she could twirl in the living room with her daddy throwing compliments and laughing aloud before putting her feet on his so he can show her how to dance. She already knows how to be pretty. She tilts her head to see the back, the dirty fender carrying the purple bag, and stares at the license plate. I wonder if she can read, and if she can tell that I have already crossed two provinces—almost 2,000 kilometres.

I take my eye off her to pay my bill. I walk outside to see her leave with her dad. It's warm. My jeans are sticking to my skin, and the chaps have expanded in the sun and created a warm air pocket around both legs. There is only one other car at the pump and no traffic. The wind seems to be bringing dust, random trash, and the smell of gasoline.

I get to the bike and crouch; I want the same angle she had. It does seem impossible from here. The squeaky noise from the warm leather of my chaps and jacket takes me out of my head and makes me look at the pair walking to their car.

⁀

I remember when my dad and I went to look at a motorcycle when I was a little girl. We parked in the driveway and walked down to the garage, and the salesman took it out for me to sit on. It was so beautiful and perfect. It was small, mostly white, with a red seat and trim. After encouragement, I sat on it. I wore my purple rubber boots and grey sweatpants for the occasion. My dad's eyes met mine, he had changed his mind: it was too dangerous for his little girl.

⌒

I get up with so much more ease than I bent down. I saddle on the bike and let the engine warm up to a normal roar. The vibration goes from my hips to the rest of my body. I zip up my jacket to protect myself from the wind. I stand on my two feet and push right and left on the handlebar to make the bike sway under me. I kick the stand and sit for more road.

At night, I stand in front of the mirror in my room. The dim light forms shadows on my face, revealing my tired eyes and sunburned skin. I put my helmet on the dresser in front of me. I unzip my heavy jacket. I lift my tired right leg to the chair to unzip my chaps. The other leg follows and feels heavier.

I undo the buckle and let the chaps fall to the ground. The sound resonates with my spirit; it was a long day. I take my legs back to the chair to unzip my boots. In the half-dark room, I stare at my face. My eyes are red, hiding behind a mess of hair contained in the bandana.

Here I am. My armour is off. I raise my two hands next to my head. Slowly, staring at the mirror, I put my hands on each side of my bandana and raise it. It keeps its round shape. I lower it slowly in front of my eyes; it feels important. My hair falls out, loose. I gently put down my crown for the night.

Chantal MacCuaig
Cover Girls
AN EXCERPT FROM A PERSONAL ESSAY

I was born in 1986, on a Tuesday in May. That same month, the now defunct *Life Magazine* released an issue celebrating "Hollywood's Most Powerful Women." Pictured on the cover were Jessica Lange (37), Sally field (39), Barbra Streisand (44), Goldie Hawn (40), and Jane Fonda (48). The women were photographed huddled together, dressed in matching black turtlenecks, the page cut off just below their shoulders so all that was visible were their smiling faces and feathered hair.

Somewhere far away from Hollywood, in a hospital room in London, Ontario, a nurse wrapped my squirming body in a pink blanket and placed me in my mother's tired yet loving arms. She was only 23 at the time. And even though I had arrived two weeks late and broke her tailbone as I careened into the daylight, she smiled down at me like I was the only thing in the world that mattered. Her first born, her little girl.

⁀

I was a happy child who grew up in the suburbs on the East Side of one of those cities people don't often leave. It was the '90s and a time where, in the world of a young girl, not much existed outside of best friends and boy bands. The anxieties that consumed me were having to read aloud in class, who I would sit next to on the bus, and—the most ever-present concern—when I would grow breasts. Aside from these worries, I was content being myself for most of my early life; I wouldn't have thought to be anyone else. That all changed one day—seemingly overnight—when I started to notice things. Feel things.

There began my search for guidance.

⁀

It started in elementary school. Eleven or twelve. I had taken an interest in the *Soap Opera Digest* magazines that my mother always reached for at the grocery store checkout. At that time, the internet was still relatively unknown to me; it hadn't yet the power to provide answers to the inner workings of a young girl. So, I sought out information wherever I could. For hours I sat cross-legged on my bed flipping through the glossy pages of the magazines as if they held clues to the mysteries I wanted to unlock.

The covers featured actors with big hair, symmetrical faces, and full lips. Headlines proclaimed, "Sizzling Romances" and "Betrayal!" and promised torrid love triangles for those who tuned in. The dynamic was often two women getting into what the writers referred to as "a catfight" over a man—slapping each other in dramatic fashion. Though sometimes the inverse would occur. Two men would compete for the affections of a virginal woman with wanting eyes. She was usually given the choice between a straightlaced man with a Ken Doll face or a misunderstood bad boy who rides a motorcycle.

For as long as I can remember, my mother watched *The Young and The Restless* in the time between arriving home from her office job and dinner. She would walk through the back door and kick off her high-heeled shoes, fold her legs under her on the sofa, and press play on the episode she had set to record on the VCR earlier in the day. I would lay on the carpet pretending to do homework while absorbing the melodrama, wide-eyed, while love scenes set to saxophone music saw characters throw caution to the wind in silk sheet-covered canopy beds. It was during that time I started to daydream about falling into a romantic, all-consuming kind of love.

At school, the boys wore baggy jeans and punched each other in the crotch. During recess, they wiped orange, cheese-flavoured Doritos dust from their shirts and tried to kick balls at us from across the field. For reasons only known to this prepubescent girl, I desperately craved their attention. I hadn't yet experienced what other girls in my class had: being *chosen*.

I had my eye on a tall boy named Lucas who wore basketball jerseys over white T-shirts and walked with a mellow swagger. I sat behind him in class. He had chestnut-coloured hair and freckles in the shape of Saturn on the back of his neck. During one of our first school dances, he asked me to slow dance under the dim lights of the gymnasium. A dream. Even though I was wearing my platform sneakers, he was still much taller than me, and it felt as though I was reaching for the sky when I placed my shaking hands on his shoulders. We swayed and avoided eye contact while "Wonderwall" played, and our entire relationship flashed before my eyes.

"Well, how was the dance?" my mother asked on the car ride home, a tender curiosity in her voice.

"Good," I told her, without elaborating.

I was too busy gazing out the window, noticing the stars in the sky as if for the very first time. In my bedroom, I wrote his name in my diary in large looping cursive with a purple gel pen. Drew small hearts and scribbled, *it's finally happening!* Suddenly, and with ferocious urgency, all my future hopes and dreams rested on a boy who I knew nothing about, except that he probably liked basketball.

For the rest of the school year, I tried with deep concentration to get him to turn his head and look at me in class. He never did, at least not that I noticed, and I had made it my all-consuming hobby to notice. After every failed attempt to get his attention, I wondered what I was doing wrong. I returned to my mother's soap operas, seeking answers.

In 1998, I was balancing on a fraying tightrope of overwhelming emotions and unpredictable moods. That year, to establish more control over my library of resources, I begged my mother to let me sign up for a yearly magazine subscription. She agreed, with a stipulation: "Only one, so choose wisely."

After much deliberation, I picked the American teen magazine *YM*. I collected issues with covers featuring Katie Holmes (19), Aaliyah (19), and my most coveted issue, Sarah Michelle Gellar (20). Pictured dressed in a sheer lavender shirt, she clutched her hands to her chest in a guarded manner, a smile on her face. The headlines read "50 Guy Mysteries" and "Love Lessons: How to Know If He's Right for You."

Buffy the Vampire Slayer was formative for me, as was the show's star. Buffy Summers was the fiercest character I had come across who also had a wardrobe I desired and spoke with the wit and confidence I wished to possess. That was the first time in my life I remember wanting to be someone else. I carefully cut out the magazine cover photo and taped it to my bedroom mirror. For weeks I stared at the image and contemplated how I could look more like her, embody her.

My mother wouldn't let me dye my hair. She said I was too young for that sort of thing. That I should "love the person I am on the inside and the outside." I rolled my eyes at her and walked to the drugstore to purchase a bottle of Sun In, a lemon-scented spray that promised to lighten any shade of hair. The instructions were to apply, then head outside and let the sun work its magic. I doused what smelled more like kitchen cleaner than citrus fruit in my naturally dark strands and starfished on a beach towel in the backyard for an entire afternoon. At the end of the day, I was left with brassy brown hair and a sunburn.

I stood in front of the mirror, eyes darting between my own reflection and Buffy, baffled by what I saw. Despite my best efforts, I appeared almost completely the same. I had already envisioned the splash my new hair would make when I returned to school; there's a scene in the movie *Can't Hardly Wait* when Jennifer Love Hewitt slow-motion walks into a party, the music swells, and suddenly there's a soft breeze in the room—exactly like that. My expectations were sky-high. I decided more extreme measures would need to be taken.

I borrowed a pair of fabric scissors from my mother's sewing kit, returned to the mirror, and snipped at the long pieces of hair that framed my face, trying to create a layered cut with wispy side bangs. At the time it seemed possible that this decision could change my life. But the more I cut, the more frustrated I became with how things were going. I removed the photo from the mirror and folded it into the front pocket of my overalls, along with allowance money I kept in a jar on my dresser. Then I rode my bike to the hair salon to fix the mess I had created.

An hour and twenty dollars later, my new hair looked as though it had been cut in the darkness where my hopes and dreams now resided. On my sombre bike ride home, I could feel the wind on my neck where I couldn't before.

I cried myself to sleep that night while my mother consoled me. Rubbing my back, she looked down at me and promised that it wasn't the end of the world. Everything would be okay.

Alisen Santa Ana

Special Love: Before My Cult Leader Went to Prison

AN EXCERPT FROM A MEMOIR

We stood in long nighties and slippers, camomile tea in our bellies, huddled excitedly in the centre of his mostly pink living room—ice-pink sofas, rose-pink carpet, and blush-pink drapes. I watched the other nine girls' eyes sparkle under the glow of a nearby lamp, their warm cheeks flushed, faces beaming. I beamed, too. At fourteen years old, third generation Kabalarian, I had no doubt we were the luckiest children in the world. Especially since Dorothy—one of the eleven women who lived with Mr. Shearing, our spiritual leader—called our mothers earlier in the day. She informed them that Mr. Shearing requested an impromptu sleepover with the girls from his Young Philosopher's Teenage Class. No lessons. No lectures. A night loaded with fun and games. And Dorothy wasn't wrong. Just an hour after our mothers delivered us to his Vancouver Fairview Slopes mansion, the night was proving to be one of the most rollicking times of my life.

Our beloved leader stood in front of his piano as we eagerly waited for him to start a game of hide-and-seek. He toyed with us; briefly closed his eyes, then opened them. Kept us hanging on. Until finally he closed his eyes for several seconds and shouted, "One, ..." at which point, our young gaggle split apart, wild legs and flailing arms, everyone running in different directions. Two girls charged across the living room and hid behind a loveseat; another girl galloped toward the tea table and tucked herself underneath. I fled fast behind several girls into the kitchen, through sweet and nutty smells of sugar, butter, and stovetop popcorn. We shuffled past several women of the house who were preparing delicious treats for us to relish later. They smiled and winked as we raced through the kitchen into a hallway. A couple of girls scrambled to hide inside a main floor bedroom.

"… five, … six, … seven, …" Mr. Shearing continued to count as I rushed behind Jhuli, an older girl, down the hall. We turned right at a corner and hurried down another short hallway. Metres away, I saw that the door to our leader's den was closed. I had a quick impulse to enter, to hide inside, but the den was a forbidden place without Mr. Shearing's permission. It was where he conducted private meetings, often spiritual emergencies with his Instrument, Ronelda, who lived in his mansion. He channeled evil dead minds from the Mental Realm through her highly sensitive body whenever Kabalarians allowed themselves to become possessed.

I shadowed Jhuli to the stairs that led to the basement as our leader counted higher. We raced fiercely down the steps, her golden hair dancing over her shoulders. Once downstairs, Jhuli veered to the left and spun around in a whirling frenzy near the bookshelves, until she vanished behind a loveseat. I kept running straight ahead and then bolted into a dark pantry. Panting and exhilarated I struggled to catch my breath, then tried to stay as still as possible.

Mr. Shearing counted higher and higher, until he yelled, "… forty-nine! … fifty! Ready or not, here I come!" Nervously, I crouched in a corner of the musty room, growing colder in my nightie. I listened. One by one, evident from sudden high-pitched squeals and bursts of laughter, Mr. Shearing triumphantly found the girls hiding upstairs. I waited. Minutes later, I heard him storming down the steps, and soon his slippers shuffled over the basement floor. *Was he headed to the pantry?* I heard him holler, "Gotcha!" as he found Jhuli, her giggles shrill and broken before the basement transformed to quiet. All I could hear were the upstairs sounds of kernels popping and muffled chatter. *Was Mr. Shearing tiptoeing toward me, getting closer to the downstairs pantry?* I waited and my heart pounded. *Was it a trick?* But then I heard Jhuli abruptly giggle before she raced up the stairs. The sounds of Mr. Shearing's footsteps grew closer and closer. *Here he comes!* I held my breath.

Suddenly, tall and majestic, he appeared inside the pantry. Mindful of the lower ceiling, he moved carefully toward me, as he playfully teased, "Well, well, well, what have we here." He grabbed the sides of my waist, simultaneously saying, "Gotcha." I swelled with laughter and relief. He pulled me closer toward him, towering as he wrapped his arms around me in a tight embrace. His breath smelled sour. It usually did. *How awful that I noticed!* He continued holding me, pressing me firmly into his body, making me warmer—sweaty. My body flooded with strange feelings, making me dizzy. His hugs were always close. They needed to be. He told us that he was transferring The Power—positive vibrations of the universe—directly through his solar plexus to ours. But this embrace was tighter than usual. Too tight. So tight, that I felt like I couldn't breathe properly. His long nose grazed the side of my face. My stomach was like a stew of winged insects fluttering around. Lightly, like a wet feather, he kissed my neck, murmuring undetectable words before he kissed it again and again. He had only ever kissed me on my cheek before. His mouth tickled, but I didn't dare move and disrupt The Power.

"Special love, little one," he whispered into my ear. His syllables seemed to ignite a sensation in me that I was floating out of my body, hovering above us, watching the silhouette of our embrace. Something hard pushed into my stomach, something from below Mr. Shearing's waist. The word *penis* entered my mind. *No! How could I let myself think something so disgusting? So vile!* Mr. Shearing regularly warned us that a sexual thought was an open door to being possessed. I was vigilant—an evil dead mind was right there in the pantry, trying to enter my body, to control my thoughts, to pretend Mr. Shearing's spiritual hug was something else. *Should I confess my sexual thought immediately?* Instead, I managed to fall into Mr. Shearing's soothing magical voice, tenderly saying, "Little one, don't ever forget how much I love you. You are deeply loved. Special love, little one. Special love."

He released me from his hold and summoned me to follow him. My limbs quavered. I wobbled behind him out of the pantry. As we walked across the basement he started humming, "On the Sunny Side of the Street," a tune Kabalarians sang together during Musical Evenings– entertaining nights when Mr. Shearing hypnotized members to do embarrassing things.

Lightheaded, I walked up the steps behind him. At the top of the stairs, Dorothy and a girl rushed by, both carrying bowls of popcorn. We followed them into the living room. The other girls were drinking camomile tea, chatting, but turned silent when Mr. Shearing entered. Still feeling lightheaded, I walked to the tea-table and poured myself a cup of tea. It wasn't very warm. I drank it quickly, returned my cup to the table, and slowly walked back toward the girls.

With a giant grin, Mr. Shearing announced jovially, "It's showtime!" He turned on the TV and picked up a remote control. Bowls of popcorn and napkins were passed around. The girls placed their empty tea cups on the tea-table. Dorothy collected and returned the dirty cups to the kitchen. Shortly after, she appeared for a quick goodbye and retired to her bedroom.

Mr. Shearing sat in his chair and beckoned us to move closer, to sit near him. Several girls scurried and sat on the floor at the sides of his chair, while a few older girls plunked down directly in front of him. I sat on the carpet furthest away from our leader. I watched him bend forward to place his arms around Jhuli's chest. He helped her wiggle closer until she sat leaning comfortably against his knees. As popcorn bowls were passed around, mouths were stuffed; the living room filled with noisy chewing. I took a few bites of popcorn. *Too salty. Too buttery.*

I watched Mr. Shearing caress Jhuli's hair. While his wife Loro bustled into the living room carrying two plates of cookies, he moved his hands to massage Jhuli's shoulders.

Loro passed me a plate, then stepped closer toward Mr. Shearing. She smiled warmly and passed the other plate of cookies to Jhuli. Affectionately, she wagged her finger and chirped, "Now, you girls be good. Tell Mr. Shearing anything that ails you. He is your only true friend." Mr. Shearing gave his wife a wink, and we all waved her goodbye. Loro disappeared up the spiral stairwell that led to the upstairs bedrooms— another place we were forbidden from entering.

I wasn't feeling hungry but grabbed a cookie and passed the plate to a girl sitting beside me. I took a small bite. It tasted bitter, like baking soda. The batter wasn't properly mixed through. Discreetly, I tucked it inside my napkin and when no one was watching, stored it behind my back. It wasn't very late, but I started to feel drowsy. Some of the girls looked sleepy as Mr. Shearing started the movie. A Walt Disney production. A film I had already seen several times before about twins—*The Parent Trap*—a story about trickery and mistaken identity.

Carrie Walker
I Am a Rat

When I first opened the hatch to the crawlspace and looked in, the traps sat in the shadows. I had secured them with string and a rock so that the rats couldn't drag the traps into an unreachable corner then die and rot. The strings were taut. Was there something there? A body? I pointed my phone towards the void and a picture appeared on the screen clearer than what I could see with my naked eyes. I texted my husband, "Two."

"Wow, well done, you are a killer!" he texted back.

Don't I know it, I thought to myself.

I went to the garage and fetched a paper bag, gloves and a respirator. Last time, I had left them too long. Traps set, I'd failed to check on them. I'd gone out of town, and when I came home the house smelled off. There had been only one body that time, a dried brown puddle beneath it. But these two were fresh. Aside from their crushed necks, they looked like they were still alive. Their black eyes were bright. I wondered if, after I pulled the trap from their necks, they might reanimate and scurry away, or bite me. The latter would be deserved. After all, it wasn't their fault they'd found entrance to the crawlspace. That was my negligence. And yet, having made their way there, I had to hunt and trap them.

⁀

I like rats. They're not my favorite animal, though I think they could be if they were held in higher regard by our society. They are proximate, which means they have more going for them than most other wild creatures. How can I love a tiger having never been near one? And knowing that it is foolhardy to approach a tiger, I could only ever love one from afar. It is said that proximity breeds familiarity, and with familiarity comes fondness—so long as this familiarity reveals desirable traits. If it does not, then we default to the more commonly expressed adage, and we breed contempt.

What am I to despise in a rat? Of all the wild creatures I have known, the rat is the boldest. Only a rat has sprung from a cardboard box that I have nudged with an extended foot, leaping across the corridor in front of me in the light of day. Only a rat has dragged a chicken bone to nibble on under the workbench in the garage. Only a rat has scurried back and forth beneath the low wooden boardwalk by the side door while the dog pounces at its edges, enthralled and enraged. Rats have risked everything to lick peanut butter from my traps, and they have triumphed. Sometimes.

When I was a teenager, I had a rat as a pet. It was my first pet, in that it was mine alone, unlike the cats and the dog that were shared by the whole family. My rat lived in a cage meant to house fairer rodents: gerbils, hamsters, guinea pigs. He was white with a black head and a black cross-shaped mark on his back. I named him Skypilot, but my brother quickly renamed him T.R.—The Rat. It was a better name. T.R. was social, to a degree. He didn't mind being held. He lived on a diet of cat kibble.

One day, I entered my bedroom and found one of the cats in his cage. She had managed to squirm in through the small hatch at the top. T.R. stood nonplussed in the corner. The cat had eaten all of his food. Another time, I went on a trip leaving my stepmother in charge of him. During my absence, he escaped and crawled up the back of my desk into one of the drawers, where he consumed most of the contents of a tube of black printing ink. A few weeks later, he developed a tumor, and died.

I had learned in elementary school that, according to the Chinese zodiac, I was born in the Year of the Rat. To have secured one of only twelve spots of the zodiac demonstrates the strength of the image of the rat. Some characteristics of those of us born in the Year of the Rat, are as follows: ambitious, hard-working, charming, talkative, adaptive, and clever; we are smart, but we lack courage.

Although I hold no store in zodiacs, Western or Chinese—no matter how much I may relate to their proposed attributes—it is possible that my fondness for rats is a result of implicit egotism. This theory suggests that humans gravitate towards things that resemble themselves. Implicit egotism isn't considered unhealthy. It is good to love oneself, at least a little. Then again, perhaps it is low self-esteem that allows me to align myself with a creature so maligned.

⌒

My current pet is a dog. A rat terrier. She and her kin were bred to kill rats. Why was I attracted to this breed? I say I am fond of rats, even as I describe the steps I have taken to destroy them. I procured a beast bred for this exact purpose, and yet, my rat terrier is useless. She has killed no rats. She's never hurt anything bigger than a grasshopper. Her single close encounter with a rodent, in this case, a squirrel—an encounter so close that she was faced with a choice, to kill or not to kill—had her running back to me with her tail between her legs. She seemed to be terrified when faced with the ultimate decision, will I destroy this creature? Having killed rodents myself, I wonder, how can I avoid this? That afternoon, I didn't reset the traps.

That night, there was a scratching sound in the wall behind the bed. The dog leapt to the floor. She nosed the outlet, and growled, then ran to the closet. *Is it in here?* Another scratch and a scurry. She barked at the wall, furious, then frustrated. So frustrated, she left the room just as she does each time she fails to catch a wayward fly buzzing in the night.

⌒

When I released the corpses of the two rats from the pair of traps, their two necks pinned and crushed, I wondered, how long had they lain there dead? And, what was the sequence of events that led them there? Did they, in the far reaches of the crawlspace, catch a scent, look at each other, and declare, "peanut butter!" prompting a quick race to the spot near the hatch where the traps were laid? Did they then each take station at their own yellow peanut-buttered plastic pad, thus releasing the sprung steel that broke their necks? Did each trap snap at the same time, or did one rat approach first, and the second shortly after? Did the second one know that its kin had left the low plastic-lined habitat of the crawlspace, if not bodily, then in spirit? Did it know and hesitate? Did it know, but tell itself, "I will do better, I will secure the peanut butter, trip the trap, and live?"

In the morning, I will scour the perimeter of the house and search for entry points. I will bend down low, creep along, and imagine, how can I gain access to the warm, dry, dark space below? My whiskers whiff at the screened vent in the concrete foundation. Wouldn't that be a nice place to nest? No way in. Circle round. Here by the hatch, I feel the warm air again. Is there a way? I stand on my hind legs, and sniff. What's this? Yes, here, where the plaster has fallen away from the frame, there is a hole. Can I wriggle through? Easily. I am in! I scamper about in my new home: safe, warm and dry. I ignore the scent of stale peanut butter and death.

Codi Darnell

Waking Up

AN EXCERPT FROM THE MEMOIR "AFTER I FELL"

It was dark. The deep black of a windowless room with the lights out and door closed. I was always afraid of the dark. Even as a teenager, I had a lamp at the end of my bed that stayed on as I slept. But the darkness here was calm and still. It was the type of rare and peaceful solitude that makes a mother wonder *why* and creates the dilemma of having to choose between enjoying the calm or seeking out the reason for it—usually a toddler emptying a box of something into a toilet.

I'm good here, I thought. I'm sure everything is fine.

The hum of lights blended with whispered conversations in a chorus of white noise that penetrated the silence.

Just ignore it. It's nothing.

I felt someone take my hand as Ian's voice broke through the din. "Codi?"

There was an edge to my husband's quiet voice that told me he had already found whatever trouble awaited me, and the tranquility of the dark dissipated into the fear I was accustomed to. I followed his voice across the void and thought: you need to open your eyes.

My eyelids were heavy and slow to rise. Through the lines of my own eyelashes, I saw him looking down at me.

"Hi," I said in barely a whisper. My tongue felt thick inside my mouth and my throat was raw. His smile was a mix of relief and sadness. His shoulders relaxed as I met his gaze, but the exhaustion was evident in the shadows around his eyes and in the way his jaw was set.

As light flooded in, worry was replaced with confusion.

Where am I? Why am I so tired?

An IV pole stood beside me with a bag of clear fluid on its hook. I followed the tubing that hung from the bag until it disappeared beneath the blankets that lay rough against my skin. I pulled my arm out and saw the tubing give way to a needle implanted firmly in the back of my hand and remembered two male nurses struggling to get it in place, apologizing profusely after every attempt.

"Don't worry," I'd said. "I'm used to it. Before my last c-section it took them seven tries to get it in. Besides, I have bigger problems than a few extra needle pokes right now."

They smiled with me and relaxed. "Thanks for understanding."

I didn't remember them ever getting the needle in place, but there it was.

But why?

I blinked and looked up to the ceiling where the bright fluorescent light illuminated my memory and the events of the last 24 hours unraveled like a film strip on fast-forward.

༄

It happened so fast. We only wanted to get outside for a few minutes before dinner to tour the progress of our house addition, after being stuck inside all day, nursing colds and hiding from the rain.

The five of us crossed the backyard. Water droplets still clung to each blade of grass and pine needle, the air laden with the strong scent of both. My eighteen-month-old daughter squirmed in my arms, and I called to Ian, "Can you take her please?"

He turned back towards me and reached his arms out. "Come here, Evi Girl. Come see Daddy."

"Nooo," she whined, and turned into me. I peeled her off me and pushed her towards him, following the two of them up the plywood ramp where the boys stood waiting for us.

I lagged behind, watching the boys' blond heads swivel back and forth as they wandered through the maze of exposed 2x4s.

"Is this a bedroom, Mommy?"

"Where is the kitchen?"

"Is the digger coming back?

I smiled. To a four- and six-year-old, this was like Bob the Builder came to life in their own backyard.

Evi had settled in with Ian, and I took in the familiar image of my husband with one of our children in his arms. Then, everything turned sideways.

All it took was one misstep and I was flat on my back, ten feet below where I stood just moments before.

I didn't even have time to scream.

For a moment I just lay there, staring back up through the opening— a rectangular cutout on the floor where a staircase would eventually be built. All I could see was sky and the branches of the tallest trees in our backyard, half of them still naked and the other half starting to bud at the tail end of an unseasonably warm winter. We hadn't yet seen our yard in the spring.

I watched the wind manipulate the clouds around the sky like a toddler pushes unwanted food around a plate, until Ian stepped into view with Evi still in his arms. I heard the boys scream, "Mommy!" and Ian disappeared again, ushering them back to the house.

I yelled up to them, "Mommy is okay. Don't worry. Mommy is okay."

Their footsteps disappeared and I repeated softly to myself, "Mommy is okay."

There was no blood or twisted limbs, but a belt of fiery pain stretched around my ribcage like an unwelcome embrace. Everything below it lay motionless against the cold, compacted dirt.

I knew I couldn't move my legs. The word "paralyzed" flashed into my mind but was quickly replaced by an image of my three kids, and I thought to myself: it's just your legs. You can still be a mom. It's just your legs.

The next several hours were full of scans, physical exams, and doctors saying very little beyond, "We'll know more after surgery." Through it all, I held tightly to my original sentiment: it's just your legs. But with every evasive answer, I let myself hope, just a little, that it wouldn't be my legs at all.

～

Now, with the surgery finished and Ian standing over me, I needed to know.

"How did it go?"

"Everything went well."

"But ... what did they say?"

He opened his mouth, but nothing came out. He dropped his eyes to our intertwined hands. "Um. The doctor said he talked to you."

I shook my head. If he did, I didn't remember.

Ian squeezed my hand tighter and took a deep breath. "You aren't going to be able to walk again."

It was the confirmation I thought I was prepared for. But as the tears I swallowed over the previous 24 hours burst violently free from their holding tanks, I realized I wasn't prepared at all.

Ian bent over and rested his forehead on mine. The tears poured from the corners of my eyes and streamed into my ears and down the back of my neck, soaking both my hair and the pillow behind me. I gasped for air.

"You need to breathe, Codi." Ian pulled back, wiped my eyes and ran his hand over my head. "You need to breathe."

Everything else in the room disappeared. All I saw, felt, and heard was the two of us. He held my hands in his. He kissed my forehead and put his mouth to my ear. His breathing was steady as he whispered, "I know. Shhhh. I know."

I wanted to pull him closer, to make room on the tiny bed and curl myself into his body–lay my head on his chest. I molded my hand around the back of his neck, pressing my fingertips into his flesh, anchoring myself to him. To us.

I had no words, just an image in my mind of me and the kids running barefoot in the backyard. It's just your legs streamed into my thoughts but instead of the comfort it brought hours before, it now felt mocking.

It was my legs. My legs. How could I live my life without my legs?

I closed my eyes tightly, as if I might be able to shut out the barefoot images. But the reel played over again and again until my weeping eyes grew heavy and my hand slowly released from around Ian's neck.

I fell asleep grateful, for once, for the darkness.

Danielle Christopher

Elvis and Ice Cream

The sun wakes me up. It is a perfect summer day with nothing planned. The other side of the bed is empty. Michael is at work. I hear the girls coming down the hall.

"Good morning." The kids pile onto the bed. After some giggles and cuddles, I ask who is hungry. We go downstairs in our pajamas. It is a summer break perk to not have to get dressed right away. I pour the cereal. As I grasp the fridge handle to put the milk away, my eyes freeze on the calendar on the door.

It is August 15.

I put the milk back in the fridge door and close it. I breathe and do a body check. I am happy and calm. This is new to me.

It is the thirty-seventh anniversary of the worst day of my life. It was the last time I saw my mom alive. She lost her battle with breast cancer that night. I remember the entire day as a repeat episode on TV. We would place flowers at her grave. As an adult, I would distract myself with work, spend the day shopping or watching movies. When I became a parent, I had my kids to keep me busy. I knew she would have been an amazing grandma and spoiled the kids like crazy.

I ached for my mom to lean on, to hear her mom advice. I wanted to know how I was as a baby. I couldn't hear my mother's voice anymore. I fed my baby her bottles while sitting in the food court spying on grandparents spoiling their grandchildren and the pain pierced hard. When I hadn't had a break for a long time, I would hear other moms complaining when their moms couldn't babysit, and swallowed my bitter and angry responses.

I began writing about how life really was without my mom after my kids were born. The venting feels cathartic, especially in the twilight with a sleeping baby in one hand, and my smartphone in the other. I love writing blog posts in between diaper changes and naps. I share when I wanted my mommy as a mom myself. I connect with other moms who miss their own mothers. We rant about the stages of grief. It doesn't matter if a mom is still alive or estranged; the pain of abandonment is real and valid to us all.

"*Mom!*" My thoughts are interrupted by my oldest beauty yelling from the kitchen table.

I jump out of my thoughts and answer, "What?" My heart starts beating again. The feeling of my hands and legs returns.

She is watching me with a look of curiosity in her smile. "Close the fridge. You are wasting energy, remember?"

Smiling, I close the door. Screw it. I want to make today better than ever. I ask my girls to get ready for a day of fun. I do not want to spend the day sad like before. My mind is filled with going to the water park, stopping at the toy store and having ice cream for dinner in the backyard. I hope it is a day my girls will remember and can re-write this anniversary for us. I can be the mom my girls need me to be. I know my mom was that for me for as long as she was able.

For the first time since August 15, 1984, I am not consumed with sadness on the anniversary. It occurs to me she has always been here. All this time I worried about being a mom when the whole time I already had the best mom to model myself after. She wasn't the best cook, me neither. She wasn't the best homemaker; me too. I let go of cleaning the house before playdates. That is a waste of energy. My mom is always there for me, even in death. She is there in my parenting and in unconditional love; I still feel her.

I pack the kids' backpacks with snacks, water bottles, changes of clothes and favourite toys. I select a playlist and Elvis Presley blasts through the speakers. I remember Mom playing his tunes loud either at home or in the car. I spy the girls in the backseat bouncing to the familiar music. I look forward to a celebratory day with them. Smiling, I start to sing along. Today will be a new memory, a good one.

We pull up to the toy store first in case there are toys we can get to play at the park. The girls squeal out their delight. Strolling through the aisles, the beginning to "A Little Less Conversation" comes on. I begin to tap my leg. The girls are looking at me strangely. I shake my hips in an Elvis style. They laugh. I must look like a dork, and I do not care. They explore the store as I hum along to Elvis. It occurs to me she passed away close to Elvis's death date. He died on August 16. She was that big of a fan. Mom may have sent the tune to show she is here. I think she would approve of ice cream for dinner, too.

Growing up, I hated it because it separated me from the other kids. I would be given another task while my classmates made a Mother's Day gift as if I didn't know what they were doing. I felt like a freak at the circus. Friends made comments about how they don't want their moms to die, or it must suck. Yes, it sucked. It still sucks.

I always think about what Mom would think or say about everything going on. I didn't want to have kids. My husband did. Given that I had endometriosis, which meant I couldn't conceive easily naturally, I was okay with that. My two girls proved that the doctor is not always right.

I became what is now known as a helicopter parent. I understand too well the pain to want your mom. I knew every moment, every giggle, breath, and milestone. I began to see things differently: I was grateful to not have to drag my weary body, and husband, to loud family dinners. We were the village for her. Being at home on the couch in pajamas became the new date night.

Days before we were expecting our bonus baby to arrive, my maternal grandma passed away in her sleep at the care home. It dawned on me that I would never have that experience with my mom, see her grow old, or put her in a home. I will always and forever see my mom as 38 years old.

I will always have pity days of "could have," "should have," and "would have," but it has altered my world today. My body is not twisted in depression. If I had that other life, one with her in it, I wonder if I would have met my children. I might not have my stories, but I am making memories with my own daughters by being here to experience their childhood stories.

The girls find me in the stuffies aisle. Their arms are filled with packages of toys and figurines. I turn us around toward the cashier. I swipe my debit card and they fight on who can carry the bag. Give it to the kids to bring me back to reality. I relieve the bag from their tug-of-war and place it in the trunk. Once we are buckled back up in the car, I put music on.

Two hours later, after wearing ourselves out running around the water park, we are in the backyard with large bowls filled with three kinds of ice cream and chocolate sauce. There is a slight breeze in the air which makes it a perfect temperature.

"Mom, can we do this again?" I see their smiling faces. I catch myself smiling when I nod in agreement. I wipe the melting ice cream dribbles from my face with a napkin. I look forward to doing this again with them.

I will always miss my mom. I now know that she will always be here. The best way to honour her is by being the mom she was to me. And that feels like medicine to my healing heart. I didn't need a parenting book to rely on, I just have the sparkle in my kids' eyes when we hug. Being motherless does suck and that is okay to say. Motherless may be what got me here now, but it doesn't define who I am today.

The Christmas Teacup

A PERSONAL ESSAY

Christmas unofficially started on our street every November 1st when Mr. Erlendson turned on his Christmas lights. This was long before the big box stores brought Halloween decor out in July or, by mid-October, displayed Christmas decorations next to Halloween costumes on the store shelf. Back then no one put Christmas trees up in November. Lights and holiday gatherings were saved for December. The Christmas season officially started in our house when my mom started making shortbread.

See, both my parents had birthdays in December, the 7th and 22nd. It was always important to make sure we didn't mix the two, so each got their special day. We usually ate birthday cake while putting up the Christmas tree for Dad and tried not to wrap Mom's presents in Christmas paper.

Our house was decorated from top to bottom. No Griswold lights, but the inside was filled with all these special pieces. Snow globes and banisters wrapped in garland with red velvet bows. A tree that twinkled with rainbow lights, filled with handmade ornaments. Every little shelf had a Christmas caroller or ceramic Santa. Nothing fancy or catalogue-worthy, but what did gain us glory on Ocean Cliff Drive was Mom's Christmas baking.

One special item. Her shortbread.

Everyone in town knew about Doris Bell's shortbread. Kinda famous, it was; talked about and salivated over throughout the year.

Was Christmas really about being on Santa's list? No. Not in our town. You wanted to be on Doris's list. Because this meant you would possess a tin of her shortbread in December.

Okay, okay, shortbread. I get it. We've all tasted it. We've all tasted at least a dozen different kinds of shortbread.

But as my dad always said, "No, no. This is different. You have never had this."

Technically, it's traditional Scottish shortbread—the only piece of Scottish heritage my family attaches itself to. You can leave the haggis and Robbie Burns celebration to the rest of the family.

The recipe isn't a secret. But whether you can get it right is another thing. It's a 120-year-old family recipe from my paternal great-grandmother, passed down the line. When my mom joined the family she would watch Nana Bell roll out her shortbread every Christmas season. As the years went on, Nana's arthritis made it too difficult for her to knead the dough, so Mom carried on the tradition.

The recipe: salted butter, flour, and berry sugar. Berry sugar is a little finer than regular white sugar. But please don't ask if it's icing sugar; it's not. No cake flour, brown sugar, vanilla, or salt. It is not a sugar cookie cut into pretty shapes and dipped in chocolate. It is not whipped, and there are no little maraschino cherries on top. No mixers or any fancy kitchen tools, just a Royal Doulton teacup. This is the not-so-secret ingredient; the flour and sugar are measured by a teacup. The joke being you could just pour the contents of the teacup into a measuring cup so you would know the exact measurements.

While Dad would roll his eyes and shake his head, Mom would graciously say, "No, you need the teacup. The magic's in the cup." She would then roll out the dough, cut it into almost-squares, and then poke two fork prongs into the top.

Mom made shortbread for everyone: her co-workers, Dad's co-workers, our teachers, our hairdresser, the tellers at the bank, and all our friends. Every party or holiday open house, Mom brought shortbread.

Everyone always took two because one was usually already in their mouth while they slid a second off the plate.

When I was in my early twenties, we would be out late for Christmas parties and I would come home to what looked like a shortbread factory. Dough on the counter, batches cooling, and Mom counting out cookies as she put them into her dollar-store tins.

Mom was a night owl and she never went to bed if we weren't home. Ever. She always waited up. So in December she would bake and the rest of the year we came home to her watching Food Network baking competitions. But in December, no late night drive-thru was needed to cut through the booze—just home for two Advil washed down with a few cookies. Best hangover cure. I promise.

My favourite, though, was when we would find blocks of butter on the front steps with a note: *Doris, I bought butter, please make me your shortbread.* I believe the butter record still stands at seventy pounds from Christmas 2002. If I do the math, one pound of butter makes about sixty cookies. Forty years of baking equals over 100 thousand cookies.

I have yet to make a batch of shortbread, but I know my cookie destiny. I also know Mom brought the Christmas magic. She was the magic-maker. I know this now as a mother. I also know I have a few thousand cups to fill.

Jennifer J. Allen

Special Shopping

My mother spent the summer locked in her bedroom after Rob left her for an older woman. On weekends, Mom visited nightclubs with her girlfriends and flirted with other men, hoping Rob would find out and come running back. But he was gone for good and so was his money, which meant we had to go back on welfare.

"Find something nice," Mom said. I lifted Marc, my baby brother, into the Zellers cart and gave him an Arrowroot cookie. "But no black."

"What's wrong with black?"

"You always dress like you're going to a funeral. It's depressing."

Stephanie, my little sister, climbed up the front of the cart and bounced. "I like pink."

"That's because it looks good on you, baby girl," said Mom. "You're a summer."

I waited for Stephanie to settle down so we could start the game. Our goal was to fill the cart with all the back-to-school clothing we could ever wish for, then walk away, leaving everything behind. The game had no time limit and no level of difficulty. It also had no prizes. My mother called it "Special Shopping" though I didn't understand what was so special about it.

Nearby, school supplies sat untouched on shelves. Soon, kids would pick through the scented markers, sparkly pencils, and star-shaped erasers in matching plastic cases. Our government cheque wasn't due for weeks. By then all the good supplies would be gone. Just once, I wanted the first choice. I wanted to shop for real.

"I don't get it," I said.

"Get what?" my mother asked.

"This game. It makes no sense."

Mom's eyes welled and she threw her hands up. "I'm trying, Jennifer. I really am. But your attitude isn't helping."

"Sorry," I mumbled.

"I could just cry." But she already was. And I was worried she'd make an even bigger scene or run out the front door.

"Sorry," I said. "I'm sorry. *I really am.*"

Mom dabbed her eyes with a tissue, smoothed out her hair, then led us deeper into the store.

I pushed my siblings to the children's department filled with clothing in loud colours and even louder prints. Stephanie hopped off the cart and rummaged through the bold stripes, zigzags, and polka dots. She tossed a T-shirt into the cart then took off for more.

Mom turned to me, eyeing my sweatshirt, stretch pants, and runners with no laces. "You really need new clothes."

"I know I do."

"You'd also make friends if you dressed better."

"I don't need friends." I had a makeshift bedroom in the basement/laundry room, a black-and-white TV with twelve channels, and my cat for a companion. The heavy metal posters on my wall were the windows to my world. I had it made.

"What you need," said Mom, pulling a purple shirt off the rack, "are jewel tones. They'd look good with your dark hair and light eyes."

She handed me the shirt, which, admittedly, was nice. And purple wasn't too far from black. I ran my fingers along the collar and down a sleeve. The colour was identical to the birthstone on my ring finger. For the first time, I wondered how to put together a proper outfit.

"You'll need pants," said Mom.

I nodded. Hangers clattered and scraped the clothing bar as she flipped through the merchandise, looking for just the right pair.

"Here." She handed me black pants with purple flowers.

"Black?"

"At least they have colour."

I held out the shirt and pants. They looked like something a model in a flyer would wear. I imagined starting Grade 7 in this outfit. Maybe a boy would think I was cute and the popular girls would become my friends, just like they did with Kim Taylor when she got a perm. Everyone wanted to be her partner and play with her at lunch and recess.

Stephanie added more to her small but growing wardrobe. I set my things on top.

"You'll need more than that," said my mother. "Pick out anything you like. This is how rich people shop."

Together we created three more outfits. Mom taught me how to style and accessorize them with scarves, belts, and earrings. After, we picked out a pair of black dress shoes that went with everything.

The "Special Shopping" game finally made sense. My mother had found a way for us to have fun together while I learned something along the way.

She took a step back and considered our haul. "I think that's it."

"Good. Let's go. I'm starving." It was almost lunchtime. But when I went to pull Marc out of his seat, Mom stopped me.

"Why? We're done."

Stephanie climbed on to the front of the cart and Mom pushed my siblings toward the linens.

I ran to keep up. "You said we'd walk away."

Mom tucked us into a back corner amongst the shower curtains and towels. Her tone turned serious. "Girls, I need you to listen closely. Remember when I said this was just for fun?"

We nodded.

"This can all be ours if you stay quiet and follow my lead."

Then, like a magician pulling silk scarves from a magic hat, my mother reached deep into her purse and retrieved an empty shopping bag, followed by another, and then another. Then she held one out to me, but I hesitated. "Take it," she said.

I tried to speak. I wanted to ask her what she thought she was doing. And ask if she was serious. But Mom kept shaking that empty Zellers bag in my face. I grabbed it.

"You," she instructed, "will help me fill these as quickly as possible. And you," she said to my sister, "will stand at the end of the aisle and cough if you see someone. If anyone comes, stop what you're doing and act like you're looking for something. Do you understand?"

I stared at her. I knew stealing was wrong—the fear rushing through my body wouldn't let me forget—but in that moment, I was up against something far worse than the law.

If I said no, my mother would cry again or stop talking to me, just as she'd done before. Or worse, she'd go back to her room for God knows how long and I'd continue to care for my brother and sister. We needed our mother.

I gave Marc another cookie to keep him quiet, then shook the first bag open. I shoveled as much as I could into it before reaching for another. Zellers, I thought, where the lowest price is the law, yet we still couldn't afford to shop here. I wanted out of the store.

With the bags full, Mom pulled one last thing out of her purse. "Here," she said. "Pretend like you're reading this."

"A Safeway receipt?"

"It's nice and long," she said. "Act like you're double-checking the cashier's work when we leave."

We made our way to the exit where Mom greeted everyone with a smile and a "Hello!" I kept my head down and my eyes on the paper, trying not to speed walk out the front door.

"Stop it. You look suspicious," said my mother from the corner of her mouth.

Stephanie held the door open and Mom sauntered through with her sundress bouncing in the summer breeze. I followed behind, resisting the urge to push past her.

Jennifer Chrumka

Prairie Ghosts

"He told me he wanted to die. He stood in the living room, looked me straight in the eye and yelled: *I just want to die.*" My mom shares this with me over the phone without meaning to. It slips out, partly because I'm a journalist and I know how to ask questions and because she's tired. She's so exhausted I don't recognize her voice. It sounds thick and heavy, weighted by a weariness that comes from stress. I can tell she hasn't had the time to really consider the words because after she says them, she sighs like she's exasperated, like the words have been rebuffed by frustration.

We're talking over the phone, a province away, about my dad. Since his diagnosis of dementia, most of our conversations are about him. We've watched him slowly transform into a version of himself that's often hard to recognize. Surrendering to his reality means letting go of the father I grew up with while he is physically right in front of me.

My mom has been trying to get my dad to walk with his cane because he's been falling more often. So far, only on their plush brown carpet and usually in the bedroom they've shared for nearly sixty years. After reminding him, and warning him, then scolding him that if he falls, he could really hurt himself, she said, "If you don't do it for yourself Paul, do it for my sake, for the kids' sake." And that's when he snapped. As she reluctantly shares that he wants to die, I feel like I've lost my breath. It's not how I want my dad to go—rapt in this kind of angst—and it's not what I want my mom to witness.

Alzheimer's disease snuck up on my family because my dad kept it hidden in circular stories and clever humour. I questioned why he kept rehashing memories from the past, but decided it was the normal process of aging, that since retiring from a long career, he finally had the time to look back on life and wasn't that a beautiful thing. And I watched as his life became more insular—he stopped reading books, then magazines, and finally newspapers. He stopped having friends over for loud and lavish dinner parties. These days, when friends or extended family do come to the house, he stays sitting in his armchair in the living room no longer offering to serve a drink or shake their hand. It became undeniable that something was wrong when he started crying. Growing up I had only seen my dad cry once—at his brother's funeral—now it's all the time. He tears up when listening to music, when he talks about his life on the farm, anytime he hears a touching story.

During one of my most recent visits home, we took a drive through the prairies south of Calgary. "Just for the sake of it," my mom suggested. It's what we used to do as kids, piling into our old Buick that comfortably sat the six of us and the family dog. In the back seat we'd speak in code as my parents listened to folk music from the '70s and looked out over golden grasslands. This time I was in the driver's seat, and it was my dad speaking in code. He was wearing his aviator sunglasses, the same style as always, and a medic alert necklace that flashed red and green like a beacon. My mom was sitting silently in the backseat with the window rolled down a crack so she could enjoy a bit of peace while my dad wove in and out of memories of growing up doing hard physical labour at such a young age.

⤙

It was a classically beautiful prairie day—late November with a Chinook arch off to the west that carried warm air in on the wind. Driving through the low-slung foothills, through stands of white birch and aspen groves, and past a buffalo ranch, we saw a sign for the Okotoks Erratic, also known as Big Rock, and my mom (who rarely ever swears) said from the backseat: "Holy shit. We have to stop."

A vague memory came to me of a giant rock in a prairie-flat field that we used to scramble up as kids. "What big rock?" my dad asked. "I don't remember a big rock."

It sounded so ludicrous, but we were close, so I kept driving. "You'll see, Dad," I said. It will come back to you, I hoped.

Ohkotok means "rock" in the language of the Blackfoot people. The Okotoks Erratic is a large angular quartzite boulder split in two that weighs about sixteen thousand tonnes and stands about nine meters high. It's said to have been slowly carried on the back of a glacier 18,000 years ago all the way from Mount Edith Cavell in Jasper.

I hadn't thought about the landmark in decades, but now it came back to me—memories of my brother and I sneaking through the smooth, dark inner alleys of the split rock, exploring crevices, and climbing what we could. "Be careful, goddammit be careful!" my dad yelled to us as we laughed and pretended to fall. I don't ever remember making it to the top, but I do remember standing from a height tall enough to look down upon my father. The rush of it all, standing above this giant, so physically strong and steady in my small world.

Even from above, I worshipped him.

⌒

On this late fall day many years later, I took the turn onto Highway 7 heading west toward the site and after a few minutes, it came into view for all of us at the same time. My mom was the first to react by laughing from the backseat. It looked awkwardly out of place—two boulders, resting toward each other as if in whispered conversation. I was about to state the obvious, that in my memory it was so much bigger, when my dad slammed his pale fist down on his knee and said, "God Almighty, I remember this!" I turned around to see my mom smiling then shrugged and said, "Might as well check it out."

My dad dutifully grabbed his cane and started teetering down the path of crushed gravel toward the site while my mom and I hung back as if watching a child ride a bike. I was less interested in Big Rock than I was in my father, like some fallen warrior, this shadow of himself who walked hunched over his cane like a question mark.

As we got closer, we could see a few small groups of climbers and boulderers. Their colourful crash pads circled the rocks like prayer mats.

"Holy God, it's beautiful. Is it ever beautiful," my dad said beaming, looking across the unrestricted views. From the rocks, there was an undeniable attraction that drew us in, like a supernatural force had us under a spell of shared awe.

After we looped around the back of the rocks, I followed my dad off the footpath, onto a big open field of brown prairie grass. I watched nervously as he took unsteady steps, navigating gopher holes, his head swinging from the rocks to the horizon, to the gently swaying grass at his feet to the rocks again. He dipped in and out of memories of shooting gophers and skunks with his brothers on the farm.

My mom was looking across the open fields toward the edge of the Rocky Mountains off in the distance. I sensed she wished we could carry on and drive the rest of the day, that we were at the start of a long road trip, an adventure that would break the pattern of her unwanted routine, but it was time we got my dad back home.

"I forgot how beautiful this countryside was," he said slowly. "So wide open." I watched as my father pointed his face toward the sun and straightened himself out. I was overcome by the same feeling I had as a kid, that even while he appeared diminished, I would always worship him.

I was thinking about what to say, how to share what I was feeling, when a breeze picked up and a warm gust of wind landed on my shoulder like a hand from behind, like a man whispering, "I know." My dad turned away from the sun to look at me, to faintly smile, with tear-filled eyes. Everything so very alive.

Kathleen Racher

Snapdragons

It is a beautiful Yellowknife day in early June. The kind of day north-erners dream about during the long dark winter. Endless blue sky in all directions. Birch trees full of green leaves that contrast against the trees' shiny white bark. The air is still and warm but when the rays of the sun touch your skin, you can feel your first tan of the season forming. This brilliant sunshine had inspired me to buy some flowers to plant in my front garden. I am running late, but want to drop off the flowers before they wilt in the car.

As I pull up in front of my house, I see a woman walking toward me on the sidewalk. Her clothes are dark with so many layers that I imagine she must be overheating in them today. She looks down at the sidewalk while she walks, causing her long dark hair to fall forward and cover her face. As I get out of my car, she surprises me by lifting her head and giving me a friendly "Good morning!" Her smile is so big—almost too big for her petite frame and face. But what I find most beautiful about her smile is how uncomplicated it is. Not like the awkward but polite acknowledgement that strangers give each other on the street. She looks me straight in the eyes and greets me like an old friend.

But her "Good morning" confuses me a little since it is at least three in the afternoon. I manage a brief smile and a hello as she walks past my car. After a few steps, she stops abruptly then turns back to me and says, "No, wait, it's afternoon, isn't it?" I laugh and get busy carrying my plants up to the patio at the front of my house. I expect that she will just keep walking, but she continues to stand at the end of my driveway. The smile is gone now, and she says, "You know, I am having a real bad day. I could really use something nice like a flower."

I look down at my bedding plants; I have already been anticipating the joy of watching brightly coloured snapdragons grow in soil that was covered in snow only a few weeks ago. But the plants are only a few inches tall now and I worry that taking some of the blooms off will stop them from growing to their full, glorious height.

I silently weigh my hopes for these flowers against hers and decide to give her one yellow and one red bud. The buds are small but still perfect and pretty. Having fulfilled her request, I start to head back to my car. I stop when I see that she has started to cry.

"It's just that my brother died a few weeks ago and I miss him so much."

"Oh," I say. "That's rough. I know what it is like to lose someone."

"And I left my community and am having trouble finding a place to stay. I don't know what to do right now. Maybe I should go home, but then I will miss him more."

I nod and make sympathetic noises, but I am distracted by the fact that my car is still running and chugging out greenhouse gases. I worry about being late for a hair appointment that I had to book a month in advance. The smell of alcohol on her breath starts to erode my patience.

She says, "I just want to die."

I snap to attention. I open my mouth to tell her that everything will be alright, but a sob forms in my throat and I can't speak. Instead, I search her eyes, and I see that she means what she says.

"What is your name?"

"Bev."

"My name is Kathy."

⁓

I remember the night when I first became aware that my mother was unwell. I was seven years old and watching TV by myself; my mother was in bed. It was dark, and time to sleep, but my mother hadn't come out of her room. So, I ventured down the long dark hallway to her room and tiptoed in to see her. The room was so quiet that I started to shake with fear. I called out for her, and she whispered back, "Don't worry, Kathy. It is going to be all right." And I instantly knew that it was *not* all right. I was right, too. It never was all right after that for my mother and me.

When I was older, I understood that my mother was sick with depression. But at the time, all I knew was that she frequently wanted to die. Wanted to leave me. I couldn't bear the thought of living without her, so I began to focus on how to keep her alive. I had several strategies.

There was the "act like a perfect happy kid so she feels like she is a great mother" strategy. My goal there was to boost her confidence, but her response to this was that she didn't deserve me.

Then there was the "hide the valium and water down the vodka" strategy. She was furious when she discovered her pills were missing and I ended up having to give them back.

The strategy that I had the most hope for was the "remain vigilant so you can rescue her if she tries something." This last one worked a few times, but she was never grateful—quite the opposite.

The thing is, in the end she made her own decision; I was not able to save her. Only after her death did I realize that there was one strategy that I never tried with my mother: honesty. Not once in all our years together did I tell my mother how I felt. Not once did I ask how she felt. Not once did either of us acknowledge what was happening.

I tell Bev all of this. I tell her about my own struggles with depression. I tell her that these struggles are not over for me and all I can do is to manage this illness, manage even times like Bev is having today. Times when ugly, cruel thoughts swirl around my brain, like a tornado that keeps picking up speed, devastating my confidence and destroying all memories of happier times. I tell her that, in those moments, I am so desperate for the tornado to stop and sometimes death seems like the only way.

"But Bev," I say, "like real tornadoes, these moments don't last forever. I have learned to just take shelter somewhere safe and let the storms in my head pass. And, so far, they have always passed."

Both of us are crying now, letting our tears fall to the ground. I have started stroking her arm and she doesn't stop me. "Yeah," she says. "I have been drinking today and I'm tired. Maybe it would be good to go lay down and see how I feel later." My shoulders relax a bit then. Maybe she will be okay. Maybe.

We walk down my driveway together toward my car. Then she tells me that she was praying to God for help as she walked down the street toward me earlier. And she wonders now if God sent me to her today.

Not being a religious person, I am skeptical about her conclusion. But then she stuns me with her next statement: "And maybe your mother sent me to you today to show you how hard it is to feel this way and how easy it is to feel like you want to die." She looks at me then and says—with such confidence that it takes my breath away—"Every mother loves her child, and she loved you, too."

And despite being in the middle of the COVID pandemic, we hug each other tightly. And I feel love for this person that I have only known for maybe twenty minutes. My heart is beating fast, and I am not sure how to let her go. It is Bev who ends the hug. Then she flashes me her brilliant smile again and continues walking down the street. I drive off to continue my busy day, thanking whoever might have been watching over us today.

Laura MacGregor

Lament

I do not believe in an interventionist God. It's not that I don't believe in God. I do. I think? I just don't believe in a divine being who hovers in the Great Beyond, attentive to our trivial, earthly problems. I know people who believe otherwise. I am related to them. Their God answers prayers, big and small. She is involved in the minute details of their lives: ensures sunshine for a Saturday afternoon picnic, vacant parking spots during the Christmas rush, and heals major illnesses. I would like such a God.

But that has not been my God. My God has been the one in the bunker, the one you pray to just before you watch your best friend get blown to bits. She has been maddeningly absent, particularly when the shit is hitting the proverbial fan.

So, I don't believe in an interventionist God, which means I don't know how to make sense of the time She sent an angel.

The dream happens when I am five months pregnant with my third child. In the dream I awaken in a hospital bed, my fingers clutching coarse bed linens. I notice the glare of an overhead fluorescent light. I am wearing a blue hospital gown. A paper bracelet encircles my left wrist.

Beyond my bed are three additional beds, each containing a woman and baby. Each woman is wearing pastel pajamas and cradling a newborn swaddled in a matching blanket.

Next to my bed is a wheeled crib. Clipped to the upper corner of the transparent bassinet is a small card with a blue teddy bear. Printed in neat block letters below the smiling bear are the words "Baby Boy MacGregor." The crib is empty. Uncertainty is replaced with panic when I move my hands to my belly to discover it is slack and doughy.

A woman wearing a white dress walks into the room. "You're awake," she says.

"I had a baby. Where's my baby," I demand.

She pauses for a moment. "We don't know. But we're looking everywhere. We'll find him."

And then I wake up.

Night after night, I bolt awake, heart hammering. My hands seek out my belly to confirm our child is still safely held in the boundary of my body, cradled in the curve of my pelvis. We plan to call him David, a baby brother for Robert and Matthew.

I know the dream speaks the words I am unable to say out loud, not even to my husband. It is as if giving voice to my fears will speak them into existence, so I tell no one. My deepest longing is to be one of those mothers wearing pastel pajamas holding a healthy infant. But I am terrified history will repeat itself, that I will awaken in a hospital room to a nurse who is unable, or unwilling, to tell me anything, only that I had a baby. I am afraid of hearing again that my baby is already in an ambulance speeding away from me before my anesthesia wears off. Where was God then? Perhaps She had to stir up some sunshine for a birthday party?

After Matthew's birth, Bill and I briefly wondered if having a third child was a good idea. But we are both the oldest of three children, and three kids has always been our vision of a perfect family. As we learned the laundry list of Matthew's diagnoses, the visions we had of our family, of hiking and camping together, crumbled.

You can't plug a feeding pump into a tree. But we were determined our dream of three children would not be among the fallout. So, we stopped using birth control and decided to leave the decision in the hands of the God who had abandoned us. Which meant that one evening in mid-July, I walked into the basement office where Bill was finishing a report and handed him a plastic stick with two bright pink lines. He stopped typing, stood up, and wrapped me in his arms.

The comments begin as soon as Bill and I announce we are pregnant. *How could you do it again? You're so brave. I couldn't.* I insist that I am confident, that I trust this baby will be born healthy. But the dream spooling through my subconscious every night suggests something else.

Three weeks before David's scheduled birth, the dream abruptly changes. It begins with the same opening scene. I feel the rough bedclothes. I am wearing a blue hospital gown with a paper bracelet on my left wrist. The three neighboring beds are still occupied by carefully coordinated mothers and babies. I glance to my left. The crib is still empty.

But this time when the woman in white enters the room, the overhead fluorescent light bathes her in a halo-like glow. The rest of the room fades into the background until all I can see is the nurse surrounded by light. And this time she is holding a baby. My baby. She hands me my son wrapped in a blue-and-white-striped blanket.

"Here he is, Laura. He's perfect. And you don't need to worry," she says. "His name is Daniel."

The next morning, over the single cup of coffee I allowed myself while pregnant, I finally tell my husband about the dream. "I think we should change the name to Daniel. The angel told me that we got the name wrong," I say.

"You really think so?" Bill asks. "If we look to the Bible, the stories of David and Daniel talk about the same thing. David topples the Goliath; Daniel tames lions rather than being eaten alive. They're both stories about men who overcome something that feels insurmountable, a bit like this pregnancy. I think your dream is telling you that not only is the baby perfect, but the name *David* is as well."

The words of the angel/nurse comfort me and I do not have another dream. Twenty-one years later I still believe that I was visited by an angel who offered comfort during one of my most vulnerable moments. Except I don't believe in an interventionist God who sends angels.

Doreen McCormick

Microwaves

In the 1990s, life in our house was just a titch crazy. There were four kids plus me as solo parent, so every second of my day was accounted for—some of them more than once.

I often took shortcuts: when driving, when managing the kids, at home. I was always looking for a quicker way, out of necessity and, as some would accuse, an insane level of impatience. In the need for speed, the microwave was my ally.

One year I had the kids make homemade Christmas gifts: shadow boxes filled with sand and seashells. Life being hectic in the run-up to Christmas, we were gathering sand at the beach on December 23. We ended up buying the seashells at Granville Island to avoid frostbite. And then I realized that we couldn't use the sand until it was dry, which is where the microwave came in.

Suffice it to say, I do not recommend drying five pounds of sand in your microwave. It makes your entire home smell like low tide.

There was also the day that Gerry (a patient man who even withstood my rejection of the word boyfriend) went to nuke a mug of water for instant coffee. I was in the living room when I heard the microwave door pop open, followed by a high-pitched, "Ew! What the hell is this?"

Instantly, I started to giggle. I'd made spaghetti squash for dinner. Despite having poked it with a fork per standard operating procedure, the squash had detonated. Post-detonation, I had moved on to putting dinner on the table. The microwave was still full of stringy squash stalactites and embedded spaghetti-like strands. It was unlike anything you've ever seen before—unless, of course, you're one of those special people who blows things up in your microwave recreationally.

I once bought my daughter Mel a cute cotton summer dress, on which she promptly spilled watercolour paint. The next time she asked for her favourite dress, it was buried in a load of wet laundry. Mel didn't want a different dress, and we were running late. I decided that microwaving would be our fastest option. And indeed, it was.

After a few minutes' drying time, I hit the "open" button. I was forced to jump back to avoid the boiling steam cloud that rocketed out at me. The dress itself was too hot to handle. Not to be deterred, it was Captain Barbecue Tongs to the rescue! I tonged the dress out of our microwave/autoclave and spread it out to cool. That's when I saw the red gobs that had once been adorable heart-shaped plastic buttons.

Quickly, before Mel noticed, I set about re-forming the molten shapes into something approximating hearts. Once the dress was no longer scalding, I threw it over Mel's head, and we were out the door. The day was saved—although the buttons turned out less like the cute version of a heart, and more like the anatomical one.

One night, Gerry and I were at my place relaxing in front of the TV. The kids were in bed, the dishwasher was on, and the last load of laundry was drying. All was well—that is, until I smelled something odd. I followed my nose toward an odor of burning plastic.

I went to the laundry room and checked the dryer. There was nothing out of place. I sniffed my way back to the living room.

"Gerry? Do you smell something burning?"

"What?"

"A plasticky smell. Do you smell something?"

He walked toward me. "Yeah, I do." Like me, he headed for the dryer.

I went to the kitchen. The dishwasher had steam puffing out its vent. I opened it. Nothing out of place there, either.

"Did you check the dishwasher?" Gerry asked from the doorway.

"Yeah, that's not it … but it's getting stronger."

Gerry went upstairs to the hallway outside the bedrooms. Mel and Nik had been known to melt Barbie accessories in their wall heater. They enjoyed putting a tiny shoe or hairbrush in at the top to produce molten plastic. I'd discovered their secret while vacuuming when I found a fused plastic puddle of dayglo pink, yellow and blue. (This behaviour was obviously something they'd inherited from their father.)

Gerry stood aside and I checked the girls' room. Their heater was cold to the touch. Same with the other rooms. All good.

I gravitated back to the kitchen, where the smell was stronger now. Suddenly, I spied flickering from the microwave. I stepped forward, popped open the microwave door, and flames shot out, licking up toward my face. I slammed the door shut and snatched the plug from the wall.

Gerry arrived to find me standing transfixed. "What is it?" he asked. "What's burning?"

When the flames sputtered out, I popped the door again. The white plastic of the microwave walls were burnt and bubbled like cheese on an overcooked pizza. Wisps of smoke trailed out the door. The plasticky smell was overwhelming. In the middle of the turntable was a melted and charred plastic shower scrunchy—the kind for scrubbing skin.

"What the hell's that doing in there?" Gerry asked, peering over my shoulder.

"I put it there," I admitted sheepishly.

"You put it there? What for?" Gerry's voice jumps an octave when he's excited. It was in its upper registers now.

From my point of view, the blame fell squarely on the shoulders of Montel Williams, talk-show host. In the previous week, I'd seen his show on "Germs at Home." He'd presented horrifying statistics on household germs, replete with magnified, blood-thirsty looking images.

"I was sanitizing it," I explained to Gerry. He fixed me with a steady, incredulous look.

"I was watching Montel, and he said that you should put these things in the microwave for a minute to kill all the germs on them."

"For how long?"

"Well, he said a minute … but when I put this one in, I accidentally set it for twenty minutes, and I was going to stand here and take it out again after sixty seconds, but …" Gerry continued to stare me down.

"I guess I got sidetracked."

Gerry shook his head. Wisely, he made no comment. After all, I have a proven track record of putting pretty well anything that's not metal into the microwave. This time it didn't work out, but we both knew there would be more experiments in the future—once I bought a bigger and more powerful microwave.

Last Night at Work

ADAPTED FROM A JOURNAL
DATED FEBRUARY 27, 2014

Last night at work was one of those nights that is memorable for being extremely unpleasant, but also very lucrative. I worked with a pock-marked man named J. I described him this morning to a friend as looking like a gremlin, but what I meant to say was Freddy Krueger. Just the skin, though, not the expression. His was pouting and placid, like a baby.

I realized somehow that the potential was there to make a lot of money. It's hard to explain how that happened, because we never technically agreed to work together. I kept repeating to him that my time cost $150 per hour, and he kept repeating, What do I get for that? What you're getting right now, I kept saying. We did that for five hours.

We never had a conversation beyond arguing about whether he could touch me, and he never stopped trying. He snuck big, mushy kisses to my face and hands, spanked me and swatted my breasts when he caught me off guard. Sometimes I yelled at him, and so did the girls nearby. It was insufferable, but he kept wanting me to stay, so I stayed.

Why? A bird in the hand, I guess you could say. Because it's easier to wrestle with a soggy middle-aged man and hate it, than it is to find another $800 client on a Wednesday night.

⁂

He ordered shots of tequila without my asking for them, at least ten over the course of the night, with drinks at the same time. He seemed to love feeding me shots, he would applaud and embrace me after I took them.

When it was my turn to dance on stage I was so drunk that I had to go barefoot so I wouldn't trip. All this time, we're being taken care of by a waitress, Anouk. She was good with him—patient and attentive, despite the fact that he insisted on calling her Paco, and yelling "Hola! Paco!" and clapping at her every time he wanted something. He also kept calling her French rather than Quebecois, while saying hateful things about the French.

He was paying me on his card, so given how drunk he was, I carefully got him to confirm at each hour's passing, with Anouk as our witness. He couldn't seem to determine how he felt about paying for company. He kept me around by promising me "so much money," but every time I sought his consent to begin another hour, he would pout and kind of shut down, angry at me for bringing up money.

After a few rounds of this, I quit caring about being subtle (again, I was wasted), and I would repeat the question of whether he wanted to add another hour very loudly and clearly until both he and Anouk had said okay.

There's a problem with receiving credit card payments that I had on my mind. Besides taking five percent, the club deducts your house fees before cashing you out. The owner, Sam, often applies bogus house fees, which means that I stood to either lose a chunk of my money, or have a nasty fight at the end of the night.

I tried to pre-empt these possibilities by discussing it with the manager, Jack (actually a decent guy, believe it or not). He assured me that— on top of the five percent—I would only need to pay that evening's house fee, fifty bucks. But large gains always attract negative attention from Sam, so I was still concerned.

⌒

By around 2:20 a.m., J kept getting out of his chair to sort of lumber around aimlessly. He was such a mess. Anouk and I determined to settle our bills with him right away. He tried to close out his bar tab without tipping Anouk, who was owed around $80 after putting up with his shit since about 8:00 p.m., and helping him to run up a nearly $400 tab in the process. That's when his meltdown began. He turned on her, screamed that she was a crook, told us that we were all money hungry and uncaring. He must have griped about my bill too, which was $750. Sam heard the whole thing; he was sitting right there next to the credit card machine.

Sensing disaster, but seeing that J had indeed signed his bill, I cajoled him back to the couches, just to get him away from Sam. I danced for him, and his anger over the check gave way to glassy-eyed contentment.

But I was angry at him. How dare you treat the waitress that way? She was so nice to you all night. He barely understood what I was talking about. He denied having said anything, said that he didn't even care about money. He told me how amazing he thought I was. "Awesome" was his word, actually. I pleaded my own case too. You're just in here to have fun, but you could get me in trouble with a real bad guy.

Shelley—that's my mentor at Club Wanda's, dancer name Delores—told me early on never to forget that we work in a psych ward. From the careless, intoxicated clients, to the aggravated bouncers, to the coked-out, paranoid DJ, to the wicked owner, and many of the other dancers, our job is to deal with irrational, combustible personalities.

You strive for a sort of professional invisibility in a place like that. Look every bit as good as everyone else, and don't stray too far from reigning aesthetic codes. Be friendly, be focused on your work, and be consistently yielding, but not too much, and don't do anything distinct to get it, either. Don't be dirty, or overly flamboyant, don't talk too much. Don't overcharge, and never, ever perform contact. Don't leave early. Mime deference, fear of Sam, respect for Jack. Speak French. Work regularly. Even the most extreme of party girls—being excessive is not so frowned upon—abide by these rules.

I'm lax about my schedule, and bosses probably know that I don't give a damn about them. The truth of how I feel about Sam is that I loathe him, consider him an evil, dangerous, yet also pickled and impotent old man. A good candidate to play the devil in a movie. He has just that look: what were once good features and an air of leisurely, Mediterranean dignity, now warped by alcoholism and festering hatred, ensconced in a permanent cloud of cigarette smoke. The girls and I used to fantasize about a cable TV series in which he would be shot by an unknown shooter in the first episode, J.R.-style, and we would take over the club.

Sam remembers my name when I line up at the end of the night to collect my money. I wore my glasses, thinking to make myself inconspicuous, to no avail.

He drilled me with questions about my time: when I had begun working, how many times I had danced onstage, even—grossly—how many times I had gone to the bathroom, as if I had ruthlessly cheated J out of all of these customary, obligatory moments away from him. He was drunk, I said, he had agreed to all of it; Anouk had kept records. He loved me. Seconds after paying his bill he was happy again.

Sam continued yelling at me, threatening my job. He instructed the bartender, Caprice, to deduct $250 from my money. She looked terrified.

"Caprice, Jack and I talked about this," I said in a low voice.

"Well," she muttered, "that's not the situation right now."

Caprice has probably been bartending at Wanda's since the late '80s. She has incredible personal style, sort of Prince/Camille Paglia/Madonna, like a true 1980s Madonna. We have a fine relationship. And yet, in this moment, I hated her so much. You dumb bitch. How do you keep this job for thirty fucking years, where you're lorded over and terrorized and forced to extort dancers, whose money—whose cheap, utterly needed recompense—we earn naked, for men.

But hey. I understand that I don't need to make nearly a grand in a night. No one else gets to. I walked with more than $500, and that's still a lot of money, almost rent in a day. That's why we submit to these hazards, I guess, like speeding tickets. Take them as reminders to operate in cash. Accept this crazy, volatile environment. Because there are just not a lot of jobs where you can show up whenever you want, and make money like that.

Akiko Hara

Lydia

AN EXCERPT

"I'll spit at you!"

Lydia threatens me, her small triangular face defiant. She has anchored herself in the corner of my office, while her mom Jean and I remain at the child-sized table across the room. On the table, Lydia's favorite game Shopping List is abandoned, her practice cards scattered. *L, L, Lemon. L, L, Lollipop. L, L, Lego.* We are in the middle of a speech therapy session. Lydia, four and a half years of age, is doing a great job remembering to press her tongue tip against the "bumpy place" just behind her upper front teeth to produce /l/, her new sound. Then she suddenly declares she doesn't want to play anymore and marches away.

Lydia and I have been working together for over a year now. During our first phone call, Jean had warned me that Lydia was very shy with strangers and might not talk in my presence. Lydia was afraid that other people might not understand her, or worse, might make fun of her.

I understood her fear completely. As a child, I, too, had difficulty pronouncing some sounds. The /s/ sound was one of them. Speech therapy didn't exist in Japan back then and I didn't know how to fix my pronunciation. I kept my funny /s/ sounds for a long time. "You sound like a foreigner," a teacher commented on my speech. I became self-conscious and avoided speaking in public as much as I could.

I told Jean, "It would be perfectly okay if Lydia didn't want to talk at all during our first meeting." I added, "I understand how she feels."

Jean agreed with my proposed goal for our first session. We both wanted Lydia to feel safe and comfortable and have fun in her first session. I looked forward to meeting her.

I remember our first meeting clearly. Lydia came to my office wearing brand new pink sneakers. In contrast to her bright, sparkly sneakers, her face was cheerless, her eyes downcast, her lips pursed. Yet it did not take long for her to warm up. All I had to do to get her talking was admire her pretty pink shoes. Without a word Lydia did a small jump on the spot. Her shoes lit up and flashed.

"Wow!" I said and begged her to jump again.

She did. This time, a much bigger jump. Now she had a big grin on her face. Her eyes sparkled. After that, she talked nonstop for thirty minutes.

Jean and I exchanged a quick glance and a smile when Lydia surprised us by talking. I sensed good humour in Jean's understated manner. Behind her plain round glasses, her eyes sparkled just like Lydia's. Once she saw Lydia warm up with me, she went to settle in the adult-size chair at the back of the therapy room, allowing me to build rapport with her daughter.

Lydia told me many things. She said her name is *"Yedia." "I yike my madic tues. My fabot caya's pint. I yike detti n toy towy."* She liked her magic shoes. Her favorite colour was pink. And she liked Jessie in *Toy Story.* I found that Lydia had excellent expressive language skills but her pronunciation needed some help. She had difficulty saying /s/ and /l/ and a few other sounds.

We began speech therapy, first working on the /s/ or "snake" sound. I taught her to do the "alligator teeth" and hiss like a snake. Sssss! She learned to say "star" instead of *"tar,"* "story" instead of *"towy,"* and "spider" instead of *"pider."* As she was beginning to use her snake sounds at the sentence level, I taught her another new sound: /l/ for Lydia.

She made good progress over the next year. Everything seemed to be going well, until the arrival of a new baby brother at home. She began having meltdowns during therapy sessions. Jean told me that Lydia might be feeling insecure again because she's been busy with her baby.

Today, Lydia doesn't want to play her favourite game because she thinks she is losing. This is strange. In my speech therapy sessions, the child always wins. As long as they are winning the game, the child doesn't mind practicing the same speech sound over and over and over again. Given that Lydia has won all the games we've ever played, I'm surprised to see her getting so anxious about losing.

Now, with Lydia pouting in the corner of my office, Jean tries to coax her.

"Come on, Lydia. Let's play. I think you are winning."

"No!" Lydia shouts, so loudly that my colleague two doors down hears it. Then she announces, "I hate you guys!"

"Lydia!" Jean reprimands her daughter. "We don't use that word to people. Remember?"

I catch Lydia's face turn sad for a second, then defiant again, as she bravely recomposes herself. I am shocked as much as Jean is, for a different reason. Intellectually, I know Lydia is just upset and doesn't really hate me. Emotionally, I notice I'm hurt. *I thought she liked me.* I cannot let it show on my face. Because if I do, she will know that what she is doing is working. I hide my shock and keep my neutral facial expression. This is easier for me than for Jean.

I tell Lydia as calmly as I can, "When you are ready to play again, you can come back."

Seeing me unaffected by her strong words, she yells again, "I'll spit at you!"

Did she just say that!? For a few seconds, I forget I am a speech therapist and she is my client. I must have let my shock show on my face. I catch a slight but clearly triumphant smile on Lydia's face. I take a moment to ground myself again. When I do this, two thoughts come to my mind: first, from where she is, it's unlikely her saliva will get me; and second, she pronounced the word "spit" instead of saying "pit." It was so spontaneous. I secretly celebrate her mastery of the /s/ sound.

Jean is not celebrating. Her face tenses up and she is about to say something to her daughter. I gesture for her not to. "How about ..." I suggest. I have a plan. Jean nods. I am grateful that she is open to my suggestion at this very difficult time. I suggest that we give no attention to Lydia's outburst. At the same time, we are going to make the game look really fun, so much fun that it will entice her to come back. I want Lydia to learn that shouting is not effective. I want her to come back to the game of her own accord.

Feeling Lydia's piercing gaze, Jean takes Lydia's place and we resume the shopping game on our own. We make our voices over-animated. We cheer for each other every time we find an item that matches the shopping list. We dare not look at Lydia, who continues her vigilance from the corner of my office.

After we play like this for a while, I say to Jean, "It would be so nice if Lydia joined us." Jean agrees. Then we look at Lydia and ask her if she would like to join us.

I'm greeted by Lydia's tense face, held together with her last effort. Then her face crumbles. Exhausted from her strenuous effort to maintain the angry look, she lets her fortress fall apart. She starts sobbing. Alone in her corner. I feel a sting of guilt when I see the big tears roll down her face. *Did I overdo it? Was this too hard for her? What do I do now?*

I don't have to figure it out, because Jean knows exactly what to do.

"Do you need a hug?" Jean offers in her gentle voice. Lydia nods. Jean walks to her, sits down, and gathers her daughter in her arms. Lydia's small body relaxes. My body relaxes, too.

"Come back and play," says Jean.

Lydia nods again. She gets up and comes back to the table. When she reclaims the seat next to mine, my heart is full. I show this on my face and in my voice. "I'm so glad you came back!"

We pick up the Shopping List from where we left. *L, L, Ladder. L, L, Ladybug, L, Lion.* Lydia aces through her practice cards. She wins the game. In fact, we all win. For today.

Nicole Succar Sedan

Will It Be Me?

A REFLECTION ON AGING

He rolls into my line of sight just as I am taking a break from looking at my laptop. I can't help but stare at him. I forget my manners, although it doesn't matter, he can't see me, not really. The person pushing his wheelchair leans over to speak to him, whispering very close to his ear. I imagine she's asking him what he wants from the café. She parks the wheelchair at a table on the patio, but it's so cold out there. I see he's wearing layers upon layers of clothing, plus a blanket, plus leather gloves, plus a hat, but he still looks cold. Maybe it's just his face that is frozen, but frozen in time, it seems, not frozen from the cold.

He holds on to the edge of his hat for what seems like an eternity, pressing it between the thumb and index fingers of his right hand. My hand is getting tired just from looking at his. It goes on and on, for much longer than it needs to. My eyes are fixed on his raised arm, I wonder how much it must hurt, and right then, as if he could hear my thoughts, he lowers it. I sigh out. What a relief. For a moment there, I truly thought he was frozen. He looked like a marble statue inviting your hand to glide over it, to feel its coolness, its textures, its shapes, and you do, but with that tiny, faint voice in the back of your head telling you to be careful just in case he wakes up and grabs you by the wrist.

I look at him, straight into his eyes, hoping to awaken something, but nothing happens. His gaze is fixed on something invisible, or maybe on something visible only to him. What is it? A memory? A dream? A person? A blank? A reflection? It's as if he is staring at what little time he has left or at death waving to him at the end of a short tunnel. I realize, then, what unsettles me about his look. It's as cold as his body seems. I've seen that stare before, and it made me feel discomfort and sadness. My great-grandmother, who survived several strokes that left her frail, confined to a wheelchair, and unable to do even the basics on her own— eat, walk, talk—had that same stare. Her eyes worked, but she couldn't make them focus.

The companion comes back, sits in the chair beside him, sets a coffee and a pair of cookies down on the table. She got two of those heart-shaped, hole-in-the-middle, short-bread cookies filled with raspberry jam. They're my favourite.

She offers him a cookie. He remains frozen. She talks to him. He doesn't respond. She tries again. Still nothing. Why doesn't she just let him be, I wonder.

But what if that's not what he wants? What if he wants her to talk? Her voice might be his comfort. It's me that should let them be. I decide, then, to talk to him as well, to murmur something under my breath, a soft, light whisper the wind can carry over to his ears and wake him up.

His eyes are still fixed on nowhere or somewhere. And right then, a thought crystalizes in my mind. Will that be me? Will that be me? And who will be the person keeping me company? My husband? My niece? When will that be me? Ten years? Twenty? Thirty? Sooner? Later? Will that be my dad? Or my mom? Who will be in each role? Him in the wheelchair, her drinking coffee? The other way around? Or both in wheelchairs, and me, or my brother, drinking the coffee? Will that be my grandma? She's 91 and strong, no wheelchair, no frozen gaze, but my other grandma didn't have the same luck. Toward the end she was all but paralyzed, also staring at something, or someone, only she could see. Maybe the dead husband? Maybe the dead daughter? Who knows what ghosts we carry around with us.

I hear laughter and hellos—it's a group of people shuffling around the table behind me. The noise pulls me out of my gazing, reeling in the thoughts that are peeking down the edge of the rabbit hole. It's a group of older adults, four or five of them, who sit so close to me the invitation to eavesdrop is implied. They're chatting about computers or technology. They laugh and joke. A younger man arrives and sits with them. Warm greetings go around before they start to inundate him with questions about a server or how to copy files or look something up on the internet. He is ever so patient and responds to all the inquiries, taking the time to probe further, clarifying what is meant by this or that.

I am astonished by his patience. I don't think I have it. Or maybe I do, but I always wish I had more. The line snaps and my thoughts slide down the rabbit hole yet again. Will that be me? Will that be me? Not me answering the questions, me asking them. I'm aware I'm closer to the age of question-asker rather than question-answerer. It's like my dad says: from your thirties to your sixties, time passes by in a flash, and a young mind suddenly finds itself trapped in an old body. So the question should be when will that be me, not if that will be me.

My eyes shift back to the old man. His companion has finished her coffee and looks content. He still looks the same. Nothing, nothing has shifted. She brings the dishes into the café, returns to the table, picks up his gloves, puts them on his hands, does the same with his hat, adjusts his blanket, and off they go. The other group is still behind me, the younger man's soothing voice answering every question.

I am left feeling impatient and unsettled after being afforded a glimpse into the reality of aging, of my own aging. I feel gray and cold, my mood matches the weather outside.

My wise ones live far away, and distance blurs the footprints time leaves on them, while distorting my own perception of its passage. Every one of their wrinkles, every grey hair, every age spot is supposed to be a reflection of my own aging, but if I can't see them, if I can't experience or feel them, what sense does their aging then have? In their aging I am supposed to see my own, and to come to terms with the reality that if we are all aging, some of us will soon start to leave. Who will that be? Will it be them? Or will it be me?

Abby Pelaez

Barbados: Lionfish

AN EXCERPT FROM A FOOD MEMOIR

I wasn't sure what either of us was hoping to get out of meeting each other. Our mutual friend hadn't mentioned any hint about a match for friendship, love, or networking. We met at Café Sol at the other end of Dover where many British tourists stayed. At first I thought they were wealthy. Later, locals and tourists told me that they were, in fact, middle class.

He was a welcoming and interesting lunch companion. He showed up carrying a plastic bag with a deboned and gutted lionfish, which he'd caught a couple hours earlier. I appreciate someone's unusual hobbies, even underwater fishing of invasive species. The fish's protruding dorsal spikes were cut off so it no longer had the starburst-shaped mane for which it was named. Its striped skin reminded me of a zebra.

We split shrimp tacos and took advantage of the margarita happy hour while sitting on an open-air shaded seat overlooking one of the cerulean bays. "Tell me about that dead fish on the table," I joked, pointing at the limp lionfish.

"Oh, yeah. I speared it on a dive. They're invasive, so we're allowed to do that."

"Like, underwater? With an oxygen tank?"

"Yes, exactly. I dived with a local and he taught me how. I caught this one myself. There are tons of them."

"Wow." I allowed myself to be impressed since he'd done it under the guidance and permission of a local diver and it wasn't an endangered species. "Did you gut it yourself?"

"Yup. I'm going to throw it on the grill tonight."

He had learned to scuba dive here, having old family friends whom he would visit after our lunch meetup. After finishing a partially funded semester in Indonesia during undergrad, I learned to scuba dive in Thailand, the cheapest destination to get PADI Advanced Open Water-certified.

"Where else are you going besides Barbados?" he asked, with the professionalism that an office employee would use to clarify project scope and deliverables.

"Just here," I replied, dazed. I'd lost all sense of corporate jargon and manufactured urgency a week into island life. "Basically the month of February, then to California."

"Huh. Why there?"

"My mom and brother live there and I'm going to see them. Not sure how long, maybe a few months."

"What are you doing with the rest of your time here?"

He had landed days ago. I'd already given him a summary of what I'd done when we talked by text: sailing, snorkelling with sea turtles, reading on the beach, eating fish platters at Oistins market, visiting St. Nicholas Abbey to learn about histories, surfing, seeing Rihanna's childhood home and current mansion … I'd done or planned half of the experiences I wanted. This week I was reading, swimming, and forcing myself into a writing habit.

I shrugged. "Honestly, not much; I'll just hang out. Go to the beach. Work on my writing." I picked up a shrimp taco with three fingers and the other hand supporting it.

"What are you writing?"

"A collection of short stories. I like creative writing but sometimes it's hard. That's one of the things I'm working on during my sabbatical. I want to finish this project."

"What are the stories about?"

What were they about? So far I had six stories, some the product of assignments in a creative writing class. They covered a range of themes including love, boundaries, the immigrant experience, trust, and critique of capitalism. I had no idea what their common denominator was.

"Well, they're a collection of fictional stories with different characters and settings in each one. And they explore different themes of the human condition." Did I sound pretentious at 'the human condition'? "Mostly they're my thoughts on those things, dramatized in stories."

He leaned back. "Oh." He nodded. "Well, I wish you all the best with your project!"

"Thanks," I said. We sipped our mango margaritas. I was not matching the energetic pace of his line of questioning and knew I should ask him something too, but I was overwhelmed. I'd been living alone in Barbados for eight days, yet I'd already relaxed to the point that I was content to co-exist in silence. He was an agile mover, an opportunist who assesses, networks, and wraps up quickly. Our conversation was reaching dead ends where we had to return to mutual topics to try a new jumping point for discussion. When an unstoppable force grazes an immovable object, can they exist together? Can the immovable object pull the unstoppable force off-course in an orbit around the object, or will the unstoppable force pass on by?

Before I could figure out what to ask, he summarized his work history, eager to fill the silence I savoured. I shared that I was not planning to stay in banking. I told him I'd try to be a writer and get into the lucrative field of data analytics.

"Why not just be a writer?" he asked. "Why bother with data analytics?"

I said I had no previous passion for data analytics but also had none for banking; it was simply engaging enough to be an interesting way to pass seven hours. An okay job was a good trade for a bigger paycheque, especially since cheese and Netflix had inflated in cost this year. Besides that, I have many hobbies to save time for and expensive dreams to fund.

Honestly, after a childhood being told I couldn't have things others had because it cost too much, I was okay to have a job I didn't hate for small luxuries and to grow savings fast.

"What about you?" I asked. "You said you quit after three years. What will you do when you get back?" Three years is the longest I've ever stayed in any role; before that I've either quit, chosen not to extend the contract in favour of a semester of school, once been promoted, or twice been laid off (at casual gigs shelving books and making bath bombs). I didn't understand how people could stay in the same job for decades. Maybe if I didn't go on this sabbatical I would have.

He was optimistic and unbothered. "I don't know. I'll probably find another job. I'm ready for a change of industry."

Same. I was less optimistic, though. I remembered being eighteen, submitting fifty applications and getting half as many interviews before I got an office assistant co-op job. The job market had become even more competitive since.

"You know, you shouldn't say you're *trying* to be a writer," he advised. "You're here, and you're writing. You're doing it. You *are* a writer."

"Hmm ... yeah, you're right," I said, realizing he made a good point.

I hadn't yet formed a consistent habit and I wasn't paid or in demand, but I was putting in the effort.

This is supposed to be my Hemingway-esque, writer-in-the-Caribbean phase of life.

No. I applied his advice: This *was* my writer-in-the-Caribbean phase. This was my time to read and write fiction on a beach and sail in turquoise waters all day like a lackadaisical, literary pirate. "Thanks, I think I will say that. I *am* a writer. It's an author that I'm trying to be."

"And you'll get there," he encouraged. "If you believe in it and put work into it, you'll make it happen."

"That easily?" I raised an eyebrow. Although I could tell he wasn't interested in my stories and was being polite, I sensed a genuine conviction in his words. He didn't think about the possibility of failure, about the risk of lost time?

"Yeah, why not? It's what you want. You have to trust that you'll make it happen."

"I know, but there's so much competition. A lot of it is luck and timing. You have to have someone read it who likes it, and you have to be ready with pieces that people want."

"That's the same with everything, though. And there isn't just one shot you'll have to get your book published; if you miss one, there will be another opportunity."

My doubt must have shown on my face. *Get a good job and you won't struggle. We immigrated so you could have a better life.* I was resourceful because I adopted a scarcity mindset. I had viewed saving money as a mountain that painstakingly grew and took eons to replace, until I entered the workforce.

Then I saw money as a wave going in and out that could be replenished. A clean wave like the eternal ones at Dover Beach around the corner of my two-room shack. Maybe I needed to lean into the trust that opportunities would come back. Maybe I needed to think things were abundant instead of scarce.

Kimberley McNeil

I Want to Be Like You Someday

AN EXCERPT FROM "YOGA IS NOT AN OPTION"

"Thanks, everyone," I said as I struggled to find the words.

My eyes began to well up. Alicia walked over and hugged me. That was my cue to go around and hug everyone else, the perfect distraction from crying. *Phew, that was close.*

I had recently left a job at the university. My research coordinator position had been slashed because of funding cuts. The work had been meaningful but it was the people who had kept me going every day. I'd miss my coworkers more than my quick goodbye would let on.

I had met them at a time when my life hadn't been going very well. I'd lost my mother to cancer six months earlier. Along with the grief, I had been dealing with the end of a decade-long relationship and the burnout from a yoga teaching career that had left me emotionally and financially gutted. My colleagues hadn't realized what they were getting themselves into when I was hired.

A few weeks after the job ended, my former director, the lab's principal investigator, hosted a potluck at her place. All my former coworkers attended. We ate, we drank, we laughed as hard as always. At the end of the night one of the lab's undergraduate students, an intelligent, spirited, confident young woman named Alicia, handed me an envelope.

"We made you something," Alicia said as she handed me the gift.

"Ah, guys. You shouldn't have. Thank you."

With everyone's eyes on me, I opened the envelope. Inside was a beautiful handmade card made of several layers of folded paper. The pages made a sort of booklet. Staples held them together in the middle to create a spine. Each page had a handwritten note on it. As I quickly thumbed through the sheets, my eyes picked out words like "appreciate," "miss," "fondly," and "better posture."

I decided to save the card until I was alone. I didn't want to risk going into the ugly cry. No one needed to see a 30-something woman bawl.

⌒

The day after the party, I convinced myself to read the card. I choked up as I flipped through the sheets. The notes were filled with everything from inside jokes to heartfelt messages to more serious confessions:

It's been so much fun working with you! I'm going to miss our morning lab conversations and just you in general. If you ever want more eggs, just let me know. Lots of love, your favourite Russian (Polish) spy.

It's been so awesome working with you this last however-long. The lab is a lot less homey and awesome without you here— we're all confused about what we should be doing, and no one will explain the jokes to us. Thank you. (No, thank you!)

Good luck with future stuff. (This colleague got points for brevity.)

You are one of the most compassionate people I've ever met. I admire that you're always so eager to learn with an open mind. There's a lot to learn from your optimism. The lab won't be the same without you. We'll miss you very much. p.s. Eat your veggies.

One line stood out from the rest: *I want to be like you someday.*

The note had been written by Alicia, the same young woman who had handed me the card the night before. I thought, *Joke's on her. If only she knew the truth.*

If only she knew that after coming home from the potluck, I had fallen prey to another sleepless night. If only she knew that hours after I had gone to bed and insomnia had taken hold, I had spiralled into anxiety. My body had tensed, my jaw clenched, and my breathing became shallow. I had caught myself and exhaled, trying to cue my muscles to relax.

I had started mindfulness breathing—breathe in, pause, breathe out, pause, breathe in, pause, breathe out, pause—but the calming effect didn't last. I started again, this time using a longer technique—deep breath in for four counts, pause, deep breath out for four counts, pause, deep breath in one, two, three, four, pause, deep breath out one, two, three, four—it helped, albeit briefly. The feeling was akin to standing on the edge of a cliff. I leaned forward slowly, slowly, slowly until I fell off.

And then, as my prefrontal cortex lost the battle against my amygdala, my thoughts plummeted into hopelessness. It had been around that time, in the very early hours of the next morning, that my brain started tallying up the ways I had screwed up my life. Not long after that, my mind reminded me of my long list of failures; how I had failed at school, how I had failed at finding a real career, how I had failed at my relationship, how I had failed financially. And, to ensure I got the message, my mind rattled off the reasons I was a complete and utter fuck up: I was lazy, I was unfocused, I was stupid, I was everything wrong about a person.

I reached for my cellphone. It was in its faithful spot on the bedside table. I texted the one friend who knew what I had been going through.

Are you awake? I waited.

I'm not doing well. Nothing.

It was 2:00 a.m. There was a slim chance they'd be awake but there was a chance. After waiting a moment without a reply, I had to accept they weren't awake after all.

Eventually, after the waiting and the tallying, I had given in to the self-inflicted pain and bawled. I rolled onto my side gripping my pillow as if begging it not to leave me, to save me. Its cotton sheets were soft and forgiving against my skin. In dramatic contrast, my body stiffened into the fetal position. It was as if I had looked upon Medusa herself and turned to stone.

My tears soaked the pillowcase. The dampness turned cool. After using up what must have been every ounce of moisture in my body in the way of sweat, tears, and saliva, I started to dry heave. My body heaved and heaved and heaved. Then, when the internal battle was over, after the mental exhaustion from hours of berating myself had finally set in, I fell asleep. If only Alicia knew that after coming home from that party, during my subsequent mental collapse, I had spent some of those excruciating early-morning hours thinking about killing myself. Thoughts of suicide weren't new, they reserved themselves for the particularly tough nights, which were now becoming more frequent.

How many sleeping pills did I have left? Let's see: I took one the other night and another one last weekend so that should leave me with 27, give or take. That should be enough. The tablets never helped me sleep but they would put me to sleep forever.

At that point in my life, I had been struggling with undiagnosed depression for more than 25 years. Looking back, depression overtook me when I hit puberty. The deep sadness, the self-criticism, and the hopelessness materialized around the age of thirteen.

It would take going in and out of therapy for years, failing at my yoga career, going through savings, losing my mother, losing my relationship, and losing my self-worth to hit the bottom of a deep emotional pit.

The depression had been part of me for so long that I figured it was me. I considered my indecisiveness, my tardiness, my perfectionism, my mood swings, and my self-criticism to be character flaws. I assumed I was inherently flawed. It never occurred to me that these were in fact symptoms of depression, indications of something else, an illness that could be treated.

I hoped Alicia would never end up like me someday.

Correction. I hoped that if she did end up like me someday, she'd find the courage to ask for help. I hoped she'd be brave enough to tell the truth after living through one of those lonely, sleepless nights. I would wish she would be vulnerable enough to share the full extent of what she was going through with her therapist. I would hope she could release herself from the shame. I would pray she'd find the words to describe what she was feeling so that she could get properly diagnosed. And, when she wasn't properly diagnosed and things didn't get better, I would hope she'd keep looking for help. I would pray she'd stop accepting her reality so that life could get a little easier.

I'll get my finances in order so it's less of a hassle when I'm gone. I should sell my stuff before ending it. Who should I give my yoga props to? Why can't I ever motivate myself to accomplish anything? Because I'm a lazy, pathetic loser, that's why. I can't do anything right. I've wasted my life. I'm such a fuck-up. What will people say after I'm gone? I can't do this anymore. I don't want to live like this anymore.

My ex-lab mates had no idea what it meant to see them every day. They helped distract me from myself. Our conversations and coffee breaks helped keep me alive.

If only they knew the truth. Perhaps the one who didn't know the truth about me was me. On my worst days, I tried to convince myself that everyone around me would be better off if I were dead. Luckily, I never succeeded.

I'll leave it at that—no point risking the ugly cry.

Pammila Ruth

Take My Money Make Me Thin

AN EXCERPT FROM A MEMOIR

Science is a wondrous thing. Right here in my bathroom, before my very eyes, lies an example of Newton's third law of motion. Every action has an equal and opposite reaction. As the numbers on the scale rise, my heart sinks. Science at its best.

I'd have liked to start this book off with me sitting at the kitchen table chatting about how well my last diet went–how I got to my goal so easily, sharing all my tips and tricks of the journey and then how I maintained it for over a year. But I'm not there. I've been there. A few times, as a matter of fact. That conversation, however, needs to be put on the back burner for a while until we can sort through a few distracting issues.

While sometimes I have been known to self-sabotage, I've generally already had my fate sealed regarding most weight-loss fads, gimmicks, and schemes. The cards were stacked against me from the beginning. They are also stacked against anyone who wants to go down that road. It's not our fault! The diet industry is bent on making us fail.

So why am I here? I'm here to help you not fall into the same traps I did. To not fall for the multi-billion dollar diet industry that revolves around making us feel like we need to be something else. That we need to be that perfect number on the scale, that dress size, or that we just aren't good enough.

Obviously, I'm not here to sell you on a get-thin-quick scheme. I'm not going to hand you a magic pill or even promise that I can help you reach your weight goal. I'm here to share my story of thirty-plus years in the diet game in hopes that it can help you skip some of the existing schemes you may find in your own journey.

Whether you are a beginning dieter or are already on the path I have been on, I hope that by reading this, you will bypass some of those that did not work, or try the ones that did (while skipping the self-sabotage parts). If, like me, you are already a professional dieter and have been on this road many times before, have no fear: this book will still be for you, if only to let you know that you were not travelling that road alone. Let's make up with our bodies and stop beating ourselves up. Cake happens; let's move on.

This book isn't a weight-loss guide. Seriously, you already know how to lose weight. You do. The length of this book would be no more than a sentence if I were to out-and-out tell you how to lose weight, or at least what I actually had a doctor tell me once: Eat less, exercise more. There. End of book.

Life, of course, is not so cut and dry.

I am not a doctor. Hell, I'm not even a nutritionist. But after thirty-some-odd years of experimenting, yo-yo-ing, and beating myself up, diet after diet … after diet, I can assure you I've been there and know what not to do. So I can save you time, disappointment, and of course, *money* if you take this book to heart.

~

I grew up at what was considered a normal weight. Well, under, actually. I was born a preemie back in 1965 at 31 weeks. That was a big deal back then. But, as the doctor said to my mom, after doing everything they could for me medically, "It's in God's hands now." (Spoiler alert: I survived.)

After four months in an incubator, I was still terribly, terribly small, and my parents fretted over me constantly, worried I wasn't eating enough. I quickly became a very picky eater because they just fed me whatever I wanted; anything was better than nothing, right?

In my last year of elementary school, I was still the smallest kid in the building. To top off my already undaunting stature, I was also the most uncoordinated and least-interested-in-sports kid on the planet. Well, my best friend Tina was second on that list, given only that she could make a mean cartwheel out on left field during school baseball games. My best athletic feat was running in a gallop. I thought I was pretty cool.

I spent my teenage years undoing any nutritional lessons taught through my childhood–as few as there may have been given the circumstance–by surviving on fries with gravy, black coffee, and cigarettes. My astounding athletic ability to gallop had subsided into teenage angst and a quest to be actually cool. Luckily, due to my part-time waitressing jobs and having to walk to school two kilometres for middle school and later 4.5 kilometres to high school (uphill both ways, of course), my weight stayed steady at 100–105 pounds, the minimum weight for my height to be within the healthy weight category on the body mass index. One inch taller, and I'd have once again been considered medically underweight.

I never worried about what I did or didn't put down my gullet. At home, my mom was lucky to get anything green into me besides frozen peas in my midnight snack of stir-fried rice or iceberg lettuce for my dagwood bologna sandwiches on white bread. At school, lunch consisted of myself and three friends combining our dimes and nickels and splurging on a small order of fries from Bailey's Burger joint down the road. I was becoming a carbohydrate addict and a relatively lazy one at that.

When I met Rick (my now husband) in 1986, I had no reason to believe my weight would ever change. However, when we moved in together, I quickly began to gain weight. His mom had taught him how to cook for a *large* family. They were only a family of five, but they had large appetites.

The odds started piling up against me; the weight did as well. Thirty pounds within six months, to be exact. On top of Rick's fabulous cooking (which he thoroughly enjoyed, by the way) he was as picky an eater as

I was, so there wasn't much along the lines of a balanced diet. And then we got a deep fryer (who knew deep-fried pierogies were so delicious?).

I quit my waitressing job and got a sedentary job at one of the big banks. I was doomed. I had no nutritional skills, no fitness knowledge (galloping to work in your twenties, even in the '80s, was very faux-pas), and no idea how to combat this gain. I had nothing in my toolbox. I avoided cameras like the plague and would sulk for hours if I caught a glimpse of myself on film or in the mirror. *Who was this person?* I used to be quite the ham when the camera came out.

Then, self-deprecation began to seep out into the physical world. I filled my diary with some of the most insulting, heartbreaking, bullying words to myself. Reading them today still cuts me to the core. Belittled, berated, betrayed by my own self.

Cow, lazy bitch, fat ass. Would I have spoken to a friend that way? No. No, I wouldn't have.

A few months before our wedding, I had had enough. My body was already starting to feel it. I was tired all the time; I ran out of breath easily. So my doctor encouraged me to quit smoking.

"You will never be as unhealthy fat as you will be as a smoker," he said when I voiced my concern over my gaining even more weight if I quit. Hmmm. We can debate this in my next book.

Yup … I gained even more weight when I quit smoking. Wedding dress shopping with my mom was not fun. I wanted sleek and sexy, but my body no longer dictated that (mind you, I was 5'3", so sleek was never my forte), but that's what I so very much wanted. I ended up with a big fluffy Southern belle dress. Cute. Cute as a daisy? No. Cute as a marshmallow.

I needed to do something, and I needed to do it quickly. I had three months to make this wedding dress look at least sexy, because if I couldn't even look at photos of my regular self, how could I look at my wedding photos in this marshmallow dress?

I pictured the oversized framed photo of the wedding party on my wall: my bridesmaids all gorgeous in their mint green and yellow dresses (oh, how I miss the '80s); Rick and his handsomely tuxedoed entourage; and a black marker scribbling me out of the photo, like something an obsessed stalker in love with the groom would do.

I needed to find a quick fix. I had no concern about the aftermath. I just needed it done so I could be that beautiful bride I saw in my mind's eye. At. All. Costs.

And this, my friend, brings me to the true beginning of our journey: my obsession with getting back what I thought I once had—the perfect body.

Susan Hawkins

Aftermath

AN EXCERPT

My father's death a few weeks earlier had completely shattered our family's rhythms. In the weeks that followed, even though I still went to school every day, everything else in my world was askew. It felt as though I had survived a bomb blast and was stuck inside a debris field: stunned, wandering about without any direction. At first, I was disoriented and numb; this was followed by a dull ache that never went away.

Our apartment was shrouded in silence. My mother wept quietly and often. My brother Norman retreated. His asthma grew worse and he spent most of his time alone. He didn't say much, only pointed out that we should move the extra chair from the kitchen table. "We won't be needing it anymore."

He never cried, at least not in front of me. Years later, he told me that he didn't have a single happy memory of our father, that all he remembered was the drinking and the chaos.

All three of us struggled to find new patterns. My mother still worked part-time in the mornings as a bookkeeper at a nearby steel warehouse. She hated her job but knew she needed to earn a living to support us. I was twelve, my brother was two years younger; she had a long road ahead of her.

During the afternoons while we were still at school, she would go through my father's things. Every day when I arrived home from school, there was something else of his that had been removed. Objects somehow had realigned themselves. Ashtrays vanished from the coffee table, books of matches disappeared. Day by day, my father was leaving our apartment forever.

The worst for me was when she went through his clothes. The suits that he wore to the office hung in the hall closet along with his white shirts. All gone. When I stared at the gaping space they left, my mother told me that men from the Salvation Army had come and taken them away. She justified this by saying that someone else would put them to good use, that it was wrong to leave them just hanging there. I seethed at this. To me, it was a summary dispatch, yet another burial.

Most of his personal possessions were confined to the top dresser drawer in their bedroom: his Navy medals, a watch, a few papers, a poem I had written for him years earlier. His entire 44 years of life was summed up in that small space. My mother removed most of the items, returned my poem, and gave his medals to my brother. I was struck by how little remained.

One afternoon I saw his navy wool sweater sitting on their bed. I grabbed it and felt its scratchy wool against my face. It was part of a set; she had knit a smaller matching one for my brother. The back of it was a sailing sloop, its snow white sails set against the deep blue of the sea. My mother sewed dresses for both of us because she couldn't afford to buy new ones, but she knitted for pure pleasure, saying that she loved the feel of the soft wool on her fingers.

She reluctantly handed over his sweater and told me to keep it folded neatly on a shelf in my closet. Instead, I tossed it onto my massive roll top desk and slammed the lid down so she couldn't see it. She despised my messiness and hiding things seemed like the best way to avoid her nagging reproaches. The desk was my private spot.

After school, I would take the sweater out and run my fingers over the thick, dense wool. It had covered his shoulders, hugged his ribs, and kept him warm against the wind. He treasured it and now it was mine. I knew he wasn't coming back but at least I had something of his next to me.

One afternoon when I arrived home from school, the top of my desk was open, the sweater gone. I stormed into my mother's bedroom demanding my sweater back. She looked at me, her face stiffening and told me she gave it away.

"How could you do this to me?" I shrieked. "It was the only thing I had left of him, I can't believe you could be so mean!"

Taking the sweater away seemed like an act calculated to cause me the most possible hurt and pain. Her answer was typically lame. She thought it was unhealthy the way I had obsessed over it, that my father was gone and that I needed to accept it.

"What's done is done," she said quietly. I recoiled from her hand brushing against my shoulder. I burst into tears, slammed every door in the apartment and fumed at her heartlessness.

Poetry

C. Eliot Mullins
Drown

Do you remember
what it felt like
the first time
you looked back
and didn't see
the shore
ocean
nipping
at the tips
of your fingers
piercing your skin
tingeing the water pink
watching
your cells
absorbed
into the vastness
Do you remember
what it felt like
to dissolve

Do you remember
the first time
the rushing river
ran the waterfall
of your veins
the burn on the back
of your tongue
can you taste it now

Do you remember
how we got
our shit together
seven times
in seven cities
seven sixty-day
chips lining the dash
seven pay-or-vacates
scotch-taped to
seven doors
the soundtrack
of our existence
whispering
*you're not gonna
make it*

Do you remember
the picket fence
we passed on
because people like us
can't live
in places like that
the precarious progression
of peril
where we lived
and you died

Do you remember
the day we came
apart
smoking in my car
on your morning break
while I told you
we were losing
the last house
Do you remember
deciding
not to cry
because the break
was only ten minutes

Do you remember
almost being snowed
under
knowing you
were supposed
to be grateful
but wanting
to ride one
more millimetre
into the magic

Do you remember
the exact second
you knew love
was not
a sufficient substitute
for oblivion

How we met

When they ask, I tell the safe version. The clean version. The version where it was not an act of betrayal and the end of a quarter-century marriage with children. I tell it pretty. So pretty. *That's so sweet,* they say. I tell it perfect. I leave out the part where she nearly took her own life. And that sometimes I wish she had taken mine. I think of the poems no one will read because they say what we did. I think of wanting to love her and not knowing how.

Veronika Gorlova
Anatomy Fables

The body is a storyteller, oracle, bard. It's a prolific fabulist, your very own Aesop.

One day, you lift your arm and there is something in your armpit. Was it there before, when you raised it up in the dark, dancing in that mass of people?

The stories like to hide around the edges of your curves, in all your sweet succulent spaces. They like humidity and moisture. Sometimes they're like words on the tip of your tongue. Other times they're in between your legs, pulsating or resisting.

There was a story in the way your sex was warning, all teeth and barbed wire fences. flashback and foreshadow, fused together. Remember how you kept stumbling over that sinister fairy tale, only to retreat? Remember how it took a remembrance to bring back your wetness?

Stories that lament the loudest crave comprehension. But the ones you know by heart might need to be reconstructed, reclaimed, reformed.

There is a story in the way you pack into an igloo when a gentle hand makes contact with your largest organ. But it's not the story you think you know.

There is a story in those bruises, like splotch art continuously shifting places on your skin. This one is hard to pin down, like their origins. No memory of how they were painted, and maybe that's the premise.

The horror fictions that facilitate your nightmares, that possess you, haven't been branded into your flesh like the name of a cult leader. They aren't sharpies on a white board, they aren't even a thirty-year mortgage. Their text is transcendental; watch it transpose, or wane and withdraw.

Even your most myopic tales maintain magical faculties.

Everything we do is recalled by our animal, is chronicled by our anatomy, even if we cannot name it, even if we do not feel it. It endures, it modifies our memoirs—those histories recorded all over our bodies as conjecture and conundrum.

Shh ... be still.

Can you hear them?

Encephalon Hothouse

My mind is a minefield brimming with rose bushes. My hands
        hemorrhage then heal, as I work to clear paths
           out of the thicket.

You'll see me: a pool of milk in the midst of wine
and olive. My ear to the ground, listening for

      that fatal heartbeat.

You'll see me again, only for an instant,
        before my body bursts into cinders—too firm-footed.

Milk turns to charcoal, catapulting through the cranium, lands
        in untouched shrubbery, hides amongst the thorns.

I've died many deaths and been reborn, the renewal infinite.

Sometimes my hands unearth pieces of my former selves,
        foreboding gifts shrouded in flowers.

Black chalk mixes with liquid metal, creates an
        insoluble paste. I pave a path with it, a russet road
           of the undead.

When I get tired, I paint on my skin, an anatomically-accurate
heart directly above my real one. Lie down on my back,
close my eyes, listen for

      the heartbeat of the living.

You'll see me: a snowflake in the middle of a nursery,
      a corroded heart
      beating right through my chest.

Jules Wilson

I Come by This Naturally

from the tone of my skin
from the stride in my step
from the depth of my voice …
I come by this naturally

from the breadth of my nose
from the strength in my frame
from my style and my slang …
I come by this naturally

from the depth in my eyes
from my braid full of locks
from the roar in my laugh …
I come by this naturally

from the crease in my skin
from the sculpt of my chin
from my dimples, my grin …
I come by this naturally

from the gaps in our wealth
lower outcomes of health
prison sentences dispensed …
I come by this naturally

from suspensions school dealt
the jokes at my expense
the refusals to rent ...
I come by this naturally

from exclusions to clubs
the profiling in sports
the you're not good enoughs ...
I come by this naturally

from the you shouldn't tries
we don't welcome your kind
why are your morals slight ...
I come by this naturally

from the where are you froms
misappropriation of my contributions
surprise that I'm a Canadian citizen ...
I come by this naturally

as taught by our society
the weight of my identity
contrived and collapsing
like a dense black hole of despair

labelled endangered
with goals of extinction
my conservation, like
a black rhino, is rare

unworthy of humanity
still we made a note to sing
haunting harmonies expelled
healing over suffering

unworthy of equal access
we sat in to call for change
barbaric acts unanswered
justified the point we made

unworthy of voting rights
militarised we were to march
we occupied your headlines
your hypocrisy worldwide watched

unworthy of due process
your bullets pierce our chests
your carnival-rigged self-righteous
you can no longer claim contempt

to say you haven't heard our cries
to stand proud, deaf, and resolute
would you trade your life for mine
speak up now and tell the truth

yes I come by this naturally
because the choice is in *your* hands
until you choose to invest in change
powdered residue is what I'm left

like I said before
and I'll say time and time again
I come by this naturally
Yes—I come by this naturally

Angelle McDougall

Last Time

FOR BRAD AND TIM

In the park I watch you
pick up your daughter and help her
go down the slide.
When was the last time
I did that with you?
What day did you become
too big or too heavy or too old
for me to pick up
or sit you on my knee to read *Moira's Birthday*,
or blow on an owie to make it better,
or share a big chair to watch *The Lion King*,
or rock you to sleep?

I remember the first time
I looked at your sweet little face
and held your bundled weight in my arms,
your first smile at me, your first tooth,
the first haircut you gave yourself
that made your hair stick up,
your first wobbly steps in the hallway.
I recall these things in vivid detail,
but no matter how hard I try,
I don't remember the last times.
Fresh tears threaten and my throat

fills with regret.

If I had known it was the last time,
would I have paid more attention?
Would I have taken a moment
to breathe it in, to commit to memory
what you were wearing, how you smelled,
the look on your face, the weather outside?
Would I have made it special somehow?
Maybe etched it on the wall
next to the height marks?

She's running now and giggling
while you chase her and swoop her up
into your arms, spinning her around
before setting her down,
and she scampers away.

The sun peeks through
my overcast thoughts
as I realize it has to be this way.
That knowing ahead of time
would have made it too hard to let go.

Rekindled

FOR MOM

Perpetual breeze eases from
the lake in sync
with the rhythmic whispers
of rolling white waves.
Seagulls scream and swoop,
exclaiming over fish carcasses
washed up on shore.
On the cliff above,
a copse of maples
cultivated from conjoined samaras
collected from Dad's backyard.
Now, ten years older,
ten feet taller, they
continually clean the air
of dust and fumes
created by decrepit cars.

The rectangular lot's centre
has a quaint cabin
with a covered deck.
Tables and chairs filled
with family—playing cards,
cleaning freshly picked berries,
or reading the newspaper
while listening to CFCW.
As dusk creeps across

the sky, we settle
around the metal wheel
piled with split spruce.
Sparking bark spits sap
and fills our mouths
with the sharp tang
of sulfur, smoke, ash.

Flames mirror our faces
as enveloping darkness, made
deeper by firelight,
creates a natural room
fit for sharing secrets
and telling tall tales—
an open-air confessional
with only heaven's stars
and the silent moon
to hear our words.
We regale each other
in hushed reverent tones.
Quiet laughter rumbles with
"Emil sunk the gator ..."
"Jeanne's coming to visit ..."
"Louis caught a mariah ..."

The flame's blue eye
watches as tears from
smoke, laughter, and pain
are wiped away leaving
soot-streaked cheeks. Later,
the inky sky lightens
and wrens warble welcome.

Spruce bones crumble, turn
to ashy embers, whisper
last wishes before dying.
Stories dwindle, heads nod.
We amble home, glowing,
carrying the fire like
lanterns in our chests,
blessed and refreshed with
hearts and minds rekindled.

Jaeyun Yoo

Stargazing

we drive at dusk
to Porteau Cove

stand at the edge
of the big bowl

brimming with moon jellies
and silver-green fish

look up
at the Great Bear's light

from a hundred years ago
look up

at the time-travelling
tail-star of the Swan

I look left
at the crescent dimple

on your stubbled cheek
the same smile

your *yeye* once had
in a grainy photograph

emerge 2022

you look right
at my black hair

windswept
like calligraphy

of my pensive
ancestors—

when we are
long gone

back to being
water and salts

the night sky
will be a flower bed

constellations
bright as baby's breath

will look down
at centuries ago

see how we steered
our eyes away

from Cassiopeia
and instead, kissed

Margaret Anderson
More Than Zinnias

Another floral arrangement arrives,
backseat occupant in a rusty
Corolla. In the kitchen, she washes
dishes, leans toward the window.
Engine sputters to a halt as it drops
fart-like pops into the quiet dusk.
Gardenias were last week's offering,
his latest attempt to make up by flower.
It's a big apology tonight. She can tell
just by the way the delivery
kid struggles to carry the box.
Lately, her boyfriend is careless,
moans women's names in his sleep,
nicks off outside for private calls.
Once, carnations and daisies eased the pain.
Poetic apologies on a card used to make her
quick to forgive. She's forgetting how. He
recycles excuses in stems and petals.
Sometimes, the new flowers come before
the old ones have died. She refuses to be a forget-me-not
untended, a faded hydrangea bloom lost among
vases of wilted promises. She opens the box,
wanting far more than pistils and stamen.
Exhaling regrets, she plucks a blossom,
young and fresh. She's more than
zinnias in a heart-shaped pot.

Echo Chamber

echo chamber in my head
resounding words my mouth has said.
hour after hour, reverberating.
around, around, the clamouring

resounds words my mouth has said
spoken in haste, voiced with regret,
around, around. in the clamouring,
your whispers rise and calm the clatter

of words spoken with haste, voiced in regret.
murmured in our bed with languid laughter
your whispers arise to calm the clatter—
love songs sung to the ears of evening.

murmured abed with languid laughter
chanting a chorus of secret matters—
love songs sung for my ear this evening.
bodies drawn close, heads together, quiet

chanting of our chorus—secrets matter.
hour after hour, reverberating,
bodies drawn closer, heads together, quiets
the echo chamber in my head.

I pretend it is raining

I stood on the sofa, toes tucked between cushions,
elbows perched where Mom rested her head
  like Mike, my brother,
  would spy at the fence as
  our neighbours fought
  over burnt hot dogs
  with loud roars of blame
  Mike found entertaining.
I watched the storm take
our house through a car wash,
amused by the rain.

I hunched at my desk, pink nails bitten,
no power for cramming just bright flares of lightning
  like campfire flames
  under marshmallows.
  Sisterly teasing
  devolved into catfights.
  Dad's reprimand forced us
  to resort to eye rolls.
Clouds' grumbled threats
breathed out into echoes,
tension eased with the rain.

I escaped from my textbooks with a gaze out the window,
witness to gathering night-ripened storm clouds
  like frat boys crowded
  on half-lit back porches
  with laughing young coeds

drunken with yearning
to do something outrageous
during long nights of chaos.
Thunderclaps raved,
then shame-walked to silence,
entranced by the rain.

I leaned in the doorway, arms crossed and exhausted,
beds cradling children, moon shrouded by mists
like black curtains drawn
across the front window
which sheltered the calm
of the family within.
Strife gone for the evening,
hushed moment of stillness.
As the patter of raindrops
soothes us to slumber,
we are safe in the rain.

I lay on my sick bed, sight slowly fading
under fluorescent lighting machine noises insistent,
like a ringing alarm clock
or signals at crosswalks,
they call out my life signs,
announce my leaving
as I ponder sad faces
and incurable cancer.
In the midst of the maelstrom,
I feel fear in the storm break;
I pretend it is raining.

Noodling

He pours tea,
steady stream tumbles
from the porcelain pot
like falling river water
at Tahquamenon,
steeped brown by cedars.

> One summer's day there,
> I dipped my hand in a pool,
> surface sun-warm, depths cool.
> My wiggling fingers lured
> a perch blithely swimming by.
> It did not resist as I closed my hand.

He offers the tea,
his eyes holding mine
still waters between us,
my fingers a lure
next to his on the cup.
No resistance.

Marin Nelson

Carlotta in the Gallery

No one swims at the swimsuit shoot.
Another model smokes a warning
my way: *after the pedestal
comes the push*.

The photographer sips from a cloudy glass. He says
the light leaks when I enter the room.
I'm not sure how to make this interesting
for you.

Mmm, he says. Tanned neck tan,
scorched like the amber sipping liquid
pooling the coaster. And then,
I'm glad you brought that up. I'll show you.

I know I'm being acted upon.
He steers me to an art gallery,
blindfolded, but not more blind
than usual. I can't see

the paintings, but he says I can touch
them. Anything is allowed here
in the gleaming darkness.
Small blots of oil and turpentine

ignite, catching an unknown
light. I can't see the source,
only textures of mottled pain
gathered enough to form a painting.

The crackle of an acrylic scab coming free,
my mind's pastorals and still lifes
dissolve into imprints of the last shapes
of light my retinas retained.

There are bodiless names in this room,
living in an acronym or a harsh initial
scratched into canvas. I want nothing more
than to be among them but

I'm left with the soft scraping of my palm,
nails digging into lacquer, caressing
the rigid contours of a frame.
I thumb the goosebumps

on the sculptures and wonder,
can granite feel desire?
Next week is Ghost Ranch, New Mexico
where the drains clog with sand. They'll play

a bolero, and I'll lean and drag myself
under arches. When no one looks
I'll eat fat crisped sage, hold it in my mouth
and think *I hope my life will be like this forever.*

Vermillion

Do you miss it
the feeling
of being sought?
What has taken its place?
Whatever the opposite of mystery is.

She applies a lip in Vermillion. Is the colour
too young? She closes her journal, they order
grapefruit juice, and she recounts what was
just written, ink still
fresh enough to stain

the next page.
Her husband doesn't want a second child. Impact on
the economy, the environment. She laughs at her own
despair. The lips of her friend part
and seal. She reaches out but stops

just short. The server places a teapot on the table
along with a small hourglass. Thick slices of avocado
yield to the knife
rippling green
like a dress lifting.

So, the red lip, a black coffee. A wrist tattoo beneath a
selvage edge.

Mystery,
I'll bleed it.

    Orbs of water surged out
    of clenched moss
    in a nectarine grove in Northern Quebec.
    Below the old volcanic hills
    the earth was wet and fragrant.
    Behind the picking shed
    two fruit pickers
    struck skin.

    He explained
    the temptation is to devour it fast
    but if you're slow about it
    it tastes better. There's a lingering and you
    can notice the texture
    of skin in your mouth
    how some parts
    are firmer
    than others.

She's been bruised ever since.

Everything is painted white in the café,
the crown moulding, white. Some of the paint
gums in the slats. A sprinkler juts roughly
out of the ceiling. A couple stands up and debates
whether to remove their cups and soiled
napkins off the table. They change the subject,
put on their coats, leave. Outside, cars
grip the asphalt.

Vivian Maier Repository

Shadows are sprayed on the warehouse floor
where men huddle with hushed abduction
tones and suitcases of cash
to negotiate a nanny's work. But they didn't have to
wipe December beach noses or clean soiled sheets

'til they were spic and span. A fractured archive of
light spreads itself against screaming rabbits,
ornate women with pearl throats and hair stacked
above a high and broken-toothed
Chicago.

Who do you see in your self-portrait?
Heavy boots, long dresses, El Dorado for the French?
Or everything I just said, but with a duct-taped mouth
and a pleading look through a light-forgotten grate?
Adjust the exposure.

Walking through the noise, a child tugs,
It's cold now and I'd like to go inside.
Hush now. If you tilt a lens through the dim window
you can see them purchase

a woman's silence.

Tanaz Roudgar
My Body Is a Metaphor

My body is a busy street
in Tehran, Iran
polluted with smoke and male dominance
50% CBD 50% indica-dominant hybrid, because I control the pollution
on a Tinder date,
I control the connection
with a head
and submission that looks like his favorite position.
On these streets there are no rules, but the police are powerful,
they make their own rules and
punish
people who don't abide.
My mind is the police
controlling the traffic of people coming to and going from my life,
punishing the bad thoughts, the free thoughts, the habits.

My attitude is a soft grunge song
with immigration rage
not-getting-cultural-references shame
"Have you ever watched *Friends*?"
"No."
Friends turn away, creating their own band.
My body is white foundation
red eyeshadow
smoking cigarettes

soldier boots crushing
sharp rings penetrating like black scream
if they don't want to be friends, they can be intimidated instead,
like being handcuffed by the police.
My sensations are the Vancouver weather
slicing wet drops
hitting my forehead
tick, tick, tick,
slipping
not a haven
need a haven
need a home
what the fuck, Vancouver?
My body is smoky skies in August from wildfire
ashes from a burnt tree
weed in the air

My spirit is a silent meditation retreat
no distractions
no running away
"We are alone, aren't we?"
says my meditation teacher
vibrations vibrating faster than my vibrator
more pleasant
pain paining more than the heartbreak of 2018
unpleasant
my body
finding a new trail
hugging a tree and knowing softly they are hugging me back
content knowing it's just me here

content with the breath
the taste of dancing wind over a thirsty flower
the touch of freedom on my head, free of hejab
waking up to the body as it changes

my body has been many different metaphors
it is a metaphor, I am the poet
constantly trying to grasp it, make sense out of it, explain it
so you get me, so you see me, so you love me
what if my body is just a body
outside of labels and identities and colours
existing as dancing molecules and energy in the party of love
bigger than attachment styles, needs, and metaphors
is my body satisfying without describing what it's good at,
where it was born, who it fucks
alive with imagery and sound and rhythm

Am I a poet when I just am?

Natasha Overduin
refusing words

Nan is calling from her armchair in Toronto
coughing into my ear
joking about cadavers
and her trip to the coroner
while I'm busy
fussing over career opportunities and
perusing Vancouver Island real estate
with my partner and our sweaty toddler
planning for the future
refusing words
that start with *c*
and end with *r.*

We tour too many homes
we can't actually afford
noting which lawns are well cared-for
and those pocked by chafer beetles and cat's-ear.
We admire an ivy-drenched brick rancher with a cellar,
a modern condo with a striking cantilever.
We get dubious guidance from a realtor who, like Nan,
is a chain-smoker.
We buy a bungalow on a weedy lot lined by red cedar.

In our first April downpour
a light coffee stain appears in the ceiling.
It mutates the plaster, heads slowly towards the chandelier
each day gaining a few more centimetres.
Experts assure us the damage may be treatable
if we cut out every corner.

Try not to panic, Nan says,

it's just

a slop of humans, *a–z*

a/an

    abscess of oligarchs
    burpee of crossfitters
    convoy of truckers
    dash of bike commuters
    empire of politicians
    flute of poets
    ganache of fake-eyelash girls
    hush of golfers
    inertia of civil servants
    jam of flight attendants
    knowing of survivors
    lineup of Costco members
    maul of dog walkers
    narration of dungeon masters
    overkill of ultra-marathoners
    peasantry of tenants
    quirk of bookshop browsers
    riffle of birders
    snore of librarians
    teacup of grannies
    upswell of climate activists
    vortex of stoners
    warble of gardeners
    xanthan gum of gluten-free bloggers
    yahoo of first-year undergrads
    zig-zag of toddlers

when I meditate, what I find (ghazal)

The ocean shakes her white ringlets.
Waves froth the sandy shores of my mind.

Belaying, I scrabble rock,
the slack grows. I climb higher, out of my mind.

Waiting in a fogged-in airport lounge for
a Boeing—but I don't mind.

Just sit. Breath. In. And out. Stay
with your breath. Quiet the mind.

Oh, Joy—there you are!
You've been out-of-sight, out-of-mind.

It's busy, like shopping malls used to be—
people т-bone, cut lines—*Hey! Do you mind?*

Pack and re-pack the trunk. Our shit just won't fit.
Rear-view vision I may or may not bear in mind.

Poems crash toward me.
A herd of wild horses thunders my mind.

The bus lurches as I step over the yellow line. Grasp
at plastic. Brace feet. Steady, mind.

Rain jackets pedal past in every shade of Skittles. I rinse my
lungs in fresh October. Peace of mind.

Wriggle in a hammock, reaching
for that itch in the back of my mind.

Voices echo where the furniture used to be.
I sold everything with the future in mind.

I vomit chunks of apple crisp and grilled cheese.
The floor is slick with my sick mind.

Hi, Tasha, my sister's voice says from a corner of the
darkness. A hug wraps the sobbing shoulders of my mind.

Karen Drummond

My Monna

I'm planted in the crack of the sidewalk
looking up the steps to your door.
Steps I ran up each summer as a kid
in my bell-bottom jeans
awaiting a big hug,
bowls of Licorice Allsorts
and trips to the Pop Shoppe
for black cherry and lime rickey
in tall glass bottles.

I don't want to go in now.
I want to escape to the cove
at the end of the street
just as I did so many times before
with my siblings and cousins,
when the adult banter was
too boring to bear.

We'd pick blackberries,
climb the rocks,
search for tidal pools
with little crabs,
seek out bits of smooth coloured glass
on the rocky beach,
like so much was at stake,
like we were mining for gold.

Then we'd finish up by collecting kelp
for your garden,
loving the salty sea scent
and rubbery feel of it,
swinging it in circles over our heads.

But I'm not a kid anymore
and I must go in that door,
knowing you won't be on the other side.

I'm greeted by a white-haired man
in your recliner, and my aunt setting out
cucumber sandwiches.
I'm still and staring,
but my cousin sees me.
He introduces me to people,
some I met thirty years ago or so
and others I've only heard stories about.
We politely exchange memories.

In the kitchen, I open the freezer.
Nope, no whipped topping
for dessert.
I hold the door ajar
and remember your favourite story
about me. I can hear you say:

> *Oh, you were so funny,*
> *you used to get so mad at me,*
> *you'd put your hand on your hip,*
> *stomp your foot and say,*

"No laugh, Monna, no funny,"
and that would make me
laugh even harder.
I close the freezer door and
sneak down the back steps,
take off my black patent heels
and walk to the end of the street.
I breathe in the salty night air
and dip my toes in the cold water.
Over the waves, I hear you laughing.

Texarkana Chorus

Deep breaths don't bring sleep, only a nose full of brand-spanking new air-mattress vinyl. I splay out and replay day one of this vacation: our gold Catalina spewing smoke into the sky, Dad kicking the tire as we droop roadside in the Texas sun. I wipe my forehead, roll on my side and close my eyes again, remembering the air-conditioned café, the latticed cherry pie, and detouring here, 200 miles too soon. I listen to the crickets chirp and start to drift before a quiet snuffling comes from the other side of the tent. It gains momentum until the snuffle becomes a full-on snort. By the second snort, a chorus begins. Each snort is followed by a deep, resounding bark from the red four-man Coleman beside us. Snort, bark, snort, bark, dad, dog. I scowl at the five bodies around me. How can it be that I'm the sole witness to this? Just then my sister's eyes blink open, blearily gazing my way. *We don't dare wake him, do we?* If we do, the chorus would be replaced by a soliloquy of swearing. *No.* Denied sleep, we still dream. Maybe tomorrow will be the day we step over ominous eggshells to start living the image.

> Brush off the stale night
> sweat, a pink sky and new songs
> on the horizon.

Dongkoo Lee

Proposed Bridge Replacement Project

I.

The bell tolls from the clock tower
of a city hall toward the margin of a town.

It is noon here,
and midnight there, when she hangs
up the phone with me.

_____ can't see her enter her dark room;
_____ can't see her lie down beside the extra pillow.

This is the way she is everywhere, and
called (or incorporated) into time, or air.

2.

A river flows as if it has no questions.
The inking sound permeates my eyes, blurring
the outlines in the town.

Now I stand in the middle of the incomplete
pedestrian bridge, open for
its designer—time.

In the water, there is debris
of the demolished old bridge piers.

A couple of mallards swim, approaching,
I am gradually disquieted—the sharp-edged rebars
and erratically bent dowels.

But they are okay now.

Near the dislodged past,
walleyes swim upstream, seemingly in stasis (as we live),
against the strong spring current
to lay their eggs.

The air of a raw and mutable wonder
emerges from there, in the face of its reiterated metaphor,
as though noon and midnight might emerge as *noonight*.

3.

I kneel and see the slope and the evenness
of the newly-placed bridge decks, and imagine the feet
and wheels of an occupied future.

Whoever we are, whether we wish to go back
or forward, we will meet here to cross the river.

Beyond the galvanized chain link fence,
people walk out of where or when they used to be and
fill the empty square—looking out at the incomplete bridge.

Ross William Bartleman
Demolition

the four of us pile into
the Ford Fairlane
for the drive out
down the Big Hill

Sunday roast with Yorkshires
her sizzling dark brown
pillowy puffs of heaven covered in gravy
banana cream pie made with
Jell-O caramel pudding you can't buy anymore

summers working in the family store
the dull tin sign of old reads:

> **W. ANDISON**
> **GENERAL MERCHANT**

a pioneer from the old country, England to be exact
a purveyor of dry goods from another time

when he was on his last legs
and I was a toddler
we'd round the crabapple tree
and climb the stairs to the screened veranda
open the door to my mom's childhood a music box
of unrelenting expectations

as a young boy
the vinyl record player
in a vintage wooden cabinet
held a certain magic
as the diamond needle
followed the grooves
on one side or the other of
The Sound of Music
Anna Russell Sings! Again? ...

thousands of hours
listening, learning,
singing, memorizing

a nascent gay adolescent
immersed in a rose-scented bubble bath
filled with everything from
Julie Andrews to Brahms
to Gershwin to Shakespeare
and everything in between

my grandfather's adding machine
staring at me from the piles of
tax returns on the desk in the billiard room
solitaire, cribbage, and crokinole at the kitchen table
badminton and croquet in the yard
walks to MacKay's
for three-scoop ice cream cones
Cochrane bricks
and majestic stones
from the Canadian Rockies
holding this part of my history together

Alice is the last to go
my maternal link to the past
extinguished, the house demolished
to make way for two rows of
sacrilegious townhouses

what was created and sustained here
for close to a hundred years, up in smoke

no more drying the dishes
she hands me one by one
no songs in the air after dinner
my mother at the piano
no disquieting family photo
in the second bedroom
no narrow red stairs
leading to the basement pantry
no learning how to make pastry
with just two big cups of flour

no powerful sweet scents
of the verdant plants
no swirling humidity
in the greenhouses
no layered grime
on the shop floors

no end
to the desecration

Untethered

I.

Falling through the floor
                    and into another dimension
I am floating
            above the earth
                       reaching out for everlasting peace
This is unfamiliar territory
                this state of being
                      unattached
untethered
                    cut off from
my Mother

with the brutal force of a sharp blade

II.

There is blood everywhere
seeping out onto the ground
engulfing me
carrying me away from this womb
to unknown shores

This river of blood
returning me at long last
to the sea, a return home

III.

When I come to, years later
I am a grown man
or so it seems
Yet this is clearly not the case
as I watch myself
searching in every moment
to recreate the suffocating bond
I had with my mother
no matter who shows up in her stead

Mom is long since dead
the victim of
a vicious attack on her brain
that no amount of
surgery, radiation, and
chemotherapy could repair

Not even I,
her cherished first-born,
could save her

And so, I am a motherless son

Alone and isolated
in this perverse psychic dance
longing for some illusory wholeness
waiting for a reunification
that can never be

Anna Chadwick

Black Wings Beat

not a single step
not a soul to be seen

this northern place is not my home
I embrace the hushed stillness
so rare in my rushed world

I imagine the frozen lake beneath me
as an immaculate blank slate

then, solace slips

a cacophony of caws call down the lake
a conspiracy of ravens
look for the leftovers
of last night's wandering wolves

black wings beat
soaring hunters seek
in a circle of silhouettes

my fleeting silence shatters
and this terra nullius
whips away with the wind

wind whispers, then whistles
flicking white fog down the lake
to meet my face with a bitter bite

a sharp shiver runs through my body
my bellowing heartbeat
batters my bones

I step slowly, ice cracks
the lake gulps and bubbles

the land whispers its secrets
through haunted scars

as shrill wind screeches
through collapsed cabins

Meandering

I remember the day,
    my dear daughter,

when tears cascaded
    down your cheeks
        the day you ran
                zigzags
        across the lake
    black wolves
in your wake
    their yellow teeth
        snapping at your
                silver snow boots

            you said you could smell
        the stink of rabbits
on their steamy breath

growing up
    is never a straight line

        the next day
            you invited
        the winter wolves
    to our hearth
the wild wily guests
    ate your toy stuffed bunnies

                    licked their wounds
                              sawed logs by the fire
                    ate the cat
          they had to retire

humming with the
          melodic murmur of
                    dancing damselflies
                              you chased
                    the soaring sapphires
          past the gauze birch trees
into the willow bush
          sipped juniper tea
                    with black squirrels
                              only to be banished
                    by buzzing bees
          and biting black flies

growing up
          is never a straight line
                    the day a chortling chum
                              flicked off your fishing line
                    after a flash
          of its pearly tail
you flew
          into the frigid water
                    emerged shivering
                              legs quivering
                    you told us
          you invited
the convivial fish home
          to eat caribou steaks

for dinner
the day
your feet
met sidewalks
and cement
there were
so many lines
so many lights
so many signs
you cried for months
begged us
to go back
to meandering
in the wild
one day
we'll wander back
but I wonder
if the wily wolves
will still wander in for dinner

Libby Jeffrey

To the Diner at the Legion

I peer in, welcomed by the wide-open
dance floor made to order. It's a venue—no,
a bingo hall. Dart tournament. Jets game.
Meat draw. Diana is dressed to get the job
done, tells me so with her bright eyes
and running shoes. No more than thirty seconds
and I'm at a sprawling table
for eight.

Black coffee, white mug, no saucer. More creamers,
jams, and ketchup than an edible finger-painting session
could offer. Blue marbled tabletops, wood siding. Black
chairs with metal legs, that baritone screech they make when
nature calls. Fireworks of laughter and debate light
up tables five and seventeen. I'm table nine, seating
for eight, yet just me with my top seven
imaginary friends.

One man, also alone, stares out with a smirk
instead of down his phone. We are ignored
yet attended to, in just the right way. Now, that's comfort.
That's Grandpa's secret sauce. Now, that's
a diner.

Ata Island, 1977

Wynken, Blynken, and Nod one night
Sailed off in a wooden shoe—
Sailed on a river of crystal light
Into a sea of dew.
—Eugene Field

Six desks sat empty as a murmur
passed through the village. "Those boys!
They stole!" A cranky yellow boat they packed,
one rucksack with only bananas,
coconuts, cookstove. Pushed off the dock
with secret smiles, hopes higher than a kite.
The young one, thirteen, invited since
he knew how to steer. And he did, until in darkness,
calm seas, his heavy lids won the fight.
Wynken, Blynken, and Nod one night.

They woke to a storm as it set in.
Sail shredded to spaghetti, old rudder
cracked next. Food ran thin and coco husks
caught raindrops: one sip per morning,
one more per moonrise. Eight days until
the eldest, weak, bleak, saw anew
a speck on the horizon. Ship splintered to
toothpicks when it hit the mass of rocks.
Any chance of an adrift rescue

sailed off in a wooden shoe.

Furious, the hungry one fought two sticks
for a spark. "We need teams in shifts,
together we can," said the talkative one
as he hollowed parched tree trunks to catch
each drop. The quiet one said, "We need
no quarrels. Neither day nor night. A fight
begets a time out." They agreed to split and
stare out to sea until peace was the only way back.
Just then, the first fire sparks took flight
and hope *sailed on a river of crystal light.*

First flickers maintained, the bored one
turned steel boat strings to guitar playthings.
All songs they knew became their hymns. Sunup,
sundown, the funny one humoured rescue. He built raft
after raft, as the young one tested and crashed.
So it goes, how, under skies ocean blue,
the six, sixty years later will say—still friends—
"Best days of my life." They secretly smile, they
are shelter to each other. All thanks to
a cranky yellow boat sailing *into a sea of dew.*

Gap Year

My aisle neighbour moved to an empty seat
during turbulence. He whispers, *You get some sleep.*
The weeping must have been a little much.

The first of many nights that begin
with good intentions. Talking circles over
beer glass rings, he hopes I'll drink too much.

I see Mom in the street but then realize it's a stranger.
If you can't be smart, be safe, they said on the day I left.
I wasn't smart. I was lucky. Not by much.

Each second, a fun mistake. Girlish giggles
to mask the nerves. *How many people have you …*
met with *a lady never tells*—much.

Phone call home. Please pick up. *Got a job!*
Short commute. Irish pub. Ireland! Brave voice,
teary face. *I like it. So much.*

The neon Chinese take-out became religion
'til I brought my humble hangover to the Methodist teatime.
Have you got friends in Dublin? I admit: not much.

I only know drunk men in this city, she says
with her County Down lilt. *I need female friends.*
Libby's lungs fill. *Oh, I'd like that. Very much.*

Jason E. Coombs

False Cognates

Side a

False cognates are pairs of proper nouns that seem to be
spouses because of similar values and attractions,
but hear with disparate histórias; they come from distinct
cultures to form family.
When listening becomes lazy, they may lead to the abrupt end
of a bilingual love story.

SIDE B

The *hawk* she called out
with a *rock* you heard
as *walk* against the blue
of sky. an idiom reserved
for bilingual couples
fluent in each other,

their mother tongue rolls
in the sheets with sonorous lingo
giving birth to a child of costume.
it grows lively until taken
for conjecture. repeat *de novo*

desculpe—to express guilt actually,
atualmente replaces sorry with hope.

say that again fills the between
them like six feet of distance
separating the desirous
outside a capacity-reduced No Frills
—the need outweighs the wait.

when intend is pretend
and pretender is *fingir*
you have become
each other's false cognate.

Not Paranoia

Side a

plastic thought is
a vinyl record in cons-
tant skip
turning harmonic vibrations into the hole your stomach
tries
to fill with a bi-
te of hear-
t eleven minu-
tes before you bump the needle
to dream another nine
to
try
to forget the
tex-
t no-
t yours
to see because i-
t sucks yesterday's cer-
tain-
ty in-
to
to-
nigh-
t's insomnia

SIDE B

the untouched turntable came back
with instructions from the manufacturer:
"learn to meditate"

Two-Hour Lunch

SIDE A

Two someday adults roll up the curb
across the sidewalk, step skateboards
up to their hands past teachers' cars
that bite their tongues.

Mr. Whittle's white Ford Festiva
would have backfired after hearing:

> "What time is class?"
> "1:45"
> "I thought it was 1:35;
> we're only five minutes late."

The backpackless boys saunter
up the hill to the school side door
at the pace of coworkers sulking
to the office after a two-hour lunch
on the Friday before a long weekend.

Sophia finishes gnawing on her salad
of tall grass; we make our way back
to the apartment in time for our nap.

c. nicol
traffic

driving back from the hairdresser taking the truck route because it's usually faster they know how to drive these guys but man cut them off and be ready for a solid blast a cubist vibe a fist of notes that have nothing in common crushed together that hate each other but no one pays any attention except the train who also doesn't give a shit who sends a sympathetic major 5th of a response across four lanes of traffic both ways as we stop at a light and I look over and up to see the driver's face but there's just an elbow with a fist of fingers with grease and ground under hard as nails and hell will freeze over before those fingers ever straighten again a perpetual clutch holding on for dear life and they can make something out of nothing and everything out of air out of determination and pride and no expectations and respect and fear and there's a guy shaped like a question mark with a shopping cart full of stuff trying to cross the four lanes of traffic his head a mass of white bristles sticking back like he's trapped in a wynd tunnel then we move forward again inch by inch covering ground making progress trying to get home and the guy with the cart is there already smiling and waving at us as we drive our cars wherever we are going I want to pull over talk to the guy with the cart and ask him how do you make what you need how did you survive and man I really love your hair.

Cutting Board
(OR THE FOURTH WALL)

after ten years together
I try to fix up the house
paint it black

he tells me there's money
in the top drawer
I grab a handful of twenties
make my way to the mall

wicker and silk flowers
and an oval cutting board

I find sympathy for the devil
inside the house sleepless
for four days and
four nights

arranging armaments
polishing props and
propaganda extolling
death before dishonour
fueled by fraudulence
high octane blow
cut with desperation

on the other side of
the fourth wall the
nursery growing full
of misplaced belonging

my cat her kittens
falling through the space
where the floor
and wall miss

under the house
I gather them up
in a box and take them
to the shelter to be put

out of my misery
give me shelter

he returns after two weeks
pacing from room to room until
he discovers the nursery
unfamilial

I listen hard for murmurs of love
my heartbeat an arrhythmic tattoo
and I am lost all is lost I am a
beast of burden

then he is born
he is my sunshine

emerge 2022

I leave and take
the wicker brittle now
the silk flowers cocooned in oily webs
the cutting board uncut

moving through the fourth wall
to my own house

to a room of my own.

Contributors

FOREWORD

Jónína Kirton, a Métis Icelandic poet, graduated from Simon Fraser University's Writer's Studio in 2007 and is currently an adjunct professor with the UBC Creative Writing program. She was 61 when she received the Vancouver 2016 Mayor's Arts Award as an emerging artist in the Literary Arts category. Her second collection of poetry, *An Honest Woman*, was a finalist for the 2018 Dorothy Livesay Poetry Prize. Her third book, *Standing in a River of Time*, released in 2022, merges poetry and lyrical memoir to take us on a journey exposing the intergenerational effects of colonization on a Métis family.

AUTHORS

Jennifer J. Allen is a memoirist with a compelling urge to turn her unconventional upbringing into art. Her writing has earned her a scholarship and a finalist placement in the Penguin Random House Award for Student Fiction. She holds diplomas in professional writing and criminology—both of which prove useful in her memoir endeavours. Jennifer is a member of the Creative Nonfiction Collective Society and Vancouver Writers Fest.

Margaret Anderson grew up in a large family with a father who quoted poetry on a whim. Following her love of language, Margaret earned degrees in speech-language pathology and works in private practice. She is a graduate of the Writer's Studio at Simon Fraser University and writes texts for the English for Speakers of Other Languages program at the Canucks Family Education Centre. A Michigan native residing in Vancouver, B.C., Peggy is grateful for her supportive husband and two children.

Niyanta Baniya is a writer, dancer, and Korean drama enthusiast. Originally from Nepal, she moved to Canada in 2007 and currently lives in Surrey, B.C. She loves to read, sing, and go on walks for creative inspiration. Niyanta is excited to be taking her first steps into the world of literary writing with the Writer's Studio.

Ross William Bartleman is the founder and artistic director of Time+Space Creative. He is a performing artist, poet, playwright, singer, and photographer. On stage, he has played everything from a meteor to a *Jet* to a bridesmaid. He has also appeared in *Human Library* (PuSh) and *Virtual Humanity* (Zee Zee Theatre). In August 2022, his debut solo work entitled *27 Lost Years: Diary of a Compulsive Hoarder* was presented virtually as part of the 75th Edinburgh Festival Fringe.

Nikki Berreth, who originates from the heavily forested lands of rural Northern Alberta, writes cross-genre fiction with a healthy dose of science. Now living along Canada's west coast, she tries her best to impersonate a sea sponge by living a simple life while soaking up all the knowledge and experiences that float her way. She's a science communicator and informal educator who spends too much time entertaining the public with her most recent research findings. Unlike a sponge, she's a gifted storyteller and has performed her work for spoken word audiences, Science Slam events, and scientific conferences across North America.

Shiva Bhusal grew up in Nepal. He loves reading and writing, playing table tennis and cricket, and dabbling with portrait photography. Shiva currently lives in Bellevue, WA, and works as a software engineer.

Chase Boisjolie is a writer whose day job is teaching English as a second language to international students. A San Diego native, he relocated to Vancouver in 2018 after completing a degree in literature from the University of California, San Diego. His work explores the ever-growing political and social divisions in society, particularly those in the United States in the past decade. He hopes to use writing to create a portrait of humanity.

Adele Bok is a South African writer living in Tunisia. She enjoys coffee and long walks on the beach, in whichever order her day provides them.

Anna Cavouras is a reader and writer living in Toronto. Her work has appeared in *Studio Magazine*, *Boneyard Soup*, and with the League of Canadian Poets. She is a judge with Reedsy Prompts, editorial assistant for Minerva Rising Press, and a former writer-in-residence at firefly Creative Writing. Anna holds an MSW and is a graduate of the Writer's Studio at SFU. Her current project is a novel about revolutionary tattoo artists of the future. You can find her walking around with her feminist agenda in her bag and on Instagram as @a.cavouras.writer.

Anna Chadwick is a clandestine creative writer, hoping to one day emerge with published writing from behind closed doors. She resides in Victoria, B.C., and is also a university researcher, art therapist, and clinical counsellor. She finds inspiration for poetry and lyrical creative writing from nature, northern life, liminality, and the talented writers of SFU's Writer's Studio.

J. R. Chapple is an artist and writer living in Vancouver, B.C. Her creative career has taken her to various places around the world, creating stories with words, movement, sculpture, and sound.

Danielle Christopher has been featured in *West Coast Families, One Village, Simply Gluten Free, Write, The Mighty, Flash in a Flash, Vancouver Mom, Yummy Mummy Club*, and various other publications. She has essays in the anthologies *Worth 1000 Words, Parenting with PTSD, Parenting Without Judgment*, and *Wisdom Has a Voice*. She is a non-fiction student of the Writer's Studio 2022. Danielle lives with her two kids, two cats, and one husband in Langley, B.C. She is @DanielleASigne on Twitter.

Jennifer Chrumka is a Canadian freelance writer who lives in Kamloops, B.C. For most of her career she's worked at CBC Radio where she's won several journalism awards and produced documentaries that have aired on shows like *The Current, The Sunday Magazine*, and *Unreserved*. She has her master of journalism degree from UBC and is most recently a graduate of SFU's Writer's Studio.

Jason E. Coombs is a Toronto-based poet who, when he is not reading, studying, and writing poetry, spends his time helping build a chocolate business. He also runs an emerging poetry podcast called *Eh Poetry Podcast*, where poetry lovers can listen to poetry like they listen to their favourite music: on repeat. His work has been published in the anthologies *Worth More Standing, Mothertongue: a multilingual anthology*, and *The Covid Verses*, as well as in the digital poetry magazine *Sledgehammer Literature*, among others.

B. A. Cyr was born and raised in Edmundston, New Brunswick. From a teacher of biotechnologies, she evolved into leading a mission organization in Vancouver. She now has a pastoral role locally and internationally. Her work with young adults is the catalyst for her writing.

Codi Darnell spends her time balancing writing with motherhood, marriage, and wheelchair life. But the best words usually spill out of her as deadlines inch closer and other responsibilities vie for her attention. You will find her work on CBC, Filter Free Parents, Family Fun Canada, and VancouverMom.ca. She is currently working on her first memoir from her home in British Columbia, where she lives with her husband, three children, and two dogs. You can follow her on Instagram @codi.darnell.

Kim Dhillon always wanted to write fiction and joined the Writer's Studio to write her first novel, which explores dynamics within a mixed-race, immigrant family in the 1980s. She also writes contemporary art theory, poetry, and essays with work published in *Prairie Fire*, *c Magazine*, *frieze*, and *Fillip*. She won the 2019 Banff Centre Bliss Carman Poetry Award. Her first book is *Counter-Texts: Language in Contemporary Art* (2022, Reaktion Books). You can find her on Instagram @kimsukiedhillon or at kimdhillon.com.

Stephen Douglas writes stories that illuminate our desires to belong, to be loved, and to fulfil our passions. His characters discover meaning and resilience in overcoming trauma or loss. Former editor of *Psychologica*, he has authored articles on topics ranging from recovery from trauma to the impact of colonization. A Toronto native, Stephen draws inspiration from the streets of Vancouver and Toronto, his thirty-year career as a psychotherapist, and themes found in the world of nature.

Karen Drummond is an aspiring poet finding her way back to creative writing after a long hiatus. Creative writing provides a welcome distraction from a demanding job and the joys/challenges of raising teenagers. Other distractions include travel, theatre, live music, and hiking up mountains near home (Calgary, Alberta).

Nicole Dumas (she/they) has spent the past four years living, writing, and teaching in the villages of Kitkatla and Ahousaht. She recently returned to Vancouver, on the unceded territories of the Musqueam, Squamish, and Tsleil-Waututh peoples. She wrote a chapbook of poetry called *Hard Body Candidate for Soft Embrace* about her time as a soccer referee.

Louise Dumayne lives off-road and off-grid in the remote Yukon wilderness. She is the winner of the 2021 Lush Triumphant Short fiction Award, received Highly Commended recognition for the 2018 Words & Women Short Story Competition, and was short-listed for the Federation of BC Writers Short fiction Award; this piece will be published in the 2022 contest anthology. Louise's work also appears in *Understorey Magazine and Words & Women: Four* (*Unthank Books*), and is forthcoming in *Riverside Review*, a short fiction anthology (Klondike Institute of Arts and Culture).

Sarah El Sioufi is an Egyptian Canadian writer living just outside of Toronto with her husband, daughter, and rascally dog. Her writing explores the dangers and triumphs of being a teenager. An early version of her manuscript, titled "Reading Between the Lines," was the 2021 Muskoka Novel Marathon Winner for Best Manuscript. Sarah is passionate about writing and it brings her great joy to express herself through her work. She also considers it her own personal form of therapy.

Cristina Fernandes authors dark and twisty novels. Originally from Lisbon, she survived a decade of deep winters in the far Canadian North before settling in the pleasantly damp Pacific coast wilds. Contributing to the disarray of her home are an unfailingly adoring pug and two opinionated daughters. Also, a puppy of undetermined breeding who they are all still coming to terms with. A graduate of SFU's Writer's Studio, Cristina's stories explore the many ways humans love and damage one another.

Lauren Galbraith-Gould is a Vancouver-based writer whose work is influenced by her fascination with mythology and folklore. Blending fact and fable, her emotionally engaging stories compel readers to recognize themselves in the unfamiliar. She is currently working on a historical fiction novel set in 17th-century Scotland, where the border between our world and another is closer than it seems. When not forgoing sleep to write, Lauren is taking photos, reserving flights, or checking out too many library books.

Veronika Gorlova is a queer, autistic, Jewish writer currently living on the unceded territories of the Musqueam, Squamish, and Tsleil-Waututh Nations, also known as Vancouver, B.C. She immigrated to Canada from Ukraine when she was five years old and has lived in many parts of the country. Her day job is as a fundraising professional for a local nonprofit, but her real passion is poetry.

Michelle Greysen writes in the wide-open spaces of the Canadian prairie with her heart grounded in her West Coast youth. As a freelance writer with many magazine features and bylines on a variety of topics, and a corporate publishing background, she is also an award-winning realtor. Her published literary fiction short stories have earned notable nominations. Michelle's current works include a historical fiction novel, "Shunned," creative non-fiction works, and a short story series. She "writes what it reminds you of."

Sierra Guay is a writer from Lisbon Falls, Maine (USA). She currently lives in North Carolina with her fiancé, Kevin, and their dog, Henry. Her recent work explores the consequences of grief and encourages readers to question their notions of normal. In 2022, Sierra won third place in the town of Farmville's annual Hometown Haiku Contest. Most of her work lives in her head or appears on the many sticky notes covering her desk.

Darian Halabuza is a writer of dark and eerie fiction. She lives in Winnipeg, Manitoba. After taking an interest in short stories in school, she began creating novels on a writing website named Wattpad. Eight of her thirteen novels have been featured on the website, and have won a number of small awards. Darian likes to explore difficult topics in her stories, enjoying the deep dive into a character's psyche and understanding the dark side of humanity.

A.J. Hanson is a writer, mother, echocardiographer, and beginner homesteader who is passionate about sharing stories of nature and ecology. Writing sci-fi and eco-fiction, she seeks to provide a sense of hope, even in dark dystopian worlds. The founder of The Motley Writers Guild—an eclectic collective of writers—she lives in Northern British Columbia with her husband, three young kids, six chickens, and ten very clever ducks.

Akiko Hara, born in Japan, is a Vancouver-based writer who is also a registered speech-language pathologist. Her inspiration for writing often comes from her work with children and families. She writes creative non-fiction; her work in progress is titled "Speech Therapy." Her short story "The Art of Parting" was published in the *Globe and Mail* in May 2022. Another article is scheduled to be published in the CBC First Person column in August 2022.

Susan Hawkins is a Canadian writer currently living in Gig Harbor, Washington. Her *emerge* piece is an excerpt from her upcoming memoir, "Finding True Bearing," a coming-of-age story set in Montreal during Quebec's Quiet Revolution in the 1960s. Her work was recently shortlisted in the annual Pacific Northwest Writers Association Unpublished Manuscript Literary Contest in the memoir/biography category.

Tamar Haytayan is a photographer and writer working from personal and intuitive perspectives. Themes central to her work are the explorations of memory, mortality, and grief. Tamar is Armenian, born in Lebanon, spent her formative years in London, UK, and moved to Vancouver in 2003. Her work has exhibited at the Armenian Center for Contemporary Art, PhotoHaus Gallery, Philadelphia Photo Arts Center, The Women's Art Show, The Center for Fine Art Photography, Los Angeles Center of Photography, and The Blue Sky Gallery.

Sharon Inkpen is a writer, an educator, a mixed media artist, and a terrible dancer from the suburbs of Vancouver. Her fiction wholeheartedly embraces the peculiarities of life and relationships. When she is not laughing at her words on the page, Sharon is teaching tweenagers, making art from found objects, or joyfully attempting to move her feet in rhythm to music. She hopes to one day move her arms too.

Ella Jean is a queer, LGBTQIA2S+ fiction and poetry writer. Their ambition is to publish uplifting, sapphic novels—safe spaces for readers to escape to. Born and raised in Vancouver, B.C., Ella began writing and creating stories at age ten. They have ambitions to write and direct a screenplay, as she is also deeply passionate about film. When they aren't scribbling down various story ideas, you can find Ella outdoors in the mountains, by the sea, or in a lush forest.

Libby Jeffrey is an emerging writer and settler on Treaty 1 Territory (Winnipeg). In 2020, Libby self-published *Babybytes: Becoming a Mom as the World Locked Down.* She has been published by the Mum Poem Press and The Eco Hub, and was selected for Writes of Spring (Winnipeg International Writers Festival) in 2021. Libby is the founder of MomAlong.ca, a writing group for self-identified moms. She lives in Winnipeg, Canada, with her partner, her son, and Sharky M. Cat.

Lisa Jones is a writer, student success advisor, and a volunteer with various women's organizations. She's currently undertaking her masters in social work, and is the mother to one human and one fur child. Her fiction has been published in *kerning | a space for words*, and she has work forthcoming in *Blank Spaces Magazine*. Lisa lives with her family in Uxbridge, Ontario, where she enjoys short hikes, moderate kayaks, and finishing the cheese before company comes.

Rachelle Jones lives in Vancouver, B.C., on the unceded traditional territories of the Musqueam, Squamish, and Tsleil-Waututh Nations. She has a Bachelor of Arts in communication from Simon Fraser University and currently works in the Vancouver film industry. Things that make her very happy include making a new street cat friend, a good thrift shop find, and a lazy morning coffee with her partner.

Dianne Kenny is grateful to live, work, and play on the unceded Coast Salish territory of the T'Sou-ke Nation. She is thrilled to participate in the Writer's Studio community and to have a piece included in *emerge*. She is grateful to all her friends and teachers past, present, and future for their nurturing encouragement.

Leena Khawaja loves to eat, write, and run. Leena moved from Karachi to Toronto when she was seventeen. She considers herself to be half-and-half and hopes that through writing she can help other immigrants with similar experiences feel seen and heard. Moving to British Columbia mid-pandemic was the best decision Leena ever made. In nature, she found her inspiration and writing spark. Leena is working on her first novel with the help of the Writer's Studio program.

Dongkoo Lee was born and raised in Korea. He moved to Canada in 2019 and currently works for a construction company. After a long period of silence, Dongkoo was inspired after Louise Glück won the 2020 Nobel Prize in Literature. He is honoured to have participated in the 2021–2022 poetry cohort with the Writer's Studio at SFU. He lives in Peterborough, Ontario, with his wife, Mina, and their tiny black poodle, Leo.

Meredith Lingerfelt is a writer and former dancer from Washington, DC. She worked in restaurants, studied, and stripped in Montreal and New York City for much of her adult life. She now lives with her fiancé in Vancouver, British Columbia.

Bing Jie Jenny Liu is a writer, photographer, and project manager in Vancouver, B.C. She holds a degree in mechanical engineering from the University of British Columbia. Born in China, Jenny immigrated to Canada and now lives in Vancouver with her husband, daughter, and their pet chickens. She enjoys playing piano, growing vegetables, and having deep, one-on-one conversations. She blogs at Stuff-I-Love.com.

Entao Liu is a bilingual writer living in Beijing. She got a graduate degree in landscape and architecture and worked for a magazine for a few years. Entao spends most of her time reading, watching birds, and identifying plants. She now writes full-time and works mainly on short stories.

Julie Lynn Lorewood is a young adult fiction writer, originally from Fall River, Nova Scotia. A career in cartography gave her the opportunity to travel across Canada before she made her home in Vancouver, British Columbia. Julie is drawn to writing books that capture the excitement of adventure, the whimsy of first love, and the magic of imagination. When she isn't writing or creating maps, Julie loves taking her dog on long hikes and playing board games with her fiancé.

Caitlin McCarthy wears many creative hats. She currently lives and works in Vancouver as an actor, writer, and producer, among other things. She has authored work for live performance, including The flame Storytelling Event and the Vancouver Fringe Festival. During her time at the Writer's Studio at sfu, Caitlin has written both fiction and non-fiction. She is a graduate of the University of Toronto and Studio 58, and, if given the choice, she would probably become a professional student.

Doreen McCormick has waited a long time to share her off-kilter viewpoint of the world, but now that the kids have left home she's found the time to spread her wings and embarrass them on an even larger scale. Should they ever gang up on her and launch a civil suit, this material might just be their Exhibit A.

Chantal MacCuaig is a writer living on the unceded territories of the Musqueam, Squamish, and Tsleil-Waututh Nations (Vancouver, B.C.). She also works as a communications manager in the television production industry and as a graphic designer. Her writing journey started in the '90s through writing fan mail to the Spice Girls, and now she is working on a collection of personal essays in which she explores the pop culture that raised her.

Angelle McDougall is a poet living in Port Coquitlam. She also writes fiction and creative non-fiction. Some of her works have been published in print in *Circle of Magic: A wpc Press Anthology*, as well as online at *Weird Christmas* and *The Drabble*. Angelle also keeps detailed journals of her travels around the world with her lovely writer husband.

Kirk McDougall is a speculative fiction author living in Port Coquitlam. His stories are published in *Island Writer Magazine*, *Circle of Magic: A WPC Press Anthology*, and on the Port Coquitlam City website. He regularly travels through space, time, and alternate realities. He explores space battles, high-tech murders, and magical tech support. But his favourite place to be is on the balcony writing beside his lovely poet wife.

Laura MacGregor is a wife, mother, researcher, knitter, and hiker. She spends her days working in the fields of disability, caregiving, theology, and ethics. In her free time, she enjoys walking around provinces. Literally. "Lament," her first published piece of creative non-fiction, was written while completing the Island Walk circumnavigating Prince Edward Island.

Kimberley McNeil was born in the culturally diverse land of poutine and smoked meat (Montréal). She migrated across the country to Calgary in 2002 to see if the Rocky Mountains were all they were cracked up to be; they were. Since then, she self-published a book (*Happy Joints*, a teaching guide) and explored various careers, including wildlife biologist. In the end, she landed on copywriter (fewer mosquitoes). Now, she writes and paints, not at the same time.

Laura Mervyn has a rich knowledge of the subject of her novel: the lives and journeys of people striving to escape addiction. Laura's past includes her years as a drug-involved youth and a long career in social work. Her keen observations of human interaction allow her to immerse readers into the lives of ordinary people who also happen to be addicts. Laura writes from her home, overlooking trees and ocean, on Salt Spring Island, B.C.

Ruth Midgley writes fiction, usually of the speculative and eco variety, as a way to explore themes of environmental degradation and human–nature relationships. Ruth holds a degree in environmental studies and conservation biology, has worked as a field biologist and a nature conservation advocate, and now works on climate action for local government. She writes short stories and is working on one too many novels. Ruth grew up in Alberta and currently lives in Victoria, B.C.

April dela Noche Milne is a Filipino Canadian illustrator and writer. She studied fine arts at Langara College and graduated with a BFA in illustration from Emily Carr University. She is the artist for the graphic novel *The Blue Road: A Fable of Migration* and the children's book *The Imperfect Garden*. You can find her on the internet in general, but more specifically you can visit her at AprilMilne.com.

Elizabeth Moira was born in Twickenham, England. She spent some time in the Persian Gulf with her husband just before and during the beginning of the Iranian Revolution. Her novel "As Long as I Can Breathe I Am Alive" reflects that time. She is halfway through her second novel, "She Pressed Send." Elizabeth Moira has six children, lives in West Vancouver, and, among other things, is a member of a classic rock choir on the North Shore.

Heather Morgan is an Irish writer from Cork. Her writing is proudly influenced by Irish culture and includes a plethora of scallywag characters. She grew up listening to her grandmother telling humorous stories and poems. Her work includes fiction, non-fiction, and poetry. She is passionate about including themes of sex, gender, relationships, addiction, and mental health within her writing. And she hopes to make you giggle along the way.

C. Eliot Mullins (she/her) is an educator, mental health therapist, friend of cats, lifelong Pacific Northwesterner, mother of two adult sons, and extreme introvert. She embraced her identity as a poet after coming out of the closet at the age of 49. Her work has appeared in *Lavender Review*, *Jeopardy Magazine*, *Interconnectedness: A Whatcom Writes Anthology*, and *Cathexis Northwest*. She resides in Washington State with her wife and assorted animals, feral and tame.

Maria Myles lives in Vancouver, British Columbia, and has recently completed her BSc from Thompson Rivers University. She is a freelance writer and her work has appeared in *Stonecrop*, *Other Worldly Women Press 2020 Summer Anthology*, and *Detour Ahead*. When she is not writing, she can be found practicing Imanari rolls and omoplatas at North Vancouver Brazilian Jiu Jitsu. Her photography assisted monostichs can be found on Instagram at @mariaismyles.

Marin Nelson is a poet and professional writer living and working on the unceded traditional territories of the Musqueam, Squamish, and Tsleil-Waututh Nations, commonly known as Vancouver. She has had work published in *Reed Magazine*'s 2018 edition, and is honoured to be included among so many talented writers in this year's *emerge* anthology. She'd like to give a heartfelt thanks to her mentor, Kayla Czaga, and her poetry cohort for lending their brilliant and beautiful perspectives to her work.

Alicia Neptune is a communications specialist, artist, and long-time diary keeper. After exploring creative writing in high school through NaNoWriMo, poetry slams, and songwriting, she went on to study communications at Capilano University. Her writing has appeared in *The Capilano Courier* and the online edition of *Vancouver Magazine*. During her time at the Writer's Studio, she turned her focus to short stories and flash fiction. Her recent work explores life's intimacies and vulnerabilities through the lens of speculative fiction.

Kathleen Newson has worked in the non-profit sector in the UK and Canada. She is a writer exploring the nooks and crannies of the human condition. She lives in the mountains with her family and books.

c. nicol currently works as a psychotherapist in Port Moody and at two inner-city schools in Surrey, B.C. From the beginning, it became clear that reading and writing provided her an opportunity to transcend challenging life experiences and later, stupefied, to be carried to safety. The evolution of her own narrative seeks purchase within the human condition inviting connection and catharsis. When not writing or listening, Claire is swimming in lakes with friends.

Kieran O'Connor is a self-proclaimed geek inspired by all different types of stories, including books, movies, and games. His current project is a fantasy coming-of-age story set in the world he created during his numerous Dungeons & Dragons campaigns. Though set in a fictional world, his stories explore very real themes and conflicts and will immerse you in the adventure.

Natasha Overduin is an emerging poet. Professionally, she is trying to figure out how to help move the dial on reconciliation and watershed sustainability. She is a great cook, a mediocre gardener, and a weird horse person. She lives in Nanaimo with her dog, cat, and husband.

Isaiah Papa enjoys creating fantasy worlds through his writings. His works and interests focus on characters navigating cool magic systems and overwhelming capitalist, imperialist societies. When not writing, he indulges in watching cartoons and showering his girlfriend's corgi (Sparkie) with lots of love.

Abby Pelaez makes sense of the wonderful absurdity of life by writing short stories and memoir pieces. These explore queer love, the immigrant experience, and ghosts asserting boundaries (among other things). Her short story "Socialism and Robots" was self-published within a Vancouver anthology called *Sweat.Ink* (2017). Her articles appear in *Check Your Head*, *The/La Source*, *YouthInk*, and *The Ubyssey*. She hopes to publish a collection of short stories and standalone novels. A versatile zillennial, Abby has dabbled in community organizing, banking, sewing, and gardening (among other things). Read more of her work at AbbyPelaez.com.

Chris Powell is a native of the B.C. Interior who moved to Vancouver to study computer science and engineering at UBC. After several decades in IT, he went on to study film production, journalism, technical writing, and speculative fiction. His greatest conflict is that his love of science, technology, and writing requires he sit at a desk, while his love of physical activity and nature demands he never sit at a desk.

Shantell Powell is a two-spirit Inuk and a member of the Turtle Clan. She grew up on the land and off the grid. She is an advocate for Indigenous human rights and Land Defense, multidisciplinary artist, forager, swamp hag, and finder of strange things. A graduate of Yale University's LET(s) Lead Academy and the University of New Brunswick (fine arts, classics, and English drama), her writing can be found in such journals as *Augur*, *Cloud Lake Literary Journal*, *Feminist Studies Journal*, *Prairie fire*, and *Yellow Medicine Journal*. You can find her on Instagram as @shanmonster.

Kathleen Racher is a scientist who always dreamed of either writing a memoir or becoming a nightclub singer. Although she grew up in Vancouver, she has been happily living in Yellowknife since 2000, using her frequent walks on the ice to work out the plot of her stories. Her contribution to this year's *emerge* is her first publication in the genre of creative non-fiction.

Tanaz Roudgar is a human with identities such as: immigrant, bilingual playwright, poet, and actor for film, theatre, and intersectional media. She loves writing about sexuality, immigration, and belonging. Tanaz's mission is to spread awareness and share BIPOC queer voices, love, and togetherness. Tanaz is now dismantling and healing from systems of oppression, colonialism, and capitalism like a warrior goddess on the unceded and stolen lands of the Coast Salish peoples (a.k.a. Vancouver).

Pammila Ruth lives on the beautiful Sunshine Coast in the land of *The Beachcombers* (Gibsons, B.C.). When she found herself unemployed at the beginning of the pandemic, she decided to rekindle her love of writing, something she thought she had lost. Encouraged by her family, she started with a few courses here and there with SFU's LIB55+ program, and then plunged headfirst into the Writer's Studio, hoping to never look back at the nine-to-five, because #sheisawriter.

Cate Sandilands is a professor of environmental humanities at York University. She teaches and writes about the cultural, social, and emotional dimensions of environmental issues, including in her edited multi-genre collection, *Rising Tides: Reflections for Climate-Changing Times* (Caitlin Press, 2019). Cate has loved Jane Rule's work since she was an undergraduate student and now divides her time between Toronto and Galiano Island, B.C., which was also the home Jane shared with her life partner, Helen, for thirty years.

Alisen Santa Ana is a Vancouver-based writer living on the unceded territories of the Musqueam, Squamish, and Tsleil-Waututh Nations. She holds degrees in philosophy (BA) and counselling psychology (MA). Alisen recently left a long career in mental health to pursue education in non-fiction/creative writing. She roots her work in feminism, existentialism, and empathy. Currently, she is writing a memoir about growing up in a cult. She is a member of the Looped Poetry Collective and the singer/lyricist of Ghost Shepherd.

Jennifer Scarth is a physician by training and has spent the past thirty years in the practice of medicine. Writing fiction and poetry has been in the background. Her publication to date is a chapbook contribution, back in the early years of her maternal career. Favourite writing moments: having a character walk into her mind and having time to pursue them. Favourite maxim to date, from TWS22 workshop: "if you're lost, you're chasing plot."

H.E. Scott has indie published two fantasy novels with book three coming in 2022. Scott also writes historical fiction and is working on a novel about convict transportation from 18th-century England to Colonial America. Scott lived two years in France and three years in Hong Kong, which has given her a historical perspective for her writing. Scott recently completed a master of arts in global leadership through Royal Roads University and works with a non-profit for disabled Canadian veterans.

Shelby Sharpe is a lover of adventure and discovery. Having fallen victim to wanderlust at a young age, she draws much of her inspiration from the places she's travelled and visited. She is a long-time fan of speculative fiction and fantasy, and writes predominantly in the YA genre. She imbues excitement and exploration into her writing, creating wonderful worlds to escape to and get lost in. Shelby was born and raised in the Pacific Northwest, and she continues to call it home.

Nikica Subek Simon was born and lives at the crossroads of cultures. Learning foreign languages helped her connect with the mysteries of the wider world, which led her to work as a translator. Currently, she works in libraries. In her free time, and when not writing, Nikica loves reading, gardening, knitting, and making soap. Nikica and her family call Winnipeg in Treaty 1 Territory their home.

Nicole Succar Sedan is a Colombian Canadian writer living in Vancouver, B.C. She holds a bachelor's degree in ciminology and a minor in biopsychology from Simon Fraser University, and she is a recent graduate of their Writer's Studio creative writing program. Since moving to Canada she has participated in running a variety of family businesses. Her multicultural background affords her a unique life perspective that informs her writing, which is largely focused on issues of social inequality and cultural traditions.

Si Mian Melody Sun is a Chinese Canadian writer living in so-called Vancouver. Born in mainland China, she immigrated to Canada with her family when she was fifteen years old. With a master's degree in publishing, she recently started her career as an executive assistant at an indie publishing company. Melody's writing usually features immigrant life, identity crisis, classism, and feminism. Besides writing, Melody is passionate about reading, connecting with book lovers, and disassembling the patriarchy.

Aimee Taylor is a writer who has been living with metastatic cancer since 2013. She completed a BFA in the Creative Writing program at UBC and attended the SFU Writer's Studio to work on her memoir, which navigates the delicate balance between hope and fear in the world of terminal illness as a parent of young kids. Aimee is heavily involved in the young adult cancer community and advocates for 2Spirit LGTBQ+ rights in palliative care. She lives with her wife and nine-year-old daughter in Vancouver, B.C.

Jackson Wai Chung Tse 謝瑋聰 is an award-winning consultant and interdisciplinary artist, creating work in media, performance, and literary arts. Fascinated by complex relationships, queer identities coexisting with cultural values, and Chinese diaspora in the West, Jackson has published essays and reviews in *Grip!* and the *Holy Male Magazine*. Born in Hong Kong, Jackson has worked as an oilsands engineer, a living statue, and a brain researcher. Now, he resides in Vancouver, B.C., and writes about how to love.

Denise Unrau resides on a collective farm on the traditional territory of the Semiahmoo. She has spent her life telling stories and teasing out answers to questions that have come from growing up in a small religious farming community on the Prairies. Her story "Transcendent Expectation" placed third in *Room*'s 2022 fiction Contest.

Amy Van Veen is a writer and editor who has lived in British Columbia's Lower Mainland for most of her life. When her creative energy isn't spent baking her way through cookbooks and teaching her dog, Walter, to high five, she edits other people's words and writes stories. After typing out her Dutch grandmother's handwritten life story, she started writing a novel exploring the interconnected lives of three generations of women, and how the past impacts the present.

Carrie Walker is a visual artist who can't stay away from words. This entanglement has led her to make zines, artist books, and countless drawings with titles that are too long. Walker is currently writing a memoir about her relationship with her mother. This emotionally fraught work is offset by maintaining the social media accounts of her rat terrier, Guess, who has a penchant for carrying giant sticks. She recently began writing about plants, a ruse that she has concocted in order to spend more time outdoors.

Voted class president in elementary school, **Christina Walsh** was destined for a career in politics. But the job she loves most is writing, and helping other moms write their stories, too. Christina co-founded The MomBabes, a writing community that has co-authored two anthologies. Christina is currently working on her memoir, which she hopes will be a cherished family heirloom. She usually has a lukewarm coffee in hand and is a big fan of Dolly Parton. Christina lives with her husband and two girls in Squamish, B.C.

Gerald Williams, a Canadian, has spent most of his adult life in Japan as a professor of education. Upon returning to Canada, he began writing plays. His works have been selected for the Samuel French Off-Off Broadway Festival and the Tennessee Williams Tribute Festival in Columbus, Mississippi. He has recently turned his attention to fiction, and, along with a series of short stories, is working on a satirical novel about lonely, wealthy women who borrow children from poor single mothers.

Jules Wilson is a Black Canadian poet of Grenadian and Nigerian ancestry. His woven wordplay invites you in, with voyeuristic curiosity, to self-locate against vivid backdrops, exploring themes like equity, the beautification of blackness, and nature's nurturing. With training in HR and social work, he currently leverages his poetics to help others unpack modern challenges related to allyship, anti-racism, and identity. Outside of poetry, he is an avid pet guardian and parent embracing family adventures into nature.

Don't tell anyone, but though **Nora Wood** is an accountant by day, she spends most of her waking energy thinking about words and character arcs rather than numbers. Currently, she is rebelling against her technical training by working on a novel of pure fiction and loving that there are no mathematical proofs required! Nora lives in Winnipeg with her husband, daughters, and their Labrador retrievers.

Ethan P. Yan has been conjuring stories rooted in both reality and fantasy since he was a toddler. A writer steeped in fiction novels, he has been experimenting with shorter forms of fiction since coming to TWS. His dream of publishing a full novel endures to this day, but he's begun honing his focus on developing character before plot within shorter mediums. When he's not busy making stuff up, he can be found either teaching or out enjoying good food.

Jaeyun Yoo is a Korean Canadian poet and psychiatrist whose work has appeared in *Canthius*, *The /tɛmz/ Review*, *Prairie Fire*, *Grain*, *Contemporary Verse 2*, *EVENT* and others. She is a member of Harbour Centre 5, a collective of emerging poets. Their collaborative chapbook, *Brine*, was published in 2022. She lives and writes on the traditional and unceded lands of the Musqueam, Squamish, and Tsleil-Waututh peoples. Find her at @jaeyunwrites on Twitter.

Production Credits

Publisher
Laura Farina

Publisher emeritus
Andrew Chesham

Managing editor
Emily Stringer

PRODUCTION TEAM
Cadence Mandybura—Production Editor
Abby Pelaez
Sierra Guay
Pammila Ruth
Dianne Kenny
Nicole Dumas
Sharon Inkpen

EDITORIAL TEAM
Section editors
Raoul Fernandes—Poetry and Lyric Prose
Dayna Mahannah—Fiction and Non-fiction
Christina Myers—Non-fiction
Leah Ranada—Fiction
KT Wagner—Speculative and Young Adult Fiction

Acknowledgments

The students of the Writer's Studio would like to thank our mentors, guest instructors, program facilitators, staff, and apprentices of the Writer's Studio for their guidance and support in the creation of these works.

Thanks to the new and returning TWS alumni who bolster this community of writers through their contributions to emerge, including our editors Raoul Fernandes, Dayna Mahannah, Cadence Mandybura, Christina Myers, Leah Ranada, Emily Stringer, and KT Wagner. Thanks to Jónína Kirton for her thoughtful foreword. Thanks to Blaine Kyllo for his beautiful design work.

Thanks to Joanne Betzler, Grant Smith, and the Yosef Wosk Foundation for their generous support, which helps us bring alumni and students together for the production of this anthology. Their assistance strengthens our community. Thanks also to John Whatley and SFU Publications for their continual support of the students and this publication.

Thanks to Betsy Warland for thinking so deeply and insightfully about the practice of writing. Her influence is felt in many of these works.

Thanks to our friends and family who support our writing journeys in myriad ways.

The writing in this anthology would not have been possible without the generous assistance of Zoom and other people's cats.

LAND ACKNOWLEDGMENT

This book was composed on the traditional territories of many Indigenous peoples, who have been caretakers of these lands and their stories since time immemorial. As we bring together a multitude of voices in this anthology, we reflect on the voices that have traditionally been excluded, and commit to uplifting those voices now and in the future.

We're grateful to the Indigenous peoples on whose lands we live and write, including: the T'Sou-ke Nation; the Semiahmoo Nation; the Yellowknives Dene Nation; the Penelakut Nation; the Hwlitsum Nation; the Kitkatla and Ahousaht; the Tsawwassen Nation, Treaty 1 Territory; the Hul'qumi'num and SENĆOŦEN speaking peoples; the Stó:lō Nation; the Kwikwetlem Nation; the Qayqayt Nation; the Katzie Nation; the Kwantlen Nation; the Duwamish and Snoqualmie; the Amazigh peoples; the Mississaugas of the Credit; the Anishnabeg, the Chippewa, the Haudenosaunee and the Wendat peoples; the Lekwungen peoples; the Songhees, Esquimalt, and W̱SÁNEĆ peoples; the Matsqui Nation; the Tk'emlúps te Secwépemc situated within the unceded ancestral lands of the Secwépemc Nation; the Blackfoot Confederacy, including the Siksika, Piikani, and Kainai Nations; the Stoney-Nakoda, including the Chiniki, Bearspaw, and Wesley Nations; the Tsuut'ina Nation; the Snuneymuxw, Snaw-naw-as, and Stzuminus peoples; the sx̌ʷəbabš; the Tr'ondëk Hwëch'in Nation; the Tuscarora people; the Lheidli T'enneh; the Neutral and Haudenosaunee peoples; the Nooksack and Lummi peoples; the Ktuanxa, the Syilx, and the Sinixt; and the Coast Salish peoples, including the xʷməθkwəy̓əm, Skwxwú7mesh, and Səlílwətaɬ Nations.

Elzevir A*a* Q*q* R*r*

The interior of *emerge* is set in DTL Elzevir. Originally created in the 1660s, Elzevir is a baroque typeface, cut by Christoffel van Dijck in Amsterdam. As noted in Robert Bringhurst's *The Elements of Typographic Style*, baroque typography thrived in the seventeenth century and is known for its axis variations from one letter to the next. During this time, typographers started mixing roman and *italic on the same line*. The Dutch Type Library created a digital version in 1993 called DTL Elzevir. It retains some of the weight that Monotype Van Dijck, an earlier digital version, possessed in metal but had lost in its digital translation.

The interior of *emerge* is printed on Rolland paper, produced by Rolland Inc, Canada. The cover for *emerge* uses Kalima CIS paper, made by Tembec Inc, Canada. Both papers are Forestry Stewardship Council (FSC) and Sustainable Forestry Initiative (SFI) Certified, and are acid free/elemental chlorine free.

emerge

AVAILABLE AS AN EBOOK

Since 2011, *emerge* has been available
in print and ebook editions.

Visit

amazon.com

and

kobobooks.com

Manufactured by Amazon.ca
Bolton, ON

33689912R00259